Enchantment of E'vahona

Part II-The Abyssal Dominion

T.A. McEvoy

T. McEvoy

For permission requests, contact:
tmcevoy1121@yahoo.com

U.S. Copyright Registration: Pending
Library of Congress Control Number: 2026906868

Cover design by NovelStormDesigns (Etsy)
Map illustration by Rob Donovan (Snikt5 on Fiverr)

First Edition — 2026
Printed in the United States of America

9781964250236

Imprint: T. McEvoy

Dedication

Tom Vick

To my wonderful boyfriend, Tom—

Thank you for reading every draft of this book, even when they were barely stitched together.

Since we met, my life has grown brighter in more ways than I can express.

Your steady encouragement, fierce loyalty, and unwavering belief in me mean more than words can say.

And special thanks for fending off the marketers—though I think you may have scared them away for good!

You are my anchor, my champion, and the reason I keep moving forward.

A Word Before You Begin

The Living Dragons of Vacari

I have always loved dragons.

In the world of Vacari, they are far more than beasts or distant legends. They are living, thinking, feeling beings—each with choices to make, burdens to carry, and destinies to shape.

Here, dragons are not simply part of the world's backdrop. They are part of its soul. They speak, they feel, and they decide their own paths. Some stand as fierce protectors, others as cunning schemers... and a few may surprise you in ways you do not expect.

I understand that this vision may not resonate with every reader, but it is the heart of Vacari. These dragons are not merely creatures within the world—they are woven into its breath, its heartbeat, and its very existence.

Thank you for stepping into their story. I hope you enjoy meeting the dragons of Vacari as much as I have loved bringing them to life.

Welcome to The Dragons of Vacari series!

You're in the right place if you love high-stakes adventure, legendary dragons, and a richly crafted world steeped in magic, mystery, and danger. The Dragons of Vacari is a sweeping fantasy saga filled with intense dragon battles, deep friendships, ancient secrets, and the ever-present struggle between light and darkness. Whether you're here for the action, the emotional journeys, or the evolving lore, this world was built to draw you in—and keep you coming back for more.

Planned as a nine-book epic, *The Dragons of Vacari* unfolds gradually, with each volume expanding the world and deepening the story. While the series is interconnected, every installment can be enjoyed as a stand-alone adventure. Readers who follow the journey in order, however, will discover layered mysteries, evolving character arcs, and long-building revelations that reward the path book by book.

From the noble dragons and their bound kin to treacherous alliances, awakening powers, and ancient threats rising from the shadows, this is a tale meant to challenge heroes—and readers alike.

While you await the next release, you can explore more of Vacari through exclusive content on my YouTube channel. Just search for "Theresa McEvoy" for behind-the-scenes lore, worldbuilding, and character insights. You can also find me on TikTok under T.A. McEvoy.

https://www.youtube.com/@theresamcevoy612

Your patience and support mean the world to me as I bring each chapter of this story to life. Thank you for joining me on this adventure—I hope you enjoy the twists, turns, and surprises that await!

— T.A. McEvoy

World Map

Vacari – The Living Realm

Series Motto

The Creed of Vacari

You were never supposed to do it alone.
Hope will always triumph over despair.
Love over destruction.
Unity over division.

Contents

Prologue

Whispers of the Dominion

The wind howled across the ravaged plains of Afor, carrying th stench of ash and old blood.

Malrik drew his cloak tighter around himself, the once-proud sigil c Vuarus, God of Shadows, now little more than a ghostly scar stitche into the fabric. Long ago, he had been High Priest of the Shadow Temple. Now he was only a wanderer in lands hollowed by war, chasing th same rumor from ruin to ruin.

The darkness was stirring again.

Every whisper had led him here Flameford, a city reborn from ruir where black wings were said to sweep the skies in silent formation. Som claimed the dark dragons had united beneath a single will. Others murmured that a hidden master had returned to command them.

Malrik did not know which tale he feared more.

He only knew he had to see the truth.

The path ended at a tower of fractured stone veined with molten fire its wounds glowing faintly red as though the earth itself still bled. Powe clung to the air ancient, familiar... and dangerous.

With each step up the spiral staircase, the years pressed heavier upon s shoulders. The iron door at the summit opened at his approach ithout a touch.

Inside, the shadows breathed.

Runes flared across the floor, forming a circle of command. At its nter stood a figure shrouded in darkness that shifted like smoke caught tween worlds.

Malrik lowered his hood. For the first time in many years, uncertainty nd something perilously close to dread—flickered through him.

“Forgive my intrusion,” he said, forcing steadiness into his voice. “Ru- ors reached even the ruins I walk of a power rising here. One who bends e dark dragons to their will. I came to learn whether such tales were uth... or the ramblings of the desperate.”

The figure turned.

Shadow slid across her face like living silk.

Malrik’s breath caught. His pulse stuttered.

“...You.”

A faint smile touched her lips not warm, not cruel, but inevitable.

“Yes.”

The word settled between them like a seal broken long ago.

“But you will remain silent,” she continued, her voice calm and un- elding. “I have restored the Abyssal Dominion. The dark dragons an- ver to me once more. The noble ones will fall and with them, every ally ho clings to false light.”

For a heartbeat, the world seemed to tilt.

Malrik sank to one knee, memory and reverence bending him as surely fear.

“Then I am yours to command,” he said, his voice rough with surren- r. “As I once served the Shadow... and the power that stood behind it.”

Her gaze sharpened, cold and absolute.

"Understand this," she said. "My name is not to be spoken. My form not to be questioned. To the world, I am neither man nor woman on the darkness that binds their fate. Let them argue. Let them guess. L them tremble."

A tremor rolled through the tower, deep and slow, as though som thing vast had shifted beneath the world's skin.

Malrik lifted his gaze toward the fractured window. Beyond it, win eclipsed the moon, their shadows sweeping across the land.

The Dominion had awakened.

And the age of shadows had begun.

Chapter 1

Whispers Beneath the Realms

The sky above the borderlands between Flameford and Fel Thalor burned in quiet dissonance embers drifting through a veil of mist, as though fire and frost waged a war too ancient for the world to remember its beginning. The land bore the scars of that struggle: obsidian ridges slicing through frozen stone, fissures breathing slow, aching curls of heat.

It was here, in this wounded seam of Vacari where no dragon claimed dominion, that the Dark Ancients gathered in wary silence.

The air shuddered first.

Then came Zylron.

Molten light spilled from his wings as he descended upon the blackened earth, scales shimmering like living metal, sulfur rolling from him in a suffocating tide. The ground seethed beneath his claws.

From the mist behind him, frost whispered.

Glaciera emerged, her vast form carved from living ice, every movement measured, inevitable. Her breath unfurled in crystalline vapor that hissed as it met Zylron's heat.

From the shadows between the stones, black smoke coiled and unraveled, resolving into the silhouette of Nocturna, silver veins glimmering faintly beneath her obsidian hide.

When she spoke, her voice did not sound it lingered, like a memory carved into bone.

"We linger too openly, Zylron," she said. "Even the air remembers us now."

Zylron's molten eyes narrowed.

"Let it remember," he snarled. "I will not whisper my purpose while Abyss-born ears infest the wind."

A deep, sodden rumble rolled through the ravine. Roots tore free of the soil as Xalzorath rose verdant decay given form, moss clinging to dark scales, blackened dew trailing from his wings.

"This ground is well chosen," he murmured. "Fire repels frost, frost tempers flame. Few will linger long enough to listen and fewer still will understand what they hear."

Glaciera's gaze drifted toward the horizon, distant lightning mirrored in her eyes.

"Then speak," she said coolly. "We did not gather to admire the weather."

Zylron exhaled, molten vapor coiling into ash between them.

"Thundria's fall," he said. "And Zarathos' claim upon the Topaz Dominion."

The name lingered heavy, unresolved.

Nocturna's tail coiled, stirring dust and shadow.

"Destiny rarely surprises," she murmured. "He was shaped for that throne. Gem-blood is volatile brilliant, but prone to fracture. Still... he remains Vacari-born."

"Which makes him dangerous," Glaciera replied without inflection. "Grief corrodes judgment. Pride, once wounded, sharpens into a blade."

Xalzorath's eyes gleamed like murky gold.

"A blade may still serve justice," he said. "If Thundria fell unjustly, Zarathos has cause to reclaim what was taken. But justice is irrelevant to the Mysterious One. We are summoned only when obedience advances their design."

Zylron's claws bit into stone. The earth hissed beneath him.

"And yet Void and Abyss dragons roam unrestrained," he growled. "They fracture accords, defile borders while we, who remember Vacari's shaping, remain bound by riddles and unseen chains."

Nocturna's laughter slid through the gloom, thin as drawn steel.

"Loyalty may be our oldest weakness," she said softly. "The leash tightens with every indulgence granted to outsiders."

"Enough."

Glaciera's voice cut the air like frost-edged glass.

Cold flared along her wings, the temperature plunging in a sharp, lethal hush.

"We do not sever what we do not yet comprehend," she continued. "But we will observe. We will prepare. And when the hand moving against us reveals itself..."

"...it will meet frost and flame united."

Zylron inclined his head, molten fissures pulsing like a forge's heartbeat.

"Then it is decided," he rumbled. "Each to their dominion. Each to listen but not kneel."

Nocturna unfurled her wings, shadows rippling like liquid night.

"Before we scatter," she said, "know this. The Obsidian kin lair beneath Flameford far deeper than most dare descend. Stone and magma speak to us there."

Her silver-veined gaze shimmered.

"An entrance has been carved beyond the city's edge hidden, warded. The Mysterious One and their Abyssal watchers will sense nothing. Let them believe the depths still sleep."

Zylron regarded her with a flicker of respect. Xalzorath's tendrils rustled with approval. Glaciera inclined her head, frost dusting the scorched stone.

"Good," Zylron said. "Then the Void remains blind to what moves beneath its feet."

Glaciera swept her gaze across them, bright as starlight on ice.

"It is settled," she said. "We return to our lairs. But if the Mysterious One's games grow too bold call. We gather here. Not Flameford."

"I will not be summoned again like an unruly hatchling."

A low, molten chuckle rolled from Zylron. Even Xalzorath's rumble carried dark amusement.

"Agreed," Xalzorath murmured. "Here. Between flame and ruin."

Silence followed uneasy, ancient, bound by shared defiance.

Then they departed.

Nocturna melted into shadow.

Glaciera dissolved into drifting frost.

Xalzorath sank into moss and soil.

Zylron rose last, wings spilling molten brilliance across the broken plain.

As he vanished toward Fel Thalor's horizon, the air fell still once more thick with ash... and the promise of unspoken rebellion.

The Infernal Throne of Fel Thalor

The skies above Fel Thalor bled with twilight flame. Rivers of molten rock carved through jagged peaks, their slow, deliberate flow pulsing like the veins of an ancient heart. Heat shimmered across the cliffs, warping the air into spectral mirages of wings and fire.

This was Zylron's dominion.

Nothing entered it uninvited.

He descended in a storm of flame, the air cracking beneath the weight of his wings. When he struck the ground, the stone fractured, steam hissing upward in reverent spirals around his talons. His scales burned like living magma, gold veins flaring with every breath. Every motion proclaimed ownership.

The cavern yawned before him a cathedral of molten stone sculpted by centuries of his temper and will. Obsidian columns twisted skyward, their edges glowing faintly where lava kissed their base. The heat was merciless, even to him and he welcomed it. It was the pulse of his power. The heartbeat of his reign.

At the cavern's heart lay his hoard.

A mountain of gold and crystal, gemstones fused by fire into glassy rivers winding between relics of conquest. There was no chaos here. Each treasure rested where he had decreed it should remain: crowns torn from fallen kings, armor stripped from slain wyrms, enchanted blades whose magic now slumbered beneath the weight of his supremacy.

Zylron prowled across the glittering expanse, wings half-unfurled, molten light scattering over curved gold and jeweled edges.

He did not move like a guardian of wealth.

He moved like a sovereign surveying his realm.

"Weakness invites theft," he rumbled, his voice rolling through the cavern like thunder bound in stone.

"And theft is answered with ruin."

He halted at the edge of the hoard, where the floor collapsed into slow-churning lava. Heat rippled against his face, thick with sulfur and iron. His molten eyes narrowed, pupils contracting as he studied the distant shadows near the cavern mouth.

Nothing stirred.

No breath.

No sound.

Still, he watched.

Vigilance was law.

He spread his wings, stirring a gust that scattered coins and embers alike. Beneath the shifting gold, an obsidian mirror set into the cavern wall revealed itself a relic torn from a temple long reduced to ash. Within its dark surface, his reflection wavered: monstrous, regal, eternal.

"Let the others trade whispers and bargains," he said.

"Words burn."

"Power endures."

The mirror shuddered beneath his gaze, molten light crawling across it like flowing gold.

A tremor rolled through the cavern the distant thunder of the volcano's heart. Zylron lifted his head, drawing in ash-laden air as magma roared below like a chained beast.

"Good," he growled.

"Even the mountain remembers who reigns."

He returned to the center of the cavern and coiled atop his golden mound, wings folding around him like the closing gates of a forge. Molten light spilled across his scales, casting rivers of fire along the cavern walls.

All fell still, save for the low hum of molten veins and the echo of his slow, deliberate breathing.

In the silence, his thoughts returned to the gathering the tightening leash of the Mysterious One, the obedience demanded of dragons who had carved their freedom in blood and flame.

His jaw tightened.

"Let them send their commands," he muttered.

"This fire does not kneel."

Outside, the volcano answered with a deep, rolling growl that echoed across the peaks of Fel Thalor as though the mountain itself acknowledged its master.

The Mire-King's Domain

The mists of Etharyon clung to the world like a funeral shroud. The sun never truly pierced the canopy; what little light survived bled green through veined leaves, sinking into black water that rippled without wind. Moss and rot perfumed the air, mingled with the metallic breath of unseen death.

From the heart of that fetid stillness, the waters stirred.

Slowly at first then rolling outward as something vast displaced the mire.

Xalzorath emerged.

His dark scales devoured the light, reflecting nothing. Wings unfolded like tattered sails of shadow, shedding rivulets of swamp water as he lifted his head to taste the air. The motion sent ripples crawling across the pools.

Every living thing froze.

Even the insects fell silent, as though the marsh itself knew to hold its breath when the Mire-King returned.

He spoke softly, his voice a rasp of stone drawn through mud.

"You remain loyal," he murmured.

"Good."

The water trembled.

Beneath its surface, unseen shapes shifted lesser kin of the deep acknowledging him in mute obedience. Xalzorath advanced, each step dissolving into ripples that whispered through the swamp.

The first entrance to his dominion lay hidden beneath roots thick as towers, their slick surfaces glazed with moss and glistening fungus. Warm, wet air exhaled decay and ancient magic. Xalzorath lowered his head and released a slow breath of corrosion. The roots recoiled, parting to reveal a narrow descent into darkness.

He slipped through like a serpent returning to its hollow.

Below, the swamp surrendered to a cathedral of stone and water.

Fungal lanterns clung to cavern walls, their dim glow scattering restless reflections across black pools. Columns of stone rose from the depths, draped in vines and bones; ancient carvings half-devoured by moss whispered of civilizations long claimed by the mire.

This was Xalzorath's true lair.

A second entrance an underwater passage leading to the open lake beyond lay hidden beneath reeds and illusions that bent the mind. Many had drowned seeking it.

None had reached him.

He climbed the central rise of stone, water sliding from his claws, and surveyed his dominion. The cavern answered tremors rippled outward, bubbles sighed from unseen vents, and the lair itself listened.

"Fire and frost clash above," he murmured.

"And still... they forget who governs below."

He unfurled one wing. Droplets cascaded like black diamonds. Amber light smoldered in his eyes as he regarded the upper tunnels.

"Zarathos hunts vengeance," he said softly.

"Let him."

"Pride is patient bait."

The water shuddered as a massive, blind eel-like sentinel surfaced scarred, ancient, obedient. It circled the base of the stone rise, awaiting command. Xalzorath spared it a single glance, then turned away. The creature sank without a sound.

"Watch," he whispered.

"Mark every trespass."

"The Mysterious One plays games above the soil let them."

His gaze hardened, slow and merciless.

"Down here," he said quietly,

"I decide what endures."

The water carried his will through the flooded labyrinth until even the air above the swamp seemed to pulse in response.

Satisfied, Xalzorath coiled upon the central stone, wings draping like living shadow. The faint light dimmed. The mists thickened.

The swamp fell utterly still.

In the silence, the Mire-King allowed himself a thin, cruel smile.

Patience was his sharpest weapon.

And in Etharyon, patience could last an eternity.

The Storm in the Mountains

The peaks of Etharyon tore through the clouds like jagged spears, each crowned in lightning. The air itself lived here thick with ozone, every breath steeped in the metallic promise of thunder. Winds screamed along the cliffs, carrying the scent of rain and scorched stone. High above it all, lightning coiled in spirals of gold and white, converging upon a single mountain that pulsed with stormlight.

This was Zarathos's dominion, where the sky bent in reverence... and fear.

Within the mountain's hollow heart, crystalline walls caught the storm's flicker, scattering shards of light across vast chambers. The lair was fortress and cathedral alike: veins of gold and amber threaded the stone, forming natural conduits that hummed with captive electricity. Each strike upon the peak above drew a deep, resonant answer from the cavern the breath of a god bound in crystal.

Zarathos, the Topaz Ancient, coiled upon his hoard a sea of molten gold, jewels, and enchanted relics still shimmering with stolen stormlight. His scales burned with fractured brilliance, golden topaz deepening into molten amber along every plate. His eyes blazed like captive suns as he lifted his head toward the thunder beyond the arch.

"Still..." he murmured, fury threading the word like a blade.

"She does not answer."

Lightning crawled along his horns. He exhaled, and the air hissed with static.

He rose.

The storm answered.

Thunder tore through the mountains as though ripped from his chest.

"They whisper of me," he said softly venom beneath velvet.

"They believe grief dulls the storm."

"That wrath may be buried beneath gold."

His gaze hardened, blazing.

"Fools."

"I am the storm."

His tail swept across the hoard. Coins fused in sudden flashes of heat. He paced through arcs of living light like a god stalking the ruins of his own temple, reflections of conquered ages dancing across his scales.

In the far corner, a smaller Topaz dragon crouched half-buried beneath crystal shards, wings folded in rigid deference. Its eyes flicked nervously as Zarathos approached.

"The others watch from afar, my lord," he whispered.

"Even the Mysterious One grows wary of your silence."

Zarathos lowered his head until the air between them trembled with charged power. Sparks leapt across the younger dragon's hide. It flinched.

"Let them fear," Zarathos growled.

"I do not serve silence."

"I command it."

Stormfire flared in his eyes.

"The storm does not ask permission to break the sky."

The smaller dragon bowed lower, smoke curling from his scales.

"As you command, my lord."

Zarathos turned away. His gaze locked upon the storm-wracked horizon beyond the cavern's arch, where peaks vanished into mist and lightning carved fleeting sigils across the clouds.

"Thundria," he whispered the name half snarl, half prayer. "They believe your death ended the storm."

His wings unfurled.

The chamber ignited in reflected fire. Bolts of lightning leapt from wall to wall, weaving a crown of living brilliance above him. When he roared, the mountains answered thunder ripping across Etharyon's night.

"Let them learn otherwise."

The storm did not fade.

It never would while Zarathos, Fallen Gem of the Peaks, yet drew breath.

The Lair Beneath the Flame

The obsidian cliffs near the Cerulean Expanse lay shrouded in sea-born mist. Waves sighed against the black stone, their rhythm masking the faint tremor of something ancient stirring below. To any wanderer, the cliffside seemed solid and unyielding a wall of dark glass where even daylight hesitated to linger. But to Nocturna, the rock itself breathed, its pulse slow and patient as her own.

She descended in silence, her vast wings folding close as she alighted upon the jagged ledge.

The sea wind hissed across her scales, glinting faintly along the silver veins that marbled her obsidian hide. With a low rumble, she pressed one talon against the stone. Darkness rippled outward in concentric rings, revealing what mortal eyes could never see a fissure narrow as a blade's edge.

"Sleep well, guardians," she whispered to the cliffs, her voice a quiet caress of night.

The fissure widened.

Stone parted soundlessly, swallowing her whole.

Beneath the surface, the world changed.

The air grew heavy, molten warmth mingling with the cool breath of the deep earth. Walls shimmered with faint light. Obsidian stretched in smooth corridors threaded with molten gold and pale azure crystal the last echo of the Cerulean Expanse's reach.

Each step she took awakened faint vibrations through the stone, as though the labyrinth itself acknowledged her passage.

This was the domain of the Obsidian Dragons an endless warren of black stone and mirrored corridors where perception itself could betray the unwary. The pathways twisted and reformed when intruders entered, guiding them deeper into confusion while concealing the true heart of the realm.

Hidden vents exhaled sulfurous heat. Pools of liquid glass rippled like black mirrors, ready to harden at her command.

Nocturna passed beneath vast archways formed from fused magma, their surfaces etched with ancient draconic sigils that glimmered faintly as she approached.

"Too quiet," she murmured, her voice rolling through the stone like distant thunder.

"Even silence can conspire."

Far below, a faint echo answered a pulse of awareness from her kin scattered throughout the lower depths. Solitary though they were, they felt her presence. The hidden network stirred; unseen watchers resumed their eternal vigil.

She reached the inner hollow at last.

A vast cavern opened before her, crowned by a dome of obsidian crystal. Above, molten veins pulsed through the ceiling like captured lightning. At the chamber's center rested a basin of still black water.

Nocturna lowered her head and gazed into its surface.

Her reflection fractured into a dozen mirrored forms.

"The world above shifts," she murmured softly. "Zarathos takes the Topaz throne. The mysterious one stirs the Abyss... and still they do not see us."

Her eyes glowed faintly, silver bleeding into darkness.

"Let them ignore what lies beneath their feet," she continued quietly. "Let them believe the underground sleeps."

The air thickened.

Across the cavern walls, darkness flowed like ink in water. The labyrinth responded instantly traps resetting, passages realigning, silent sentinels returning to their endless watch.

"Watch them," she breathed. "If anything moves through the cracks of their arrogance... I will know."

Her words faded into the tunnels, carried through the stone like commands etched into the bones of the world.

Nocturna coiled beside the black basin, folding her immense wings around her body like a cloak.

Above her, the molten veins slowly dimmed.

One by one, the last embers of light faded from the chamber.

The lair sank into perfect darkness her chosen realm, where shadow obeyed and even silence bowed.

The Return to the Frost

The wind howled across the peaks of Firornak, carrying the weight of a storm that would never end. The sky burned the color of steel, and snow did not fall it shattered, each shard slicing the air like splinters of glass. Beneath that merciless firmament, Glaciera rose from the shadowed slopes of her chosen mountain, her wings tearing clouds apart as she reclaimed her dominion.

Below, the world lay entombed beneath leagues of snow and silence. Rivers froze mid-flow. Stone vanished beneath frost. Even the breath of the land slowed in her presence. Once, she had ruled from cold halls carved into ancient cities where mortals knelt and fed her tribute.

She had grown weary of their walls...and their arrogance.

Now she had returned to Firornak where cold was law, and life bowed before it.

Her landing struck the mountainside like a frozen thunderclap. Snow collapsed in shimmering veils, unveiling the entrance to her lair: a wound of pure white ice carved into the mountain's face, faintly lit by the echo of her crystalline breath.

She entered without sound.

Within, her domain unfolded like a frozen cathedral. Spires of ice arched skyward, glittering with pale, refracted light. Each step rang with the fragile chime of breaking glass. Along the walls, her treasures lay entombed: silver crowns, white opals, enchanted crystal shards all arranged with ruthless, immaculate precision.

She halted before a pedestal of sculpted ice near the chamber's heart.

Empty.

Waiting.

"Soon," she whispered her voice sharp enough to cut breath. "Another will prove worthy of preservation."

Her claws traced the pedestal's curve. Frost bloomed in their wake. The air itself seemed to recoil at the thought Keisha, frozen in flawless stillness, defiance sealed into eternal art.

Glaciera withdrew, her breath spiraling into mist that crystallized before touching the floor.

"The Eladrin call themselves eternal," she murmured. "Ice remembers what eternity forgets."

The lair responded.

Stalactites cracked and reformed. Walls shifted with silent obedience. She moved among her hoard, passing pillars of solid ice where lesser beings—intruders, fools, the unfortunate stood locked in their final moments, eyes wide with preserved terror.

A thin, precise curve touched her maw.

"Mortals. Dragons."

"All melt."

Her gaze hardened, merciless and pristine.

"All except me."

She ascended to the highest chamber, where a vast aperture opened to the night sky. From there, she surveyed endless white peaks, frozen rivers like silver veins, stars dulled beneath drifting snow.

Her wings unfurled. Frost thundered through the air. She inhaled, tasting the distant tremor of the world restless dragons, murmuring storms, the subtle, unwelcome influence of the Mysterious One.

"Let them play," she said softly.

"While they burn, rot, and drown in shadow... I will build a monument to silence."

Snow gathered along her wings like jeweled mail. Her eyes, cold and crystalline, reflected only her own perfection.

Far below, the wind roared through the valleys the breath of something ancient and unending.

At the heart of Firornak, Glaciera closed her eyes.

The storm would endure.

The world would freeze in time.

And when her chosen prize was claimed, the mountain would remember her judgment forever.

Whispers Beneath the Moon

Far from the domains of shadow and storm, the night over Vacari shimmered with quiet vigilance. Twin moons hung pale and watchful, their light threading the clouds with silver truth. The world slept... but not all eyes were closed.

In the woodlands near Etharyon, a lone Moon Elf crouched atop a ridge of white stone, breath misting in the cool air. He watched the horizon where the peaks clawed at the sky, their crowns ablaze with gold lightning. The storm there did not roam as storms should it circled, bound to something vast and wrathful.

His gaze drifted to the marshlands below.

A shadow shifted beneath the mist, heavy and sinuous, disturbing the waters of Etharyon's swamps.

He shuddered.

He did not need to name it to know: Xalzorath.

Two dark powers stirring within a single region storm above, mire below spoke of unrest even the elves feared to voice.

Northward, near the glowing horizon of Fel Thalor, a pixie darted through the crimson haze, her wings scattering sparks of living light. She followed a trail of heat until the sky split with thunder. Looking up, she glimpsed a dragon of flame and gold, his wings carving molten scars across the heavens.

Zylron.

He vanished into the volcanic peaks. The pixie's glow dimmed as she turned and fled.

Some sights were not meant for fragile wings.

Farther still, above the frozen reaches of Firornak, a Platinum Dragon on patrol burst through a wall of snow. Frost clung to his scales as he hovered over the blinding white. He had seen her Glaciera gliding through the storm, her form gleaming like a living glacier. No other dragon left such silence in her wake... nor such cold.

By dawn, all three reports reached Radiantus within the crystalline spires of Lyra'el.

The Platinum patrol's account was delivered in solemn reverence.

The pixie's message arrived as a flickering orb of light, whispering in her voice.

The Moon Elf's words came written in silver ink, borne by wind and ward.

Radiantus listened, his serene gaze fixed upon the horizon where dawn pressed against storm. Aurelius stood beside him, wings folded, eyes reflecting the same quiet unease.

"They have scattered," Aurelius said softly.

"No longer bound by shared purpose... yet stirring within days of one another."

"That is not chance."

Radiantus inclined his head, dawn glinting across his radiant scales.

"No," he replied. "Four shadows moving apart cast longer darkness than one bound flame."

Silence settled between them, broken only by the breath of the morning wind.

"We will watch," Radiantus said at last. "If they move again, we will answer."

Aurelius turned his gaze toward distant horizons toward Etharyon's peaks, Fel Thalor's fires, and Firornak's frozen crown.

"They will move," he murmured. "The only question is... for whom."

Dawn spilled its light across Vacari, chasing away the final threads of night.

Yet beneath that tranquil glow, the shadows of the Dark Ancients remained waiting, watching... and remembering.

Chapter 2

The Cavern of Ash

The volcanic winds of Flameford howled like a living beast, carrying the stench of scorched stone and sulfur across a ravaged sky. Beneath the mountains deep where fire slept and the air itself glowed faintly red lay the Cavern of Ash, a vast hollow of blackened rock and dying flame. Its walls pulsed with dull heat, veins of molten ore threading the stone like sluggish blood.

There, the Ancients waited.

Zylron stood near the cavern's heart, molten wings folded tight against his back, embers drifting lazily around him. His eyes burned, watchful and unyielding.

Opposite him lingered Glaciera a contradiction given form. The air near her hollowed into cold, frost creeping across stone wherever her presence touched. Between them, the ground steamed, froze, and scorched in equal measure.

They were not alone.

A figure cloaked in shadowed robes leaned against an obsidian pillar Malrik, once High Priest of Vuarus. The runes stitched into his garments flickered faintly, like embers long denied extinction. He did not speak, but his gaze moved between the dragons with measured, unsettling awareness.

Zylron's molten eyes slid toward him.

"So," he rumbled, "the Mysterious One sends mortal hands now."

"Has the world grown so small it lacks dragons to command?"

Glaciera's lips curved in a thin, glacial line.

"Malrik has worn many faces before, Zylron," she replied coolly.

"Perhaps he has simply grown weary of watching his masters fail."

Malrik remained silent. He met her gaze without flinching and for a fleeting heartbeat, something old and perilous flickered between them. He had stood before them both in an age when Vuarus's name was spoken without fear… and without forgiveness.

The air shifted.

The cavern trembled.

Lightning tore through the storm above. Through the narrow fissure crowning the chamber, a vast shape descended wings glinting gold beneath stormlight.

Zarathos.

He struck the stone in a thunderous crash, ash spiraling upward as his claws carved scars into the cavern floor. The storm followed him inside lightning crawling along jagged ridges, filling the chamber with flares of gold and white.

He folded his wings with deliberate precision, eyes sweeping over those assembled. Sparks leapt beneath his steps as he advanced.

Zylron inclined his head a courtesy edged with defiance.

"The storm arrives," he said dryly.

Zarathos's reply rolled like distant thunder.

"And the fire still smolders."

"How inevitable."

He halted beside Zylron, their combined presence turning the air molten and heavy. His gaze flicked toward Glaciera, then toward Malrik, lingering just long enough for ash to settle around his claws.

"I see the Mysterious One's taste in envoys remains questionable," he murmured, electricity tracing his wings.

"But at least it is not Voraxia or Vorathos."

"I have little patience for their arrogance today."

A thin smile cut across Zylron's muzzle half amusement, half challenge. "Then today may yet prove tolerable."

Frost crept farther across the stone as Glaciera exhaled softly. "If tolerable is possible among this assembly."

Outside, thunder rolled laughter from unseen gods.

Silence followed.

Heavy.

Charged.

The storm deepened beyond the fissure, lightning crawling across volcanic ridges. Heat and frost waged their silent war between Zylron and Glaciera, the air hissing with restrained violence. Zarathos stood between them, every breath a distant thunderclap, his gaze fixed on the fractured opening above where molten light bled into shadow.

Malrik remained motionless, expression unreadable beneath the flicker of amber runes stitched into his robes. If he felt the pressure building against the cavern walls, he did not reveal it.

The cavern waited.

So did they.

And all of them knew one presence had yet to arrive.

Then the air changed.

It grew... wrong.

Flames guttered. The molten glow sickened to a bruised red. The scent of ozone and iron thickened in the chamber, followed by the whisper of rending silk.

Two vast shapes emerged from the fissure dark wings folding through smoke. One shimmered with voidlight; the other rippled with shadows that devoured their own reflections.

Vorathos struck the stone first, obsidian armor glistening with starlight that did not belong in Flameford's fire.

Beside her, Voraxia descended in twisted grace, scales of deep violet-black threaded with veins of blood-red flame. The air warped around them.

Even the ash recoiled.

Zarathos's eyes narrowed, molten light flickering dangerously. His tail lashed once against the stone, scattering sparks.

Under his breath just loud enough to carry he muttered, "Splendid. The ones who do not even belong here."

Zylron's molten gaze gleamed with dark amusement, though his voice held no warmth. "Careful, Zarathos. They might mistake that for welcome."

Frost ghosted through the air as Glaciera exhaled. "I would sooner welcome silence."

The newcomers did not answer at once.

Voraxia's gaze drifted lazily across the assembly before settling on Malrik. His jaw tightened beneath her attention.

Vorathos merely smiled eyes like voids, reflecting nothing but her own amusement.

Lightning flared through the cavern mouth. The storm twisted, drawn toward the mountain. Shadows stretched across the floor as static thickened the air.

Zarathos turned back toward the fissure above, his voice rising over the gathering thunder. "Enough delay. One still skulks beyond the storm."

The words hung summons and challenge entwined.

From beyond the thunder, a whisper answered melodic, smooth... and exquisitely false. "Oh, but I never miss an entrance."

Light fractured.

The first illusion bloomed along the cavern's edge.

The air shimmered as Ixalia the Mirage descended through the storm. Her wings caught the lightning, scattering it into a thousand ghostly reflections that flooded the chamber like living glass. For a heartbeat, it seemed a host of dragons had arrived instead of one each illusion breathing, shifting, whispering with her laughter.

She landed without a sound.

The illusions folded inward until only the true dragon remained: scales glimmering with iridescent hues that refused to settle on any single color.

Her eyes shifting opal veiled in smoke swept over the gathered Ancients.

"What a charming reception," she purred, voice steeped in melody and mockery. Flame, frost, storm, rot... and void. Such exquisite company."

Zylron's claws bit into the ash.

"If this is charm, Mirage," he said coldly, "I dread your honesty."

Lightning crawled along Zarathos's horns as he turned slightly away.

"Spare us the performance," he growled. "Dazzle the Abyssal kin if you must. We have no patience for tricks."

Ixalia's smile curved slow, knowing, dangerous.

Before she could reply, a shadow eclipsed the cavern's crown not the shadow of a dragon... but of something far older.

The heat dimmed.

Lightning guttered into nothing.

Even the molten veins along the walls cooled to dull, lifeless stone.

The Mysterious One had arrived.

They did not step into the chamber they unfolded from the darkness beyond the fissure, a form woven of smoke and pale light. The air bent around them. Sound itself withdrew. Instinctively, the dragons drew their wings close; even Vorathos's smirk faltered.

When they spoke, their voice was calm... measured... absolute.

"Enough."

The word struck the cavern like a physical blow.

Power rippled outward. Wings snapped tight to scales. Fire died. Frost sighed into vapor. Lightning vanished.

Their gaze turned to Malrik, who stood rigid beneath its weight.

"You were once of Vuarus," the Mysterious One said.

"A priest who named obedience sacred."

"Tell them does devotion still burn when your god is ash?"

Malrik's jaw tightened.

He did not answer.

His silence was defiance.

A low rumble rolled from Zylron's chest half laughter, half warning.

"Ancient history, shadow-master," he rumbled.

"Some of us remember that age better than you."

"Spare us your sermon."

"Speak your command."

He flicked his wings, scattering dying sparks.

"The sooner you finish," he continued, "The sooner we breathe air untainted by Abyss-born who do not belong here."

Frost ghosted across the stone as Glaciera exhaled.

"Agreed," she said coolly. "End this farce."

The Mysterious One's gaze drifted across them all fire, frost, storm, rot, illusion, void.

The air bowed beneath their will.

"Very well," they murmured, a trace of distant amusement threading the calm.

"Since you are so eager... We begin."

The cavern darkened. The final ember withered.

Silence thickened until it gained weight. Magic stilled beneath an unseen hand.

Their gaze returned to Zylron. Heat and shadow coiled together.

"Remember," the voice said softly, "Who permits your flames to burn at all?"

The molten veins flared once like chains drawn taut.

Zylron's scales blazed in defiance, fire surging against the dark... then collapsing as invisible pressure crushed it. He did not bow. But his claws scored the stone until fractures webbed beneath him.

"I remember," he growled, fury bound in iron.

Something like approval or satisfaction passed through the Mysterious One's presence.

They turned away.

The crushing weight receded like a withdrawing tide.

Silence reclaimed the chamber.

Then, softly deliberately "Zarathos."

The Topaz Ancient lifted his head. Gold fire burned in his eyes. Static prickled across his scales as the storm recoiled from his name, spoken within another's dominion.

"Your kind will journey south," the Mysterious One said. "To the Emberwoods."

The cavern held its breath.

"There, you will observe the Copper...and the Copper Ancient."

"Study their defenses. Their wards."

"Their secrets."

A pause.

"You will not strike."

"Not yet."

Lightning crawled along Zarathos's horns. His jaw tightened, thunder coiling in his breath.

"You would have us watch and wait," he muttered. "While the light-born still walk free mocking our..."

The words died in his throat.

The Mysterious One tilted their head.

The air around Zarathos warped.

Power struck without motion an unseen force slamming into his chest, driving him to one knee. Lightning tore from his wings, snapping violently against the cavern walls before choking into smoke.

"You will obey," the voice said no louder than before, yet filling the chamber like thunder given flesh. "Your storm answers to mine."

For a heartbeat, only the hiss of dying electricity remained.

Then Zarathos exhaled slow, ragged and lowered his gaze.

"As you command," he said through clenched teeth.

The Mysterious One lingered a moment longer.

Then they turned away a motion that was both dismissal and decree.

"There will come a day for flame and ruin," they said calmly. "But not this one."

Their oppressive presence eased. Heat crept back. Molten veins flickered weakly into life.

Still, none of the dragons moved.

They had been reminded power did not rest with them.

Zylron's molten eyes burned upon the fading silhouette, hatred unspoken yet seething beneath his scales.

Glaciera's frost crept once more across the stone near her perch, her expression unreadable save for the faint tightening of her jaw.

And Malrik, standing in the lingering shadow, watched in silence his gaze reflecting memory… and quiet dread.

The cavern remained hushed, still trembling from the echo of Zarathos's submission. Smoke curled across the floor, weaving between claws and scales before dissolving into gloom.

The Mysterious One turned slowly, their attention settling upon Ixalia.

The Mirage Dragon stood flawless and composed yet even her illusions wavered beneath that unseen weight.

"You," the voice said softly, "Will turn your sight to the hidden realm E'vahona."

The shifting reflections around Ixalia froze, suspended like fractured glass. Her amber eyes narrowed.

"You ask for the impossible."

The Mysterious One did not answer.

Ixalia tilted her head. Color rippled as her illusions resumed their lazy orbit.

"Kadona's protection veils E'vahona," she said coolly.

"Even gods name it myth."

"The Eladrin warp reality itself to hide their sanctuary."

"You cannot command vision where the world refuses revelation."

The figure's presence darkened. The air vibrated with a depth too deep to be sound.

"You will find it," they said.

"Unravel the veil."

"Break their confidence."

"Shatter the faith that shields their city."

A thin, humorless laugh escaped Ixalia.

"Even you do not know where it lies," she replied.

"If you did, you would not send me chasing ghosts."

The cavern stilled.

No flame stirred.

No frost cracked.

Even breath felt forbidden.

Only Zylron's molten gaze gleamed with the faintest flicker of amusement.

The Mysterious One did not move.

When their voice returned, it was quiet far too quiet.

"Careful, Mirage."

"Illusion is fragile."

"Especially when one forgets who permits the light that sustains it."

The light around Ixalia shattered.

Her reflections froze mid-motion, splintered and suspended in the air. For a heartbeat, her true form stood revealed—raw, radiant, furious beneath the crushing silence.

Slowly, she lowered her head, steel reclaiming her voice.

"As you command," she said tightly.

"The Mirage Dragons will scour wind and mirror."

"We will trace the threads that lead to E'vahona... and pull until the veil tears."

The Mysterious One regarded her a moment longer.

Then a single nod.

"Do so," they murmured.

"Break their faith and their walls will follow."

Ixalia exhaled, her breath thin as smoke. Her illusions folded back into place, flawless deception restored.

From the shadows, Glaciera's voice drifted soft, faintly amused.

"For your sake, Mirage," she said, "I hope you find more than snow and whispers."

Ixalia's gaze slid to her, a curved smile forming. "Whispers are my craft."

A brittle ripple of laughter followed as thunder rolled above Flameford, sealing the echo of her vow.

Silence returned.

Then the Mysterious One turned toward Malrik.

"You will come with me," they said. Flameford must burn again as it did in the age of Phoenix and Vuarus."

"Restore what remains of their sanctum."

"Do not alter this place."

"The Cavern of Ash remains untouched."

Malrik bowed his head, expression unreadable. "As you will."

Shadow and heat twisted together as the Mysterious One's form rippled then vanished. The oppressive presence lifted, leaving only the echo of their will trembling through the stone.

Outside, thunder rolled across the volcanic peaks.

Voraxia and Vorathos stepped beyond the cavern's mouth, their silhouettes etched against the blood-red sky. Stormlight slid across their scales like liquid night.

Voraxia glanced toward Ixalia, her voice low almost gentle.

"Whatever aid you require, Mirage... you have it."

"Even the Abyss knows when shadows must move together."

For once, Ixalia did not mock. She inclined her head.

"Then let us see how deep the darkness runs."

With a beat of her wings, she vanished into the storm, fractured light scattering until even her outline dissolved into cloud. Voraxia and Vorathos followed, swallowed by molten haze.

Within the cavern, silence returned—heavier now, emptied of the Mysterious One's presence, yet more suffocating for it.

Zarathos broke it first. Lightning flickered along his horns as he turned to the others.

"What kind of power was that?" he asked quietly. "I have bowed to no being... not since I claimed my storm."

Zylron's molten gaze met his.

"We have all wondered," he said.

"Even the Abyss keeps its distance."

"We know power when we see it but this..."

He exhaled, the sound like stone fracturing.

"We do not know what it is."

"Or who."

Frost whispered as Glaciera shifted.

"Perhaps that is the design," she murmured.

"Fear cuts deepest when it wears no face."

For a long moment, no one spoke. Outside, the storm throbbed like a living heart.

At last, Zylron spread his wings, sparks scattering.

"We return to our lairs," he said. "There will be time to seek answers."

One by one, they departed frost melting into heat, stormlight fading along stone, molten glow receding into shadow.

When the last echo died, the Cavern of Ash fell silent once more an empty wound in Flameford's heart, waiting for the command that would set the world ablaze.

From the shadows beyond the fissure, the Mysterious One watched them go neither fully shadow nor flame, but something between.

"So proud," they murmured.

"So certain their will is their own."

"Let them believe it."

Behind them, Malrik moved with methodical precision. Kneeling beside the molten fissure, he traced ancient sigils into the ash with a heat-blackened finger. The markings pulsed then sank into the stone, awakening a dull glow beneath the mountain.

"Flameford will burn again," the Mysterious One whispered.

"Not as it was... but as I decree."

Malrik pressed both palms to the ground. Fire coiled outward, igniting dormant runes beneath the floor. The mountain sighed molten breath stirring like something ancient awakening.

A faint curve touched the Mysterious One's unseen features.

"Let the world believe the dragons move freely," they said softly.

"In the end... all flames bend toward the same hand."

The fissure glowed crimson as thunder rolled once more.

Outside, the storm swept the last dragons from sight.

Inside, the first sparks of Flameford's rebirth crawled across the cavern walls.

The Mysterious One dissolved into smoke and light. Only their voice lingered faint, echoing, inevitable:

"Soon, Vacari will remember its master."

The cavern flared bright and then it went dark.

Chapter 3

Reforging Flameford

Flameford was alive again.

From the heights of the Tower of Shadowalker, the Mysterious One surveyed the molten sprawl below. The city's bones glowed with the red light of rebirth basalt towers rising anew, rivers of molten fire threading the reshaped heart of the once-ruined capital.

The tower itself had never fallen.

It had waited.

Patient.

Hollow.

Remembering.

Now its halls whispered once more with the breath of dominion.

At the tower's base, Malrik labored among circles of ancient sigils, their pale glow washing over his weathered features. His hands trembled—not from weakness, but from reverence.

"It feels different this time," he murmured.

"As though the flame remembers the hand that shaped it."

The Mysterious One turned from the balcony's edge, their voice smooth, cold, unyielding.

"The flame remembers me, Malrik."

"And it remembers him."

They drifted closer, their presence bending the air.

"You were his priest."

"I was his weapon."

Malrik lowered his head as history settled across his shoulders.

"Then the temple will rise again."

"Yes," the figure replied softly.

"But not as it was."

They stopped before him.

"It belongs to me now."

"The Shadow taught me..."

"...and I surpassed it."

Deep beneath the city, the Temple of Vuarus stirred.

Once a sanctum of worship, it had fallen to ruin after the god's fall obsidian statues shattered, flame-altars long cold. Now, beneath Malrik's hand, it breathed again.

Molten light seeped through fractured seams in the stone. The carvings of Vuarus still watched from the walls—but new sigils burned over them, the mark of the Mysterious One seared into ancient stone.

The once-pure obsidian flame now burned silver-black, reflecting its new master's will.

Malrik pressed his palm to the altered fire.

"You gave me purpose," he whispered.

"He taught me power."

"Between you both..."

"...I was remade."

A presence gathered behind him.

"You were spared," came the quiet reply. "Power belongs to those who endure it."

Malrik closed his eyes. The words settled like a benediction.

The air grew colder despite the magma's glow.

The Mysterious One circled the altar like a wraith, dimming the chamber's light.

They murmured.

"Why her?"

"Why did Vuarus desire the elf?"

Malrik's breath caught.

"Keisha."

"The red-haired one," the voice replied. "She haunted his final thoughts."

Malrik's expression tightened.

"It was never blood or ritual," he said quietly.

"It was her spirit."

"Her defiance."

"Her bond to creation something he could never own."

"So he sought to break her," the Mysterious One said coolly.

Malrik nodded.

"To hollow her."

"To make her a vessel."

"And Glaciera assisted," the figure murmured.

"She froze Keisha's body," Malrik said.

"To weaken her soul."

The black flame hissed, coiling higher.

"But it failed," the Mysterious One said contempt sharpening every word.

Malrik's jaw hardened.

"Because Lysander learned of the design."

"He warned the noble dragons."

"They came not from mercy... but from unity."

Silence swallowed the chamber.

Then shadow spilled like ink.

"Then she will die," the Mysterious One said, voice like molten glass.

"Not for who she is... but for what she cost."

Malrik turned toward the burning sigil.

"They claimed they were protecting creation."

"They protected weakness," came the cold reply.

"They stole his eternity for their illusion of peace."

"And for that... the noble dragons will burn with her."

The black flame surged, twisting into the hollow skull of a dragon devouring the chamber's light. The Mysterious One lifted their hand and the fire bowed.

"Vuarus ruled through fear," they said softly.

"I will rule through vengeance."

Malrik stepped forward, molten light burning in his eyes.

"I understand," he said low, unwavering.

"I crave vengeance as deeply as you do."

"For Vuarus."

"For Phoenix Shadowwalker."

"Their names will not fade into whispers."

The Mysterious One studied him for a long moment.

Then, slowly, they inclined their head.

"Good," they murmured.

"Then you will learn to turn mourning into momentum."

"We will not merely remember them..."

"...we will teach the world why they fell."

Malrik bowed deeper.

"Even if it tears the Dominion apart," he swore, voice hard as stone,

"Keisha will die."

"Even if the noble dragons perish beside her."

"Her death will unmake their light."

The Mysterious One's smile was a blade.

"Then it is sworn."

The black flame surged higher. Sigils of god and heir burned side by side one crumbling into ash, the other blazing with newborn dominion.

Above, the Tower of Shadowalker throbbed like a heart reclaiming its rhythm. Below, chained caverns stirred, and something ancient shifted in its sleep.

Outside, night sealed itself over Flameford.

The Abyssal Dominion had a name again and with it, a promise that would not be broken.

Chapter 4

The Silver Reforging

Dawn shimmered across the veiled skies of E'vahona, its light bending like glass upon the silver spires rising from mist and memory.

Beyond the crystalline towers, the open fields trembled with the rhythm of wings the living song of dragons in flight.

The Silver Ancients, guardians of illusion and truth, soared above their riders-in-training. Their scales caught the newborn radiance and scattered it across the horizon like liquid light.

Below, the Eladrin riders moved in flawless unison, silver-threaded armor gleaming as though woven from moonfire.

High above them, Talleoss climbed the morning sky, argent wings carving ripples through the haze. His roar rolled across the valley not a challenge, but a declaration of pride.

Upon his back rode Lady Seraphina, silver hair glinting like starlight, azure eyes steady beneath the pale rim of her helm.

Not far below, his mate Silvara wheeled in a graceful arc, mirrored scales reflecting the dawn. Her rider, Lord Thaldir, matched every movement with quiet precision autumn-gold hair streaming behind him, pale-blue eyes fixed as dragon and rider spiraled in seamless harmony.

Upon a nearby rise, Keisha, Ong, and Lord Karrenen stood in shared silence, watching as sky and spirit moved as one.

The earth beneath them hummed with ancient enchantments that shielded E'vahona, a gentle reminder that even beauty must be guarded by vigilance.

Keisha's smile was soft, threaded with pride.

"They've come far," she said quietly. "Their bond feels... inevitable. As though it has always existed, and they are only now remembering it."

Ong folded his arms, eyes following Talleoss's ascent.

"It's more than training," he murmured. "They are not just learning. They are reclaiming something the world nearly lost."

Lord Karrenen inclined his head, memory shadowing his gaze.

"Aye," he said softly, the word weighted with centuries.

"It recalls the First Age when the Silver Ancients chose their riders, and the Eladrin were chosen in return. It was never about command. It was about understanding."

His eyes lifted as Seraphina guided Talleoss into a rising loop that parted the clouds.

"The Eladrin did not seek to rule the dragons," he continued.

"They sought to honor them. And the Silver ones wise beyond measure recognized their own spirits reflected in that reverence."

He paused, voice softening further.

"To witness it again... is to feel history draw breath."

Keisha turned to him, warmth, and quiet certainty in her tone.

"History never truly fades, Father. It waits for the right hearts to remember."

A faint smile touched Karrenen's lips, though his gaze remained on the sky.

"Then may they remember well," he said. "They will need that unity in the days ahead."

Morning deepened, the veil painted in silver and rose.

The dragons cried out once more not the call of war, but of promise.

And for a fleeting heartbeat, E'vahona seemed untouched by shadow.

Keisha's gaze lingered on the silver expanse of sky, where dragon wings gleamed like mirrored light against the morning mist—as though the future itself were holding its breath.

For a heartbeat, she was no longer in E'vahona. She stood in Lyra'el, the night before the last battle.

Her father's voice returned to her quiet, steady as the winds of war whispered through crystal halls.

"Nin úva telanth ilthi... náni uin nar ilthi náren sira."

(I could not bear to lose you... not as I lost your mother.)

The memory struck deep soft, unyielding.

It had been one of the few times she had seen him afraid.

Not of war... but of loss.

She turned to Lord Karrenen, tracing the years etched into his face. When their eyes met, understanding flickered there. He knew precisely which memory had found her.

A faint, knowing smile touched his lips.

"You remember," he said quietly.

Keisha nodded. "How could I forget?"

He drew a slow breath, weighted with unspoken years.

"There is something I have long meant to tell you," he said gently. "Perhaps now is the hour."

A few paces away, Ong tilted his head. "Do you want me to step aside?"

Karrenen shook his head.

"No. You should hear this as well, Ong. What I am about to share is not Keisha's burden alone. It concerns the truth of what came before Lyra'el fell."

The valley seemed to grow still.

Even the Silver dragons above slowed their flight, their shadows drifting across the light like pale ghosts of the past.

Keisha exchanged a glance with Ong. Her heart tightened.

Whatever came next, she knew it would reshape more than memory.

Karrenen's gaze softened as it returned to his daughter, nostalgia glimmering in his silver eyes.

"Serena and I were children together," he began. "She was always anchored by her bow steady, disciplined, unyielding. None in E'vahona could rival her aim... or her patience."

A small, sorrow-touched smile curved his mouth.

"You carry that same fire whenever you draw a string."

Keisha did not speak, but emotion trembled across her expression.

"As we grew older," Karrenen continued, "I came to love her. But Serena was never one to be hurried. Duty, craft, people these were her compass. I told myself she was not ready. Perhaps that was my folly."

His gaze drifted toward the silver horizon, seeing another age.

Ong let out a soft chuckle, earning a fond, warning glance from Keisha.

"Your mother moved like a whisper through the moonwood," Karrenen went on.

"Even among the Eladrin, her bow was legend."

He inhaled slowly.

"One night, the Druchii crossed our borders arrogant, reckless. She hunted them alone."

His voice softened.

"She expected only enemies... and found something else. A human."

A warmer smile touched his lips.

"He lay beneath a fallen moonwood wounded, surrounded. The Druchii circled him like jackals. Before he ever saw her, Serena loosed two arrows. Two bodies fell."

Karrenen's eyes brightened with memory.

"When she stepped from the shadows, bow still drawn, she asked him, 'Why are you here, mage?'"

Keisha leaned in, breath caught.

"He answered," Karrenen said, the corner of his mouth lifting, "'I was trying not to die. That was failing... until you.'"

Even Ong smiled.

"He claimed he had been following ley lines, not trouble. She told him he had crossed into death."

Karrenen's voice warmed.

"When she brought him before the council, the elders wished to leave him where he fell."

"But Serena would not allow it. She said, 'He is wounded, not wicked. Mercy is not weakness.'"

His gaze softened with the years.

"I agreed to bring him into E'vahona on one condition that he never remember the way."

A faint smile flickered.

"Serena gave him a moon-draught so he would sleep until we arrived."

He let out a quiet breath.

"When he awoke, she gave him rules enough to frighten a lesser man. But Eldric called her his stern savior wrapped in moonlight."

A quiet laugh lived in his chest.

"She pretended not to hear. I saw her smile when she thought no one watched."

Keisha's laugh trembled caught between tears and wonder.

"He could have left once he healed," Karrenen said softly.

"But he stayed. He took the vow.

Became one of us."

His eyes met Keisha's.

"In time, he earned not only her respect... but her heart."

His voice lowered, reverent.

"That is how it began your mother's fire meeting his flame. Two lives that should never have crossed... and yet they did."

He held Keisha's gaze.

"From that crossing, you were born a bridge between light and will."

Silence followed sacred, full, breathing.

"You were there for all of it," Keisha whispered.

Karrenen nodded.

"They were happy. Genuinely happy."

He drew a slow breath.

"And when I saw that... I never spoke the words I once carried for her."

He looked at Keisha with open, unguarded honesty.

"Some loves are not meant to be claimed. Only honored."

His voice softened.

"You were born of their joy. And though it cost me what I once dreamed... I would never trade what came of it."

Ong hesitated, gentle but sincere.

"Forgive me," he said quietly, "but did you ever hate Eldric for taking Serena from you?"

Karrenen's smile was gentle worn by time, yet unbroken.

"No," he said softly. "He gave her joy. That was enough."

His gaze softened, distant with memory.

"Whatever love I carried was never meant to bind her," he continued. "It was meant to see that she never walked alone."

He drew a quiet breath, eyes drifting beyond the veil of years.

"Later," he said, "Serena and Eldric came to me. They asked if I would become your guardian, should anything befall them. I agreed without hesitation."

His voice grew heavier.

"I did not think fate would claim that promise so swiftly."

The air stilled, as though even the dragons sensed the weight in his words.

"Then the war came," he murmured. "The Druchii captured Eldric under Malegrim Shadowwalker's command. They demanded the location of E'vahona. He refused."

His voice lowered.

"For that silence... they executed him."

Keisha's breath caught. Her hand tightened at her side.

"They meant to kill Serena as well," Karrenen continued, shadow edging his gaze.

"But the Eladrin learned of his capture. We arrived too late to save him... but not too late to bring her home."

His voice softened.

"You were so small then," he said gently. "Barely old enough to remember her face."

He paused, grief settling like ash.

"In time, Serena came to me again. She said she was leaving to hunt Malegrim Shadowwalker. To end him for what he had done to Eldric."

A quiet ache threaded his tone.

"I begged her to stay. But her will was forged of steel. She could not be turned."

His eyes softened, pride braided with sorrow.

"When she did not return... I took you entirely into my care. Losing her nearly broke me, Keisha. But I had you. And through you, I found purpose again."

He met her gaze, voice trembling despite his composure.

"I vowed I would never lose you as I lost Serena."

Silence followed long, fragile, sacred.

The wind whispered through the grass, carrying the distant, steady rhythm of dragon wings.

At last, Karrenen offered a faint, unguarded smile.

"I never told you our history," he said softly, "because I did not wish the past to weigh upon your heart. But in Lyra'el, when the truth escaped me... perhaps it was simply time. Some truths refuse to remain buried."

Keisha held his gaze. Light from E'vahona shimmered between them silver, forgiving, eternal.

She stepped closer.

For a heartbeat, no words came.

Then she embraced him.

"I was fortunate," she whispered. "I had two fathers who loved my mother... and me. For a time, I was angry with her for leaving. But not anymore."

Her voice softened.

"I still wish she had stayed. But I understand now why she could not."

Karrenen's arms closed around her.

She smiled through tears.

"And besides... I gained another father. One who taught me more than I ever wished to learn. Even magic when I was sure I could not... or would not."

A faint, fond laugh escaped her.

"But you insisted. And, as always... you were right."

She pulled back just enough to meet his eyes, tears glinting like starlight.

"Thank you for telling me, Father."

Then, in the flowing cadence of the Eladrin tongue:

"Amin mela lle, atar."

(I love you, Father.)

Karrenen smiled not as a lord, but as a man who had waited a lifetime to hear those words.

As the last echoes of her voice faded into the hush of morning, the sound of wings returned steady, proud, and pure.

Overhead, Talleoss and Silvara wheeled through the sky, their riders guiding them into formation as sunlight scattered across argent scales.

Keisha and Karrenen turned to watch, the space between them settling into quiet peace. Beside them, Ong lifted his gaze, a faint smile touching his lips.

Below, the Eladrin riders dismounted in disciplined unison, their dragons bowing low in acknowledgment.

Along the path winding between the crystal terraces, a procession of Eladrin elders and master crafters approached, robes threaded with silver runes glowing in the morning light. At their head walked an elder with white hair as drifting mist, carrying a long rune-etched staff bound in copper bands shimmering with enchantment.

At the field's heart, she knelt and, with solemn reverence, laid the weapon upon the earth.

One by one, the others followed, placing their gleaming staves beside hers until a radiant circle of ancient power crowned the ground.

Karrenen's expression softened with pride.

"Call them down," he murmured.

Keisha lifted her hand.

A ripple of pale light flowed from her palm not a command, but an invitation.

The dragons descended with elegant precision, wings stirring the air like banners of light. and the Eladrin riders dismounted in disciplined unison, their dragons bowing low in acknowledgment

When the riders stepped forward, Karrenen gestured toward the waiting circle.

"These," he said, voice carrying across the field, "are the Eladrin Spellweaver Staves.

"Forged of enchanted wood, etched with living runes that breathe with the essence of E'vahona itself. Each amplifies its bearer's magic—focusing elemental force, raising wards, or granting the precision required for true mastery."

The nearest crafter bowed low. The runes along the staves brightened, pulsing in harmony with the dragons' deep, resonant rumble.

"They were once the weapons of the first Eladrin dragon-bonded," Karrenen continued.

"Lost when the veil of E'vahona was sealed. We have remade them not as relics... but as symbols of what we once were... and what we must become again."

A hush fell across the field.

The dragons lowered their heads in recognition, silver scales reflecting rune-glow like mirrored moonlight.

Keisha stepped closer, softening her voice.

"They are beautiful."

Karrenen smiled faintly.

"Beauty, yes. But purpose above all. May they guard you, as they once guarded the Light."

One by one, the riders knelt, receiving their staves with reverence.

When Seraphina's hand closed around hers, the runes flared silver-white, answering her spirit. Around her, others followed their staves igniting in hues that mirrored their elemental bonds: frost, flame, wind, warding light.

High above, the veil of E'vahona shimmered like living crystal, as if the realm itself approved.

Keisha lifted her eyes skyward, voice barely more than breath.

"The past never truly fades... It only waits to rise again."

Karrenen looked at her, warmth in his gaze.

"And today," he said softly, "it begins anew."

The dragons roared not the cry of war, but of awakening.

And beneath their wings, the Eladrin dragon-bonded stood reborn.

Chapter 5

The Maze and the Mischief

The horizon shimmered where Fel Thalor's volcanic peaks met the glowing edge of the Emberwoods.

Here, the world was caught between flame and life ash drifting like crimson snow over forests that burned with color rather than fire. The trees were veined with molten gold, their leaves deep scarlet and amber, and the air carried a faint, honeyed warmth that hummed with enchantment.

From the storm-wracked heights descended Zarathos, the Ancient Topaz Dragon, thunder still crackling across his wings. Three of his kin followed, their scales gleaming like polished citrine beneath fractured sunlight.

Below them stretched the border-ward known as the Maze of Blossoms a vast tangle of living vines and luminous flowers pulsing with copper light. Petals shimmered in layered reds and golds, releasing slow curls of fragrant mist. The maze itself seemed to breathe, its winding paths shifting like thought.

Zarathos struck the earth with a heavy landing, talons sinking into glowing loam.

"A wall of petals?" he snarled. "Is this the Copper's idea of defense?"

One of the Topaz drakes rumbled uncertainly.

"It appears... delicate, my lord."

Zarathos bared his fangs.

"Then it will perish delicately."

Power gathered in his chest, the air tightening with electric strain. With a roar that split the canopy, he hurled a bolt of lightning into the heart of the maze.

Vines blackened. Blooms folded inward, collapsing into ash and light.

Then the maze restored itself.

Every petal returned.

The air filled with jasmine and ozone, sweet, and mocking.

Zarathos's eyes burned.

"Again."

A second strike flared gold-white, shearing the floral walls to nothing.

They bloomed anew.

A third brighter, louder, edged with fury and still the maze stood whole, blossoms opening wider as if in quiet taunt.

High within the red-gold canopy, Emberwood Pixies darted between glowing leaves, laughter chiming like glass bells.

One, scarcely larger than a leaf, covered her mouth with both hands.

"At this pace, he will scorch his own crown," she whispered.

Another snorted, flicking gold dust into the air.

"Three strikes already. Should we tell him Raelithar's will binds it?"

The first shook her head, eyes dancing.

"Let him try a fourth. He gleams most brightly when he is furious."

A third pixie sighed and streaked away copper light threading through the forest.

Moments later, the upper canopy bowed beneath a deep, resonant hum.

Through shafts of amber light descended Raelithar, the Ancient Copper Dragon. His wings glowed like molten metal; his scales already shimmered with quiet amusement before he spoke.

"Well now," he drawled, voice smooth as tempered bronze, "it seems the Topaz still struggles to tell the difference between dominion… and disaster."

Zarathos snapped his head up, lightning crawling along his jaw.

"Raelithar."

His tone was poison.

"Your games are wasted on me."

Raelithar circled lazily overhead, sunlight flaring across his wings.

"Games?" he mused. "No, my gilded friend. Only a reminder."

He dipped one wing toward the maze below.

"The Emberwoods bow to no dragon who mistakes arrogance for strength."

Pixie laughter shimmered through the leaves. Even the forest seemed to hum in quiet amusement as Zarathos's tail lashed the earth.

Raelithar's gaze locked on the Topaz Ancient. The air between them tightened, alive with heat and tension.

"It would seem," the Copper Ancient continued, "you have chosen the wrong side."

His grin sharpened, emberlight glinting in his eyes.

"Tell me, Zarathos why lead them down the same road to ruin that Thundria walked?"

Zarathos's snarl cut the air, sharp with static. The younger Topaz dragons recoiled, sparks flickering along their wings.

"Do not speak her name. You know nothing of what she sacrificed."

Raelithar tilted his head. Amusement cooled into something quieter and far more dangerous.

"Sacrifice?" he echoed. "From where I stood, it looked like pride. And pride burns faster than fire."

The vines rustled. Petals brightened as if in agreement. The pixies fell silent.

Raelithar lowered himself, wings folding, eyes unflinching.

"I warned Thundria once," he said softly.

"As I warn you now. The one you serve does not build. They consume."

"You think you align with power, but you have only offered your storm to feed another's shadow."

Zarathos bared his fangs. The ground cracked beneath the pressure of his fury.

"Watch your words, Copper. You speak as though you stand above the Dominion."

Raelithar laughed deep, knowing.

"Oh no, Topaz. I do not stand above it."

His eyes burned with fierce turquoise fire.

"I stand beyond it."

The Emberwoods stirred around him trees bowing, petals trembling as if the forest echoed his defiance.

Raelithar drifted closer, copper light washing the clearing.

"Do not polish failure into martyrdom. She aligned the Topaz with Phoenix and Vuarus."

"She believed herself untouchable beneath their wings. Her death was not noble. It was the price of arrogance."

Zarathos hissed, lightning crawling across his scales.

"You dare—"

"I do," Raelithar cut in, voice flat as forged metal. "Because I was there. She tried to destroy Aurelia, the Crystal Dragon. And that... was her undoing."

The words struck like a silent blow.

Zarathos's fury flared and for an instant, something flickered behind it.

Unease.

Raelithar's voice softened, though steel remained beneath it.

"Your vengeance will not return her. It will only carve your name beside hers in the ruins of history."

The Maze of Blossoms shimmered. The pixies held their breath.

Raelithar's tail lashed, scattering molten dust.

"Blind dragons make excellent pawns," he said quietly, "for masters who promise them purpose."

The tension snapped.

Lightning exploded from Zarathos's wings, ripping the air like shattered glass. He surged forward, talons cracking the earth. "You dare lecture me..."

Raelithar's eyes gleamed, tempered amusement returning like a blade sliding into its sheath.

"Careful," he murmured, almost kindly. "You tread close to the line your mistress forbade."

Zarathos roared.

"I bow to no Copper trickster!"

Bolts of raw lightning tore from his jaws only to splinter harmlessly against the veil of molten radiance flaring from Raelithar's claws.

Raelithar's wings unfurled, vast and gleaming like hammered bronze. Red-gold light flooded the forest.

"Enough."

His voice was no longer amused.

It was ancient.

"This is my domain."

The maze pulsed blossoms curling inward, petals trembling like shields as the forest stirred.

From copper-shadowed trees, shapes emerged: Raelithar's flight, scales gleaming in hues of burnished flame and molten rose. They took position above the maze, silent and ready.

Raelithar lifted a single claw.

His dragons stilled at once.

Zarathos sneered, wings flaring wide.

"So the ancient coward summons his brood. You think I fear them?"

Behind him, the younger Topaz dragons surged into formation, lightning crackling into a jagged crescent of stormlight.

Raelithar's smirk returned slowly.

"No," he said softly. "You fear nothing. And that is precisely your problem."

His gaze hardened.

"Cross this line, Zarathos," he warned, "and the Emberwoods will rise against you."

"Even the earth knows which dragons it calls kin."

The vines shifted. Thorns extended. Petals turned like watchful eyes toward the Topaz flight.

Zarathos hesitated.

Only for a breath.

Fury flickered then calculation.

Raelithar's grin sharpened.

"Wise," he murmured. "Keep your claws clean. There are worse things than me waiting if you do not."

Zarathos glared, lightning crawling along his wings.

"This is not over. You will see me again, Copper."

Raelithar's answering smile was molten and unafraid.

"I never doubted it. But when you return... carry a message for your master."

He rose above the maze, copper scales blazing in Emberwood light.

"Tell the one who hides in shadow this is not a war they can win."

"The Abyssal Dominion has fallen before. It will fall again."

"New names, old powers the ending does not change."

Zarathos's growl rolled through the trees.

Raelithar only laughed.

"And one more thing, Topaz. Radiantus and Aurelius search the echoes of the past."

"When they uncover who commands the darkness..."

"No veil, no illusion, no dominion will hide them."

Zarathos's claws dug into the earth, sparks hissing where lightning met root.

Raelithar's grin widened.

"And bringing dragons who do not belong in Vacari will not strengthen your cause. We already know Ixalia has entered our skies."

For the first time, Zarathos faltered not from fear, but from the realization that his enemies watched more closely than he believed. "Leave my sight, Copper," he snapped.

Raelithar dipped his head, regal and dismissive. "Gladly. The scent of arrogance grows tiresome."

With a final glare, Zarathos signaled his flight. The Topaz dragons rose in a spiral of thunder and gold, vanishing toward the peaks.

Raelithar remained until the last glimmer faded.

Then he exhaled, the fire in his eyes dimming to warm embers.

"Let them run back to their master," he murmured. "The shadows grow bold again... but light has a long memory."

Above him, the Emberwoods sighed petals drifting like embers through copper air.

And the Ancient Copper Dragon turned toward the heart of his domain, laughter echoing low and knowing through the crimson leaves.

Chapter 6

Echoes in the Sky City

High above the Cerulean Expanse, the floating city of Lyra'el drifted like a shard of heaven carved from crystal and starlight. Light poured through its glass-wrought walkways, weaving living constellations across runes etched into marble older than kingdoms. Winds whispered through open arches, carrying the distant echo of dragon wings.

Within the Hall of Aether, where the sky shimmered in veils of blue and silver, Radiantus, the Platinum Ancient, stood gazing toward the far horizon. His wings rested like mirrored shields, catching sunlight until he seemed forged from dawn itself.

Soft footsteps approached.

"Aurelius," Radiantus murmured without turning. "You have felt her presence as well."

The Celestial Dragon stepped into the light, white-gold scales radiant as sunrise, eyes holding the stillness of eternity.

"Yes," Aurelius said quietly. "Ixalia has entered Vacari."

The air tightened as though the world itself listened.

Radiantus inclined his head.

"A Mirage Ancient... after centuries. We have not faced her kind since the First Shadowing. Their illusions do not merely deceive. They fracture memory and bend truth until even dragons doubt their own sight."

Aurelius's expression darkened.

"The dark flights do not release Mirage Dragons without purpose. Her presence alone reshapes the field of war."

Radiantus's wings unfurled slightly, platinum light rippling.

"They have loosed worse of late," he said. "But Ixalia is no simple weapon. She is a design."

Aurelius stepped closer.

"Have Talleoss and Silvara been warned?"

"They know," Radiantus replied. "The Silver Ancients already sense distortions along the boundary veils. They believe her purpose is bound to E'vahona."

Celestial light threaded Aurelius's wings.

"If Mirage Dragons hunt the hidden realm," he murmured, "then the stakes rise beyond war. Illusion set against illusion but theirs is born of shadow, not truth."

Radiantus lowered his gaze.

"They seek what even the gods could not claim," he said. "The veiled heart of the Eladrin. If Ixalia pierces even a fragment of that concealment..."

He exhaled slowly.

"...the balance itself may fracture."

Aurelius turned toward the eastern sky, where faint distortions rippled tremors only an Ancient could perceive.

"She already tests the borders," he said. "The fabric between realms trembles where she moves. Whatever they seek... it was never meant to be touched."

Radiantus closed his eyes, magic flowing through him like breath.

"The Dominion grows bold," he murmured. "To set illusion against a city woven of it."

He opened his eyes again, resolve settling into his voice.

"The Silvers stand vigilant. But they cannot stand alone."

Aurelius inclined his head.

"Then our search must not end with Ixalia. We must learn why she was unleashed."

Radiantus turned, platinum light tracing his spine.

"And who commands her. Whoever stirs the dark flights now stands closer to their goal than we feared."

Radiantus's gaze drifted toward E'vahona's unseen horizon.

"Ixalia's path may yet lead to Keisha," he said quietly. "The one in shadow has never hidden their fixation upon her."

Aurelius's expression hardened.

"Then she is the key," he said. "If Ixalia hunts E'vahona, she hunts Keisha... or what Keisha represents."

Radiantus nodded.

"The last living bond between Serena and Eldric. And the bearer of the Eladrin prophecy."

Aurelius turned fully, celestial eyes bright with resolve.

"Then the hour has come. We cease circling guesses. We uncover who this shadowed master truly is and how they are bound to Vuarus... and Phoenix."

The name Phoenix Shadowwalker echoed through the hall like a buried flame.

Old memory crossed Aurelius's gaze wings of shadow, a god undone by hunger, a Dominion nearly reborn.

Radiantus's claws tightened against the marble.

"Phoenix's fall buried many secrets," he said slowly. "Secrets Vuarus never wished to be revealed. Whoever leads the dark flights now was shaped by him... trained by him... or bound by some pact yet hidden."

Aurelius exhaled, starlight drifting like breath.

"And if they seek to raise the Abyssal Dominion through ancient rites," he said, "ignorance becomes our greatest enemy."

His gaze sharpened.

"We must unearth the past."

Radiantus inclined his head.

"Then we begin."

He spread his wings, the hall flooding with radiant light.

"The Silvers guard E'vahona. The Coppers guard the Emberwoods. The Crystals watch the skies."

His voice deepened.

"But the Celestial and the Platinum... we guard the truth."

He turned from the balcony.

"And truth has slept long enough."

They entered the Aetherium Scriptorium, where starlight drifted like dust and ancient tomes hovered in silent suspension. Scholars bowed as the two Ancients approached.

Radiantus spoke, his voice ringing like a bell in stone.

"We require the sealed records of Vuarus his rise, his rites, his disciples, and his dealings with the Abyss."

A hush fell.

The elder archivist stepped forward, robes threaded with living crystal.

"Those records predate the First Wars," she said carefully. "Some were sealed when Vuarus first sought dominion beyond the mortal veil. The Council of Light locked them away."

Aurelius inclined his head sharply.

"They sealed them because his corruption was already taking root."

Radiantus's horns glowed faintly.

"Then unseal them," he said. "The Dominion rises again and its master walks Vuarus's path."

Another scholar stepped forward, trembling.

"What knowledge do you seek, Platinum One?"

"Everything," Aurelius answered. "His rites. His ties to the Abyss. The names of his followers. The places he vanished before returning, wielding shadow like breath."

Radiantus's voice deepened.

"And the final records of the war in which Talleoss faced him. That battle ended Vuarus's life but not his legacy."

A nervous murmur rippled through the chamber.

"Those records were sealed," the archivist whispered, "because even the Council feared such knowledge could inspire another."

Aurelius's wings tightened.

"Their fear buried the truth," he said. "And that secrecy has become our enemy. We cannot fight what history refuses to reveal."

Radiantus stepped closer.

"Restore every fragment," he commanded. "Every sealed scroll. Every memory crystal."

"Begin with Vuarus's earliest years—before he claimed the Shadow... before he forged the Abyssal Dominion."

The archivists bowed, runes igniting with resolve.

"It will be done," the elder archivist vowed. "Before the next moonrise, you shall have the first reconstructed chronicle."

Aurelius lifted his head, celestial light echoing from the walls.

"The truth of Vuarus will reveal the truth of the one who walks in his footsteps."

Radiantus nodded, gaze drifting toward the horizon where the veil rippled faintly under Ixalia's unseen hand.

"And when that truth is uncovered..."

His wings unfurled in silent promise.

"...we will know how to end them."

Chapter 7

Echoes of an Impossible Bond

The veiled light of E'vahona drifted across the upper terraces, casting ripples of silver over carved stone. Lanterns of woven spellbloom hung from crystalline boughs overhead, their glow soft as moonfire. Beneath the vast canopy of an ancient moonwood, Lord Karrenen walked beside Lord Thaldir, the elder's silver-and-copper robes whispering through the grass.

Thaldir moved with the measured stillness of one who had spent centuries studying truths others feared to name. His pale-blue eyes held the calm of deep water reflective, patient... and dangerous when disturbed.

They paused near a cascading fountain where illusory water shimmered like falling starlight.

"It has been many years," Thaldir said quietly.

"Yet the echoes of that time remain."

He drew a slow breath.

"Six months in the grasp of Vuarus and Phoenix..."

He hesitated.

"Even speaking of it risks stirring shadows best left asleep."

Karrenen's jaw tightened, though his voice remained steady.

"Some shadows grow more dangerous the longer they remain unspoken."

Thaldir folded his hands behind his back, gaze lingering on the shifting light.

"You wished to speak of Ong."

Karrenen inclined his head.

"It concerns what occurred during Keisha's captivity," he said.

"When she was taken broken, stripped of strength piece by piece she reached out."

He paused.

"Not with a spell."

"Not with voice."

"With spirit."

For a breath, Thaldir's composure fractured.

"And he heard her," the elder murmured.

"Yes."

Thaldir's eyes sharpened.

"That should be impossible."

"Even among the Eladrin, soul-calling is vanishingly rare. It occurs only when two spirits are bound beyond affection through destiny, life-thread, or bloodlines woven before memory."

Karrenen looked toward the distant training fields, where Ong sparred with two silver-cloaked warriors, unaware of the weight gathering around his name.

"That is precisely why I sought you out," Karrenen said quietly.

"Such a bond between two Eladrin is uncommon."

His gaze softened.

"But between an Eladrin... and a human?"

Thaldir allowed the silence to settle like falling snow.

"Unprecedented," he said at last.

He stepped closer, lowering his voice as though the trees themselves might listen.

"Ong was not born to our magic. He carries no veilblood. No ancestral resonance."

"And yet when Keisha reached beyond agony, distance, and despair... he answered."

A crease formed at Thaldir's brow.

"That is not the bond of lovers."

"Nor the devotion of companions."

"It is something older..."

"...and far more dangerous."

Karrenen exhaled slowly.

"I felt it even then."

"And the longer I watch them, the more certain I became her soul reached for his... and his reached back."

Thaldir studied Ong in silence.

"A bond like that," he murmured,

"does not merely alter lives."

"It alters fate."

Karrenen nodded, the weight of it settling heavily in his chest.

"That is my fear."

"If their spirits are entwined beyond what we understand... then Ong stands at the threshold of something far greater than he realizes."

Thaldir turned to face him fully.

"You believe the bond is still evolving."

"I do," Karrenen replied.

"And I fear the world will test it soon."

The elder was silent for a long moment.

Then, scarcely above a whisper:

"If an Eladrin can call a human soul across agony, time, and distance..." then the boundaries we believed immutable may never have existed at all."

Karrenen's gaze returned to Ong, who paused mid-spar, as though sensing unseen eyes.

"Whatever this truth is," Karrenen said quietly, "we must be ready."

"Because if the Dominion learns what occurred during those six months—"

Thaldir finished the thought, voice firm with cold certainty:

"They will not seek to understand it."

"They will weaponize it."

The wind shifted.

The moonwood whispered as though it, too, feared what fate had begun to weave.

It carried with it a faint pulse through the veil not sound, not magic... but awareness.

The sensation brushed the edge of Keisha's senses, and she slowed mid-step upon the terrace, gaze narrowing.

"Karrenen," she said softly.

"You're looking for me."

Karrenen exchanged a glance with Thaldir.

"Yes," he replied.

"You both are."

Ong approached from the training circle, sweat glinting faintly along his brow. He slowed when he saw their expressions—too grave, too familiar with old wounds.

"What's wrong?" he asked quietly.

"Something important," Thaldir said.

"And something only the three of you can speak to."

They moved beneath the shelter of the moonwood, into a quiet alcove where silver leaves shimmered like suspended stars. Ong remained standing, tension already coiling through his shoulders.

Karrenen began gently.

"We were speaking of your captivity, Keisha... and of what occurred between you and Ong during those months."

A flicker crossed Ong's eyes memory, dread, and something deeper than either.

Keisha's jaw tightened.

"That time," she said carefully, "is not something I dwell on."

"And yet it cannot be ignored," Thaldir replied.

"Because what occurred between you defies everything we understand of Eladrin magic."

Ong looked away, jaw clenched.

"Do we really have to talk about this?" he muttered.

"That time..."

His voice faltered.

"...that time was hell."

Karrenen's tone softened.

"We know. But truth matters, Ong."

"You heard her. Not her voice her spirit."

Ong stared at his hands scarred, steady, trembling despite his effort to still them.

"Yes," he said quietly.

"I heard her. Every night. Every time I closed my eyes."

"It was not sound. It was like something inside me was being torn open... trying to reach her."

Keisha inhaled sharply.

"But I couldn't find her," Ong continued, voice tightening.

"I searched until my legs gave out. It was not a direction it was a pull."

"And every day I failed to reach her..."

He swallowed.

"...it felt like I was failing her."

Silence pressed close, heavy, and sacred.

"When Vuarus summoned us," Ong said at last, eyes distant, "he did not bargain. He did not pretend mercy."

"He showed us Keisha half-frozen, barely conscious and said he would release her if we revealed the location of E'vahona."

Keisha's breath hitched as her fingers tightened around Ong's.

Thaldir's expression hardened.

"That aligns with everything we know of him," he said coldly.

"He sought the veil's collapse above all else."

Karrenen's voice lowered, heavy with memory.

"He demanded that I reveal the path. And when I refused..."

"...he turned to Ong."

Ong's fists clenched.

"He told me a human would break first," Ong said bitterly.

"That I would care nothing for Eladrin secrets."

"That I would trade a world to save one woman."

A breath sharp, controlled.

"He didn't understand me."

Keisha's eyes shimmered.

"I wanted to save her," Ong said, raw honesty breaking through.

"Seeing her like that... it shattered something in me."

He paused.

"But giving him E'vahona would have destroyed everyone she loved."

"Everything she fought to protect."

Karrenen nodded once.

"We could not trade the soul of our people for one life even hers," he said quietly.

"To do so would have delivered E'vahona into annihilation."

Ong's voice dropped to a whisper.

"And so we walked away… believing that was the last time I would ever see her alive."

The moonwood leaves rustled softly overhead, silver light trembling as if the realm itself remembered.

Keisha's breath hitched, tears burning at the corners of her eyes.

"And even then," Ong said quietly, his voice gentling,

"even when I thought she was gone… I still heard her."

"Faint. Distant. But never silent."

His gaze lifted to hers.

"Like her spirit refused to let mine go."

Thaldir regarded Ong with a mixture of awe and unease.

"A soul-call such as that," he murmured,

"should not have crossed species. Should not have crossed realms."

"And yet…it did."

He looked at Ong as though seeing him for the first time.

"You refused to betray E'vahona," Thaldir said.

"And yet you never released Keisha."

"That is not ordinary devotion."

A pause.

"That is something far rarer… and far more dangerous."

Keisha tightened her grip on Ong's hand, her voice trembling.

"You saved me," she said softly. "Even when you thought you couldn't."

Ong shook his head.

"No," he replied.

"You saved me."

"As long as I could hear you, I knew you were alive."

"And if you were alive…"

His voice broke.

"…then I couldn't give up."

Thaldir's gaze moved between them reverent now, and wary.

"What binds you may very well reshape the fate of realms," he said quietly.

The moonwood leaves whispered overhead, silver light shifting like breath. Thaldir allowed the silence to settle before speaking again, his tone lower, older—a voice meant for ancient halls, not open gardens.

"Ong," he said,

"what you and Keisha share is not affection."

"It is not even love, as mortals understand it."

"Nor is it merely the bond forged through shared suffering."

He stepped closer.

"It is something that should not exist."

Keisha's breath caught.

"Our souls are not shaped the same," Thaldir continued.

"Eladrin spirits are woven of veil and memory."

"Human souls burn fast bright, fierce, and brief."

"We do not intertwine across that boundary."

"Not fully."

"Not without consequence."

Ong swallowed.

"Then how—"

"Because," Thaldir said gently,

"you crossed a line no human ever has."

His eyes met Ong's unwavering.

"You heard a call meant only for veilblood."

"You answered it."

"You followed it."

"And in doing so, your spirit reached across a divide that was never meant to be bridged."

Karrenen nodded slowly.

"That is why we asked you here," he said.

"There are... conversations unfolding among the elders."

"Deliberations. Preparations."

Thaldir folded his hands before him, posture shifting into something ceremonial—as though voicing a truth meant only for prophecy and council chambers.

"A bond such as yours does not weaken," he said.

"It strengthens."

"And if left unchecked, it will begin to strain the differences between your lifespan, essence, fate itself."

Ong's breath came shallow.

"So what are you saying?"

Thaldir held his gaze.

"I am saying that the world will not ignore this bond," he replied quietly.

"Nor will the Dominion... if they come to understand it."

Keisha stiffened.

"You mean Vuarus."

"No," Thaldir said.

"I mean something older."

"Something that predates him."

A hush fell.

Not silence but the kind that feels like destiny holding its breath.

"There are prophecies," Thaldir continued carefully.

"Fragments. Half-seen truths. Broken visions left unfinished by time."

His gaze darkened.

"Most were sealed."

"Dismissed."

"Or buried because they frightened those who first glimpsed them."

He looked at Keisha and Ong.

"They do not speak of conquest."

"They speak of convergence."

"Of boundaries bending."

"Of a bond that should not exist... and yet must."

The words settled like falling ash.

Keisha felt their weight press against her chest not as fear, but as recognition, as if some quiet part of her had always known.

Karrenen's voice was low.

"This knowledge is not for the world," he said. "Not yet."

Thaldir inclined his head.

"Nor even for you fully," he added. "Not until the moment arrives when knowing becomes necessary."

Ong frowned, frustration threading his voice.

"So we're supposed to wait?"

Thaldir's expression softened but the gravity did not.

"No," he said.

"You are meant to live."

"To choose."

"To strengthen what binds you by will... not by fear."

His eyes sharpened, ancient, and unyielding.

"But understand this if the Dominion learns what you are to one another..."

"They will not see love."

"They will see leverage."

"A key."

"A weapon."

The moonwood rustled overhead, silver leaves trembling like breath held too long.

Keisha tightened her grip on Ong's hand.

"Whatever this is," she said quietly, "We face it together."

Thaldir studied them the Eladrin heir of veil and memory, and the human who had reached beyond the limits of his soul.

At last, he nodded once.

"That," he said softly, "may be the most dangerous truth of all."

And above them, the moonwood whispered as though the world itself were listening.

"We are preparing," Thaldir continued quietly, "to offer you something a human has never been granted."

The words carried quiet thunder.

"Something our people have withheld for millennia. Something only the highest of the veilblood have ever known."

Keisha's eyes widened, her voice barely more than breath.

"Thaldir... you don't mean—"

He lifted a hand gently, halting her.

"Not yet," he said.

"We will not name it not until the decision is final."

His gaze turned to Ong, ancient and measuring.

"But understand this, Ong of Vacari the Eladrin do not take such steps lightly. What we are considering is reserved for those who stand at the heart of our people. For those whose existence has become entwined with ours."

He held Ong's gaze steadily. "And you, through a bond that should not exist... now stand at the edge of such a place."

Ong stared at him, awe and disbelief colliding in his expression.

Keisha slipped her hand into his, her voice trembling with wonder and fear.

"Ong... they're preparing to change everything."

Thaldir inclined his head.

"And what comes next," he said quietly, will depend not on our lore... but on your choice."

Ong turned sharply to Keisha, eyes wide. "Keisha... what are they talking about?"

Karrenen stepped forward, resting a steadying hand on Ong's shoulder.

"Tell me, Ong," he said gently, how much do you know of Eladrin culture particularly our relationship with immortality?"

Ong blinked.

"Immortality? As in... never dying? That immortality?"

Karrenen chuckled softly. "Of a sort."

Ong's gaze snapped to Keisha, alarm blooming.

"Wait does that mean..."

He gestured at her, panic rising. "Does that mean Keisha was never in any actual danger all those times I panicked? When she was frozen? Poisoned? Nearly sacrificed? When she fell from a..."

"Ong, please" Keisha groaned, heat rising to her cheeks.

But Karrenen shook his head, smiling with a warmth few ever saw.

"No, Ong. Eladrin immortality guards against age. Against disease. Against the slow erosion of time."

His gaze sharpened gently.

"But not blades. Not ice. Not poison. Not dragons. Not war."

Ong stared at him, stunned. "So... she could still die? All those times... she was really in danger?"

"Very much so," Thaldir confirmed with a sympathetic nod.

Ong threw his hands up in exasperation. "Then what good is immortality?!"

Laughter rippled through the courtyard Karrenen first, then Thaldir, and finally Keisha's bright, breathless giggle. Even the moonwood seemed to shimmer with shared amusement, silver leaves trembling in the soft light.

Thaldir composed himself, though a smile still lingered.

"Its value," he said gently, is not in invincibility... but in time."

"Time to learn."

"Time to build."

"Time to protect what matters most."

His gaze returned to Ong warm, solemn, and heavy with meaning.

"And time," he added quietly, is exactly what your bond may soon demand."

Ong swallowed, turning to Keisha. Her eyes shimmered with emotion she did not try to hide.

"So..." he whispered, "I would stay with her? Always?"

Keisha nodded, squeezing his hand.

"You would."

Thaldir's expression sobered.

"But understand the cost. Humans measure life in decades. We measure it in centuries. Your father, your kin, and any human you love will age while you remain unchanged."

Ong froze.

"And unless taken by battle," Thaldir added gently, "they will pass while you endure."

The truth struck like a slow tide.

Ong stared at his scarred hands, then lifted his gaze to Keisha, who watched him with hope and fear entwined.

Thaldir placed a hand over his heart.

"That is why immortality is a choice. A sacred one. A burden as much as a gift."

"And it is being offered because your bond with Keisha has already broken the boundaries of our lore."

Ong looked at her, voice barely breath. "You'd want me to stay that long?"

Keisha answered without hesitation, fierce and luminous.

"Yes." For as long as you choose—yes."

And in that moment, Ong fully grasped the weight of what lay before him.

He drew a steadying breath and looked from Thaldir to Karrenen, then back to Keisha.

"So, this immortality..." he said quietly, "What does it truly mean? What is the process? And what are the risks?"

Thaldir's expression turned solemn. "It is not reversible."

He stepped closer, voice deepening with ritual gravity. "When the binding is performed, your essence will be anchored to the lifeflow of E'vahona. Your aging will cease."

"Your spirit will strengthen."

"Your body will resist disease and the erosion of time."

Then, gently: "But once done... there is no return."

"No reclaiming the years you would have lived."

"No return to mortal brevity."

Ong nodded, absorbing every word.

"And immortality does not grant safety," Thaldir continued.

"A blade can still kill you."

"Poison."

"War."

"Dragons."

"The Dominion."

His gaze held Ong's.

"It is not invulnerability."

"It is endurance."

Karrenen stepped forward then, amusement softening the solemnity.

"There is," he added lightly, "one particular advantage."

Ong blinked. "Which is?"

Karrenen smiled, a rare dry spark of mischief.

"You would live long enough," he said smoothly, "to watch any children you and Keisha one day might have grow into their full Eladrin potential."

"Father!" Keisha spluttered.

Thaldir coughed, clearly entertained.

Ong smirked. "Subtle, Karrenen. Very subtle."

“Someone had to say it,” Karrenen replied, unapologetic.

Keisha flushed, but warmth lingered behind the color the quiet glimmer of a future she had never dared to imagine.

Ong exhaled slowly, the humor fading into something deeper.

He turned fully toward Keisha, studying her as though the shape of his destiny lived in her eyes.

“When you all talked about consequences,” he murmured, I kept thinking about what I’d lose.”

Her fingers brushed his.

“But now,” he said softly, all I can think about... is what I’d lose if I didn’t choose this.”

His voice thickened.

“There’s no choice for me. I won’t leave you and I refuse to become another loss you have to carry.”

Keisha’s eyes brimmed.

“You won’t be,” she whispered.

Thaldir bowed his head in solemn respect.

“Then the decision is made.”

Karrenen rested a hand on Ong’s shoulder pride, acceptance, and quiet relief in the gesture.

“The Eladrin welcome you, Ong,” he said softly. Not only into our people... but into our eternity.”

Thaldir stepped back, voice ceremonial.

“The ritual cannot be performed today. The circle must be prepared. The runes aligned. Your spirit attuned.”

Karrenen nodded. “The Spellweavers and elders will begin at once.”

Thaldir inclined his head to them both.

“At first light tomorrow,” he said, when the veil is thinnest and the life flow sings strongest... the binding will be performed. Until then rest. Meditate. Prepare.”

Ong inhaled slowly.

"Tomorrow," he echoed. "I'll be ready."

Keisha entwined her fingers with his. "So will I."

Above them, the moonwood rustled a soft, reverent music, as though E'vahona itself had witnessed the vow.

As Thaldir and Karrenen turned to begin their preparations, Ong and Keisha remained beneath the shimmering canopy, hands clasped, their futures interwoven.

The path ahead glowed like starlight.

Tomorrow, everything would change.

Chapter 8

Dawn of the Veilbinding

Dawn broke softly over E'vahona.

Not with sunlight alone, but with the awakening of the veil pale silver radiance drifting through the crystalline canopy like breath across glass. The air itself felt altered, charged with a low, resonant hum that thrummed through stone, leaf, and soul alike.

Today was no ordinary day.

Ong stood at the edge of the moonwood courtyard as first light brushed his face. His breath rose in faint clouds despite the warmth. The veil's magic sharpened everything colors too vivid, sounds too clear, emotions pressing heavier against his chest.

Behind him, the great silver leaves whispered together, their rustle carrying something almost... aware.

Keisha approached quietly, armor set aside in favor of a simple robe woven from whisper-silk. Her red hair caught the dawn like molten copper. When she reached him, she did not speak at first only slipped her fingers into his, anchoring him.

"You slept?" she asked gently.

Ong exhaled a humorless breath.

"Not even a little."

She smiled, weary but fond.

"Neither did I."

They stood in silence fear, hope, and devotion coiled between them like a living thread.

Footsteps approached, measured and composed.

Lord Karrenen entered the clearing, clad in ceremonial silver and emerald green. His expression was solemn, but warmth lived beneath it the steady calm of one who understood thresholds.

"It is time."

Ong turned, a knot tightening in his chest. "Already?"

Karrenen inclined his head. "The Circle of Veilbinding has been prepared. The Spellweavers have aligned the runes. Thaldir is waiting."

His gaze settled on Ong, seeing deeper than flesh or breath.

"Remember this," Karrenen said softly. "This binding does not make you less human."

A pause gentler, truer.

"It allows you to remain beside the one your spirit has already chosen... without being torn apart by time."

Ong swallowed.

"That's why I'm here."

Keisha's grip tightened.

Together, they walked through E'vahona's shimmering pathways. The city felt suspended in reverent stillness no calls, no wingbeats, no music. Even the dragons were absent, as though the realm itself had chosen silence.

It felt like waiting.

At the sacred terrace, Ong stopped short.

The Circle of Veilbinding lay before him.

Ancient stone bore spiraling runes like constellations frozen in motion. Elders stood in a wide arc, their robes faintly luminous with restrained magic. At the center, Thaldir waited, staff in hand, eyes deep with centuries.

"Ong of Vacari," Thaldir called.

"Step forward."

Keisha lifted her hand to Ong's cheek, her touch warm despite the veil's chill.

"I'm right here," she whispered.

Ong drew a steady breath.

Then he stepped into the circle.

The runes ignited beneath his feet.

The veil trembled overhead a vast, luminous canopy shivering with ancient power.

Silver light bloomed, spiraling outward in patterns older than language. Threads of magic rose from the stone like drawn breath, coiling around Ong's arms, chest, and lungs not binding yet, but testing.

Thaldir raised his staff. "Begin the Veilbinding."

The elders' voices joined his layered, flowing, resonant. Eladrin arcana wove through the air, thickening it with living light. The runes pulsed once... twice... then surged upward in a column of silver fire.

Ong gasped as the magic swept through him warm at first, almost welcoming...then burning.

Keisha stepped closer to the circle's edge, hands clenched. The wind tugged at her hair, lifting strands of red like living flame.

"Ong," she called softly.

He tried to answer but the veil pulled him inward.

His vision fractured.

White dissolved into silver.

Silver stretched into infinity.

He stood in a boundless expanse of light.

And across from him stood Keisha.

Not as she appeared in the world, but as the veil knew her.

Her Eladrin spirit blazed with silver fire, eyes lit by ancient truth, her essence unveiled and radiant.

She reached for him.

"Ong... can you hear me?"

"I hear you," he whispered.

The veil pulsed.

The terrace shuddered.

A sharp crack rang out one rune splintering, unstable magic flaring upward like a blade tearing through the circle.

Thaldir's eyes widened.

"Hold the lines. Ease the pulse the human spirit resists the veil's embrace."

The elders shifted their chant, counter-harmonics threading through the spell. The fractured rune steadied, but Ong staggered, breath ripping from his chest as though his very nature were being unraveled.

Keisha pressed her palm against the barrier.

"Ong, look at me. Stay with me."

Pain lanced through him intimate, piercing as though his spirit were being rewritten.

"I'm not—" His knees buckled. "Keisha—"

"I'm here," she said fiercely. You're not alone."

The veil surged.

Light swallowed everything.

Then the bond struck.

A heartbeat across eternity.

A thread of silver snapped into place between them, thin, radiant, unbreakable.

Keisha cried out as part of her spirit opened in answer not in surrender... but in trust.

Thaldir lifted his staff, voice ringing like crystal.

"Bind the spirit. Link the lifeflow. Let the veil accept this soul as equal to its own!"

The runes flared.

Ong felt something settle within him, no longer burning but vast and warm, like a second pulse aligning with his own.

Keisha felt it too.

In the endless light, she reached for him.

"Come back to me," she whispered.

He took her hand.

The terrace snapped back into focus.

The runes dimmed to a gentle glow.

The veil quieted, folding inward.

Ong stood at the center of the circle, swaying, breath ragged... but alive.

Thaldir lowered his staff.

"It is done," he said softly.

"The Veilbinding is complete."

Keisha rushed to him, catching him as his legs faltered. Ong leaned into her, grounding himself in her warmth.

"You okay?" she whispered.

He let out a shaky, breathless laugh.

"I feel... different. Like the world just sharpened around me."

He looked at her truly looked and something irrevocable shifted in his gaze.

"You felt it too," he murmured.

"Didn't you?"

Keisha nodded, eyes luminous.

"Yes," she whispered.

"I felt you."

The elders bowed in silent reverence.

A new bond had been forged.

A human soul had been reshaped not erased, not diminished, but expanded.

And for the first time in E'vahona's history...

A mortal now walks the edge of eternity.

Chapter 9

The Bond That Should Not Be

The morning light of E'vahona felt different now.

Not brighter deeper.

As though the veil itself had inhaled during the ritual and had yet to fully exhale.

Ong sat on the low stone edge of the moonwood terrace, one hand braced behind him, the other resting loosely in Keisha's. The world felt sharper than it had any right to be. Distant wings sounded closer, heartbeats felt louder, and the faint hum of E'vahona's magic whispered at the edge of his awareness like a language he almost understood.

Almost.

Lord Karrenen approached in quiet steps, his expression composed yet thoughtful, weighed by centuries and the significance of what had just unfolded.

"You're still with us," Karrenen said dryly.

Ong huffed a breath.

"Last I checked."

Keisha smiled faintly, but there was tension beneath it a protective stillness, as though part of her still stood inside the ritual circle.

Karrenen stopped before them.

"What you felt," he said gently, "was not simply the magic of the Veilbinding. It was your soul being recognized by E'vahona."

Ong blinked.

"Recognized?"

"Yes," Karrenen replied. "Not rewritten. Not replaced. But... accepted."

He looked directly at Ong now.

"You were bound to the lifeflow not as Eladrin, not as something you are not... but as a human whose spirit has already crossed a boundary most never even perceive."

Ong frowned, trying to piece together the lingering echoes inside his chest.

"It feels like..." he hesitated. "Like there is an extra heartbeat in me. Like I am standing half a step out of where I used to be."

Keisha's grip tightened.

"That's because you are," Karrenen said quietly. "Your bond with Keisha was already stretching the limits of what is possible. The ritual did not create that bond."

He let the truth settle. "It acknowledged it."

Keisha drew in a slow breath.

"Then this really is tied to the prophecy."

Karrenen's gaze softened.

"Yes. More than we ever intended to tell you... and more than we can safely reveal yet."

Ong shot him a sideways look. "You Eladrin have a real habit of saying terrifying things calmly."

A faint smile touched Karrenen's mouth.

"Terrifying things tend to become worse when spoken with panic."

Then his tone grew heavier. "There is something else you need to understand."

Ong straightened.

"When the Veilbinding took place," Karrenen continued, "the Noble Dragons would have felt it. Not as pain. Not as a threat."

He glanced upward toward the distant shimmer of the sky.

"But as a disturbance. A resonance. A note that does not belong to any melody they have heard before."

Keisha's eyes narrowed slightly.

"The Silvers..."

"And the others," Karrenen confirmed. "Silver. Copper. Crystal. Platinum. Celestial."

He looked back at Ong.

"They will sense that something in E'vahona has changed. That a human soul now stands partially within their world's current."

Ong grimaced.

"So... dragons are going to notice me."

"Not you," Karrenen corrected gently. "What you have become."

Silence settled between them.

Keisha shifted closer to Ong, her voice quiet but unwavering. "They won't see him as a threat."

"No," Karrenen agreed. "But dragons do not ignore anomalies. And they do not ignore bonds that touch prophecy."

Ong exhaled slowly. "And we'll have to explain it."

"Yes," Karrenen said. "Together."

He softened slightly.

"This is not a summons. It is a courtesy and a necessity. The Noble Dragons are allies. Protectors. But they deserve the truth when something this significant shifts within Vacari."

Ong glanced at Keisha.

"You okay with that?"

She nodded, brushing her thumb lightly over his knuckles.

"If this bond affects dragons, realms, and prophecies," she said quietly, "then we face it openly."

Karrenen watched them pride, concern, and something quietly emotional flickering in his gaze.

"You have already crossed lines that reshape fate," he said. "It is only right that those who guard this world understand why."

Ong let out a slow breath, half nervous, half awed. "So first immortality rituals... now dragon briefings."

He looked at Keisha with a crooked smile. "Looks like we've truly chosen the path that defies destiny."

Keisha smiled back, eyes shining. "With you? Always."

Karrenen turned slightly, gazing toward the sky where distant wings traced unseen paths.

"Then prepare yourselves," he murmured. "Because when dragons sense a change... they will come seeking answers."

"And this," he added softly, "is only the beginning of what your bond will awaken."

High above Vacari, where clouds and sky blurred into endless blue, the Noble Dragons stirred.

Not in alarm.

Not in fear.

But in recognition.

Across distant skies, something shifted a subtle resonance threading through the ley lines like a newly struck chord. It carried no scent of shadow. No trace of corruption.

Instead, it felt like light discovering its name.

A purpose awakening.

In the vaulted heights of Lyra'el, Radiantus, the Ancient Platinum Dragon, lifted his head as the sensation rippled through his scales. The air around him glowed faintly, as though responding to an unseen summons.

Beside him, Aurelius, the Celestial Dragon, paused mid-step, wings tightening in quiet awareness.

"You felt it," Radiantus murmured.

Aurelius inclined his head.

"Yes."

They stood in silence as the resonance deepened not intrusive, but inviting. Not forceful, but inevitable.

"It is not the Dominion," Aurelius said softly.

"No," Radiantus agreed. "This carries no hunger. No fracture. No rot."

He turned his gaze toward the unseen horizon toward E'vahona.

"It feels like... alignment," he continued. "A soul settling into a path it was always meant to walk."

Aurelius's eyes narrowed with ancient understanding.

"Or a bond awakening that prophecy once warned us would come."

The word lingered between them.

Prophecy.

Radiantus exhaled slowly, platinum light rippling along his spine.

"The convergence spoken of by the Seers," he said quietly. "A bond between what should never intertwine... yet must."

Aurelius's voice lowered.

"The living bridge... the thread between fate and choice."

For a moment, neither spoke.

Then Aurelius turned slightly, celestial light threading his wings.

"If this resonance touches the Noble Flights, they will sense it as well."

"They already have," Radiantus replied. "The Silver Ancients will feel it most strongly. Truth always responds first to change."

A faint pause settled between them.

"We should summon the Council," Aurelius said.

Radiantus inclined his head.

"The Hidden Isles."

Before he could speak further, the air shimmered softly iridescent and a nymph emerged, her form woven of light, petals, and whispering wind. Her wings trembled as she bowed low before the two Ancients.

"Radiantus. Aurelius."

Her voice carried urgency wrapped in reverence.

"The Silver Dragons have felt the shift," she said. "So has Kadona."

Both Ancients stilled.

"The Guardian of E'vahona?" Aurelius asked.

The nymph nodded.

"They have requested your presence," she continued. "The Hidden Isles. At once."

Radiantus exchanged a slow glance with Aurelius.

"So," he murmured, "they sensed it as we did."

Aurelius's gaze hardened with resolve.

"Then it is confirmed," he said. "This is no anomaly. No fleeting echo."

Radiantus turned toward the sky, wings beginning to unfurl.

"It is a turning point."

His voice deepened steady, resolute.

"Inform the other Noble Flights," he commanded. "Copper. Crystal. Emerald, and Sapphire."

The nymph bowed again.

"They are already being summoned."

Radiantus looked once more toward the unseen veil of E'vahona.

"If prophecy is stirring," he said quietly, "Then we will not allow it to unfold in darkness."

Aurelius stepped beside him, celestial light flaring in agreement.

"Let the dragons gather," he said. "Let truth stand before shadow."

Together, the two Ancients rose with platinum and starlight wings, cutting through the heavens as they turned toward the Hidden Isles.

And far below, unseen but resonant, a newly forged bond continued to hum with purpose a promise not of destruction, but of convergence.

The Hidden Isles drifted above Vacari like a crown of cloud and crystal, veiled by enchantments older than most kingdoms and guarded by the Noble Dragons themselves.

Mist curled along floating stone bridges. Sunlight fractured through suspended waterfalls that shimmered like molten glass. The air carried the deep resonance of ancient wings and forgotten memory.

One by one, they arrived.

Silver cut through the sky first, Silvara descending in a graceful arc, argent wings scattering truth-light across the Isles.

Copper followed Raelithar, molten bronze gleaming with quiet amusement and watchful intelligence.

Emerald wind stirred as Verdantia emerged through drifting green light, her presence carrying renewal and calm.

Crystal flared next Aurelia, refracting sunlight into prismatic halos as she settled near the central dais.

Then the heavens brightened.

Radiantus, the Platinum Ancient, descended in a cascade of celestial brilliance, followed moments later by Aurelius, whose white-gold radiance shimmered like dawn incarnate.

Last came Kimras, the Ancient Golden, his presence warm, immense, and steady, sunlight burning gently along his scales as he landed with quiet authority.

And with them came the mortals.

Keisha stepped onto the Isle's central platform beside Ong, with Lord Karrenen just behind them.

The moment Ong crossed onto the sacred stone Amara stilled.

The Amethyst Dragon lifted her head sharply, pupils narrowing as something unseen brushed her senses. Her gaze locked onto Ong—not with hostility, but with startled recognition.

"...You," she murmured, more to herself than to anyone else.

A ripple of subtle reaction moved through the other Noble Dragons. Not alarm. Not suspicion.

Awareness.

Amara held Ong's gaze a heartbeat longer, then inclined her head once before moving to take her place among the assembled Ancients.

The council formed a wide arc wings half-folded, eyes ancient and attentive.

Radiantus broke the silence, his voice resonant as struck crystal.

"Something has changed," he said calmly. "And it does not carry a shadow."

His gaze settled on Ong. "Tell us what has changed."

Karrenen stepped forward, bowing his head respectfully to the gathered dragons.

"It concerns the Veilbinding," he said. "And what occurred during Keisha's captivity... long before this day."

Radiantus turned slightly toward him.

"You knew such a bond existed before the ritual," he observed. "How?"

Karrenen's jaw tightened.

"Because it began years ago," he replied quietly. "When Vuarus and Phoenix took Keisha."

A low, restrained tension rippled through the gathering at those names.

"She was broken," Karrenen continued, his voice steady but edged with old pain. "Frozen. Drained. Slowly stripped of strength."

Keisha remained silent, but Ong's hand tightened slightly at her side.

"She reached out," Karrenen said. "Not with magic. Not with a spell. With spirit."

Radiantus's eyes narrowed slightly. "And Ong heard her."

"Yes," Karrenen confirmed.

Ong swallowed but did not look away.

"Across distance. Across agony. Across a boundary that should never have yielded," Karrenen continued. "He heard her. Followed the call. Refused to abandon it even when Vuarus demanded E'vahona's location in exchange for her life."

A deep, rumbling breath rolled through the council.

Kimras leaned forward slightly, golden gaze heavy with memory.

"It was during the time Radiantus was absent," the Golden Ancient said, his voice warm but solemn. "The boy's defiance and the bond he would not sever was already shaping fate."

He lifted his head toward Radiantus. "It was not merely devotion. It was convergence... the kind that shapes ages."

Radiantus listened in silence, then slowly inclined his head as understanding dawned.

"So that is what Aurelius has been sensing," he said quietly. "The stirring. The resonance. The echo in the ley lines."

He turned to the Celestial Dragon.

"A prophecy long whispered... now taking form."

Aurelius nodded gravely.

"The Seers spoke of a bond that should not exist a thread binding mortal will to Eladrin destiny. A convergence that could become either bridge... or fracture."

His gaze shifted to Ong not with judgment, but with solemn recognition.

"And now that bond stands before us."

Silvara's silver eyes softened, truth-light shimmering faintly around her.

"He does not feel like a threat," she said calmly. "He feels like... purpose."

Raelithar smirked faintly. "Well," he drawled, "that's a refreshing change from the usual disasters that try to end the world."

Verdantia regarded Ong with thoughtful warmth.

"The forest sensed it," she murmured. "Not disruption... but alignment."

Radiantus stepped forward, his voice steady but profound.

"Ong of Vacari," he said, "You have crossed a boundary no human ever has. Not by force. Not by ambition."

"But by loyalty. By love. By refusal to abandon what your spirit had claimed."

He inclined his head a rare gesture from an Ancient.

"This is not corruption. "This is prophecy unfolding."

Kimras rumbled softly, approval threaded through his tone.

"You were never meant to do this alone," the Golden Ancient said gently. "Perhaps that truth extends farther than any of us imagined."

A quiet stillness fell.

Keisha looked at Ong fear, pride, and hope shimmering in her gaze.

Radiantus lifted his wings slightly, light spilling across the council.

"Then we stand at the beginning of something ancient," he said. "Not a doom... but a convergence."

"And this time," Aurelius added softly, "We will ensure prophecy serves hope, not shadow."

Above them, the Hidden Isles glowed faintly brighter, as though Vacari itself were listening.

And for the first time, the Noble Dragons did not see Ong as merely human...but as part of the fate of their world.

The council gradually dispersed, leaving only the heart of the Hidden Isles drifting stone, luminous mist, and the low, resonant breath of Noble Dragons.

Ong stood near the central dais, still feeling the faint echo of the Veilbinding in his bones, as though the world now recognized him in ways it had not before.

A presence approached.

First came Amara, amethyst wings glinting with prismatic light.

Then Kimras, Ancient Gold, warm as sunrise.

Behind them descended Radiantus, Platinum, and Aurelius, Celestial, starlight trailing in his wake.

Amara studied Ong with open curiosity head tilted, eyes bright. "...You feel louder," she observed lightly.

Ong blinked. "Louder?"

"Not in sound," she said. "In existence."

Kimras rumbled with quiet amusement. "The bond has anchored him more deeply into Vacari's lifeflow."

Radiantus stepped closer, his voice calm and thoughtful.

"The prophecy speaks of a Convergent Soul," he said. "One who stands between what is... and what should never have been."

Aurelius inclined his head.

"A bond crossing species.
Crossing fate.
Crossing design."

His gaze rested on Ong not coldly, but with reverent curiosity.

"You were never meant to hear Keisha's call," Aurelius said.

"And yet you did.
You answered.
You refused to let it break."

Kimras added gently, "The prophecy never described a weapon... but a bridge."

Ong swallowed. "So... I am part of some ancient destiny now?"

Amara's lips twitched. "Do not let it swell your pride," she said dryly. "You are not becoming some crowned savior or tale for temple singers."

Radiantus's eyes softened.

"The prophecy does not promise power," he clarified. "It warns of impact. Your choices will matter more than most."

Aurelius turned his gaze toward the horizon, thoughtful.

"The dark dragons and the one who moves behind them will not sense this immediately," he said.

"They never believed the prophecy.
They dismissed it as myth as wishful thinking."

A quiet pause followed.

"But when they do notice," Aurelius continued, "they will realize the balance has shifted."

Radiantus nodded slightly.

"They will underestimate what they do not understand," he said. "That grants us time."

Kimras looked at Ong with quiet certainty.

"Use that time wisely," the Golden Ancient murmured. "You are not meant to carry this alone."

Amara circled Ong once, then leaned closer, eyes glinting with playful challenge.

"So," she said lightly, "Prophecy or not... convergent soul or not..."

She smirked. "Do not assume this means I will go easier on you in training."

Ong let out a startled laugh. "Wouldn't dream of it."

Amara's grin sharpened. "If anything," she added, "I expect more from you now."

She flicked her tail once, amused. "Destiny does not earn special treatment from me."

Kimras rumbled warmly. "That may be the most reassuring thing said today."

Aurelius gave a faint, knowing smile.

"And perhaps," he said quietly, "The very reason the prophecy chose a heart like his."

The mist drifted between them, glowing softly.

Ong glanced at Keisha, who stood just beyond the circle pride, relief, and love in her eyes.

Whatever awaited them...He would not face it alone.

And somewhere far beyond the Hidden Isles,

The shadows remained unaware that something fundamental had already changed.

As the council slowly dissolved, the Noble Dragons began to lift into the luminous skies of the Hidden Isles—gold, silver, platinum, celestial, and amethyst wings scattering light like falling stars.

The weight of prophecy faded into something quieter.

Something human.

Ong exhaled at last, rubbing the back of his neck as though trying to shake off destiny itself. Then he turned to Keisha, pulled her gently closer, and wrapped an arm around her waist.

"So let me get this straight," he muttered, half-grumbling, half-relieved. "You're immortal... but not actually safe."

Keisha laughed softly. "Ong—"

He shook his head, tightening his hold just a little.

"That just means my job got harder," he said. "Now I have to keep you alive for centuries instead of decades."

Her laughter brightened, warm and unburdened.

"Poor you," she teased.

He leaned his forehead lightly against hers.

"I'm serious," he murmured. "If you can still be hurt... still be lost..."

His voice softened. "Then I am not relaxing. Ever."

Keisha smiled up at him, eyes shining.

"Good," she whispered. "Because I don't plan on making it easy."

Nearby, Amara snorted quietly as she turned away, wings flicking with amusement.

Radiantus watched them with a faint, approving glow.

Aurelius inclined his head, starlight soft around his form.

Kimras rumbled with gentle warmth.

One by one, the dragons returned to their paths to skies, forests, cities, and hidden realms.

But Ong lingered a moment longer, holding Keisha close as though anchoring the future to the present.

She laughed again, resting her head against his shoulder.

"Come on," she said lightly. "Destiny can wait. You are taking me home."

He smirked. "Yeah," he replied. "Before prophecy hands us another test."

Together, they walked away beneath drifting mist and fading dragon-light love intact, fate acknowledged, and the promise of tomorrow still theirs to choose.

And far beyond their laughter, the larger world continued to turn... unaware that the first thread of convergence had already been woven.

Chapter 10

The Unraveling Veil

Mist curled like silvered breath along the borders of the Emberwoods and Emeraldwoods twin forests standing as sentinels between realms seen and unseen. Beneath their canopies, ancient magic pulsed subtle, patient, and older than any dragon's memory.

But today... that magic trembled.

High above the whispering leaves, Ixalia, the Mirage Ancient, carved a path through the sky. Her wings broke the light, bending air and illusion alike into wavering specters. Each beat distorted the world below trees blurred, shadows stretched unnaturally long, and reality itself rippled like a mirage under relentless heat.

Trailing her, two younger Mirage Dragons flickered in and out of existence their forms phasing like half-remembered dreams, never fully anchored to truth.

Again and again, Ixalia swept the borderlands.

First over the red-and-gold labyrinth of the Emberwoods, where copper-rich soil and volcanic warmth ignited the forest in hues of flame.

Then across the emerald-tide canopy of the Emeraldwoods, where living leaves glowed with inner light, and the air tasted faintly of renewal and healing.

Three times she circled.

Three times the veil rippled and refused to yield.

On her third pass, her wings slowed not from fatigue, but calculation. Illusions unfurled in widening arcs, probing deeper, pressing against unseen boundaries. The air shimmered violently where her magic met resistance, as though reality itself rejected her touch.

Still… the veil held.

During that final sweep, Emberwood pixies hidden within spiraled fire-lilies dared to peek from their glowing shelters. Their wings shimmered like molten sparks as the shimmering dragon carved spectral wounds through their sky.

One tiny voice whispered, breathless:

"That's not a dragon from here…"

Another hissed:

"And she is searching. Hunting."

A third pixie clutched a curled petal, trembling.

"The Copper Ancient must know. Go—go!"

With a burst of crimson dust and flickering flame, the pixies shot upward—weaving through thorn-vines, ember-blossoms, and molten branches until they reached the heart of the Emberwoods, where Raelithar, the Copper Ancient, lay coiled in a clearing of glowing stone and whispering heat.

They burst into the clearing in a scatter of sparks.

"Ancient Raelithar it is her! The Mirage Dragon! She is circling the borders again!

Three passes already!"

Raelithar opened his great copper eyes with slow control.

But beneath that calm… fire simmered.

Across the Emeraldwoods, where the light turned green and living, fairies hovered among drifting blossoms, their glow muted by unease. They too had seen the shimmering wings—felt the distortion ripple through bark, leaf, and root.

The air smelled wrong.

Illusion magic intrusive... searching... hungry.

One fairy pressed her palm to the trunk of the Emeraldheart Tree, sending a pulse of warning through its ancient roots.

"Verdantia must be told."

With emerald-bright speed, they darted through tunnels of living leaves until they reached the inner grove, where Verdantia, the Emerald Ancient, rested coiled in gemstone bark and glowing moss.

The fairies alit upon her scales like drops of living dew.

"Ancient one the Mirage Dragon has come. She circles the borders again and again...

As though hunting for a door."

Verdantia's crystalline eyes snapped open, emerald light igniting within their depths.

Two warnings.

Two Ancient Dragons alerted.

And somewhere beyond sight...

Ixalia continued her search.

And somewhere between Emberwoods and Emeraldwoods, Ixalia circled once more—her voice drifting on the wind like a silk veil drawn over a blade.

"Show yourself, E'vahona... you cannot hide forever."

The forests answered not with sound, but with tension.

Verdantia burst through the emerald canopy first, her wings unfurling in a brilliant sweep that scattered green firelight across the clearing where the two forests met. Leaves bowed in her wake. Roots stirred beneath the soil.

A heartbeat later, Raelithar descended from the copper-tinted sky, molten embers trailing from his wings as he landed beside her. Heat rolled outward from him in slow, deliberate waves.

Before them hovered Ixalia.

Her form wavered like heat over desert glass scales shifting between silver, violet, and pale gold, never settling, never fully real. Illusions layered around her like fractured reflections, each one watching from a different angle.

And still she circled.

And still she whispered "Show yourself, E'vahona..."

Verdantia's laugh rippled through the trees melodic, resonant... and edged with warning.

"E'vahona can and will remain hidden from those such as you," she declared. "Not even your illusions can pierce what was woven long before your kind ever touched Vacari."

Ixalia slowed, her fractured form drawing inward as her attention fixed on the Emerald Ancient. Her eyes—void-lit and ever-shifting—narrowed.

Before she could answer, Raelithar stepped forward, copper scales gleaming with quiet menace, a molten smirk curling along his maw.

"So," he drawled, "it is true. The mysterious puppet-master has begun scraping the Void and the Abyss for allies desperate enough to kneel."

Ixalia hissed though even the sound fractured, splitting into layered echoes that rippled through the air.

Raelithar did not so much as blink.

"I would suggest," he continued lightly, "That you inform the other invaders of a simple truth neither you nor they are welcome here."

His gaze hardened.

"Vacari has troubles enough... without parasites dragged from realms meant to remain sealed.

Verdantia moved beside him, emerald scales shimmering with restrained power.

"The dark dragons of Vacari," she said calmly, "are tolerated only because they are of this world bound to its creation, shaped by its breath."

Her gaze sharpened living crystal given purpose.

"You, Mirage Dragon... and those who crawl from the Void and the Abyss... are not of Vacari."

A pause.

"And you will not be tolerated."

Raelithar spread his wings, fire flickering beneath their membranes.

"Leave," he said, almost pleasantly, "before it becomes impossible to do so."

His tail lashed once, scattering sparks across the forest floor.

"The forests will not shield you. The Ancients will not spare you."

"And E'vahona will never reveal itself to creatures like you."

The air trembled.

Verdantia's tranquil authority.

Raelithar's simmering wrath.

Ixalia's invasive, unraveling illusion.

Three powers met and the forests themselves seemed to hold their breath.

Ixalia's wings flickered. Her form fractured into overlapping images, each slightly uncoordinated with the others. Her voice followed—layered, distorted, sliding between tones like something not meant for a single reality.

"You cannot keep secrets forever... not even your hidden jewel."

Verdantia only smiled.

"Try," she replied calmly, "and you will learn why light and earth endure..."

Her eyes burned brighter "...while illusions crumble."

Ixalia's wings folded inward.

The air warped.

A shimmer rippled across the clearing soft at first, then swelling into a rising tide of distortion. Trees bent into impossible angles. Shadows stretched into grasping claws. The sky fractured into mirrored shards, each reflecting a different, twisted version of reality.

Verdantia's vision wavered.

Raelithar's fire sputtered, confused by the shifting air.

Mirage magic ancient, invasive, born of a lineage that unraveled truth itself.

Ixalia's voice slithered through the bending world:

"Let us see how strong your resolve remains... when truth becomes fog."

The forests bled into one another. Ember and emerald blurred. For a heartbeat—even Verdantia's mind slipped—

A silver flash split the sky like a drawn blade.

Silvara descended in a blazing arc.

Her wings shone with argent brilliance, each edge cutting through illusion like sunlight through mist. Her roar followed—sharp, crystalline—a sound that did not merely carry, but cleansed.

The illusions shattered.

Mist evaporated.

Reflections collapsed.

Reality snapped back into its rightful shape.

Verdantia straightened. Raelithar exhaled, his fire steadying once more.

Silvara landed between them and Ixalia, silver scales pulsing with truth-light the same resonance that guarded the hidden heart of E'vahona.

Verdantia inclined her head in quiet gratitude.

Raelithar's smirk returned.

"She is yours now, Silver Ancient."

"Make sure she remembers the lesson," he added lightly.

With twin sweeps of emerald and copper wings, they departed returning to their domains.

Silvara watched them go.

Then she turned to Ixalia.

Her gaze locked onto the Mirage Ancient with cold, crystalline certainty.

"Your illusions hold no power over the Silver Dragons."

Ixalia's form flickered subtle, but unmistakable.

Silvara stepped forward, argent light spilling from her scales, dissolving the last remnants of distortion.

"Not your tricks. Not your phantoms... and certainly not your attempts to unravel what we protect."

Ixalia hissed, her wings trembling with fractured color.

"Do not presume to command what you do not understand," she snarled, her voice splitting into layered echoes.

"Your light blinds you to the realities I can reshape."

Silvara's eyes narrowed slightly.

"Reality is not yours to twist," she replied coolly. "Not here."

Ixalia struck.

The illusion came not as force but as corruption.

The ground beneath Silvara collapsed into an endless void. Trees warped into grotesque spirals. The sky twisted into a mirrored dome, reflecting her into a thousand fractured selves.

Silvara did not move.

Her wings rose slowly, deliberately.

Argent light surged.

The void sealed.

The trees straightened.

The mirrored sky shattered into drifting sparks.

Ixalia recoiled.

"You cannot unmake all my magic," she hissed.

Silvara advanced serene, inevitable.

"Not all illusion is yours to command," she said softly. "And not all truth can be hidden from us."

Ixalia lashed out again phantom blades, bending shadows, a shifting labyrinth meant to trap and disorient.

Silver answered.

Silvara's claws flared with radiant brilliance.

One strike.

The mirage collapsed.

Not shattered unmade.

Silence followed.

Ixalia stilled.

She had expected resistance.

She had not expected mastery.

Silvara tilted her head, calm as moonlight on still water.

"Enough."

The word carried no force.

And yet the battle ended.

Realization flickered through Ixalia's shifting gaze.

The warning returned:

Do not provoke a battle without the one who commands Flameford.

Silvara had not even begun to press her full strength.

For a moment, Ixalia considered testing further, unraveling deeper, forcing the veil to react.

But she felt it.

She could not win here.

Not alone.

Not against truth itself.

Her wings shattered into shimmering fragments as she began to withdraw.

Silvara spoke before she vanished, her voice quiet absolute.

"Carry a message to your master."

Ixalia stilled.

Silvara's eyes shone like twin moons.

"Tell them E'vahona does not fear shadows."

A breath.

"Tell them the Silver keep watch."

Her wings lifted slightly, light gathering along their edges.

"And tell them.."

The air itself seemed to listen.

"—we do not fear what hunts in the dark."

Ixalia hissed under her breath but did not answer.

She turned sharply, her form dissolving into a streak of violet and silver, vanishing toward Flameford in fractured light.

Silvara remained, watching until the distortion faded beyond the horizon.

Only then did she move.

Her wings lifted.

Her form dissolved into silver radiance and vanished back into the hidden pathways of the veil.

Chapter 11

The Fracture of Shadows

Flameford simmered beneath a pall of ash and red mist. Its rebuilt towers and molten rivers glowed with renewed malice. The air hummed with dark magic restless, watchful, waiting.

When Ixalia descended, her wings flickering through a storm of violet illusions, her landing struck the obsidian stone with a sharp, echoing crack. Molten dust spiraled upward where her talons touched the ground, disturbed by her agitation.

Malrik, sweeping embers from a newly carved sigil, stiffened.

He looked up, eyes narrowing at the fractured shimmer of her form.

"She returns," he muttered.

And she did not look pleased.

He turned at once and strode toward the Tower of Shadowwalker, cloak snapping behind him. Within, crimson light pulsed through the chamber as the Mysterious One stood over a scrying pool, shadows coiling around their form like living things.

"My lord," Malrik said, bowing low. "Ixalia has returned."

The figure stilled.

Slowly, deliberately they lifted their head.

"Then she has found something..." they said softly.

A pause.

"...or failed trying."

The shadows flared.

Without another word, they turned and moved, darkness trailing in their wake like smoke pulled by unseen wind. Malrik followed at a measured distance, unease tightening in his chest.

As they entered the Cavern of Ash, Ixalia straightened from her pacing. Her wings flickered between substance and haze, unstable, unsettled.

"My master," she began, inclining her head. "I bring—"

"You bring excuses?"

The words cracked through the cavern like a lash.

Ixalia froze.

"You were sent to locate the hidden realm," the Mysterious One said, stepping forward, voice low and lethal. "Not to wander forests like a lost hatchling."

Ixalia's illusions flared sharply, shards of light splintering outward in agitation.

"It is not the forests that hinder me," she shot back, tension bleeding into her tone. "It is the Silver Dragons. You failed to mention they guard the veil itself."

"SILENCE."

The cavern trembled. Ash sifted from the ceiling in a gray, drifting rain.

"I did not summon a Mirage Ancient to hear her whine," the figure snarled, shadows writhing violently around them. "You are illusion incarnate. Deception made flesh."

They took another step closer.

"And yet you return to me speaking of obstacles... as though they matter."

Ixalia's wings tightened, her form flickering unevenly.

"I did not run—" she snapped.

"You failed."

The word did not rise.

It fell heavy, absolute.

Ixalia's head dipped, not in submission but in the strain of holding her ground. Fury coiled beneath her shifting scales, pressing against the weight of the moment.

Then the Mysterious One stopped. Turned and fixed their gaze fully upon her.

Power surged. Not fire.

Not lightning. Something colder. Older.

It struck without movement an unseen force slamming into Ixalia's mind like a wall of ice and shadow.

Her breath hitched.

Her illusions shattered into jagged fragments, reforming only to fracture again under the pressure.

Thought itself faltered.

Her anger her defiance her carefully measured control.

Collapsed.

"Ixalia," the Mysterious One said softly now, their tone almost gentle.

The pressure did not ease.

"You will not speak of fear to me again."

The words pressed inward, deeper than sound.

"You will not question what I have told you."

Her wings faltered, half-visible, trembling between form and nothing.

"You will do as ordered."

Silence stretched.

Ixalia tried to steady herself to reclaim some fragments of will but the weight bore down harder, crushing the attempt before it could take shape.

At last, her voice broke free thin, strained. "...Yes... my lord."

The pressure released.

Not fully.

Just enough.

Ixalia drew a sharp breath, her form stabilizing in uneven waves as her illusions settled back into place controlled, but dimmer now, subdued.

The Mysterious One regarded her for a long moment.

Then slowly they smiled.

Calm.

Measured.

Terrifying in its restraint.

"Good," they said quietly.

A step closer.

"Now..." The shadows stilled. "Tell me everything."

Ixalia steadied herself. The fractured shimmer along her wings slowly reformed into controlled illusion, each ripple tightening into place as she dared lift her gaze.

When I first reached the borders of Emberwoods and Emeraldwoods," she began, voice measured once more, "the forests resisted—but they were not impenetrable. Their magic bends... when pressed correctly."

The Mysterious One folded their arms.

Waiting.

Ixalia continued, confidence returning in careful increments.

"I encountered Verdantia and Raelithar soon after. The Emerald Ancient and the Copper Ancient arrived together as though warned."

A faint curl touched her lip.

"But they were... predictable. Their senses were sharp, yes but their perception...

She flicked her tail dismissively. “Their minds were nothing exceptional. A shift of perception. A fracture of awareness. They were already beginning to lose clarity.”

A flicker of satisfaction crossed her expression subtle, but deliberate.

“They were close,” she pressed. “Verdantia’s sense of truth was wavering. Raelithar’s fire unsteady. Another moment, and they would have been navigating a reality of my design.”

Her gaze lifted, something sharper in it now. “I could have broken them.”

A pulse of shadow moved through the Mysterious One stillness, not approval... but interest.

Then Ixalia’s tone shifted.

Slightly. “...and then the Silver arrived.”

The cavern quieted.

Not with absence but with attention.

The Mysterious One’s eyes narrowed.

“Silvara.”

The name fell cold and precise.

Ixalia inclined her head, tighter this time. “Yes. Silvara. Ancient of the Silver Dragons.”

The illusions around her flickered once, twice before stabilizing again.

“She did not arrive like the others,” Ixalia continued, voice lower now. “She descended like... interruption made manifest.”

A pause.

“The moment she touched the ground, my illusions failed.”

Not weakened.

Not strained.

“Failed.”

The word lingered.

“Every distortion. Every layered construct. Gone. As though they had never existed.”

The Mysterious One's posture shifted subtle but telling.

Ixalia exhaled through her teeth.

"She did not counter me," she said, frustration threading deeper now. "She did not dismantle the spell."

"She willed it away."

Silence pressed in.

"I have unraveled minds across realms," Ixalia went on, quieter still. "I have fractured perception until dragons turned on their own reflections..."

Her gaze darkened.

"She did not even struggle."

A flicker of something unfamiliar crossed her expression.

Not fear.

But recognition.

"She told me her kind cannot be deceived by Mirage magic. That what they guard cannot be twisted... because it is anchored in something I cannot reach."

The Mysterious One's jaw tightened as shadows coiling faintly at their shoulders.

Ixalia hesitated just briefly then continued.

"At the end... she gave me a message."

The shadows around the Mysterious One stilled completely.

"Speak."

Ixalia repeated the words, each one measured unavoidable in their weight.

"E'vahona is protected by a magic older than the Mirage Dragons themselves."

A sharp, controlled ripple moved through the Mysterious One's form.

Ixalia's voice dropped further.

"She said the Silver Dragons keep watch..."

A breath.

"...and that illusion cannot break a truth anchored by ancient light."

The words settled into the cavern like ash after flame.

Silence followed.

Heavy.

Deliberate.

The Mysterious One did not speak at once.

But the shadows at their feet began to move slowly, restlessly as something far colder than anger took hold.

Deep beneath Flameford where molten veins thinned into blackened stone and the world narrowed into silence Nocturna coiled within her labyrinth.

Her obsidian scales consumed the darkness, rendering her form indistinguishable from the shadows themselves. Only her eyes violet, precise, and unblinking cut through the void.

Far above, carried through layers of stone, heat, and hollowed passageways, fragments of Ixalia's report drifted downward,

Silvara... immune to illusion...E'vahona protected... magic older than Mirage Dragons...

Nocturna did not move at first.

She listened.

Measured.

Then, slowly, a smile curved along her maw.

"So," she murmured, her voice threading through the cavern like a remembered whisper, "even the Mirage fractures against something it cannot rewrite."

She uncoiled, deliberate, controlled. Shadows shifted with her not cast, but responding sliding along the walls as though aware of her passing.

"They reach beyond Vacari," she continued softly, "pulling from the Abyss... the Void..."

Her tail traced a slow arc across the stone.

"...and yet they misunderstand the one realm they seek most."

A low, quiet sound followed not quite laughter, but something colder.

"Power taken from elsewhere does not grant dominion here."

She moved deeper into the labyrinth, passing through corridors that twisted subtly in her wake. Pathways realigned. Traps settled. The lair adjusted itself not to her command...

...but to her presence.

"Ixalia failed," Nocturna said, not with mockery but certainty. "Not because she lacks power... but because she chose the wrong battlefield."

Her eyes narrowed slightly.

"The Silver do not resist illusion."

A pause.

"They render it irrelevant."

The distinction lingered harp, deliberate.

"And the others..." she continued, voice lowering, "Abyss-born. Void-touched."

Her lip curled faintly.

"They mistake intrusion for authority."

She slowed near the entrance to one of the deeper passageways an unseen junction where tunnels branched toward the hidden routes between territories.

"I will inform the others," she decided at last. "Zylron will want confirmation. Glaciera will want patterns."

A faint flicker of interest crossed her gaze.

"And Xalzorath..." she added quietly, "...will already be listening."

Silence stretched.

Then.

"For now," Nocturna whispered, "let the one above believe force will reveal what cannot be taken."

Her wings shifted slightly, folding closer.

"It will not."

Her eyes gleamed calm, certain, patient.

"E'vahona is not hidden by distance...it is hidden by truth."

The cavern stilled around her.

Nocturna stepped forward and the shadows closed, swallowing her form as though she had never been there at all.

The shadows still trembled from the weight of the Mysterious One's power when they turned sharply toward Malrik.

"Malrik," they commanded, voice cold as obsidian, "you will find a way for Ixalia to overcome the Silvers. Search the archives. The ruins. Every remnant left behind by Vuarus."

A pause measured, deliberate.

"Something must exist that clouds their vision."

Malrik bowed, though tension tightened along his jaw. "As you wish, my lord."

He turned and strode from the cavern, boots grinding against charred stone.

Once beyond the threshold, his composure slipped.

"Magic that even Vuarus feared..." he muttered under his breath. "And I am meant to surpass it?"

He shook his head but did not slow.

Orders were not questioned.

They were survived.

Inside the cavern, the mysterious one faced Ixalia once more.

"You will continue your search."

Ixalia inclined her head, though her wings flickered with restrained unease.

"Master, the protections—"

"The protections are irrelevant."

The words did not rise.

They pressed.

Heavy. Absolute.

"E'vahona will be found. No matter the cost."

Silence followed light, suffocating. "Is that clear, Mirage Ancient?"

Ixalia lowered her gaze. "Yes... my lord."

She turned, her form dissolving into a shimmer of violet distortion as she withdrew from the cavern.

But doubt lingered.

Why this place?

Why this obsession?

What power lies behind a veil even the Silver guard?

She did not understand.

And she knew better than to ask.

Still...

She had heard it.

Not anger.

Not command.

Desperation.

And that frightened her more than any Silver Dragon.

"Obey," she whispered to herself as she launched into the ash-dark sky. "Do not fail."

When the last echo of her wings faded, silence collapsed over Flameford like a suffocating shroud.

The mysterious one stood alone.

Still.

Then they turned and the storm began.

They moved through the tunnels toward the Tower of Shadowwalker, shadows recoiling from their passage.

Inside the chamber the door slammed and control shattered.

Books tore from shelves, pages spiraling into the air.

Vials burst against the stone, spilling blackened smoke that hissed and curled.

Obsidian relics cracked beneath unseen force.

The scrying basin split apart, its surface fracturing into a hundred glittering shards.

Each movement was precise.

Each destruction deliberate.

Not chaos release.

At last, the fury ebbed.

Silence crept back into the ruined chamber.

They stood amid the wreckage, breath steadying, shadows coiling close once more.

"E'vahona..." they whispered.

Not shouting.

Not cursed.

Claimed.

They stepped forward, grinding broken obsidian beneath their heel.

"The magic within that veil..."

Their voice shifted low, reverent, edged with hunger.

"Older than the Mirage."

"Deeper than the Dominion."

"Untouched."

A slow inhale.

"It will be mine."

They moved toward the narrow window carved into the volcanic stone, gazing out over Flameford's burning expanse.

Molten rivers pulsed below, casting a blood-red glow across their face.

"With it," they murmured, "the Eladrin fall."

"No sanctuary."

"No refuge."

"Scattered."

A pause.

Then softer—

More dangerous.

"And without them..."

A faint smile curved their lips.

"...Keisha stands alone."

Their fingers tightened along the edge of the stone.

"No father."

"No people."

"No dragons close enough to save her."

Their voice lowered further, almost intimate.

"And then..."

"...she breaks."

The words lingered heavy with intent.

"I will not simply kill her," they continued quietly. "I will take from her everything she believes protects her."

"Everything she draws strength from."

"Everything she loves."

Their eyes narrowed, reflecting the molten glow below.

"She will see it all fall."

"And she will understand... too late... that none of it was ever enough."

A breath.

Slow.

Certain.

"Only then," they whispered, "will she die."

The shadows gathered around them like a cloak.

"And when she does..."

Their voice settled into something calm.

Unshakable.

"I will take Vacari."

Ash drifted past the window, swallowing the last trace of light.

Chapter 12

The Sultan's Shadow

Arcadia shimmered beneath the pale gold light of Afor's twin moons, its marble terraces glowing like molten pearl against the restless desert winds. Beyond the city's crystal canals, the air carried whispers of heat, spice... and unseen conspiracies.

Lyra stood upon her balcony, overlooking the endless dunes. Veils of azure silk drifted around her like fragments of captured sky. Her posture was composed—almost statuesque yet her eyes, sharp and serpentine, revealed the quiet arithmetic unfolding behind them.

"Rhys," she said, her voice scarcely raised, the name drifting into the chamber like the strike of a chime. "Step forward."

Rhys emerged from the doorway, arms laden with leather pouches marked by differing sigils. Sand clung to his boots; he had come straight from the outer cliffs and had not bothered to hide it.

"You sent for me, Lady Lyra," he said with a practiced bow. "I have brought what you requested."

"Good."

She gestured toward the carved obsidian table between them.

"Show me."

One by one, Rhys set the pouches down and untied them, his movements precise economical. The hands of a healer trained to measure life... and a courier trained to guard secrets.

"Scorchroot bulb," he said, lifting a twisted crimson root veined with glowing lines of ember-orange.

"Boiled into a tonic, it grants stamina and wards against dehydration. Safe in small doses deadly in excess."

Lyra's gaze sharpened, the faintest crease touching the corner of her eye.

"And addictive," she said softly, "to those foolish enough to depend upon it."

"Very," Rhys replied.

He opened the next pouch.

"Dustpetal bloom."

Soft golden petals spilled into his palm, shimmering like powdered sunlight.

"Steeped in tea, it eases fever and purifies mild toxins. Harmless on its own..." He paused. "Until venom is introduced."

Lyra gave a low hum not approval, not dismissal. Calculation.

Another pouch followed.

"Cindermoss."

A dark, ember-flecked moss released a faint curl of smoke as it met the air.

"Used in burn salves and heat-warding charms," Rhys said. "Also favored in certain rituals. It masks the scent of blood."

Lyra's gaze lingered on it a fraction longer.

"That may prove... useful."

The words were quiet, meant more for herself than for him.

Rhys hesitated before opening the next pouch, his fingers tightening briefly on the leather tie.

"Ashthorn needles."

Thin, black spines lay within, sharp as splintered night.

"Ingested raw, they cause swelling, paralysis of the throat, and stabbing numbness," he said. "More commonly used in darts... or assassin's needles."

Lyra's lips curved not quite a smile.

"Delightful."

The final pouch he handled with particular care.

"Serpentblight resin."

Thick and tar-like, it glistened faintly green beneath the moonlight.

Rhys's voice lowered.

"A single drop induces violent cramps, hallucinations, and temporary madness. Any more than that..."

He did not finish.

Lyra did it for him.

"...the heart ceases."

She stepped closer, silken sleeves brushing the edge of the obsidian table as she surveyed the collection—not as a healer might...

...but as a strategist selecting instruments.

"You have served me well, Rhys."

He bowed again, though tension threaded his spine. He knew that look the one she wore when plans nested within plans, each more dangerous than the last.

Lyra selected a small vial and turned it slowly between her fingers. Glass clicked softly beneath her nail.

Her thoughts aligned.

"In Oasis City," she said slowly, "the Sultan's loyalists are still recovering from their last... misadventure. Their vulnerabilities present an opportunity."

Rhys lifted his gaze, caution flickering across his features.

"You intend for them to fall ill?"

"No."

Lyra turned toward him, her expression serene almost gentle.

"I want them noticeably unwell. Weakened. Distracted. Confused."

A deliberate pause followed.

"Nothing fatal. Nothing traceable."

She tapped the pouches in sequence Dustpetal first, then Ashthorn, then Scorchroot her touch precise, almost affectionate.

"A careful balance of these will mimic ailments born of the desert itself," she continued. "Heat exhaustion. Contaminated water. Fatigue born of poor judgment."

Rhys exhaled slowly as understanding settled into place.

"And the Sultan will summon a healer."

Lyra's smile deepened slowly and edged like a drawn blade.

"Not just any healer."

She stepped closer and lifted a single finger, resting it lightly against his chest not a threat... a reminder.

"You, Rhys. The man who 'saved' Arcadia's caravan. The one who understands Afor's herbs. The one who sees what others miss."

Her voice softened further, almost intimate.

"The Sultan will ask you to stay. To advise him. To stand at his side while his council... recovers."

Rhys drew in a measured breath, unease and reluctant admiration colliding beneath his composure.

"You intend to control Oasis City."

"I seek influence," Lyra corrected gently.

"Just enough to keep Afor's sands shifting in our favor."

Her gaze drifted briefly toward the distant horizon toward a world far beyond Arcadia.

"Just enough to ensure that when Vacari burns..."

Her eyes hardened.

"...we are not caught in the fire."

She stepped back, veils swirling around her like drifting smoke.

"Go," she said.

"Distribute the herbs as instructed. Quietly. Carefully."

A final pause.

"And do not let them know you were ever there."

Rhys bowed, gathering the pouches with steady hands that betrayed nothing of the storm beneath his calm.

"As you command, Lady Lyra."

He turned and slipped into the corridor, his footsteps fading into the marble hush of Arcadia.

Lyra turned back to the balcony, her gaze tracing the lattice of lights glowing beneath the desert moons.

"Afor will fall in line," she whispered. "Just as every kingdom must."

The wind carried her words across the sands a promise, a prophecy, and a threat entwined as one.

When Rhys was gone and the night had reclaimed its silence, Lyra remained still, her veils drifting like strands of captured moonlight.

Slowly, her smile returned.

The herbs Rhys had brought their effects, their interactions, their hidden potential were far more valuable than he realized.

Not merely tools for political maneuvering in Oasis City...

...but instruments for what comes next.

She turned back to the obsidian table, where the pouches lay open, the scents of resin, dustpetal, and scorchroot mingling in the warm air.

"Oh yes," Lyra murmured, her fingers gliding lightly across the deadly assortment.

"These will be particularly useful. here... and beyond."

Her eyes hardened, catching the light like polished citrine.

"There is one person who stands in my way," she said quietly.

"One person the world watches too closely."

"One person whose survival bends the fate of kingdoms."

A pause sharper, deliberate.

"Keisha."

Lyra lifted a pouch of Serpentblight Resin, its thick, shimmering sap glinting like liquid venom beneath the moonlight. Then another Ashthorn Needles, thin as wire, merciless in their promise.

With quiet precision, she selected only a few ingredients, their combined scents forming a subtle, perilous blend. Nothing hurried. Nothing wasted.

She sealed the remaining pouches, her movements flawless the elegance of long discipline.

Carrying the chosen herbs, she crossed the chamber toward a curtained alcove. As the silk parted, cool air spilled outward, her private sanctum chilled by enchanted stones carved long before Afor's first dune ever shifted.

Crystalline shelves lined the walls, gleaming with scrolls, vials, and meticulously labeled satchels.

A sanctuary of knowledge.

A vault of intent.

The perfect place for shaping outcomes.

She set the herbs upon a stone tray, arranging them with the careful precision of a healer... or a poisoner.

"Knowledge is power," Lyra whispered, her fingers pausing over the glowing veins of the Scorchroot.

"And power, properly applied... removes obstacles."

Her gaze sharpened as the image formed in her mind red hair, a bow of moon-wood, a presence the world itself seemed unwilling to diminish.

"...and with the right application of power..."

Her voice lowered. "...obstacles fall."

She closed the chamber doors with a soft, final click, then returned to the balcony. Her expression smoothed into serene composure the mask the world had learned to trust.

"Vacari will be remade," she murmured to the empty air.

"And when the dust settles..."

A breath.

"...Keisha will no longer stand where she does."

The desert winds carried her vow into the night.

Oasis City shimmered like a mirage carved from stone and water. Palm-lined canals wound between sandstone towers, silver lanterns glowing even beneath the sun. Beauty endured but beneath it, unrest simmered, quiet and feverish, spreading with every whispered rumor.

By the time Rhys reached the city gates, the guards were unsettled, their glances darting, their voices hushed.

"The council still sick?" Rhys asked, his tone measured with practiced concern.

A guard swallowed. "Worse today, Master Rhys. Two collapsed in the market square. The Sultan has summoned you."

Rhys inclined his head and followed without haste.

He was guided through gilded corridors into the Throne Atrium, where silk curtains cascaded beneath a dome of painted glass. The Sultan stood upon the dais, turquoise robes flowing like water, his expression drawn tight with strain.

"Rhys of Arcadia," the Sultan said, voice edged with urgency, "you are the only healer familiar with Afor's desert herbs. My council weakens by the hour."

Rhys bowed deeply. "I will do all that I can, Majesty."

"See that you do." The Sultan's hands tightened against the arms of his throne. "You will have full access to the infirmary, the palace stores everything you require."

He drew a long, controlled breath.

"And until my council recovers..."

The vast hall stilled, every eye lifting.

"...you will advise me. You will oversee the city in their absence."

Rhys felt his pulse surge sharp, immediate but his expression remained composed, deferential.

"As you command, Majesty. I will consult you on all matters and act only in your interests."

"Good." The Sultan waved him away, tension barely contained. "Go. Save them... if you can."

Rhys bowed once more and withdrew, moving through winding corridors until he reached the guest chambers prepared for him.

The door closed with a soft, final click.

Only then did he exhale.

Relief and exhilaration coiled together in his chest as he reached beneath his robes. From a concealed pocket, he drew a thin silver tablet etched with Arcadian runes.

Two fingers touched the surface.

Light rippled.

A communication glyph flared and Lyra's image formed in the air, all sharp grace and quiet command.

"Well?" she asked, her voice smooth as silk drawn across glass.

"It is done," Rhys murmured. "The council is ill beyond the palace healers' understanding. The Sultan has granted me authority to advise him until they recover."

A pause.

"He trusts me."

Lyra's lips curved into a slow, predatory smile.

"Excellent," she said. "The sands shift faster than expected."

"He believes I will strengthen his rule," Rhys added.

"Good." Lyra's gaze sharpened, gleaming like cut stone. "Then let him believe it."

Her voice lowered soft, absolute. "You will not act beyond what I have set in motion. You are my hand in Oasis... not my will."

Rhys bowed his head, the weight of her control settling firmly into place.

"Of course, my lady."

Lyra studied him for a longer breath, measuring, ensuring.

Then her expression smoothed once more.

"Continue," she said. "Keep Oasis exactly where I require it."

The glyph dissolved into nothing.

Rhys slipped the tablet away, the mantle of borrowed power settling around him like a cloak he could not shed.

Outside, the bells of Oasis City rang clear, resonant, deceptively calm.

Inside, a single thought surfaced, unbidden and undeniable:

Arcadia and Afor are hers.

And soon...

So will the rest.

Far from Oasis City, Lyra returned to her cool chamber in a sweep of blue silk. The chosen herbs still rested upon the crystal tray. One by one, she adjusted the vials and bundles arranging them with the precision of a conductor before an orchestra.

A symphony only she intended to command.

Lyra reached for the silver communication tablet once more.

Her fingers brushed the runes.

A pulse of shadow rippled through the air.

The projection formed a figure cloaked in darkness and shifting light, their presence pressing against the chamber like a gathering storm.

Lyra inclined her head measured, controlled, never submissive.

"My lord. I have news."

"Speak."

The command cut cleanly through the air.

"Oasis City falters," Lyra said evenly. "Rhys now advises the Sultan. Control of the region shifts into our hands sooner than expected."

The shadows around the figure stilled then drew inward, as though savoring the moment.

"Very good," the voice murmured. "Afor is a critical foothold. Its fall will weaken Vacari from the desert frontier."

Lyra's smile remained unchanged. "Rhys is loyal. He will follow my instructions."

"He had better," the voice sharpened. "Ensure his ambition never rises above your will. And Lyra..."

The chamber cooled.

"...you must master those herbs. Not merely their surface effects but the poisons hidden within them. You understand why."

Lyra's eyes flickered not with hesitation, but with recognition.

"As you command, my lord."

The figure leaned closer, shadows tightening like a drawn blade.

"If all else fails... If dragons turn traitor...

If illusions crumble... If E'vahona's veil holds..."

A pause deliberate, suffocating.

"We will remove Keisha by any means necessary."

Lyra inclined her head, slow and composed. "She will not remain beyond our reach forever."

A pulse of dark approval rippled through the chamber.

"Good. Keep me informed."

The projection vanished in a flash of shadow.

Silence returned.

Lyra lowered the tablet slowly, her smile sharpening something colder glinting beneath its surface.

"So," she murmured, stepping away from the herbs, "Keisha must fall."

A faint pause.

"At least on that point... we agree."

Her fingers brushed the edge of the crystal table as memory stirred.

The first time she had stood before that shadowed figure, the air had felt just as heavy just as full of promise.

She had spoken then of Vacari… of power… of inevitability.

And of one red-haired Eladrin whose influence would one day become a problem.

Destroy her early, Lyra had advised, voice calm and precise.

Before she gathers allies. Before the dragons circle her like worshippers around a flame.

But the answer had come cold and certain.

No. She serves a purpose yet.

Lyra had obeyed.

She always obeyed… when it suited her.

A soft laugh escaped her now, quiet and edged with something dangerous.

"How curious," she whispered. "Everyone changes their mind… eventually."

Her gaze lifted, distant and calculating.

"When they finally understand what Keisha becomes."

Her veils whispered as she turned toward the spiral staircase.

"Now…"

She ascended, each step deliberate, predatory.

"There is another matter to attend."

At the summit, Lyra paused beneath the open dome, moonlight spilling across Arcadia's luminous sprawl. Beyond the city, the desert stretched endless and ancient, its dunes hiding secrets older than kingdoms.

Her eyes narrowed.

"The Moon Seraphidians," she murmured.

"The last of them must still be somewhere beneath these sands."

The wind carried her words into the night.

"And I will find them."

Lyra stepped forward into the moonlight, silk trailing behind her like the shadow of a coiling serpent.

And vanished into the desert's quiet hunger.

Chapter 13

The Cradle of Echoes

The desert had no respect for royalty.

Lyra reached that conclusion the moment the sun climbed high enough to turn the dunes into molten gold and the wind into the breath of a furnace. Her silk veils clung to her shoulders, heavy with heat, while her boots sank into sand that burned like the forge of some long-forgotten fire god.

"This realm is a personal insult," she murmured, lifting the edge of her veil from her neck. "If the Moon Seraphidians truly chose this wasteland as their refuge... then clearly they were mad."

Behind her, the distant spires of Arcadia had already dissolved into heat-haze and memory. Ahead stretched nothing but endless dunes and, far on the horizon, the faint shimmer of ancient stone rising like a mirage from the sands.

The Cradle of Echoes.

A place where memory itself was said to linger in the air, fragile as breath upon glass.

Lyra narrowed her eyes.

"That," she said softly, "had better be worth it."

The desert answered only with wind.

She pressed onward, irritation sharpening with each step. Heat wrapped around her like an unwelcome cloak, leeching patience with every stride.

"I command storms," she muttered to the sky, "yet I am reduced to marching through sand like some sun-baked pilgrim."

The air shifted.

Not danger.

Presence.

Lyra slowed, senses sharpening.

The Cradle was near.

Sand gave way to fractured stones as half-buried arches emerged from the dunes like the ribs of some ancient leviathan. Weathered pillars rose in a wide circle, etched with runes so old that even Lyra could not place their origin. The wind changed as it passed through them no longer empty, but whispering, as though echoing voices long since turned to dust.

Lyra paused at the threshold.

"Moonbound fools," she murmured. "If you are anywhere, it will be here."

She stepped into the Cradle of Echoes.

Shadows moved.

Not cast waiting.

She felt them before she saw them: a disciplined stillness woven into the ruins themselves. Then the Umbral Elves emerged, slipping from the seams between stone and shadow as though they had always been part of both.

Armor like carved midnight.

Eyes catching the sun's pale fire with quiet disdain.

Recognition struck.

A ripple passed through their ranks not fear, not quite.

But something close.

Then, almost as one, they knelt.

Heads bowed.

Weapons crossed over their chests in a gesture that was not submission... but acknowledgment edged with caution.

All except one.

She stood apart.

Dark hair spilled loose down her back, untouched by the careful precision of the others. Her attention was fixed not on Lyra... but on the air itself. Her brow furrowed as she turned slowly, studying the ruins as though listening for something no one else could hear.

Lyra arched a brow.

Around them, the kneeling Umbral Elves trembled not with fear, but with reverence edged in unease. The desert wind threaded through the broken arches, carrying fragments of ancient sound.

Still, that one figure did not kneel.

Instead, she shook her head faintly.

"No... that's not it," the woman murmured, stepping closer to a fractured pillar. Her fingers brushed the runes, then sifted through the sand at its base. "Too thin. The echo's wrong."

Lyra's lips curved.

She took a single step forward.

"You do not bow."

The woman finally looked at her.

Dark eyes. Sharp. Entirely unimpressed.

"I'm busy."

Several Umbral Elves flinched.

Lyra stilled then laughed, slow and deliberate.

"Busy?"

The woman gestured vaguely at the ruins, then the desert beyond.

"Tracking something old, hidden, and increasingly irritated that it's being disturbed," she said flatly. "And if I have to do it while being slowly roasted alive, I intend to complain about it for the rest of the century."

She dragged the back of her hand across her brow and scowled up at the blazing sky.

"I despise heat."

Lyra studied her more carefully.

Not dismissive.

Not reckless.

Focused.

For the first time, interest flickered beneath Lyra's scrutiny.

"You have sensed it as well."

Caryth gave a short nod.

"Since we arrived."

Lyra's gaze sharpened.

"Your name."

The woman straightened at last, brushing sand from her gloves with absent precision.

"Caryth Shadowmere."

The desert seemed to still at the name.

Lyra's attention flicked briefly to the kneeling Umbral Elves measuring, confirming before returning to Caryth.

"You are not the one in command here."

Caryth let out a quiet, humorless breath.

"No. Rhys appointed two others."

She gestured lazily toward the far edge of the ruins.

"They were enthusiastic. Loud. Very certain they understood what they were doing."

Her expression darkened, the edge of dry humor fading into something colder.

"They were killed three weeks ago."

A ripple of unease passed through the Umbral ranks.

"Since then," Caryth continued, her voice flattening again, "they've been arguing over who should lead..."

Her gaze shifted briefly across the kneeling Elves, "...while I've been trying to find whatever has been hiding here since before any of us were born."

Lyra went still.

She studied Caryth again not as a soldier now, but as a mind.

At last, she nodded once.

"You."

Caryth blinked. "Me?"

"You are now in command," Lyra said coolly. Then, after a measured pause, she added, "...because you are the only one here thinking clearly."

Several Umbral Elves lifted their heads, shock cutting through discipline.

Caryth frowned.

"I didn't ask—"

Lyra raised her hand.

"You answer to me... but I expect competence, not blind obedience."

Silence stretched between them.

Caryth held her gaze a moment longer measuring, weighing then allowed a faint, dry smirk.

"Then we may get along better than expected."

Lyra's lips curved slightly approval, faint but unmistakable.

"Explain what you are tracking."

Caryth hesitated only a breath.

"An elusive aura," she said. "Ancient. Moonbound. It moves like a wound in the air. Something alive... and deliberately unseen."

Lyra's eyes gleamed. "Moon Seraphidians."

Caryth's breath caught.

"Half-human. Half-serpent. Hidden since the Sundering."

Lyra stepped closer, interest sharpening into something far more deliberate.

"Tell me something, Shadowmere," she said.

"When they choose to interfere with a person... what are they capable of?"

Caryth's expression shifted not fear, but caution.

"They are not warriors like dragons," she said. "Their power is subtler. Older. Moonbound magic."

A brief pause.

"They influence dreams. Fracture memory. Warp perception."

Her gaze flicked to Lyra.

"Some legends claim they can unravel bonds... even those shaped by magic or fate."

Lyra went very still.

"And the body?" she asked softly. "The mind? The will?"

Caryth's eyes narrowed.

"They are said to poison blood without a blade. To bend loyalty. To weaken those thought untouchable."

A beat.

"To break powerful figures... without leaving a visible wound."

Silence settled.

Lyra's lips curved slowly.

"So," she murmured, almost to herself,

"They do not merely kill..."

Her gaze lifted bright, calculating, cold.

"They unmake."

Caryth watched her more closely now.

Understanding flickered.

"You're not hunting them for protection," she said quietly.

Lyra glanced sidelong, veils whispering around her.

"I do not hunt to protect," she replied calmly. "I hunt to remove obstacles."

A pause sharp, intentional.

"If these Moon Seraphidians can weaken someone the world refuses to let fall..."

Her voice lowered.

"...then they may prove far more valuable alive than dead."

Caryth exhaled slowly, tension settling into something quieter and more dangerous.

"Then whatever they're hiding from..."

Her gaze drifted across the ruins, following the unseen pull she had been tracking—

"...is hiding from me as well."

The wind whispered through the Cradle of Echoes.

Ancient. Watching.

Waiting.

The hunt had truly begun.

Lyra turned toward the dunes.

"Take a small group. Find them. The moment you do, send word."

Caryth tilted her head.

"You aren't staying?"

Lyra laughed low, amused. "No. I am not foolish enough to roast in the desert when I have capable people to do it for me."

Caryth shook her head, faintly entertained despite herself.

"Yes Lyra Dreadcrusher. Brilliant, infuriating... and absolutely unwilling to sweat."

Lyra did not look back.

She simply stepped away, silk catching the sun like molten fire as the desert light swallowed her form.

Caryth watched her go for a heartbeat then turned sharply to the Umbral Elves, her posture shifting from observer to command.

"Three search lines," she ordered. "Stay within signal distance. No one breaks formation without my word."

Her gaze swept across them steady, unyielding.

"Track the Moon Seraphidians... and anything clever enough to hide from us."

A pause.

"Move."

They obeyed.

Caryth wiped sweat from her brow, scowling up at the blazing sky.

"And I still hate this heat."

The hunt began.

Lyra walked beyond the broken arches, the desert swallowing her footprints almost as soon as they formed.

Only when the ruins faded into heat-haze behind her did her composure shift just slightly.

A slow, private smile curved her lips.

"Moon Seraphidians..." she murmured.

"Poison without a blade. Bonds without chains. Power without spectacle."

She let the words linger, tasting them.

Her eyes narrowed, bright with quiet, dangerous intent.

"So many ways to end a problem..."

A breath.

"...and so many ways to remove Keisha."

The desert wind carried the name away.

But Lyra's resolve did not fade with it.

It sharpened.

Like something already in motion.

Chapter 14

Shadowhaven Reforged

Shadowhaven had changed.

Gone were the reeking piles of net-rot, the half-sunken ships patched with mismatched planks, the taverns that once vomited drunks into alleys before dawn. The harbor still hissed with danger but now it did so with order.

With purpose.

With the razor-clean discipline only the Druchii could impose.

The Druchii.

Qellaun Dreadcrusher walked the docks like a shadow given form tall, silver-eyed, elegant in his menace. Pirates who once swaggered now stood straighter and lowered their gazes as he passed. No one complained about the repairs, the new watch rotations, the curfews that gnawed into their freedom.

Not when a careless word could earn them an audience with a Druchii priestess for "corrective sacrifice."

Even the boldest captains had learned restraint.

A returning ship eased into port, its sails stained black by the volcanic winds of Fel Thalor. As crates were lowered onto the dock, every pirate moved with deliberate care dark sigils burned into the wood: Druchii runes for venom, silence, no witnesses.

One pirate bowed, just deeply enough to avoid offense.

"Master Qellaun," he said quietly, eyes fixed on the planks. "Fel Thalor sends their trade. The herbs have arrived... and their newest venoms."

He did not look up.

Qellaun studied the crates in silence, his gaze tracing each sigil as though weighing not their contents but their purpose.

After a moment, he gave a single, precise nod.

"They will be stored below," he said. "Exactly as instructed."

Another pirate braver, or simply less wise swallowed hard.

"Sir... if I may..."

His voice faltered. "What are these poisons meant for? We have brought back enough to—"

He stopped himself too late.

Qellaun turned.

His smile was thin. Cold. Exact.

"You are not paid to wonder," he said softly. "You are paid to obey."

The pirate went pale, bowing so quickly he nearly lost his footing.

"My apologies, Master. No disrespect. We follow orders."

"And you will continue to do so."

Qellaun's voice remained calm far more frightening than anger.

The crates were carried toward the old salt mines beneath Shadowhaven, abandoned long ago until Qellaun had them sealed, fortified, and bound with Druchii wrought iron. The pirates whispered of horrors stored below.

They were only half wrong.

As the last crate vanished into the subterranean vaults, Qellaun stood at the edge of the pier, gazing toward the horizon where Fel Thalor's fires stained the sky red.

Behind him, voices murmured low, careful, meant not to carry.

"Don't cross him."

"Druchii justice is no joke."

"He's rebuilding this place," another whispered, "and if we're unlucky...we're part of the cost."

Qellaun did not turn.

He did not need to.

Fear had already done the work for him.

His voice was low, contemplative meant only for the sea and the smoke-stained sky.

"The mistress will be pleased."

A pause.

"Shadowhaven sharpens..."

His gaze drifted to the horizon, where distant fire met dark water.

"...and the poisons flow where they must."

He turned, cloak snapping in the salted wind, his steps silent and unhurried.

Shadowhaven, once a den of rot, was becoming something far more dangerous not chaos refined, but will imposed.

Under Druchii rule.

Under Qellaun's hand.

Under the design of the one who no longer needed to be seen to be obeyed.

Qellaun had barely finished sealing the vault door when the darkness around him twisted, curling inward like a coiled serpent. The air chilled; lantern flames guttered, burning blue.

A voice filled the chamber smooth, commanding, unmistakable.

"Qellaun."

He straightened at once, spine rigid, expression flawlessly neutral.

"My lord."

A silhouette formed at the center of the vault more distortion than flesh, cloaked in shifting shadow. Even Qellaun, Druchii-born and tempered for cruelty and command, felt tension coil beneath his ribs.

"I have received word," the Mysterious One said, "that the poisons from Fel Thalor have arrived."

"They have," Qellaun replied. "Secured in the lower vault. No pirate touches them. No one enters the mines without my leave."

"Good. They will be needed."

Qellaun inclined his head, though his gaze sharpened by a fraction.

"For your new creatures, then?"

A hum of approval rippled through the shadows.

"Indeed. There are... matters beneath the temple below Flameford that require attention. Malrik will come for several of the poisons and herbs. He knows precisely what he needs."

A pause.

Subtle.

Measured.

Qellaun's brow twitched barely.

He kept his posture immaculate, though something colder edged his voice.

"Provided," he said evenly, "that Malrik survives Ivory Moonbeams."

A low chuckle drifted through the chamber amused, dangerous.

"Oh, Qellaun," the voice purred. "There is no need for him to walk through Sylvan territory."

The shadows thickened, pressing closer.

"I transported him myself."

Silence followed.

Qellaun blinked once.

Slowly.

Of course.

When he had been sent to Shadowhaven, he had marched for days through hostile woods—harried by Sylvan arrows, tangled in living thorns, hunted by unseen eyes.

But the priest

He bowed his head.

"As you command, my lord."

The illusion fractured like ice, shadows dissolving into nothing.

Silence reclaimed the vault.

Qellaun remained still for a heartbeat... then exhaled through his nose, the sound quiet and sharp.

"Of course," he muttered under his breath. "The priest is carried through the trees..."

A faint, humorless smile touched his lips.

"...while I nearly bleed out in them."

He turned back toward the sealed vault, expression settling once more into cold composure.

"Typical."

Dark energy rippled.

Black flame flared.

Malrik appeared inside the vault, robes swirling, eyes sunk deep in darkness.

"Qellaun," he said, offering a stiff nod. "The poisons?"

"All here," Qellaun replied, gesturing toward the crates. "I trust you know what you're taking."

Malrik smiled the kind that made wiser men step back before they understood why.

"Oh, yes. The temple's new inhabitants require... firm handling."

He tapped one of the crates.

"This one especially. It keeps them obedient."

Qellaun's gaze lingered on the sigils venom, silence, obedience.

His expression did not shift, but his attention sharpened.

Measured.

Cataloging.

These compounds could do far more than restrain beasts beneath a temple.

Weapons.

Leverage.

Control on a scale Malrik likely had not even considered.

But he said nothing.

Malrik extended his hand. Darkness curled around his fingers like living smoke as the lids cracked open, the air briefly tainted with a sharp, intoxicating poison-scent.

"I will inform our master of your efficiency."

"See that you do," Qellaun replied, voice smooth, unreadable.

Black fire swallowed the priest, and he vanished.

Again.

Without taking a single step.

Qellaun watched the space where he had stood, jaw tightening by a fraction.

Not envy.

Not quite.

Something colder.

Measured.

He exhaled slowly through his nose.

"Priests," he muttered.

"Too much magic... too little awareness."

His gaze returned to the remaining crates.

Lingering.

Calculating.

And far more potential than Malrik intends to admit.

He stepped forward and sealed the vault once more, iron grinding into place with a final, echoing weight.

Outside, distant voices drifted in from the docks pirates whispering rumors carried on Afor's winds.

Qellaun paused at the threshold, listening.

Not idly.

Never idly.

Information, like poison, is only dangerous in the right hands.

And he intended to have both.

"Arcadia's changing..."

"...the Sultan bowing to a new council..."

"...a woman in veils... power like a serpent..."

"...Afor itself trembling under her..."

Qellaun paused.

A slow smile curved across his lips proud, sharp, unmistakably Druchii.

"So," he murmured to the sea breeze,

"My sister reshapes Afor already."

A flicker of approval gleamed in his silver eyes not warmth, but recognition.

Lyra did not seize power recklessly.

She positioned herself until power had no choice but to settle in her hands.

"It seems," he continued softly, "Lyra outpaces half the Dominion's so-called commanders."

He turned from the vault, boots striking the pier with measured authority, cloak snapping behind him as pirates scattered from his path.

But his thoughts did not move on.

They narrowed.

Focused.

Lyra Dreadcrusher never acted without purpose.

If she was tightening her hold on Afor, then she was not thinking of the present. She was preparing for what came next.

And there was only one name that continued to surface in Dominion whispers.

Keisha.

Qellaun's gaze drifted back toward the sealed vault toward the poisons from Fel Thalor.

Venoms subtle enough to mimic illness.

Toxins refined enough to slip past wards.

Compounds capable of weakening even those the world believed untouchable.

Perhaps Malrik saw them as instruments of control.

Crude. Immediate.

But Lyra...

A faint smile returned, colder now.

Lyra would see refinement.

Application.

Solutions.

Should I tell her?

The thought surfaced without hesitation cool, deliberate, calculated.

Not as a gift.

Never as a gift.

As leverage.

As alignment.

As a move placed carefully upon a board already in motion.

His gaze lifted toward the horizon, where the sea darkened beneath gathering clouds.

Shadowhaven was his.

Afor was hers.

Separate dominions.

Separate strengths.

But not separate ambitions.

"And together..." he murmured, almost thoughtfully,

"We will not follow the Dominion's return..."

His smile sharpened.

"...we will define it."

The wind shifted, carrying the scent of salt, ash, and something far more dangerous. Preparation.

And beneath the surface of it all,

The first threads of something far more precise than conquest were already being drawn tight. Not war.

Not chaos.

But control.

One quiet decision at a time.

Deep beneath Flameford, where stone walls sweated heat and the air pulsed with a slow, unnatural heartbeat, the old Temple of Vuarus had awakened once more.

Black runes crept across the pillars like living veins.

The air shimmered with oily shadow.

Far below, chains rattled slow, deliberate... patient.

Malrik descended the carved steps, a sealed urn cradled in his arms. It glowed with a sickly red light, staining his robes as though they bled. His footsteps echoed... then were swallowed by the oppressive hush.

At the temple's heart a vast pit yawned, molten light seeping through fractured stone.

Shadows beneath it shifted.

Stretched.

Breathed.

Malrik smiled too thin, too precise to be called human.

"Easy now," he murmured. "I have brought what you require."

He lifted the urn's lid.

Corrupted heat surged outward. Chains screamed against stone. From the depths rose a sound not the roar of any creature of Vacari, but something older... something that had never belonged to this world at all.

Malrik poured.

Liquefied abyssal essence, laced with Druchii poison and molten ash, spiraled downward living venom vanishing into the dark.

The creature inhaled.

The entire chamber shuddered.

“Good,” Malrik whispered. “Feed. Grow.”

He stepped closer to the edge, peering into the abyss with reverence reserved for gods long dead or not yet born.

His thoughts drifted to Vuarus.

To the horrors once commanded in his name:

Shadow Wraiths born of absence and fear.

The Maelstrom Serpent storm given hunger.

The Wraithbound souls shackled through agony.

All terrible.

All powerful.

All flawed.

“They were formidable,” Malrik said softly,

“But they lacked one essential truth.”

His gaze sharpened.

“Control.”

Not fear.

Not binding.

Not even devotion forced through suffering.

Something deeper.

Chosen.

His smile deepened.

“But you... you will not serve because you must.”

A slow, reverent pause.

"You will serve because you were made to."

The pit stirred.

A tide of shadow rose vast, indistinct, immense enough to swallow the molten glow. Eyes opened within it, dim, and ember-like, watching... learning.

Malrik lowered his head.

"Soon," he murmured. "You will be unleashed."

The chains groaned in answer.

"And Vacari will understand."

As he turned away, a single thought surfaced sharp, dangerous, and carefully buried beneath discipline.

Even the untouchable can fall.

Even the girl the dragons shield.

The idea pleased him.

He sealed the urn and stepped back.

"Sleep," he called behind him. "Your time has not yet come."

A breath rolled upward heat and venom entwined.

Malrik smiled as he reached the archway.

"And when you rise," he said quietly,

"The world will finally see what our master commands."

He extinguished the torch.

Darkness swallowed the temple whole.

The shadows parted as Malrik entered the Tower of Shadowwalker, his steps measured, his expression once more composed.

The mysterious person stood amid the wreckage of their earlier fury, darkness coiled around them like a living crown.

"You have fed the creature," they said without turning.

"Yes, my lord," Malrik replied. "It grows as intended."

A pause.

Then, carefully:

"There is something else we must consider."

The shadows tightened.

"Speak."

Malrik inclined his head respectful, but never submissive.

"You wish Keisha removed," he said. "And that desire is... understandable."

Stillness filled the chamber sharp, dangerous.

"But Vuarus never sought her death."

The mysterious person turned.

"He sought her sacrifice," Malrik continued evenly. "Not to destroy her... but to claim what she carries."

A measured breath.

"Her power. Her lineage. The essence tied to prophecy."

Silence thickened.

"To kill her," Malrik said quietly, "ends the threat."

His eyes lifted.

"But it also ends the opportunity."

The words settled heavy, deliberate.

"To offer her to the Abyss..." he continued, "...would complete what Vuarus began."

The shadows shifted not in rage this time, but in thought.

"You suggest ambition," the mysterious person murmured.

Malrik's smile was faint. Certain.

"I suggest inevitability."

He stepped no closer yet somehow pressed further into the conversation.

"Vuarus failed because he acted as conqueror," he said. "Too visible. Too certain. Too soon."

A beat.

"This requires something else."

His voice lowered.

"Patience." Precision. Restraint." Then "Control."

The word lingered.

"If done correctly," Malrik continued, "her power is not lost."

A pause.

"It is transferred."

The chamber darkened.

"...You are implying she is more valuable alive than dead," the Mysterious Person said.

Malrik bowed his head.

"Alive," he said softly, "She is leverage."

A breath.

"Broken..." "She becomes a weapon."

Another.

"And given to the Abyss..."

His smile thinned to something almost reverent.

"...she is ascension."

For a long moment, nothing moved.

Then. "We will consider this."

Not refusal.

Not agreement.

Consideration.

Malrik inclined his head.

"As always, my lord."

He turned to leave.

The voice followed him quieter now, but far more dangerous.

"Vuarus failed because he lacked restraint."

A pause.

"We will not repeat his mistake."

Malrik did not turn.

But he smiled.

And deep beneath Flameford, in chains of heat and shadow, something ancient stirred. Not in hunger alone...

But in anticipation.

As though it, too, understood Keisha's fate might yet become something far worse than death.

Chapter 15

The Shattering Dawn at Crystal Vale

Morning light shattered across Crystal Vale, each beam refracting through towering facets of living crystal until the valley gleamed like a chorus of fractured rainbows. The land itself hummed a radiant symphony only Crystal Dragons could truly hear.

But today, the melody faltered.

The towering crystal cliffs trembled first in subtle warning, then with a low, grinding rumble that rippled through the Vale like a pulse of unease.

Aurelia lifted her head.

The Ancient Crystal Dragon's prismatic eyes flared, recognition instant and unyielding. Shadows gathered along the horizon thick, unnatural, bending light into angles that did not belong in this sacred valley.

Obsidian wings.

And behind them, a storm black enough to swallow the sky.

Nocturna.

And Xalzorath.

Together.

Aurelia's scales ignited with cold radiance as she unfurled her wings.

So… they dare bring their corruption here. To Crystal Vale.

High above, on the cliffside balcony of the Vale's Spire, Gailen sprinted into view, his gold-lined mantle snapping in the rising wind. The Crystalbow at his back pulsed in answer to Aurelia's tension, humming with crystalline resonance that mirrored his heartbeat.

"Aurelia!" he called, voice steady despite the tremor rolling through the valley floor. "I see them. Both of them. Nocturna… and Xalzorath."

He exhaled once, sharp and controlled.

"They're not hiding their intent."

Aurelia lowered her head, her voice chiming like living crystal drawn across stone.

"They come to test our boundaries," she said. "And perhaps… to shatter them."

Gailen mounted in one smooth motion.

"I didn't expect the Dominion to strike so soon."

Aurelia snorted, the crystals along her spine flaring brighter.

"The Dominion lost patience long ago."

They surged skyward in a radiant surge, crystalline wings scattering shards of refracted light as they tore into the thickening gloom.

Below them, a smaller Crystal Dragon burst from the eastern spire Lunareth, swift and keen. Her scales shimmered like moon-kissed ice as she angled toward the Emerald Woods.

Gailen tracked her flight and nodded once.

"Go," he called across the wind. "Find Verdantia. Warn Thalorian."

Lunareth answered with a trilling cry and vanished across the forested horizon.

Verdantia would answer.

She always did.

Aurelia tilted her wings, climbing higher as the obsidian shadows deepened.

And the sky darkened to meet them.

Ahead, Nocturna emerged from the storm like a living void her scales devouring light, her vast silhouette carving a wound in the crystalline sky. Xalzorath flanked her, black wings trailing swamp-born miasma that fouled the air with rot and shadow.

Gailen drew a measured breath, his pulse steadying rather than racing.

"They didn't come to talk."

Aurelia's voice thrummed sharp, resonant, unyielding.

"Then Crystal Vale will not answer with words."

She roared a sound like a thousand crystals shattering in perfect, lethal harmony.

The answering roar was colder.

Darker.

Older.

A long challenge.

Crystal light and obsidian shadow surged toward one another, and the first sparks of battle ignited in the fractured brilliance of the sky.

Aurelia and Gailen cut through the air like a shard of living starlight but the darkness answered, stretching taloned fingers across the crystalline heavens.

Nocturna rose from the storm like a titan carved from obsidian, her wings beating slow and deliberate, savoring the tension she had summoned.

A cruel smile split her jagged maw.

"Aurelia," she purred, her voice echoing like stone collapsing into a lightless cavern.

"Still shining. Last we met, I recall you bleeding that light into the ground beneath my claws."

Aurelia's wings flared, refracting the sun into a blinding spear of brilliance.

"Do not mistake a scar for weakness, Nocturna."

Her voice rang sharp as a drawn blade.

"You will not touch Crystal Vale."

Nocturna's laughter rolled low, dark, and amused.

"We shall see."

Without warning, Xalzorath dove.

The Ancient Black Dragon streaked toward the palace spires like a bolt of corrupted night, wings trailing venom-thick miasma that poisoned the air. His roar shook the valley, and he slammed into a barrier of shimmering light inches from the palace dome.

FWUM.

Silver and crystal erupted in a luminous shockwave, hurling him backward mid-flight as fractured light burst like shattered stars.

Across the palace terrace, Crystal Vale's mages stood shoulder to shoulder, crystalline staves humming as power gathered in rising waves. Along the upper balconies, Moon Elves lifted their hands, runic sigils igniting across their palms as threads of moonlight braided together in luminous arcs.

The combined spellwork surged outward.

A radiant dome took shape crystal lattice fused with moonfire, luminous geometry locking into place like living architecture.

Xalzorath recoiled, snarling.

"Moonborn and crystal-bound magic?"

Disdain dripped from his voice.

"How charming... and futile."

He hurled a torrent of corrosive shadow.

The barrier held.

Light flared. Runes burned brighter. The lattice shimmered and did not yield.

Aurelia roared, the sound cleaving the air like a cathedral of breaking crystal.

"You will not breach the Vale!"

Nocturna struck.

The heavens detonated as crystal shards and obsidian flame collided, shockwaves rippling across the fractured sky.

Gailen drew the Crystalbow in one fluid motion.

He loosed a volley of luminous arrows.

They refracted mid-flight, bending through prisms of light, cleaving through Nocturna's false-shadow tendrils before they could reach the shield.

Below, the palace's great doors burst open.

Emerald light surged across the valley.

Verdantia arrived.

The Emerald Ancient descended like a living storm, wings whispering as though the forest itself had drawn breath. Her gemstone scales caught the Vale's radiance welcomed it, reflected it, strengthened it.

Upon her back, Thalorian raised his staff skyward.

Emerald magic cascaded downward, blooming along the Vale's perimeter and threading seamlessly into the barrier.

"Wards up!" Thalorian commanded, his voice carried on spell-woven wind.

Every mage answered.

Staves flared.

Runes ignited.

The shield surged outward sealing all of Crystal Vale within a fortress of intertwined crystal, moonlight, and emerald power.

From the outside the city vanished.

Hidden behind a wall of living light.

Xalzorath roared in fury, each attempted strike repelled harder than the last, the barrier answering brute force with humiliating resilience.

Nocturna twisted through the air, her mane of shadow flaring rage bleeding through the edges of her calculated composure.

Verdantia rose beside Aurelia, emerald wings unfurled, her gaze sharp and unyielding.

"You should not have come here," she warned the obsidian matriarch.

Raelithar's distant words echoed through Gailen's memory:

Dark dragons may be tolerated in Vacari... but only barely.

Now, as Nocturna and Xalzorath circled like vultures denied their kill, the truth of it pressed heavy and unmistakable.

Aurelia's voice chimed through the crystalline winds clear, unwavering.

"Crystal Vale is not yours to touch."

Nocturna hissed, shadows boiling along her flanks.

"Everything will be ours," she spat. "Even your precious E'vahona will crumble."

Aurelia's eyes hardened cold, luminous, unbreakable.

"Try."

They collided again.

Emerald flames, crystal light, and shadowed malice tore across the sky as the first true battle for Crystal Vale ignited.

This was no marching line.

No clashing armies.

This was a precision strike two dark Ancients probing for weakness, testing the Vale's strength.

And Aurelia welcomed it.

Nocturna swept low, obsidian wings slicing through refracted light. But Aurelia did not meet her head-on. Instead, she angled upward subtle, deliberate eyes narrowing.

"She'll slip into shadow in three... two..."

Nocturna vanished.

Darkness folded inward, swallowing her form whole.

Gailen did not panic.

He drew the Crystalbow, breath steady.

"Now," Aurelia whispered.

Gailen loosed.

The crystalline arrow split mid-flight into seven refracting shards, each flaring like a burst of prismatic fire. They scattered wide, seemingly aimless against the open sky.

But Aurelia's instincts were flawless.

The shards curved sharply, drawn toward a distortion no eye could see.

CRACK

A roar of pain tore through the air as crystalline light detonated against the unseen.

Nocturna reappeared in a violent collapse of shadow, scales fractured, her form bleeding light where darkness had failed her.

Her eyes burned.

"You dare anticipate me?"

Aurelia's wings flashed, brilliant and cold.

"I learn."

Xalzorath dove without warning, jaws dripping black ichor. Shadows streamed from his wings, hardening into spears of solid darkness that streaked toward Gailen and Thalorian.

Verdantia reacted instantly.

"Thalorian windward!"

The Moon Elf sprang to his feet atop Verdantia's back, Arborblade flashing into his grasp. The emerald-forged curve caught sunlight and flared bright.

He slashed downward.

A spiraling arc of verdant magic surged outward, colliding with Xalzorath's shadow spears. The impact shattered both forces into drifting clouds of black and green dust.

Xalzorath snarled, banking hard for another pass.

But Gailen had already moved.

"Verdantia banking right!"

Aurelia spun with him, seamless.

Gailen loosed again.

This time, the Crystalbow answered with a crystalline chain-shot twin bolts linked by a radiant arc of living light.

The shot spiraled around Xalzorath's wing and constricted.

He roared, thrashing violently as he tried to tear free.

The chain snapped but not before slicing deep into the membrane.

Xalzorath recoiled, shock flickering across his shadowed features.

Nocturna surged toward him at once, forcing Aurelia and Verdantia to tighten their formation.

"They're coordinating," Thalorian warned.

"And so are we," Aurelia replied coolly.

Crystal light flared.

Emerald power answered.

The battle escalated.

Gailen nodded, eyes never leaving the dark Ancients.

"Not a full assault. Just a test."

Aurelia's voice chimed like fractured crystal.

"A test they are failing."

Nocturna bared her fangs.

"We have only begun."

She lunged again but Aurelia had already anticipated her approach.

Verdantia flanked right. Thalorian swept the Arborblade downward, unleashing a scalding arc of emerald fire. Nocturna dissolved into shadow mist to evade — but not quickly enough.

Emerald flame scored her flank, burning vine-patterns into obsidian scales.

Xalzorath attempted to capitalize, diving hard only for Gailen to loose a prismatic burst that turned the air itself into a wall of refracted weapon light.

Xalzorath pulled up sharply, snarling.

For the first time, doubt flickered in his eyes.

A deep resonance rolled through the Vale the unmistakable signature of Crystal Vale's wards locking fully into place.

Thalorian raised his staff.

"Wards are complete! They cannot reach the city!"

Verdantia answered with a thunderous emerald roar that shook treetops miles below a declaration of dominance that rippled through stone and sky alike.

Nocturna and Xalzorath slowed, circling at a distance.

They had learned what they came to learn.

Nocturna hissed, her voice cutting through the air like a blade.

"Crystal Vale stands today..."

A pause deliberate, venomous. "...but it will break tomorrow."

Xalzorath snarled in agreement, his wounded wing twitching.

Aurelia hovered in the radiant air, unmoved.

"Try us."

Verdantia's eyes burned bright as Thalorian raised the Arborblade skyward in silent challenge.

For a heartbeat, the dark Ancients hesitated.

Then their shadows peeled away into the storm clouds, retreating northward leaving only the echo of their fury lingering across the skies.

Aurelia watched them go, light rippling across her crystalline form.

"They probe the edges of Vacari's defenses."

Gailen exhaled slowly, lowering the Crystalbow as its glow dimmed.

"And found Crystal Vale very well guarded."

Verdantia landed beside them, emerald scales shimmering.

"For now."

Thalorian tightened his grip on the Arborblade.

"They will report to the Dominion. Whatever comes next..."

His gaze hardened. "...will not be a skirmish."

Aurelia nodded, eyes hard as diamonds.

"Then we will be ready."

Shards of settling refracted light drifted through the air as Aurelia and Verdantia hovered above the Vale. Beneath them, the wards shimmered like a second sky crystal, moonlight, and emerald flame interwoven into a living shield.

Gailen steadied himself on Aurelia's back, the Crystalbow resting at his side. Across from him, Thalorian wiped a smear of shadow dust from the Arborblade, his expression grim.

Aurelia broke the silence.

"This was only the beginning."

Verdantia inclined her head, wings cutting slowly through the light.

"A probing strike," she agreed. "They will test every border. Every flight. Every alliance. Perhaps not today. Perhaps not tomorrow. But they will return."

Gailen's jaw set.

"Then we warn the others. Crystal Vale is not the only target. They will weaken defenses one by one until something breaks."

"Then nothing must break," Thalorian said firmly.

Aurelia turned her gaze toward the eastern forests, resolve sharpening.

"Warnings must be sent. At once."

She lifted a crystalline claw and traced a luminous arc through the air. Magic pulsed outward, racing toward the Emerald Woods.

Moments later, the branches stirred. A forest nymph emerged in a whirl of green and gold, eyes bright as dew, hair woven with blossoms of living emerald fire.

She bowed deeply.

"Ancients. You called?"

Aurelia lowered her great head.

"Go swiftly. Carry word to every bordering realm. Crystal Vale was struck by Nocturna and Xalzorath a skirmish only, but proof that the

Dominion moves. Tell them to ready their riders, their wards, their dragons."

Verdantia added, her voice softer but unyielding,

"Warn the Silver Ancients as well. They will be tested soon."

The nymph bowed again, wings of light unfurling.

"Your message will reach the forest courts, the mountain flights, and the sky cities before dusk."

With a rush of wind, she vanished among the trees.

Silence returned.

Verdantia turned to Thalorian.

"We return to Emerald Woods. They will need preparation... and reassurance."

Thalorian nodded, offering Aurelia a respectful salute before Verdantia angled her wings and soared away, emerald light trailing behind her.

Aurelia circled once above Crystal Vale's glittering shield.

Gailen rested a steadying hand against her radiant scales.

"We held them today," he murmured. "But it won't be this easy next time."

Aurelia descended toward the valley, wings folding with solemn grace.

"That is why we prepare," she said.

"That is why we stand together."

Their landing sent a faint tremor through the crystalline terraces below.

Crystal Vale had endured the first strike.

But the war had reached its borders at last.

And both dragon and rider knew. This was only the opening move.

Chapter 16

The Nymph's Warning

Moonlit mist curled along the shimmering threshold of E'vahona as the ancient wards sighed open. The illusory veil softly chimed a crystalline bell-song that marked the arrival of one who came in peace.

Through the silver-lit archway stepped a nymph of the Emerald Woods, her form woven of verdant glow and delicate flowering vines. Dew shimmered upon her skin, and her hair cascaded as ivy brushed with starlight. Anxiety shadowed her expression, though her bow remained flawless reverent and precise.

Lady Seraphina, Lord Thaldir, and Karrenen emerged from the courtyard steps to receive her. Above them, Talleoss and Silvara watched from their stone perches, vast silver forms half-veiled in moonlight, their eyes bright as argent mirrors watchful, discerning, ancient.

The nymph pressed a hand to her heart.

"Honored guardians of E'vahona," she said, voice steady despite the tremor beneath it, "I bring urgent word from Aurelia, Crystal Ancient of the Vale, and Verdantia, Emerald Ancient of the living forests."

Seraphina's smile held warmth, but concern tightened her brow.

"Please," she said gently, "speak freely. What has occurred?"

The nymph swallowed. Petals along her arms dimmed.

"There was an attack. Nocturna, the Obsidian Dragon, and Xalzorath, the Black Serpent of Etharyon, descended upon Crystal Vale. Their shadows tore across the skies."

She drew a breath.

"But Aurelia and Verdantia drove them back."

Thaldir lifted his gaze toward Silvara above. They exchanged a heavy look shared knowledge, shared burden.

"It begins, then," he said quietly.

The nymph inclined her head.

"Aurelia and Verdantia urge all realms to vigilance. They believe the Abyssal Dominion has begun to move in earnest."

Her voice softened.

"They wished E'vahona to know first for your realm remains one of the strongest bastions of light."

At her words, the wind stirred, whispering through the silver blossoms that encircled the courtyard. The sacred boughs rustled like listening spirits.

Karrenen exhaled slowly, fingers brushing his jaw as thought sharpened into resolve.

Seraphina folded her hands, her voice calm and unyielding.

"We will stand ready," she said.

"As we always have."

The nymph's gaze shifted upward, drawn to Silvara. The Silver Ancient adjusted her wings, moonfire gliding across her argent scales like flowing starlight.

"And..." the nymph hesitated, "there is one further message. Verdantia sensed a disturbance within the deeper illusions of the forest days ago as though something of the Mirage had stirred."

Thaldir stepped forward, his expression darkening.

"That would be Ixalia," he said. "Silvara confronted her three days past. The Mirage Ancient crept too close to the Emberwoods and attempted to veil herself in spell-born deceit. Silvara shattered the illusion but Ixalia fled."

"No doubt searching," Thaldir finished.

"For something specific," Seraphina said softly.

Karrenen's gaze sharpened.

"The Silver Ancients guard more than a hidden realm," he said. "If the Mirage Ancient prowls this near… she may be testing the veil itself."

A hush fell not of fear, but of recognition. A shared understanding that unseen lines of fate had begun to shift.

The nymph bowed once more.

"I have delivered all that was entrusted to me. The Emerald Woods stand ready to answer if called."

Seraphina stepped forward and touched the nymph's shoulder, gentle yet resolute.

"And we are grateful. Return home with our blessing and our promise."

Her eyes held steady.

"E'vahona will not be caught unprepared."

With a final bow, the nymph stepped back through the moonlit archway. Her form dissolved into emerald radiance as the veil closed behind her with a soft, resonant sigh.

Silence settled over the courtyard.

Taut. Watchful. Waiting.

Karrenen turned to the others, his expression grave.

"We can no longer treat these incursions as scattered provocations. Nocturna. Xalzorath. Ixalia."

His gaze moved between them.

"The pattern is clear. The attacks are coordinated and too many threads now point toward E'vahona."

Thaldir crossed his arms, eyes shadowed with thought.

"The Dominion tests our boundaries," he said. "Measuring response."

"And searching for weakness," Seraphina added quietly.

Karrenen nodded once decisively.

"Then it is time."

He straightened, resolve sharpening the air around him.

"We summon the Eladrin Council. Every elder. Every voice. They must understand what approaches before the Dominion chooses the moment for us."

Above, the Silver Dragons answered with a low, resonant rumble that echoed through the crystalline trees.

A vow.

A warning.

A promise.

E'vahona would not be caught unaware.

The path to the Council Hall shimmered with soft silver luminescence as ancient runes awakened beneath the steps of the Eladrin Lords and Ladies. Windbells whispered among the branches overhead, their chiming subdued a herald of urgency rather than ceremony.

Within the vaulted chamber, crystal pillars rose like frozen moonbeams, catching candlelight and scattering it into pale, opalescent hues. At the center waited the great round table, carved from the heartwood of the First Tree, its spiraled grain pulsing faintly with ancestral memory.

One by one, the leaders took their places.

Lord Alaric, stern and unyielding.

Lord Karrenen, fingers tapping the table in measured tension.

Lord Thaldir, Silvara's rider, eyes alert and calculating.

Lady Elowen, soft-spoken, wisdom etched into her calm.

Lady Lythia, healer and seer, leaning forward with quiet concern.

Lady Seraphina, composed and resolute, palms resting lightly upon the living wood.

The doors hummed closed, sealing the chamber beneath a veil of privacy.

Karrenen spoke first as expected.

"Ixalia represents the greater threat," he said, voice steady and deliberate. "Zarathos is prideful and overt. His aggression is predictable."

A pause.

"Ixalia is neither."

Lady Elowen inclined her head.

"Zarathos entered the Emberwoods, yes but Raelithar drove him out with little difficulty. The Copper Ancient has faced gem-blooded dragons before. He understands how to dismantle arrogance."

Thaldir's jaw tightened.

"But Ixalia is another matter entirely."

He leaned forward, eyes reflecting a faint echo of silver fire as memory surfaced.

"She wove illusions so intricate that even the forest spirits hesitated to discern truth from falsehood. Terrain shifted. Shadows multiplied. Even Raelithar was momentarily ensnared. Had Silvara not arrived when she did—"

Lady Lythia finished softly, "he could have been drawn into a fatal trap."

Alaric folded his arms.

"The Mirage Dragons have always favored deception. But Ixalia's strength exceeds what our records once held. If she prowls this close, she is either acting under command... or seeking something she believes lies hidden within our borders."

A stillness settled the implication unspoken yet fully understood.

Seraphina broke it gently.

"Silvara shattered her illusions with ease," she said, "but that does not lessen the concern. Ixalia was not wandering. Her movements align too closely with Nocturna's assault on Crystal Vale and Xalzorath's resurgence. These actions are not isolated."

Thaldir exhaled slowly.

"Ixalia fled after their confrontation. But dragons like her do not flee from fear only from calculation. She will return. And next time, she may not act alone."

Karrenen's expression darkened.

"The Emberwoods were a test. She was probing defenses, mapping response. If the Dominion now deploys Mirage and Gem dragons alike..."

His voice lowered. "...then E'vahona has shifted from distant interest to active target."

Lady Elowen traced the glowing grain of the table with thoughtful fingers.

"And Zarathos? Will he return?"

"He will," Karrenen replied. "But Zarathos obeys ambition, not subtlety. He is dangerous — but predictable."

A beat.

"Ixalia is not. She is the one we must prepare for."

"And prepare swiftly," Lady Lythia added. "If Mirage magic can slip through outer wards, then inner defenses must be reinforced."

Seraphina nodded.

"They will be. Silvara and Talleoss will strengthen the veil surrounding the First Glade. Additional watch-wards will be placed along the Emberwood boundary."

Thaldir's voice grew low.

"And we must assume the Dominion now watches us as closely as we watch them."

Silence followed.

Not fear.

Unity.

Alaric straightened, his eyes glowing like twin lanterns.

"Then let this council be clear. E'vahona is no longer merely observing the unrest of the world."

His gaze swept the table.

"We are preparing for war whether the Dominion comes by shadow, flame, illusion, or fang."

One by one, the councilors nodded.

Karrenen rose, his voice resonating through the chamber.

"Then let our preparations begin."

The final echoes faded into crystalline stillness as the runes along the walls pulsed with soft silver light acknowledging the weight of the decision forged within the ancient hall.

Before any could rise, Lord Karrenen turned to Seraphina and Thaldir, his expression firm yet quietly trusting.

"Before we adjourn," he said, his voice low but carrying the authority of centuries, "there is one further charge I would place in your care."

Seraphina lifted her gaze, composed as ever.

"Name it."

Karrenen clasped his hands behind his back a posture of resolve, not command.

"Work with Talleoss and Silvara, and with all Silver Ancients under their guidance. Reinforce E'vahona's wards and veils. Strengthen every boundary, every veil, every layer of protection this realm possesses."

Thaldir exchanged a knowing look with Seraphina.

"You believe Ixalia will seek a path around our defenses."

"I am certain of it," Karrenen replied without hesitation. "She is Mirage-born. Illusion is her native tongue. We must be prepared to disrupt her senses, fracture her perceptions, and confound any attempt she makes to locate E'vahona."

Seraphina inclined her head slowly, strategy already unfolding behind her calm expression.

"We can weave counter-illusions with the Silver Ancients. Talleoss can obscure the outer boundaries, while Silvara reinforces the inner glades."

A thoughtful pause.

"We may even craft false signatures echoes convincing enough for her to pursue."

Thaldir's smile was thin, resolute.

"Then if Ixalia returns, she will chase shadows of our choosing."

Karrenen's shoulders eased, relief briefly softening his features.

"Good. E'vahona places its trust in you both."

His gaze lifted toward the Silver Dragons above.

"Work with them. Let their power amplify your designs. The Dominion must not glimpse even a fraction of what lies hidden here."

Lady Lythia rose, her luminous robes whispering across the crystal floor.

"Then it is agreed. The Silver riders and their Ancients shall oversee the strengthening of our defenses."

One by one, the councilors stood, their reflections rippling across the mirrored stone like moonlight across water.

As they moved toward the great doors, Karrenen paused and turned back once more.

"Whatever you require runes, mages, illusionsmiths you shall have it. E'vahona stands with you in full."

Thaldir inclined his head.

"We will not fail."

The doors parted with a soft, harmonic sigh, opening onto the silver-lit courtyard beyond.

Outside, Karrenen called the gathered Eladrin to attention. When he spoke, the crystalline pathways carried his voice through the glades with gentle resonance, weaving authority with reassurance.

"People of E'vahona," he announced, urgency tempered by calm, "hear this decree. Lady Seraphina and Lord Thaldir, alongside the Silver

Ancients Talleoss and Silvara, shall oversee all defensive measures within our borders."

A hush fell then resolve.

"They will strengthen our boundaries," Karrenen continued, "reinforce our wards, and ensure that no Mirage-born dragon nor any creature of the Dominion may pierce our veils."

Murmured agreement spread among the Eladrin not fear, but fierce unity.

Seraphina and Thaldir stepped forward, standing tall as their bonded Ancients shifted above. Talleoss and Silvara unfurled their wings slightly, scattering reflections of argent light across the courtyard like falling starlight.

Seraphina raised her voice, clear and unwavering.

"We will defend this realm with all our strength. Place your trust in us and in the dragons who guard our skies."

Thaldir followed, his tone firm and grounded.

"Know this: E'vahona will not fall to shadow while we stand."

A resounding, resonant chorus rolled from Talleoss and Silvara an ancient vow of the Silver flight, echoing through stone and leaf alike.

E'vahona's defenses had begun.

Gradually, the courtyard dispersed as Eladrin returned to their duties, purpose renewed. Silver blossoms drifted from the high canopies, stirred by the currents of the Silver Dragons' wings as they rose to survey the realm they had sworn to protect.

Keisha and Ong approached Lord Karrenen beneath the soft glow of newly awakened ward-lights, their gentle radiance flickering to life along the crystalline pathways.

Keisha's red hair caught threads of gold from the lantern crystals. Ong walked beside her, posture straight and calm the quiet gravity of his new bond lending him a steadiness that felt both earned and unfamiliar.

Karrenen turned as they neared, a faint smile easing the severity of his expression.

Keisha spoke first.

"Is there anything we can do to strengthen the defenses?" she asked. "We don't want to stand idle while everyone else prepares."

Ong nodded.

"Just tell us where we're needed."

Karrenen studied them both not as youths seeking direction, but as pillars whose placement could shift the balance of the realm.

He turned to Ong first.

"There is something you can do," he said. "It would be wise for you to return to Purplefire Woods. Amara is powerful, but the Dominion's movements will ripple through every forest. Your presence will steady her... and the Woods themselves."

A measured pause.

"The Eladrin bond you now carry will anchor the land."

Ong straightened, resolve settling without hesitation.

"If that's where I'm needed," he said quietly, "then I will go. I will leave at first light."

Karrenen placed a firm, approving hand on his shoulder.

"Amara will feel your return. And Purplefire will stand stronger for it."

Keisha glanced at Ong, pride and worry flickering through her gaze then turned back to Karrenen.

"And me?" she asked softly. "Where do you need me?"

Karrenen's expression shifted not unkind, but heavier with consequence.

"You, Keisha... must go to Goldmoor."

He met her gaze fully.

"Kimras will need you. If the Dominion moves in force, the Golden Ancients must be ready. Your bond strengthens him and his presence, in turn, steadies the alliance."

Surprise crossed her face.

"Goldmoor?" she hesitated. "Are you certain you do not need me here? I can help reinforce the wards, I can—"

Karrenen shook his head gently but without doubt.

"This is not a debate. Your strength is needed with Kimras. He listens to you in ways no one else can. And Goldmoor cannot be left exposed. We no longer have the luxury of waiting."

His voice softened.

"I regret separating you and Ong so soon after the Veilbinding," he admitted. "But Vacari needs both of its anchors in different places."

Keisha drew a slow breath, the weight of duty settling in her chest. She nodded once obedient, but not untouched.

"All right," she said quietly. "If Kimras needs me, then that's where I'll go."

Karrenen inclined his head.

"Your presence will matter more than you realize."

Keisha gave one last look toward Ong a silent exchange of duty, trust, and the bittersweet pull of being drawn in different directions.

Then she turned away.

Her silhouette slipped into the silver-lit pathways, red hair trailing behind her like a flame dissolving into moonlight.

Ong watched her go. A faint ache settled in his chest, but he did not call out.

They both knew this was what must be done.

As Keisha vanished into the deeper glades, the first subtle winds of change stirred across E'vahona.

She walked alone beneath the moonlit canopy, crystalline lamps casting soft halos over moss-worn stone. The realm shimmered around her serene, beautiful… and suddenly distant.

Each step carried the weight of Karrenen's words:

Go to Goldmoor. Help Kimras. Leave now.

Her heart pulled in two directions, but duty had always spoken louder.

Ahead, curled beneath a flowering silver birch, Pumpkin lifted her sleek black head. Emerald eyes gleamed like twin lanterns, catching Keisha's approach with immediate understanding.

Keisha's breath caught.

"Pumpkin…" she whispered.

The panther rose and padded toward her, tail sweeping low. Keisha knelt, arms sliding around Pumpkin's powerful neck, burying her face in familiar fur.

For a moment, she allowed herself to hold on to the one presence that never questioned her choices, never demanded explanation.

"I need to ask something of you," she murmured, brushing the panther's cheek. "Something important."

Pumpkin answered with a low, affectionate chuff.

"Go with Ong. Stay with him." Keisha swallowed, her composure thinning. "He may need you more than I do."

Pumpkin stilled.

A displeased huff rumbled in her chest as her gaze flicked toward the path Keisha would soon take. Her tail lashed once sharply, protesting.

Then she stepped forward, pressed her forehead to Keisha's, breath warm and steady… and nudged her shoulder with silent insistence.

Agreement.

Keisha closed her eyes, resting her brow against Pumpkin's.

"Thank you," she breathed. "Take care of him for me."

Pumpkin circled her once, brushing along her side before settling back, eyes fixed on Keisha with unwavering loyalty.

Keisha rose slowly, brushing moisture from her lashes.

She glanced once toward the heart of E'vahona where Ong and her father still spoke, believing she would leave at dawn.

Dawn felt too far away.

Her steps carried her toward the stables, where the scent of hay and the glow of enchanted lanterns warmed the cool night air. Celeste lifted her head as Keisha entered, ivory coat shimmering, silver mane stirring as though touched by unseen magic.

Keisha stroked her muzzle.

"We're leaving," she whispered.

Celeste pawed the ground, sensing the urgency beneath the calm.

Keisha worked quickly, saddling with steady hands despite the storm within her chest. She did not look back toward the Council chambers. She did not seek Ong. She did not search for her father.

She knew if she hesitated even for a heartbeat she would be stopped.

And Kimras needed her now.

With a final breath, she mounted and guided Celeste toward the edge of E'vahona. The wards parted gently at her approach a sigh of wind, a shimmer of silver light granting passage to one of their own.

She slipped through without ceremony.

Without farewell.

Without being seen.

And beneath the silver-draped night, Keisha rode away from E'vahona her path already bending toward Goldmoor...

Toward duty.

Toward danger.

Toward whatever awaited her there.

Evening deepened across E'vahona.

Lanterns dimmed one by one as Ong walked beside Karrenen in reflective silence. The air still carried the weight of the council's decisions, but beneath it, something tugged at Ong's thoughts uneasy, persistent.

At last, he spoke.

"Lord Karrenen... earlier," he said carefully, "when Keisha asked how she could help..."

He hesitated, choosing honesty over comfort.

"I think... she may have felt dismissed."

Karrenen slowed, then stopped. The words settled into him like a stone dropped into still water.

"Dismissed?" he echoed quietly. "I only meant to place her where her strength would matter most."

"I know," Ong said gently. "But Keisha feels deeply. She needs to know she is needed. Being sent away so quickly might have felt like being pushed aside."

The truth struck.

Karrenen exhaled slowly.

"I should have acknowledged her," he admitted. "I should have told her why her role mattered... instead of simply directing her."

A flicker of unease crossed his eyes.

"Come. Let us find her. I would speak to her before she leaves at dawn."

They turned toward the stables but slowed as they reached the lantern-lit entrance.

The scent of disturbed hay lingered.

One stall stood empty.

Celeste was gone.

The saddle hook hung bare. The floor still held the faint warmth of hooves that had stood there not long ago.

Karrenen's breath caught.

"She's already gone..."

Ong stepped into the empty stall, fingers brushing the still-warm rail. His brow furrowed not with anger, but with quiet, growing worry.

"She didn't tell us," he murmured. "She didn't even tell me."

Regret tightened Karrenen's expression.

"I feared I made her feel unneeded," he said softly. "Now I fear I did exactly that."

Ong turned to him, resolve settling into place.

"Goldmoor isn't far from Purplefire," he said. "I will check on her once I arrive. I will make sure she is safe."

His voice steadied protective, grounded.

"She won't face anything alone."

Karrenen nodded, shoulders heavy.

"Thank you, Ong. May the Ancient Light guide you both."

His gaze lingered on the path Keisha had taken, regret etched deep.

"I only hope I have not sent her away believing she was unwanted."

Ong placed a steady hand on his arm.

"She knows you care," he said quietly. "And I'll make sure she knows that too."

Together they stood in the stillness of the stables, the empty space speaking louder than words.

By morning, they would walk separate paths.

But both now carried the same quiet worry.

And as twilight deepened, E'vahona itself seemed to hold its breath.

Chapter 17

The Road of Silver Shadows

Keisha urged Celeste into a steady, whisper-soft gallop, the mare's hooves striking the starlite path with the hush of falling snow. Behind them, the wards of E'vahona faded in shimmering arcs of silver, their gentle hum dissolving like the final notes of a lullaby.

Night stretched ahead vast, watchful, and heavy with secrets.

The deeper she rode, the more the world changed.

The first sign of the Emberwoods came as a faint glow along the tree line embers caught beneath bark, veins of fiery gold pulsing through ancient roots. Branches arched overhead in cathedral silhouettes, leaves flickering as though lit from within.

Keisha slowed Celeste beneath the burning canopy. The air tasted of warm cinnamon and wildfire magic unmistakably Raelithar's domain, steeped in the Copper Ancient's raw, untamed spirit.

Celeste snorted, uneasy but obedient.

"I know," Keisha murmured, stroking the mare's neck. "It feels different tonight."

And it did.

Not hostile.

But disturbed.

Threads of Mirage-born illusion still clung to the forest's edges faint shimmers between trunks like lingering ghosts. Silvara had torn Ixalia's enchantments apart, but the dragon's touch remained subtle and poisonous, like a bruise beneath the bark.

Keisha tightened her grip on the reins.

"Raelithar will feel it too," she whispered. "He'll warn the others."

Duty urged her onward.

Beyond the Emberwoods, the land softened. Fiery hues melted into gentle greens as the Emerald Woods unfurled across the horizon a living tapestry of bioluminescent light. Leaves shimmered with emerald glow, drifting like stars caught in the wind.

The air cooled. Dew gathered in crystalline beads along the path. Somewhere deep within, Verdantia's presence whispered through the forest a lullaby of growth, balance, and ancient wisdom.

Keisha breathed it in, letting the calm briefly settle in her chest.

"Aurelia's messenger passed this way," she murmured. "She would have felt safer here."

Celeste flicked an ear, as if in agreement.

Yet even here, something felt wrong.

Patches of light dulled unexpectedly, as though shadows had brushed past and refused to let go entirely. Verdantia's forest rarely dimmed unless it recoiled from something it could not immediately cleanse.

Keisha's pulse quickened.

"Then Mirage passed here too..."

Ixalia was covering too much ground.

Too quickly.

Keisha pressed her heels into Celeste's flanks.

They needed to reach Goldmoor.

The terrain rose, lifting into ridges of ancient stone veined with silver quartz that fractured moonlight into cascading beams. At the crest of the final rise, the world opened wide.

The bridge awaited.

A monumental arc of luminous stone spanning the vast chasm that split Vacari east to west forest to mountain, shadow to flame. It bound Purplefire Woods, Goldmoor, and the eastern realms to the Emberwoods and the living heart of the Emerald Woods.

The Bridge of Connectivity.

Each patterned step glowed beneath Celeste's hooves as Keisha guided her toward its threshold. Below, the abyss churned with luminous mist, starlight trapped and swirling in endless motion.

Legend claimed the First Ancients shaped this bridge so the realms would never truly stand apart no matter how the world fractured around them.

Tonight, it was beautiful.

And foreboding.

Keisha drew Celeste to a halt.

Wind at this height cut sharply and cold, brushing her hair back like a whispered warning. Her red braid gleamed like a falling ember against pale stone.

Beyond lay Purplefire Woods.

And farther still Goldmoor.

Her duty waited across this bridge.

So did her fear.

She guided Celeste onto the first span and a sudden chill raced down her spine.

Instinct.

Sharp.

Unbidden.

Celeste's ears pinned back.

Keisha looked up.

A silhouette unfurled from the sky wings like fractured glass scattering moonlight into prismatic shards. Reality bent subtly around her, as though the world itself hesitated, unsure which truth to obey.

Keisha's breath stilled.

Ixalia.

Ancient Mirage Dragon. Weaver of deception. Predator made of illusion.

Ixalia spiraled lower, laughter drifting like wind through broken mirrors.

"A traveler in the night," she crooned, voice shimmering through the air, "and a red-haired elf, no less."

Almost pleasant.

Almost hungry.

Keisha did not hesitate.

"Run, Celeste now!"

Celeste surged forward, hooves striking sparks from the ancient stone. Keisha leaned low, urging speed, her braid snapping behind her like a comet's tail.

Above, Ixalia circled once then descended in a smooth, deliberate glide.

"Voraxia spoke of you," the Mirage Dragon purred. "the red ember wandering where she does not belong..."

Keisha ignored her.

The bridge stretched endlessly ahead, moonlit and trembling beneath Celeste's pounding strides. Mist churned far below, but Keisha did not fear the fall.

She feared what followed.

Ixalia drifted closer, wings barely moving, her presence bending the air like a dream forcing itself into reality.

Still Keisha did not slow.

Not until Celeste's hooves struck the far side of the bridge crossing into the threshold where the path forked toward Purplefire Woods… and beyond, Goldmoor.

She hauled the mare to a halt, breath ragged.

Ixalia descended like a collapsing curtain of fractured light, hovering just above the treetops.

She laughed.

Soft.

Sweet.

Poisonous.

"Running, little ember?" Ixalia crooned. "How dull. Surely you have more spirit than that."

Keisha's hand hovered near her daggers not to fight a dragon, but to anchor herself.

Illusions were Ixalia's true weapons.

Deception, her breath.

Perception itself… her battlefield.

Keisha steadied her breathing.

Centered.

Focused.

Ready.

Ixalia's wings flared.

The air fractured.

Light split. Shadow folded. Reality wavered. And the illusions came.

Illusion One — Zylron

The air screamed.

A roar split the sky as heat slammed into Keisha like a living wall. The bridge vanished from her sight, swallowed by fire and drifting ash. Stone warped into molten rivers. Moonlight drowned beneath choking smoke and emberfall.

Before her rose a colossal volcanic form.

Crimson scales veined with molten gold. Wings shedding sparks with every thunderous beat. Fire bled through the seams of his armor-like hide.

Zylron.

His eyes burned like twin infernos, fury radiating in waves that scorched both air and memory.

He lunged.

Keisha did not scream.

She did not run.

She breathed.

"I already faced you," she said quietly, her voice steady despite the heat clawing at her.

"You were loud. Predictable."

Zylron's jaws snapped shut inches from her face and passed through her.

No heat.

No weight.

No truth.

Keisha's eyes narrowed, clarity cutting through the illusion like a blade through smoke.

"And you never learned," she said calmly.

"You rely on fear."

Her gaze lifted not to the dragon, but beyond it.

"Ixalia relies on lies."

For the briefest flicker of a heartbeat, the illusion faltered.

Not from force.

From recognition.

That was enough.

Cracks splintered across Zylron's blazing form like fractured glass. Fire collapsed inward, devouring itself in a storm of ash and dying embers. His roar twisted, hollowing into silence as the illusion unraveled.

Reality snapped back.

Moonlight.

Stone.

Wind.

The bridge returned beneath Celeste's hooves, luminous and steady.

Keisha exhaled slowly, her grip on the reins loosening by a fraction.

"Next illusion," she murmured, lifting her chin.

"Make it worth my time."

Illusion Two — Kimras

Gold light erupted outward blinding, warm, and heartbreakingly familiar.

A massive form materialized before her.

Kimras.

The Ancient of Goldmoor stood at the bridge's edge, staggering. His once-brilliant scales were torn and blackened, molten gold blood spilling across the stone in slow, terrible rivulets. His great wings sagged, their radiance guttering like a dying sun.

"Keisha..."

His voice rumbled low fractured, dimmed.

"Help me..."

Her breath caught.

Not fear.

Something deeper.

Instinct.

Bond.

For a single heartbeat, her hand moved.

Not to fight.

To reach him.

Then she stopped.

Because something was wrong.

Not the wounds.

Not the voice.

The presence.

Kimras was not merely power.

He was certainty.

A sun that did not flicker.

Even in battle... even in pain... his mind burned steady, unyielding, impossible to diminish.

This...

This was dim.

Fading.

Unanchored.

Keisha exhaled sharply, forcing the ache down before it could take hold.

"That is not him."

Her voice steadied, cutting clean through the illusion.

"Your tricks are sloppy."

The golden dragon froze.

For a fraction of a heartbeat, the illusion held as though deciding whether to persist.

Then it shattered.

Kimras collapsed into fractured motes of light, dissolving into drifting gold dust that scattered and vanished into nothing.

High above, Ixalia hissed.

The sound warped through the air, irritation threading through her otherwise composed tone.

"So," the Mirage Dragon mused, voice tightening at the edges,

"Sentiment does not blind you. Interesting..."

Keisha steadied Celeste, fingers pressing into the mare's mane. She grounded herself in breath, in muscle, in the living rhythm beneath her.

Truth.

Not illusion.

"Is that all?" Keisha called upward, voice remain steady despite the storm in her chest.

"I expected better."

Ixalia's pupils narrowed to slits, amusement curdling into something colder.

"Not remotely."

She unfurled her wings fully.

Light bent.

Shadows twisted.

Reality blurred, folding and refolding like silk in her claws.

"Let us see," Ixalia purred, silk stretched over steel,

"What remains... when your mind is laid bare."

The air around Keisha rippled.

Stone wavered beneath Celeste's hooves.

The sky peeled back in layered fragments, like veils torn from a wound.

And the true illusions began to form.

Not crafted to frighten but to break.

Ixalia carved slow, deliberate arcs through the warped heavens.

"Perhaps sentiment fails you," she whispered,

"But fear..."

A pause.

Longer this time.

Colder.

"...fear is universal."

The air twisted violently.

A shadow bloomed before Keisha vast, horned, and dripping with void-dark essence.

Something ancient.

Something wrong.

Something that did not belong to memory alone.

Illusion Three — Voraxia

The air convulsed.

Smoke and shadow coiled as a massive form tore itself into existence. Darkness thickened, shaping scale and wing until a towering silhouette loomed before her a living storm of umbra and malice.

Voraxia.

The Shadow Dragon roared, the sound rolling like thunder trapped beneath the bridge. Her jaws split wide, teeth forged of pure night, void-dark essence dripping and hissing where it struck the stone.

She lunged.

Keisha sighed.

Not in fear.

In irritation.

"Oh," she muttered dryly, one hand settling against her hip,

"Again?"

Voraxia did not vanish.

Her jaws slammed down and this time, the force hit.

Celeste reared, the impact rippling through the bridge as shadow splintered across the stone like shattered glass. The illusion did not pass through her.

It resisted.

Keisha's eyes narrowed.

"...Better," she murmured.

Voraxia circled now, slower, more deliberate. Not a memory.

A reconstruction.

Her wings carved shadows that lingered too long. Her presence pressed not fully real but no longer hollow.

"Didn't I already deal with you?" Keisha said, voice steady, testing.

Voraxia answered with a roar that shook the air.

Not memory.

Reaction.

Ixalia's voice drifted from above, sharper now, threaded with focus.

"Recognition is not immunity, little ember."

Voraxia struck again.

This time from the side.

Shadow slammed into Keisha's shoulder, not enough to throw her but enough to hurt. Enough to prove the illusion had teeth.

Celeste staggered, hooves scraping light from the bridge.

Keisha steadied herself, breath tightening not from fear, but from recalibration.

"Not real..." she whispered. Then she corrected herself. "...not fully."

Her gaze sharpened.

"You're learning."

Voraxia lunged again and this time Keisha moved first.

She shifted with Celeste, angling just enough that the strike passed wide. Her hand lifted, not to strike but to deny.

"I already know how this ends," she said, voice cutting clean.

The illusion faltered.

Just slightly.

That was all she needed.

"Memory isn't enough," Keisha said, stepping forward now, forcing the illusion to meet her instead of chasing her.

"You don't understand her."

Voraxia froze and cracked.

Darkness splintered across her form, fractures spreading through wing and scale like stress lines in glass.

Keisha's voice hardened.

"And you don't understand me."

The illusion shattered.

Voraxia collapsed into black mist, unraveling with a sharp, violent recoil — as though the shadow itself rejected the shape it had been forced to wear.

High above, Ixalia's tail lashed once, cutting through warped sky with a snapping crack.

This time, she did not hide her frustration.

"You mock me, little ember," the Mirage Dragon hissed.

Keisha lifted her chin, eyes bright, unyielding.

"Only when you make it easy."

Ixalia's pupils thinned to razor slits, prismatic light flashing like shattered gemstones.

The air thickened.

Warped.

Then split apart with a scream of cold.

"Then let us see," Ixalia snarled, all pretense gone now,

"How long your bravado lasts..."

Illusion Four — Glaciera's Frost Breath

White-blue frost exploded across the path.

The temperature plummeted in an instant breath crystallizing midair as a violent blizzard tore reality open. Wind howled with razored fury.

From the storm surged a towering form wings of jagged ice unfurling with a shriek of frozen wind.

Glaciera.

The Ice Ancient lunged

Keisha gasped.

Cold seized her instantly.

Frost crawled over her boots

Celeste screamed beneath her

Keisha clenched her fists.

"This... isn't real..." she forced out

"I won't break."

Ixalia pressed harder.

The cold changed.

No longer sharp.

Smothering.

Heavy.

It sank into her bones.

Keisha tried to focus.

On Ong.

On Kimras.

On E'vahona.

The memories slipped.

Like warmth leaving her body.

Her breath hitched.

"...No..." she whispered

Her knees buckled.

She fell beside Celeste.

Frost rimed her lashes.

Her heartbeat slowed, each pulse heavier

The world dimmed.

Sound dulled.

Even fear began to fade.

Ixalia's voice slipped through the storm close now.

Inside.

Silken.

Merciless.

"Everyone breaks.

"Even you."

Keisha's eyes fluttered.

Frost crept over her shoulders...

Her chest...

Her throat. And for a moment. She stopped fighting.

Silence swallowed the storm.

Then a thunderous roar shattered the illusion.

Golden light tore through the false frost, searing it into nothingness. Glaciera's illusory form vaporized in a single radiant blast, the cold collapsing as reality snapped back like a released bowstring.

Keisha collapsed forward, gasping as warmth flooded her limbs.

She heard her name.

"Keisha!" The single word carried more than urgency it carried fear.

She forced her eyes open.

Kimras descended like a sun breaking through stormclouds.

The Ancient Golden Dragon landed beside her with a force that shattered the last remnants of illusion. His wings spread wide, casting molten gold across the forest floor a living shield between her and the sky.

His voice thundered, fury braided with fear.

"Stand behind me, Keisha."

He lifted his gaze upward, molten fire igniting in his eyes.

"Then let us end this."

A second presence swept in.

Amethyst light streaked across the canopy scales flashing like faceted gemstones beneath moonlight.

Amara.

Her psychic power rippled outward in violet waves, a soundless resonance vibrating through root, stone, and thought itself. The air quivered as her psionic pulse struck Ixalia's spellwork with ruthless precision.

The Mirage weavings shattered like cracked glass.

Ixalia recoiled midair, snarling as illusion threads fractured and unraveled.

"Mirage wretch," Amara's voice rang aloud and within the mind, echoing like a choir of crystal bells.

"Prey on someone your own size."

Kimras stepped closer to Keisha, lowering his massive head. His voice softened, warm as heartfire.

"I felt your fear from half a realm away. Are you harmed?"

Keisha reached toward him, breath still unsteady as the last chill faded.

"No," she whispered. "You came in time."

Relief poured through him in a rush of golden warmth then his gaze snapped skyward again.

Fire ignited in his eyes.

His wings flared.

"Ixalia has hunted enough tonight."

Above them, the Mirage Dragon hissed, her form rippling like broken light. Amara circled higher, violet energy gathering in luminous halos.

Ixalia had sought a lone elf.

She found a Golden Ancient and an Amethyst fury.

The balance had shifted.

Her ancient eyes studied Kimras and Amara calculating, enraged before settling on Keisha.

"Another night, little ember," Ixalia hissed. "Your guardians arrive quickly ...faster than expected"

Kimras answered with a roar that shook leaves from every tree.

"You dare target my rider?"

His voice thundered with soul-born fury.

""Come for her again, Mirage deceiver," he said, voice low and absolute, "and there will be nowhere in Vacari you can hide from me."

Even Ixalia faltered.

Amara sighed, shaking her amethyst head.

"When will dark dragons learn?" she muttered.

"Threatening our riders never ends well."

Ixalia's form warped with rage. She bared crystalline teeth then twisted away.

With a burst of distorted color, she vanished into bent moonlight.

Gone.

For now.

Kimras landed heavily beside Keisha, talons cracking stone as the forest brightened instinctively in his presence.

"She did not harm you?" he asked.

Keisha shook her head. “No. But she tried.”

His jaw tightened.

“And she will regret that.”

The trees stirred.

A nymph emerged from Purplefire Woods, her form glowing with violet firelight, bowing deeply to Kimras.

“Lady Keisha,” she said gently, “Celeste is weary from fear and frost-illusion. I will guide her safely to Goldmoor. The path is warded.”

Keisha hesitated.

Kimras smiled dawn warm.

“Celeste will arrive safely. The forest protects its own.”

The mare nickered softly before following the nymph down a glowing path.

The forest quieted.

No illusion. No distortion. Only wind... and truth.

Keisha exhaled then looked up. “You’re really taking me the rest of the way?”

Kimras lowered himself.

“I will not allow you to walk another step alone tonight.”

A pause.

“Or ride. Especially not at night.”

Keisha blinked. “Are you scolding me?”

“Yes.” A deep, parental rumble. “You crossed Emberwoods and Emerald Woods alone, at night, with the Dominion stirring.”

“That duty couldn’t wait,” Keisha replied.

“Neither can your safety,” Kimras countered. “You are my rider.”

She sighed. “Are you done?”

“For now.”

She climbed onto his back as Amara lifted beside them a silent escort.

Together, they rose into the sky.

Goldmoor unfolded beneath them as dawn crept across Vacari.

Rolling plains of gold-tinted grass gave way to elegant spires of pale stone, inlaid with luminous filigree. Lantern crystals glowed warmly as the city stirred, unaware of how close danger had already come.

Golden Wardens bowed as Kimras passed overhead.

"The Ancient returns..." And he brings Lady Keisha."

Kimras descended not toward the palace, but toward the heart of the city.

The Garden of Resilience.

At its center stood the monument Kimras in eternal ascent, wings carved in reverent motion, and King Alex upon his back, not in dominance but unity.

A reflective pool mirrored them endlessly guardian and king soaring between sky and hope.

Kimras landed gently at the garden's edge.

Keisha slid down, boots sinking into warm earth.

"I always forget how beautiful this is," she murmured.

"It reminds us what we protect," Kimras said quietly.

His gaze lifted toward the city.

"This is where you are needed."

Keisha nodded, hand resting on his scales.

"I'm ready."

"Good," he said. "We speak to King Alex at once."

A pause.

"And Keisha..."

"Yes?"

"Next time, you do not travel alone at night."

She laughed softly relief at last. "I knew you'd say that."

"I will continue to say it."

Together, they turned toward the golden gates.

Goldmoor gleamed in the rising light.

And as the first true rays of dawn brushed the city in molten gold, Keisha stepped forward beside Kimras no longer alone, no longer uncertain, but standing where fate had always been leading her.

Chapter 18

The Mirage's Revelation

Night smothered Flameford in shifting veils of embered shadow. The volcanic ridges glowed faintly beneath the surface, their molten cores pulsing like the slowed heartbeat of something ancient beneath the earth. Smoke coiled through the air in serpentine ribbons, drifting across jagged black stone and the half-collapsed pillars that once marked the entrance to the Dominion's old stronghold.

And through that crimson haze came Ixalia.

She flew low over the cracked obsidian plain, her wings shimmering with fractured prisms of color light bending unnaturally around her as though reality itself refused to touch her. Each wingbeat distorted the smoke below, sending mirage-like ripples across the landscape.

She slipped between two towering spires of volcanic glass and descended into the heart of Flameford.

The cavernous stronghold awaited her dark, vast, and alive with heat.

At its center stood the one she had come to see:

The Mysterious Figure.

Shrouded in shadow, eyes burning like dying stars.

A presence heavy enough to bend the air.

Ixalia folded her wings, bowing her slender head as she landed upon the scorched stone. Despite her pride, the Mirage Ancient lowered herself with reverence.

"My lord," she purred, "I bring news you will find... most interesting." Her voice flowed smoothly though the memory of shattered illusions still lingered beneath her composure.

The figure turned slowly toward her, features concealed, power radiating like a quiet threat.

A pause.

Then a single command, soft and lethal:

"Wait. If your discovery is what I believe it to be... all will hear it."

Ixalia blinked in surprise, irritation flickering briefly across her shifting opal yes, but she obeyed. The figure gestured toward the darkened tunnel that split the stronghold in two.

"The Cavern of Ash."

A place reserved for Dominion gatherings, war plans, and revelations meant for every dark dragon aligned with the Abyssal Dominion.

Ixalia's breath stirred with anticipation.

"As you wish."

She glided toward the Cavern of Ash an immense hollow deep within the volcanic mountain. Ash drifted like black snow from the ceiling, layering the ground in a soft, smoldering blanket. The cavern's walls pulsed faintly with veins of molten fire, illuminating the space in shades of ember-red and bruised violet.

She settled onto the central rise of stone, her tail curling elegantly around her.

Behind her, the mysterious figure approached the cavern threshold but did not enter. Instead, they lifted one hand.

"Malrik."

From the shadows stepped a tall, gaunt figure Malrik, emissary of the Dominion, cloaked in ashen robes with eyes reflecting nothing but void. He bowed low.

"Master." His bow was precise, yet his gaze flicked briefly toward Ixalia, measuring.

"Send the summons," the figure commanded.

Malrik nodded once, pressing his palms together. Shadows thickened around him, condensing into a swirling sphere of black light. Whispered commands slipped into the magic silent, deadly, far-reaching.

Then, with a sound like cracking embers, the sphere burst into a hundred streaks of dark flame that shot across the caverns, dispersing into the night sky through jagged cracks in the rock.

The summons had gone out.

Ixalia's eyes gleamed.

Let them come, she thought.

Let them hear my discovery.

One by one, the heavy wingbeats of dark dragons echoed through the volcanic halls guttural roars rumbling like approaching storms.

Zylron's volcanic snarl tore through the cavern first.

Then Nocturna low, patient, coiling through the dark.

Zarathos followed, his presence heavy with pride.

Xalzorath's swamp-thick rasp slithered in behind them and then more... wings, shadows, breath, heat until the chamber itself seemed too small to contain them.

They were answering the summons.

The Cavern of Ash quivered as the first dark dragons entered massive silhouettes blotting out the molten veins glowing in the walls. Heat surged, smoke curling from scale and breath alike until the chamber throbbed like the heart of a waking volcano.

Ixalia lifted her head proudly, iridescent wings catching the ember-light in fractured, shifting patterns.

Tonight...she would reveal what even illusion could not break and why it mattered.

And every dragon present would listen.

Zylron arrived first.

The Volcanic Ancient stalked into the cavern with a growl that shook embers from the ceiling. Lava-like fissures glowed along his crimson-scaled hide, each breath exhaling a plume of molten heat that shimmered in the air.

His burning gaze locked onto Ixalia.

"What is this meeting about?" he demanded, voice grinding like tectonic stone.

"I was not told of any strike or change in orders."

Ixalia tilted her head, wings shimmering with faint mirage ripples. Her smile curved into something smug... delighted... secretive.

"Because the news I carry is... recent," she purred.

"And rather... illuminating."

Zylron's growl deepened, embers spilling from his nostrils.

"Then speak." Heat rolled off him in a visible wave impatience barely restrained from becoming action.

Ixalia's smile widened sharply and glittering but she made no move to explain. Instead, she flicked her tail, coils of illusory light spiraling lazily around her.

"The Master wishes all to hear it at once." Her tone carried quiet satisfaction. She was not delaying out of obedience alone, but because she enjoyed holding the knowledge.

Zylron snarled and turned as the rest of the gathering continued.

Nocturna slipped into the cavern like a living shadow, silent and deliberate, violet eyes burning with quiet calculation as they moved from Ixalia... to Zylron... to the chamber itself.

Zarathos landed with a thunderous crack of wings, pride radiating from every motion, scattering ash across the stone. His gaze lifted first not to the others, but to the cavern's heights as though the gathering existed beneath him.

Xalzorath oozed into a far corner, the scent of rot and swamp clinging to him like a curse. He said nothing but his eyes never stopped moving.

Glaciera arrived last among the Ancients, frost-kissed ash crystallizing at her feet with every step.

Ixalia's gaze lingered on the Ice Ancient longer than necessary.

Her slit pupils tracked Glaciera with unusual focus almost assessing... remembering.

A flicker of satisfaction crossed her expression brief, deliberate, and not meant to be missed.

Glaciera noticed.

Her icy frill lifted slightly.

"Why do you stare, Mirage?"

Her voice cut sharp as winter glass.

Ixalia only smiled sweetly.

"You will see."

Zylron exhaled molten smoke, impatience simmering beneath his scales.

"Enough riddles." His claws scored the stone, sparks skittering across the ash as his patience thinned.

But before further tempers could flare, the cavern itself seemed to still.

A ripple of unnatural silence swept across the chamber smothering heat, motion, and breath for a single suspended heartbeat.

Then silence deepened.

Footsteps.

Measured. Unhurried.

Each one struck the cavern like a tolling bell.

The Mysterious Figure entered the Cavern of Ash and every dragon stilled.

Shadow trailed behind the Mysterious Figure like a living cloak, every dark dragon even Zylron lowered their head, if only by a fraction, acknowledging the authority that pressed upon the cavern like forged steel.

They stepped to the center.

A single nod.

"Speak."

Ixalia straightened, folding her wings with elegant precision as anticipation lit her eyes.

The moment had arrived.

Every dark dragon watched.

The Master listened.

And her revelation was about to change everything.

Ixalia lifted her wings in a slow, graceful arc and turned toward the gathered Ancients, her voice ringing through the Cavern of Ash with crystalline clarity.

"I bring news of the red-haired elf." Her voice lingered on the words savoring the reaction before it came.

A ripple moved through the chamber heat, shadow, frost, and void shifting in restless response.

Zylron's molten fissures flared hotter.

Nocturna's shadows coiled like ink bleeding into water.

Glaciera's presence chilled the air by degrees.

Voraxia's pupils narrowed into razor-thin slits of hungry curiosity.

Ixalia basked in their attention.

"I encountered her on the Bridge of Connectivity," she purred.

"Traveling alone. Vulnerable."

Zylron snarled, embers spilling from his jaws.

"And you did not take her?" His wings flexed once, as though the failure already irritated him.

Ixalia's smile sharpened.

"I attempted the usual methods first my illusions." Her tone made it clear she considered the outcome... a curiosity, not a failure.

Several dragons leaned forward in interest. Voraxia's spined tail flicked with interest.

The Mysterious Figure remained silent. Watching. Measuring.

"The first illusion," Ixalia continued smoothly, "was Zÿlron molten, furious, poised to strike."

She cast a mocking glance at him. "It did not faze her. She dismissed it without so much as a blink."

Zylron's growl rumbled low, magma sputtering. "Impossible," he snapped, heat flaring along his scales in sharp, unstable pulses.

Ixalia gave a languid, theatrical shrug.

"And yet... nothing."

She stretched her wings slightly, savoring the tension.

"So, I tried another angle," she said softly.

"Kimras."

The chamber tightened an instinctive reaction to the name of a power none of them dismissed lightly.

Even dark dragons respected and resented the Golden Ancient's power.

Ixalia's tone softened into mock sympathy.

"I conjured him wounded. Dying. Desperate for her help."

Glaciera hissed with cold approval.

Voraxia's grin widened.

Ixalia's voice hardened.

"She saw through it immediately."

Zarathos scoffed.

"Because the elf is foolish."

Ixalia shook her head, eyes glittering.

"No. Because their bond is too strong. Illusion cannot replicate the truth between them."

A murmur rippled through the chamber irritation, envy, intrigue, frustration.

The elf had not broken.

And that unsettled them.

Ixalia turned her head with deliberate slowness, her shifting opal gaze settling on Voraxia drawing the moment out with calculated intent.

The Shadow Dragon straightened, obsidian wings flexing as living darkness curled around her form.

Ixalia's voice lowered into a velvet purr.

"I even tried an illusion of you injuring her again, Voraxia."

The cavern still fell deathly.

Voraxia's snarl rolled low, venom-laced, and dangerous.

"Again," she echoed coldly. "She remembers our last encounter well enough." Her wings spread slightly, shadow pooling beneath her claws.

Ixalia smirked.

"Apparently not with fear."

She tilted her head, mocking, amused.

"The moment she saw your bleeding shadow into the air she merely sighed and said..."

Ixalia mimicked Keisha's tone, dry and unimpressed.

"'Oh. Again.' The words lingered just long enough to sting.

A violent rumble tore from Voraxia's chest. Shadows lashed outward like barbed whips. "INSOLENT ELF—!"

Zylron barked a harsh, volcanic laugh.

Glaciera's frost-lined lips curved in cool amusement.

Even Nocturna released a hollow, rasping chuckle.

Humiliation crackled through Voraxia's fury.

She surged forward wrath coiling, shadows lashing outward as the cavern's air bent under the force of her anger.

But a colder voice cut through the cavern like a blade drawn across stone.

"Ixalia."

The Mysterious Person stepped forward, cloak trailing like spilled night.

Ixalia straightened at once.

"Yes, my lord?"

Their tone sharpened, unimpressed and lethal.

"Is this why you summoned every dragon of the Dominion?" The question was not loud yet it pressed against every presence in the cavern.

A pause.

Razor-edged.

"To inform us that your illusions do not work on Keisha?" The words fell with deliberate precision meant to be heard and judged.

A ripple of dark amusement spread through the gathered Ancients low, sharp, and edged with contempt.

Zarathos snorted.

Glaciera looked thoroughly bored.

Voraxia seethed.

Zylron rumbled in open irritation.

Ixalia's wings twitched once, pride bristling but not retreating.

"No there is more."

The Mysterious Person folded their arms, disdain dripping from every word.

"There had better be, Ixalia." Each word carried the quiet promise of consequence.

A beat.

Colder.

"Because thus far, all you have revealed... is your failure." The final word settled like a verdict.

The Cavern of Ash fell into absolute silence no breath, no movement, no defiance.

Ixalia's eyes brightened not with anger, but with delighted anticipation.

"Oh, I did fail," she admitted lightly without a trace of shame.

Her smile widened, sharp and pleased.

"But what I discovered in the attempt... is far more valuable." Her tone shifted not defensive but calculating.

The dark dragons leaned in.

Even the Mysterious Person shifted subtle, but unmistakable as interest flickered for the first time.

Ixalia inhaled slowly, savoring the moment.

"Keisha can resist illusions," she purred.

"But she cannot resist... something else." The implication spread faster than fire through dry ash.

Silence tightened like a drawn wire every predator in the cavern leaning toward the strike.

Zylron's nostrils vented smoke.

Voraxia's shadow-spines flexed.

Nocturna's gaze sharpened.

Glaciera remained still glacial, unreadable.

Ixalia let the pause stretch holding the entire cavern in the palm of her silence.

Let curiosity sharpen.

Let hunger bloom.

Finally, she spoke:

"There is one illusion that did disturb her."

The cavern stirred.

Zylron tilted his massive head.

Voraxia hissed.

Zarathos scoffed under his breath.

Ixalia's pupils narrowed into delighted slits this was the moment she had been waiting for.

“One dragon she still fears.” The words fell into the cavern like a blade placed at the throat.

Her shifting opal gaze slid slow, deliberate toward a single figure, as though unveiling prey.

“Glaciera.” The name carried through the cavern like a sudden drop in temperature.

A ripple of reaction surged through the cavern shock, disbelief, and something sharper beneath.

Voraxia snarled, shocked.

Zarathos scoffed in disbelief.

Nocturna murmured something dark and thoughtful.

Glaciera did not bristle.

Did not recoil.

Did not deny it.

She did not need to.

Instead... Her frozen frill lifted slightly.

A slow, crystalline smile curved across her frost-lined jaws, breath misting in pale, controlled spirals.

“Of course,” she said coolly, her voice like winter fracturing stone inevitable, unhurried.

“There is one thing Keisha can never forget...”

The cavern fell into absolute silence.

“...her captivity.” The word did not echo.

It settled.

Glaciera’s eyes glowed with cold satisfaction.

“Vuarus and Phoenix ordered me to keep her cell frozen,” she continued.

"Colder than breath... colder than flesh... colder than her kind was ever meant to endure.”

Frost crept outward from her talons, ash crystallizing where it fell.

"She remembers that cold," Glaciera murmured. "And she remembers who held it there."

Voraxia's wings flared, shadows snapping across the cavern floor.

"She fears you?" Voraxia spat, venom and disbelief cracking through her voice.

"Not shadow. Not the void. Not me—"

Ixalia lifted her head, savoring the fracture in Voraxia's pride.

"Yes," she purred.

"The illusion of Glaciera's frost nearly broke her." There was no embellishment in the claim only certainty.

Glaciera's smirk deepened, predatory and serene.

Ixalia continued, voice silk over steel,

"Had Kimras and Amara not intervened... Keisha would already be ours." The statement carried the weight of a near-victory.

A hush settled heavier, more dangerous than before.

The Mysterious Person's gaze shifted to Glaciera, slow and calculating.

"Perhaps we underestimated what she endured," they murmured. "...and the scars it carved into her." Not weakness. Entry.

Their tone cooled into something almost pleased.

Glaciera inclined her head slightly accepting the recognition.

Zylron rumbled with dark amusement, heat flickering between his teeth.

"Well," he growled, glancing at her, "At least she fears something ordinary."

A molten snort.

"One of the ordinary dark dragons."

Glaciera's frost shimmered brighter unbothered, unquestioned.

Voraxia snapped her jaws, shadows writhing in agitated coils.

"Normal?" she hissed. "Her fear should be me." The words sounded less like truth... and more like demand.

But the cavern already knew the truth.

Keisha feared frost.

Keisha feared Glaciera.

Keisha feared the cold that had once nearly broken her mind.

And now the Dominion knew exactly where to strike.

Ixalia folded her wings with languid satisfaction, fractured starlight gleaming across her scales her discovery now a weapon in the Dominion's hands.

"Shall I continue?" she asked sweetly, eyes glittering with quiet triumph.

The Cavern of Ash simmered with heat and shadow, the air tightening as though the mountain itself leaned in to listen. Smoke curled along the ceiling like a living thing, thick with anticipation.

The Mysterious Person stepped forward, sharpening the air to a cutting edge.

"You have found the crack in that elf," they said quietly, as though naming a flaw in steel.

A pause.

"What is your suggestion, Ixalia?"

The Mirage Dragon's smile unfurled twisting, pleased, cruel.

She turned slowly... deliberately... toward Glaciera, presenting the answer as though it had always belonged to her.

"Since she fears you," Ixalia purred, "or rather fears what you represent...

Glaciera's frill lifted, frost whispering outward like spectral snowfall.

Ixalia continued, her tone velvet over venom.

"It may be... advantageous for us to combine our talents. Your truth... and my lies."

Zylron leaned forward, molten eyes narrowing.

Voraxia hissed in irritation.

Nocturna's shadows curled and shifted, tasting the moment.

Ixalia's wings shimmered, light fracturing unnaturally around her.

"I can weave an illusion tailored to her deepest terror not imagined... remembered."

A pause, savoring it.

"But the cold that already claimed her once."

The cavern plunged into a hungry, dangerous stillness.

"A labyrinth of frost... without edge, without escape... without end." Ixalia murmured,

"Crafted from Glaciera's essence. A prison she cannot distinguish from reality because it will feel exactly like her past."

Glaciera's eyes gleamed like frozen stars recognition, not surprise.

Ixalia's voice dropped to a slow, delighted purr.

"And while she is paralyzed... while she is lost inside a nightmare of ice ...that mirrors her captivity down to the last breath she could not draw."

She looked at Glaciera and smiled wickedly.

"—that is when you strike. Not against resistance... but surrender."

Frost spiraled outward from Glaciera's talons, ash crystallizing into brittle shards.

"Freeze her in truth, not illusion. Not memory. Reality." Ixalia finished softly.

"Seal her in ice."

The cavern trembled.

"And then?" the Mysterious Person asked quietly, as though weighing the cost against the reward.

Ixalia's smile widened.

"And then," she purred,

"Glaciera may take her prize to Firornak where no warmth reaches."

All attention shifted to the Ice Ancient.

Glaciera slowly inhaled a breath so cold it seemed to burn the air.

When she spoke, her voice was a symphony of winter and cruelty.

"Encasing Keisha in ice... carrying her frozen form back to my cavern not as prey... but as possession."

Her lips curved into something vicious.

"...would be a fitting continuation of what she never truly escaped."

Voraxia snarled, shadows flaring in furious agitation, but Glaciera did not even glance at her.

Zylron rumbled in dark, molten amusement.

"An elegant plan," he growled, heat crackling between his teeth.

"Fear turned into a weapon. Cold turned into a cage."

The Mysterious Person tilted their head slightly.

"And you are certain," they said coolly,

"That this illusion can hold her long enough... to break her?"

Ixalia bowed low, pride gleaming from every fractured scale.

"With Glaciera feeding her essence into the spell?" she replied smoothly.

"Yes. The illusion will feel real... because it will not be entirely false."

Glaciera lifted her head, frost glittering along her muzzle.

"Let the elf remember the cold she thought she escaped," she said softly. "Let it finish what was started."

A murmur rippled through the cavern low growls, clicking claws, scraping scales.

Approval. Hunger. Envy.

The plan had been shaped.

And in the frozen depths of Firornak...

Keisha's fate was being forged.

Molten heat and drifting frost coiled together as Glaciera stepped forward, crystalline ice cascading in delicate spirals from her talons.

Her voice rang like cracking glaciers.

"Then I will return to my lair," she declared.

"And prepare a chamber worthy of what I claim."

A slow, merciless smile.

"She will endure eternity in ice aware, unmoving, unending."

A hush fell thick with dark anticipation.

The Mysterious Person inclined their head once.

"Very well."

Then their gaze slid back to Ixalia sharp, measuring... pleased.

A faint smile touched their shadowed lips.

"You have done well, Mirage Ancient,"

the words measured, not generous earned.

Ixalia dipped her head, wings shimmering with delighted pride.

"Thank you, my lord."

The Mysterious Person's voice rose, calm yet absolute, filling the Cavern of Ash with quiet dominion.

"Return to your duties all of you."

One by one, the dark dragons obeyed.

Zylron stalked toward the exit with a volcanic growl, molten sparks scattering in his wake as irritation smoldered beneath his scales.

Voraxia dissolved into a surge of writhing shadow, her jealousy bristling, sharp and unresolved.

Nocturna melted seamlessly into the deeper dark, her form thinning until she became little more than a suggestion a whisper where a dragon had stood.

Zarathos launched skyward with a thunderous snap of wings, pride crackling through the cavern like distant thunder.

Glaciera departed last.

Frost bled from her talons with every step, a slow, creeping promise of winter left behind in her wake.

Ixalia bowed once more before gliding from the chamber, her mirage-light rippling and fracturing as she vanished into distorted air.

Soon, the Cavern of Ash stood silent again.

Only molten veins pulsed along the walls.

Only drifting ash fell like black snow.

Only the lingering echo of a plan meant not just to break her...but to finish what had already begun.

And in that silence, the Dominion's next move settled into place.

The Mysterious Person watched the last retreating shadow vanish, as though measuring what had just been set into motion, then turned to Malrik.

"Follow me to the tower."

Malrik bowed without hesitation. His robes whispered like dying embers as they ascended the spiraling obsidian steps, the air growing heavier with each turn thick with ancient magic, ambition, and something older than Flameford itself.

Within the tower's shadowed chamber, the Mysterious Person halted at the narrow window overlooking the volcanic expanse. Rivers of molten stone pulsed below like veins of restrained fury.

A low, pleased laugh escaped them.

"Vuarus would approve," they murmured, not with reverence... but with recognition.

Malrik inclined his head, reverence and calculation threading his expression.

"Yes," he said softly.

"He would and he would have acted far less patiently."

A pause lingered deliberately.

The Mysterious Person's gaze sharpened.

"Let Glaciera keep her trophy," they murmured, as though granting permission for something already decided. Let the elf remain frozen... preserved... untouched."

"A resource, not yet spent."

Their voice cooled.

"When the Ice Ancient grows bored... when the novelty fades... Keisha will be delivered to the Abyss... intact.

Malrik's eyes glinted.

"In her frozen prison," he said quietly, understanding unfolding.

"The Abyss will feed on her magic slowly... deliberately... siphoning it away... piece by piece... breath by breath."

The Mysterious Person smiled thin, satisfied, patient.

"A gradual extraction... measured. Controlled. Invisible." they agreed.

"Not enough to kill her at once. Not enough to alert the world... until it is far too late."

A beat.

"By the time the ice melts," Malrik added softly, "...there will be nothing left to save."

"There will be nothing left of her... only a hollow shell... still breathing."

Silence settled heavy, complicit.

"Her power will become mine," the Mysterious Person murmured, certainty absolute.

Not in one reckless surge... but refined... controlled... perfected."

Malrik bowed once more and withdrew, leaving only drifting ash in his wake.

The Mysterious Person sank into the throne carved from blackened stone a seat not inherited but taken.. Shadows coiled around them like loyal serpents, eager and obedient.

A smirk touched their lips.

Cold.

Cruel.

Certain.

The game had changed... and the rules no longer favored mercy.

And far from Flameford's fire, Keisha walked on unaware that her enemies no longer debated whether to kill her...but how slowly...and how completely...to claim everything she is.

Chapter 19

The Sky Trembles

The quiet within Goldmoor shattered.

A resounding clang rolled across the city the ancient alarm bell, forged generations ago for a single purpose.

Dark dragons are approaching.

Keisha froze mid-step, breath catching as golden runes along the palace archway flared to life. Kimras' head snapped toward the sky, pupils narrowing into molten-gold slits.

A second bell followed.

Then a third.

No false alarm. No hesitation.

Keisha did not wait.

She sprinted for Kimras, vaulting onto his back in a fluid motion honed through instinct and years of trust. His wings unfurled in a blaze of radiant gold, flooding the courtyard with blazing light.

"Hold on, Keisha."

A single, thunderous beat launched them skyward, wind tearing through her hair as they surged above Goldmoor's glittering towers.

The moment they cleared the highest spire.

She saw them.

Zylron.

A volcanic colossus, wings veined with molten fissures that pulsed like a living forge.

And beside him Glaciera.

Her vast wings trailed ribbons of crystalline frost, each beat shedding shards of ice that hung suspended in the air like frozen stars.

Fire.

Frost.

Two opposing forces united.

Their presence warped the sky above Goldmoor, shadow and winter bleeding together as though the heavens themselves were being claimed.

Keisha inhaled sharply.

They were not alone.

Behind them, a formation of lesser dark dragons spread outward in a widening arc silent, deliberate, forming a tightening noose around the city.

Kimras rumbled deep in his chest, the sound reverberating through her bones.

"They come in force."

Keisha raised her hand.

Waited.

Measured.

Watched the formation tighten... the moment aligning.

Then she spoke, her voice cutting clean and absolute through the sky:

"Raise the barrier."

The command rippled across Goldmoor.

Below, mages stationed atop every tower thrust their staffs skyward. Golden runes ignited in cascading spirals, threads of radiant fire weaving upward—locking together with a thunderous, harmonic pulse.

A shimmering dome erupted around the city.

Goldmoor's Aegis.

Ancient. Unyielding. Untouched for nearly a century.

The barrier sealed with a resonant hum, light cascading across its surface like liquid gold.

Kimras angled higher, wings blazing as he positioned himself between the city and the storm.

Ready.

Waiting.

Unyielding.

A violet streak cut across the sky.

Amara.

The Amethyst Dragon burst from the horizon with sleek, lethal grace, psychic energy crackling along her wings like lightning woven from starlight. Ong rode astride her, hair whipping in the wind, his expression sharpened by focus and resolve.

Behind her a squadron of amethyst dragons followed close behind each radiating that same psionic hum that made the air itself tremble.

Kimras gave a low, approving growl.

"Good timing."

Amara spiraled past them, banking sharply as violet energy rippled outward in controlled pulses.

"Did you truly think the storm would pass without me?"

Ong caught Keisha's eye as they crossed paths a brief, unspoken exchange of relief, pride... and readiness.

We are in this together.

Keisha tightened her grip against Kimras' radiant scales, her pulse steadying into something focused. Grounded.

Kimras climbed higher, wings spreading wide as his voice carried across the forming lines.

"Form a battle line. Keep them away from the barrier. Goldmoor must not fall."

A roar of agreement answered him golden, amethyst, and allied dragons shifting into disciplined formation. Lines tightened. Gaps closed. Wings aligned with purpose.

Across from them, the dark formation advanced.

Measured.

Relentless.

The sky above Goldmoor ignited with opposing forces. Fire and frost.

Crystal and shadow.

Light... and illusion.

Keisha's heart struck once.

Steady.

Strong.

Unyielding.

"Let's meet them head-on."

Kimras answered with a roar that shook the heavens.

Together, they dove.

Zylron surged forward to meet them, molten fissures blazing brighter as his gaze locked onto Kimras. Beside him, Glaciera swept into a wide, arcing flank, her wings shedding spirals of razor-fine frost that glittered like suspended blades.

They were splitting the field.

Pressure from two directions.

Kimras angled upward to intercept Zylron, golden wings cutting through the air like radiant blades. Amara rose in perfect alignment beside him, violet energy gathering along her wings in tightening arcs.

Kimras' voice rolled like warm thunder despite the impending clash.

"Tell me, Amara... have you chosen another mountain for me to throw Zylron into this time?"

Amara barked a sharp laugh, psionic light flaring.

"There are several that would suit him beautifully."

Zylron's roar detonated across the sky, molten fire spiraling from his jaws in a violent torrent.

"NOT THIS TIME!"

Kimras folded one wing and rolled with effortless precision, the inferno tearing past in a blazing rush. Heat licked across Keisha's cheek, sharp and immediate.

She did not flinch.

Instead, she steadied.

Lifted her staff.

Runes stirred to life faint at first... then brighter.

Ready.

Amara flicked her gaze toward Glaciera as the Ice Ancient drifted closer with lethal, effortless grace.

Frost hissed through the air.

Snow spiraled in her wake.

"Today, the cold claims you... and your rider," Glaciera whispered, her voice like glaciers splitting in the dark.

Ong tightened his grip along Amara's back, jaw set.

Amara, in contrast, looked utterly unimpressed.

She flashed Glaciera with a razor-edged grin.

"Oh, it is you. I was wondering when the headache would arrive."

Glaciera's eyes narrowed. Frost gathered instantly coiling, tightening until the air around her became a storm waiting to break.

"This time," she hissed,

"I intend to act."

Amara tilted her wings slightly, smirk deepening.

"Excellent. I was beginning to wonder if you only fought with your voice."

Glaciera screamed.

A piercing, crystalline shriek that split the sky and the temperature dropped violently.

Frost lashed outward in snapping arcs, each strike sharp enough to carve through stone.

Amara reacted instantly.

A pulse of psionic force detonated from her wings controlled, precise, devastating.

The frost shattered mid-flight.

Ice burst apart into glittering fragments, scattering like shattered stars.

And then the heavens broke.

Zylron surged forward with a roar, claws outstretched, molten fire spilling from his jaws in blazing streams.

Glaciera dove in tandem, her assault no longer measured frost spiraling into lethal crescents meant to encase, not merely strike.

They had committed.

Ong braced low against Amara's spine.

Keisha raised her staff, golden runes igniting fully.

The battle for Goldmoor had begun.

Dragons collided.

Fire roared across the sky as Zylron unleashed a spiraling torrent of molten flame, heat distorting the very air as it tore toward Kimras.

Kimras did not retreat.

He drove forward.

Golden wings flaring wide, he met the inferno head-on radiance surging outward as his shield ignited like a newborn sun. Flame split and spilled around him in a violent cascade of light and heat.

To the flank Glaciera struck again.

A slicing wave of frost expanded outward, not wild but controlled, deliberate aimed to freeze the space around Amara and restrict her movement.

Amara twisted through it.

Psionic energy snapped outward in tight, focused bursts shattering ice before it could fully form, breaking Glaciera's control rather than matching her power directly.

A shockwave rippled through the sky.

Violet against white-blue.

Mind against cold.

Below them, the battlefield ignited into chaos.

Lesser dragons clashed in streaks of shadow and light, collisions echoing like distant thunder as formations fractured and reformed in rapid succession.

Above it all Kimras and Zylron collided again.

Force against force.

Heat against radiance.

The sky itself seemed to fracture.

Fire coiling with frost.

Psionic lightning tearing through collapsing air.

Golden light anchoring against the storm.

Each impact lit the heavens with violent, breathtaking brilliance.

The world trembled beneath it.

A clash of Ancients.

Savage.

Blinding.

Cataclysmic.

But still measured.

Testing.

A skirmish not a war... yet

Zylron surged first.

The Volcanic Ancient hurled himself at Kimras, claws blazing with molten heat. Kimras answered with a thunderous roar, driving forward to meet him—

Their collision shattered the clouds.

Embers rained across Goldmoor's glowing barrier like falling stars.

"You still rely on rage," Kimras thundered, wings beating hard as he forced Zylron back.

"And you still hide behind light," Zylron snarled, jaws opening as he unleashed a spiraling torrent of blistering flame.

Kimras rolled sharply.

The inferno tore past in a searing wave, heat screaming across his golden shield as it flared brighter in response. Keisha flattened against his scales, the force of it ripping the breath from her lungs.

Steam hissed along the edge of the barrier.

At the same instant Glaciera struck.

She swept in low and fast, not wild but precise.

Frost exploded outward in jagged crescents, not aimed at Amara but cutting across her path, hemming her in.

The temperature plummeted violently. Breath crystallized midair.

Amara reacted without hesitation.

A focused pulse of psionic force detonated outward, not to overpower but to disrupt.

The crescents shattered mid-flight, fracturing into a storm of glittering shards.

"So, the pattern repeats," Amara called, banking hard through the collapsing frost.

Ong rose to one knee along her back, steady despite the turbulence. He thrust his lance forward, releasing a burst of Eladrin fire that streaked toward Glaciera in a sharp, controlled arc.

Glaciera twisted aside.

Frost spiraled in her wake, but her attention never lingered on Ong.

Her gaze locked instead on Keisha.

The battlefield tightened.

Below, two lesser dark dragons dove toward the barrier, claws raking against the glowing dome.

THRUM.

Runes flared violently.

Goldmoor's mages strained, staffs blazing as the impact rippled through the Aegis. A fracture flickered along one tower's sigil then sealed as golden light surged back into place.

The barrier held.

For now.

Above Kimras surged again, seizing Zylron by the shoulder. With a roar of radiant force, he hurled him backward, golden fire trailing the motion like a comet's wake.

Zylron tumbled through the air, volcanic fury spiraling as he fought to right himself.

And then Glaciera's voice cut through everything.

"Zylron!"

The single word froze the air itself.

"DO NOT kill the elf."

A pause deliberate. Controlled.

"She is mine."

The words did not need to be shouted.

They carried.

Cold.

Absolute.

"To be my frozen prize."

The world shifted.

Not outward, inward.

The battlefield blurred.

Sound dulled.

The cold in her voice was not wind or frost. It was memory.

Stone walls.

Frozen breath.

Silence that crushed thought.

Keisha's chest tightened.

Her breath locked.

For a heartbeat she was not in the sky above Goldmoor.

She was back in the cell.

Kimras felt it instantly.

Not the words the fracture.

With a roar that split the heavens, he flared his wings wide and surged with radiant force, golden light erupting around her in a blazing cocoon.

Heat flooded outward.

Not just protection...presence.

"I have you," he rumbled, voice low but unbreakable.

The gold did not burn.

It anchored.

It pulled her back.

"You will NOT touch her!" Kimras thundered not as a warning, but as a vow.

Zylron lunged again.

Kimras was already moving.

He struck with ancient fury, slamming into the volcanic dragon and hurling him across the sky. Zylron spun end over end, fire and rage spiraling wildly in his wake.

Amara and Ong closed on Glaciera.

Ong drove his lance forward in a streak of Eladrin flame. Glaciera recoiled, frost detonating from her wings as she veered away but her gaze never left Keisha.

"Another time... little elf," she hissed.

Kimras shifted instantly, placing himself between them, blazing like a rising sun.

"There will be no next time, Ice Ancient."

His voice rolled across the battlefield ancient, final.

Reinforcements surged in.

Three gold dragons tore in from the east, answering the alarm. Below, the barrier flared brighter as the mages reinforced the wards.

The balance had turned.

Zylron steadied himself midair, molten eyes burning with promise.

Glaciera's frost spiraled inward, controlled... calculating.

Then, with a final roar of defiance, Zylron veered away.

Glaciera followed.

The lesser dark dragons broke formation and fled with them.

Within seconds the skies above Goldmoor were clear.

The golden barrier shimmered, then unraveled into drifting motes of light as the mages lowered their staffs in exhausted relief. Fire and frost faded into memory.

Amara circled once overhead, the amethyst glow along her wings softening.

"Return to Purplefire," she instructed her flight.

"Ong and I will follow shortly."

Her dragons dipped their heads in silent acknowledgment before arcing southward, their violet forms dissolving into the morning sky.

Kimras descended into the grove beside the great statue, his landing impossibly gentle for a dragon of his size.

Ong slid from Amara's back and stopped.

Keisha had not moved.

She remained seated atop Kimras, shoulders drawn inward, her gaze distant. Her fingers curled tightly into his scales, as though letting go might send her slipping back into something unseen.

Amara lifted her tail, gently barring Ong's path.

"Slowly," she murmured.

"She is still hearing Glaciera's voice."

Kimras curved his neck around Keisha, golden eyes steady warm, unyielding.

"Keisha," he rumbled softly, voice like hearthfire in winter,

"She cannot reach you. Not while I draw breath."

Keisha blinked once... then again.

Sound returned.

Color followed.

The world steadied beneath her.

Her breath shuddered.

"I... I am all right," she whispered more promise than truth.

"You are safe," Kimras replied.

That, more than anything, held.

Keisha nodded and slid from his back. Her landing wavered slightly, a tremor she did not hide.

Ong stepped forward, concern written plainly across his face.

"Keisha..."

She managed a small, fragile smile.

"Just old memories," she said quietly. "But they still feel... too real."

Kimras lowered a wing around her, shielding her from the open sky from distance, from echo, from the cold that still lingered at the edges of thought.

Silence settled.

Not empty.

Guarded.

Then a familiar black shape bounded into the grove.

Pumpkin.

Her emerald eyes locked onto Keisha as she strode straight toward her, tail flicking with unmistakable disapproval.

Ong sighed.

"Pumpkin... I told you to stay in Purplefire."

Pumpkin stared at him.

Then she thwapped her tail sharply against his leg.

Amara snorted.

Ong laughed under his breath.

"All right. Message received."

Keisha dropped to her knees and wrapped her arms around Pumpkin's neck. The panther purred deeply, the vibration steady and grounding, pulling her fully back into herself.

"You always know," Keisha whispered.

Pumpkin chuffed in smug agreement.

Keisha rose slowly, her voice quieter as she turned back.

"I don't understand why Glaciera still affects me," she admitted.

"None of the others do. Just her."

Ong answered gently, without hesitation.

"Because it wasn't just cold," he said.

"It was time. Isolation. Being worn down piece by piece."

A pause.

"That kind of memory does not fade. It stays."

Kimras lowered his great head.

"Scars are not weakness," he rumbled.

"They are truth."

His voice deepened not with anger, but with certainty.

"But she will never touch you again. Not while any noble Ancient still draws breath."

Keisha swallowed, then nodded.

Ong stepped forward and drew her into his arms. She leaned into him, the last of the tension easing from her frame. He pressed a kiss to her forehead then to her lips, steady and sure.

Amara waited, patient as ever.

"Time to return to Purplefire," she said.

Ong nodded, then mounted once more. Amara rose, violet light trailing as she carried him southward.

The grove grew quiet again.

Keisha looked up at Kimras, softening her voice.

"I'm sorry... for freezing."

Kimras nudged her gently.

“There is nothing to forgive.

You stood.”

A faint smile touched her lips.

Pumpkin pressed against her leg, solid and warm.

Together, beneath the golden statue, they watched the sun rise over Goldmoor.

The skirmish had ended.

But the war had only begun.

Chapter 20

Chosen by the Forests

Moonlit radiance spilled across the crystalline waters of Ardinia, a realm suspended between sky and sea where the air shimmered with gentle blue luminescence. The waves below lay clear as glass, reflecting every star in perfect, trembling detail. Silver windbells chimed along the branches of coral-like trees, their tones drifting like distant lullabies through the tranquil night.

At the cliff's edge stood Aeliana, Guardian of the Fae, and Protector of the Forest Realms.

Her silhouette glowed with quiet opalescence, wings like woven moon mist folded behind her. Strands of her hair lifted in the breeze, as though the wind itself moved with reverence. Her eyes deep as distant starlight remained fixed on the horizon, their weight betraying a concern rarely seen in one so timeless.

Behind her, soft footsteps approached, light as falling petals.

A young nymph, radiant in shimmering aqua hues, paused at a respectful distance. Her voice flowed like water over crystal.

"My Lady Aeliana... you seem troubled. What weighs upon your heart?"

Aeliana did not turn.

"The forests whisper of unrest," she said at last, her voice soft as wind threading through leaves. "Roots tremble where they once slept in peace. The Dominion's shadow has begun to seep into sacred groves poisoning what was never meant to be touched."

Her gaze darkened slightly.

"I have guarded the fae and the forests since the first dawn... but even I cannot stand in every glade at once."

The nymph stepped closer, brightening her expression.

"Then you seek another guardian? One to help you watch over the realms?"

Aeliana exhaled slowly, the sound carrying the weight of centuries.

"Yes. But not just any guardian."

Her voice sharpened quiet, deliberate.

"I need one the forests already trust. One whose spirit is rooted in the land itself... not merely sworn to it."

Recognition lit the nymph's face.

"Kaelorn," she said softly. "The Luminara of the Emerald Woods."

Aeliana's gaze shifted slightly, listening.

"The spirits speak of him often," the nymph continued. "He calms the restless groves. Even the oldest trees lean toward him." A gentle smile touched her lips. "And... we helped you craft a staff for him, did we not? One shaped to amplify forest magic and resist Dominion corruption."

At last, Aeliana turned.

Moonlight traced her features, revealing the quiet gravity beneath her beauty.

The memory stirred Kaelorn beneath the towering boughs of the Emerald Woods, accepting the staff forged of fae-light and living wood. Not with pride... but with humility. With purpose.

"Yes," she said softly. "Kaelorn."

A pause.

"If the Dominion reaches the forests in full... it will find him standing in its path."

For the briefest moment, something unspoken flickered in her expression—not doubt in him, but in what would be asked of him.

She lifted her hand.

The waters below rippled outward in response, as though the realm itself listened.

"He has tended the Emerald Woods with devotion," she said. "The spirits trust him. The nymphs follow him. Even the oldest roots recognize his presence."

Her voice steadied.

"He is not merely a guardian... he is part of the forest."

The nymph's smile brightened.

"Then will you summon him here, my Lady?"

Aeliana shook her head.

"No."

A single word calm, absolute.

"This is not a summons. It is a choice."

Her gaze lifted toward the distant horizon.

"And I will not make that choice from afar."

She raised her staff, its runes igniting in soft blue pulses as the wind gathered around her.

"The Dominion spreads through illusion, corruption, and shadow," she said. "If I choose wrongly, the forests will pay the price."

Her wings unfurled petals of moonlight catching the air.

"But Kaelorn..."

A faint note of certainty entered her voice.

"The forests have already chosen him once."

With a single step, she rose upon a spiraling column of wind. Light coiled around her as Ardinia opened to receive its guardian.

Below, the nymph bowed deeply.

"May the winds guide you, Lady Aeliana."

Aeliana's voice drifted back, carried on the currents of air. "They already do."

She vanished into streaks of silver-blue light, cutting across the night sky toward the Emerald Woods... toward Kaelorn's path... and the role he would soon play in the fate of Vacari.

The veil between realms shimmered ahead.

And with a soft, resonant sigh it slowly parted.

The moment Aeliana's feet touched the moss-laced earth, the forest brightened.

Leaves trembled in luminous greeting. Tiny motes of green light spiraled around her like joyful sprites. Branches lifted, bowing in subtle reverence, while the roots beneath the soil pulsed with a faint emerald glow recognizing an ancient ally returned.

A delighted trill pierced the hush.

A fairy no larger than Aeliana's hand darted toward her, trailing ribbons of golden dust.

"Lady Aeliana!" the tiny creature chimed, wings fluttering like jeweled petals. "We did not expect you today!"

Aeliana's smile softened the air itself.

"Greetings, little one. I seek Kaelorn. Do you know where he is?"

"Oh yes!" the fairy beamed, spinning midair. "He's deep in the forest checking the trees, or the roots, or the moss... or something important." She giggled softly. "He is always tending to something."

Aeliana let out a quiet laugh, light as wind over crystal.

"Yes," she said. "That sounds like Kaelorn."

She inclined her head in thanks, and the fairy zipped away through the canopy, leaving a trail of fading gold in her wake.

Aeliana moved deeper into the Emerald Woods.

The woodland parted for her.

Vines drew aside. Ferns bent low. Ancient branches shifted to open a path where none had been before. The deeper she walked, the quieter it became not with emptiness, but with awareness.

This was not a forest that simply lived.

It remembered.

It watched.

It chose.

The air thickened with the scent of dew and wildflowers, while the slow pulse of ancient tree-spirits echoed through the ground beneath her feet a steady, enduring heartbeat.

After a time, she found him at last.

Kaelorn stood beneath the vast canopy of an elder tree, one hand resting against its bark, his eyes closed in quiet focus. Sunlight filtered through the leaves above, catching in his hair a faint shimmer of fae lineage glinting like frost touched by dawn.

He spoke softly.

Not a spell.

Not a command.

A promise.

A reassurance shaped in patience and care.

The elder tree answered with a slow, contented creak, its branches settling as though eased by his presence.

Kaelorn stepped back, his posture easing, satisfaction quiet but certain.

At the edge of the clearing, Aeliana did not announce herself.

She watched.

Not as a visitor.

As a guardian judging what the forest had already begun to reveal.

There was no strain in him. No force. No need to bend the wild to his will.

He listened.

And the forest answered.

A branch lowered gently above him, as though in quiet acknowledgment. A vine curled near his shoulder, protective without being summoned. Even the breeze shifted with his movement, following instead of resisting.

Aeliana's gaze softened.

Not with surprise.

With recognition.

The forest had already chosen.

And she had come only to witness it.

At last, Kaelorn sensed her presence.

He turned, startled for only an instant before instinct took hold. He straightened and bowed deeply, hand pressed to his heart.

"Lady Aeliana," he said, his voice steady despite the faint flush rising to his cheeks. "Forgive me, my Lady. I did not sense your arrival."

He lifted his gaze respectfully, earnest, touched with subtle concern.

"What may I do for you?"

Aeliana stepped forward, studying him with calm, deliberate focus not merely as a guardian, but as one measuring the strength of the soul before her.

"Kaelorn," she said gently, "I have come because the forest speaks of you… and because Vacari may soon ask more of you than tending roots and healing groves."

The leaves stirred.

The elder tree gave a low, creaking murmur as though in agreement.

"It may ask you to defend them."

Kaelorn's brow furrowed, not with fear, but with readiness.

"Then tell me what the forest asks," he said. "And I will not turn away from it."

Aeliana regarded him for a quiet moment then inclined her head, decision settling fully into place.

"I have come to offer you a charge," she said, her voice carrying both warmth and the quiet weight of ages. "One the forests themselves have already begun to place upon you."

The glade stilled.

Leaves ceased their whispering. The breeze softened to near silence. Even the distant murmur of hidden streams faded, as though the world itself leaned closer to listen.

Aeliana moved nearer, moonlit radiance brushing the clearing.

"I have watched you, Kaelorn," she continued. "Felt your presence in the roots. Heard your voice in the quiet places. You do not command this forest."

Her gaze softened.

"You listen to it."

A branch dipped above him, as if affirming her words.

"You bring comfort where there is unrest. Balance where there is strain. Care where there is neglect," she said. "The fairies adore you. The nymphs trust you. Even the eldest trees bend when you pass."

Kaelorn swallowed, the weight of her words settling heavily across his shoulders.

"My Lady..." he said softly, "Are you certain? I—"

He hesitated, searching for truth rather than modesty.

"I am not fully fae. My heritage is... divided. Half-human. Some would say that disqualifies me from something bound to ancient magic."

Aeliana stepped closer.

"Kaelorn."

The single word stilled his doubt.

"Your heritage is not a flaw," she said firmly. "It is a bridge."

She rested her fingers lightly against his arm. Warmth spread outward, threading through roots and branches alike.

"You understand both the fleeting and the eternal. You walk between worlds without belonging solely to either," she said. "That is not weakness."

Her voice softened.

"It is balance. And balance is what the forests need."

He drew a slow breath, something within him steadying.

"You are exactly as you were meant to be," she finished.

Aeliana lifted her staff. Its runes glowed brighter now, blue-green light rippling outward in quiet waves.

"You would become my Forestborne Warden," she said.

The title settled into the air like something ancient being spoken again after long silence.

"A guardian who walks the woodlands of Vacari. One who senses corruption before it takes root. One who answers when the forests whisper... before their cries become silence."

Her gaze lifted, luminous and unyielding.

"You will stand not in my place, but beside me as my chosen steward among the living realms."

Kaelorn's breath caught, awe and disbelief warring within him.

"You will not walk alone," Aeliana added gently. "The forests do not send their wardens unguarded."

A faint, knowing light touched her eyes.

"A companion will come to you. One born of unity... not division. When the time is right."

Kaelorn blinked, that detail settling deeper than the title itself.

"A companion..." he echoed.

Aeliana inclined her head once.

"Yes."

Then she extended her hand.

The clearing responded.

Light gathered between them, soft at first then brighter. Petals trembled along unseen currents. Roots pulsed beneath the earth. The elder tree's branches lowered further, as though bowing to a moment long foreseen.

"Will you accept this mantle, Kaelorn?" she asked, her voice both gentle and absolute.

"Will you serve as the Forestborne Warden of Vacari?"

The forest held its breath.

Kaelorn lowered his gaze, emotion tightening across his chest.

Then, with grace shaped by both fae lineage and humble heart, he placed his hand over his heart and bowed deeply.

"My Lady Aeliana," he said, voice steady despite the weight settling within it,

"It would be my greatest honor to serve."

Aeliana's smile bloomed like dawn breaking through clouds, proud, and touched with ancient warmth.

"Then kneel, Kaelorn."

He sank to one knee upon the emerald moss.

The forest answered.

Petals drifted from unseen branches. Light thickened in the air, gathering in soft spirals. The great trees bowed in solemn witness, their branches lowering as though acknowledging a truth long rooted in the world.

Even the earth beneath him pulsed slow, steady, alive.

Aeliana raised her staff, its runes awakening in a luminous rhythm that echoed the forest's own heartbeat.

"Kaelorn," she said, her voice calm and absolute, "The mantle you accept is not one of title alone... but of bond."

She stepped closer.

"You do not command the forest."

Her gaze softened.

"You belong to it."

The words settled deep within him.

Then she lifted the staff and touched its tip lightly to his brow.

Warmth surged through him steady, enduring, like sunlight filtering through ancient leaves.. Rooted. Enduring.

"The first gift," Aeliana whispered, "Is the Path Unbroken."

The name carried weight.

Magic unfolded across Kaelorn's awareness not as sight, but as knowing. A quiet, unwavering thread anchoring itself within him, stretching outward through root, wind, and soil.

He felt direction.

Not north. Not distance.

But purpose.

"So that no illusion may lead you astray," Aeliana continued,

"No shadow may sever you from your path... and no distance may place you beyond reach."

Her voice deepened, carrying the quiet certainty of ages.

"Wherever the forests cry out... wherever corruption takes hold... you will find the way."

Kaelorn drew a breath as the magic settled fully into him, not foreign, but as though something long dormant had finally awakened.

"And should you ever falter," she added softly, "You will always be able to find me."

Kaelorn bowed his head, deeper this time not just in respect, but in acceptance.

"Thank you, my Lady," he said. "I will not fail what has been entrusted to me."

Aeliana's expression held quiet certainty.

"I know."

The runes along her staff flared brighter, and the forest responded in kind wind curling in gentle spirals, leaves trembling with reverent energy.

The moment sealed.

And far beyond the Emerald canopy...

The forests whispered.

Of cold.

Of shadow.

Of illusions already on the move.

"And now," Aeliana said, stepping back a measured pace, "Rise, Kaelorn... for I shall summon the companion who will stand at your side."

Kaelorn rose slowly, the newly awakened magic humming beneath his skin steady, reassuring, like the quiet heartbeat of the forest itself.

Aeliana lifted both hands.

The glade answered.

Light surged outward in interwoven currents gold, green, ember-red, molten gold, royal purple, ivory, and luminous blue the colors of every forest realm braided into a living tapestry. Wind gathered above them, spiraling into a luminous vortex fragrant with wildflowers and ancient memory.

The trees leaned inward.

Roots stirred beneath the soil.

Even the air stilled, as though the world itself waited.

Aeliana's voice rose no longer mere speech, but something older.

Music. Invocation. Command.

"By the unity of the groves, by the breath of Ardinia, by the spirits who watch unseen..."

The wind deepened. The light intensified.

"I call forth the one born of wind and forestlight. Come, Aeralinde... Come to the Warden who awaits you."

The vortex collapsed inward and blossomed.

Light unfurled in a soft, breathtaking bloom.

From its heart, something stepped forward.

Hooves touched the moss with the gentleness of falling petals. Wings unfurled like banners woven from living radiance. A mane shimmered like dawn rippling across crystal waters.

Kaelorn's breath stilled.

A Pegasus.

But not of mortal breed.

Not of simple fae crafting.

Something older.

Something chosen.

Her name was Aeralinde.

Beautiful beyond language.

Born of all forests.

And meant for him.

He stepped forward, slow, reverent, as though even breath might disturb the moment.

Aeralinde's wings shimmered in the dappled light not white, but radiant with shifting, impossible hues. One wing flowed from deep emerald into ember-red and molten gold, flickering like living flame. The other blended royal purple into soft ivory, threaded with luminous Ardinian blue that glowed like woven starlight.

Kaelorn whispered, awe softening his voice,

"My Lady… why are her wings so different? I have never seen a Pegasus like this."

Aeliana stepped beside him, her gaze warm with quiet pride.

"Because she is not merely a Pegasus," she said gently. "She is the unity of the forests made manifest."

She gestured lightly toward the radiant feathers. "The green is the Emerald Woods. The red and gold, the Emberwoods. The purple, Purplefire. The ivory, the Moonbeam Glades. And the blue…" her voice softened, "the wind of Ardinia. The bond that threads all forests together."

Kaelorn stood in silent wonder.

"She carries the strength of each realm within her," Aeliana continued, her tone deepening with reverence.

"And with it, gifts granted to no other."

Her eyes lifted, luminous and ancient.

"She can tear through illusion with a sweep of her wings.

She can sense corruption where it hides.

Through Foreststep, she may cross groves in the span of a breath.

Her presence calms wounded land, steadies magic, and shields those she carries."

Kaelorn listened as though the world itself had spoken his name.

"And more importantly," Aeliana said softly, "she is not bound by my will."

A pause.

"She is bound to you... because the forests chose you both."

A gentle nicker broke the stillness.

Aeralinde stepped forward.

Her hooves shimmered faintly against the moss, and her eyes bright, intelligent, touched with starlight settled on Kaelorn with quiet, unwavering recognition.

His breath trembled.

He lifted a tentative hand and brushed the silken warmth of her muzzle.

She leaned into him at once.

No hesitation.

No doubt.

Her wings rustled softly as she lowered her head against his shoulder warm, steady, certain.

Something within him settled.

Not earned.

Not granted.

Recognized.

A bond.

Not commanded.

Not forged.

Chosen.

Aeliana watched in silence, her expression serene, knowing.

"Rise as the Forestborne Warden, Kaelorn," she said at last, her voice soft yet carrying through root and sky alike. "With Aeralinde at your side... the forests have never stood stronger."

Aeralinde breathed gently against him, and at that moment, Kaelorn understood.

He did not belong only to the Emerald Woods.

He belonged to all the forests of Vacari.

Chapter 21

The Forestborne Warden

Morning sunlight filtered through the emerald canopy in soft, radiant shafts, each beam catching drifting motes of pollen that shimmered like suspended starlight. Aeralinde trotted beside Kaelorn, her hooves barely disturbing the moss-soft earth, her multicolored wings folded neatly at her sides. The forest seemed to breathe around them alive, listening, welcoming.

Kaelorn drew a steadying breath as he walked toward the heart of the Emerald Woods. Though this had always been his home, today it felt different. Brighter. More aware. As though every tree and root whispered his new title.

Forestborne Warden.

Even now, the words felt unreal.

Ahead, Thalorian stood beneath Verdantia's crystalline wings, half-furled like a jeweled canopy. Her emerald eyes glowed with warm recognition.

"So," Thalorian called with a smile as Kaelorn approached, "it seems word travels fast among the forests."

Verdantia rumbled, her voice a deep, melodic resonance that vibrated through bark and soil alike.

"Fast? My dear Thalorian, the moment Aeliana blessed him, the roots of Vacari whispered the news. We have known for hours."

Kaelorn blinked, startled. "I... see. I suppose I should not be surprised. Dragons rarely miss much."

Thalorian folded his arms, amusement dancing in his jade fire eyes.

"You look well, Kaelorn. Happier than I have seen you in... years."

He tilted his head knowingly. "It suits you, you know. Belonging."

Kaelorn's breath caught, the honesty disarming him.

"I've spent my whole life between worlds," he admitted quietly. "Not quite human. Not quite fae. Never certain where I fit."

His hand brushed Aeralinde's neck, her feathers warming beneath his touch.

"But now... I feel like I finally have a purpose. A place." The leaves stirred softly above him, as though the forest itself agreed.

Verdantia lowered her head, emerald scales shimmering like dew-kissed leaves.

"Purpose grows where it is nurtured. You were never misplaced, Kaelorn merely waiting for the forests to speak your name."

Thalorian grinned.

"Besides, you probably outrank half of us now in certain circles."

His gaze flicked to Aeralinde, mischief flashing in his eyes.

"Well, at least your new companion won't cause half the trouble that Valeon's fox does."

Kaelorn blinked. "Thump? Spirits above, I hope not."

Thalorian nodded sagely.

"Good. Because if I find my boots mysteriously relocated to a tree hollow again, I am blaming you this time."

Kaelorn laughed, shaking his head.

"I had nothing to do with Thump's antics, and you know it."

"Perhaps," Thalorian conceded, "but it's far more entertaining to blame you."

Aeralinde gave a soft, musical snort, as though declaring herself far too dignified for fox-level chaos.

Kaelorn smiled fondly.

"She is... special. And patient with me. Both of which I am grateful for."

Verdantia huffed gently, leaves stirring in her wake.

"She chose well. And now your duties begin. You intend to visit the forests?"

"Yes," Kaelorn said. "I want to meet the guardians and the fae of each glade... and learn what they need."

"Then go first to the Ivory Moonbeams," Verdantia advised. "The Sylvan Elves dwell there quiet, observant, wary. But they will know you by Aeralinde's wings. They will welcome you."

Thalorian patted Kaelorn's shoulder.

"Enjoy the peace while you can, my friend. I suspect being a Warden carries far more responsibility than glamour."

Kaelorn smiled softly.

"I'm ready for that."

Aeralinde stepped forward, wings unfolding in a slow, graceful sweep. Colors of forest, fire, twilight, and starlight rippled across her feathers as she lowered herself for him.

Thalorian offered a final grin.

"Do try not to get lost. The Ivory Moonbeams are enchanting... which also means distracting."

"Or dangerous," Verdantia added with a knowing rumble. "Even the most radiant beauty casts a shadow."

Kaelorn nodded once, then swung onto Aeralinde's back. With a resonant beat of her wings, they lifted above the Emerald Woods, wind rushing cool against Kaelorn's face as the canopy fell away beneath them.

The forests awaited their new Warden.

Ivory Moonbeams — The Sylvan Elves

Aeralinde's wings unfurled in a cascade of shimmering color, catching the early light and scattering it like fractured rainbows across the canopy. Before Kaelorn could even lift a hand to guide her, she launched gracefully into the sky.

"Aeralinde—wait, I didn't even—"

But she already knew and felt the pull of the forest he meant to visit.

Kaelorn settled into the saddle with a small, breathless laugh.

"Well... I suppose that makes my job easier," he muttered, settling in.

They soared above the Emerald Woods, gliding toward the pale silver glow blooming across the eastern horizon. As they climbed higher, Kaelorn cast a wary glance across the open sky, searching for any trace of dark wings.

Nothing.

Then he caught movement behind them.

A small emerald-green shape glided smoothly through the clouds a young dragon, not yet full-grown but already graceful, maintaining a careful, protective distance.

Kaelorn's lips curved with quiet gratitude.

"Verdantia," he murmured. "You truly think of everything."

The young dragon answered with a low, almost playful trill that carried even across the wind. Kaelorn made a mental note to thank the Emerald Ancient the next time they met.

Moments later, the world below shifted.

The Ivory Moonbeams appeared.

Tall ivory-white trees arched upward like columns carved from moonlight, their leaves shimmering with a pearlescent glow as though dusted with frost and starlight. Wisps of luminous mist drifted lazily between the trunks, curling around roots that looked as ancient as memory itself. The air itself felt hushed not empty, but watchful.

Aeralinde descended in a gentle spiral, her hooves touching the moss with soft, muted thumps as she landed in the heart of the glade.

Kaelorn dismounted, boots settling into luminous grass that glowed faintly beneath his steps. He sensed eyes upon him even before the branches stirred.

Two Sylvan Elves emerged from the treetops, descending with effortless grace. Their pale hair shimmered like spun moonbeams, and their robes were woven from white-threaded leaves that whispered with every movement.

The first spoke, voice calm and resonant with forest magic.

"You are the Forestborne Warden, yes?"

Kaelorn bowed lightly. "I am."

The second elf regarded him with curiosity edged by respect.

"It has been many ages since Aeliana chose one. Only the rare few earn her trust... and her blessing."

His gaze drifted to Aeralinde, whose wings glowed softly in the moonlit grove.

"And she gifted you that. Then you may be more significant than you realize."

Kaelorn flushed faintly.

"I only wish to serve the forests well."

"That is precisely why she chose you," the first elf replied warmly. "Come. We will show you our home."

They led him through the Ivory Moonbeams, their voices soft as falling petals.

"This forest is ancient," one explained. "Its roots remember every age of Vacari."

"We Sylvan Elves guard it," the other added, "but we are not its only protectors."

As if summoned by the words, faint glimmers stirred in the branches above.

Kaelorn slowed.

Aeralinde lifted her head, ears flicking forward.

Tiny bells chimed not metal, but wings.

Dozens of ivory-colored fairies drifted downward like falling petals, their wings translucent and patterned like frost on glass. They swirled around Kaelorn in gentle spirals, chiming a delicate, musical greeting.

One perched briefly on Aeralinde's mane, tapping her brow with playful curiosity before darting away in a burst of joyous sparkle.

The Sylvan Elves exchanged pleased smiles.

"It seems they approve," one said lightly.

"They do not appear for just anyone," the other added. "But they recognize Aeliana's hand when they see it."

Aeralinde lowered her head, allowing a cluster of fairies to settle in her mane. Warmth filled Kaelorn's chest not fleeting, not uncertain, but steady... a reassurance that he belonged here.

When the tour wound to its natural end, the elves guided him back to the clearing.

"You will always be welcome here, Forestborne Warden," one said, placing a hand over her heart.

"And should the Ivory Moonbeams ever require aid," added the second, "you need only return."

Kaelorn bowed deeply.

"Thank you for the welcome and the trust."

He turned to Aeralinde, who was already pawing the ground eagerly, wings twitching with anticipation.

"All right, Aeralinde," he said softly, smoothing her neck.

Purplefire Woods — Reunion With Familiar Faces

Aeralinde reared slightly, wings bursting outward in a blaze of intertwined color gold, green, red, purple, ivory, and the ever-present shimmering blue of Ardinia.

With a bright, ringing cry, she surged into the skies once more.

Kaelorn glanced back at the Ivory Moonbeams, now glowing faintly behind him like a memory of starlit peace, then leaned into the wind as Aeralinde carried him toward the violet glow of Purplefire Woods.

He had barely opened his mouth to guide her when—

"Purplefire is—wait"

—but the Pegasus was already banking south, wings angling decisively toward the rising wash of violet light on the horizon.

Kaelorn blinked... then laughed aloud.

"I suppose you already know the route. I could get used to that."

The young emerald dragon trailing them gave an approving trill as they sped across the skies. Below, the forest shifted emerald greens melting into luminous violets, trees radiating softly like lanterns caught in perpetual twilight.

Purplefire Woods.

Aeralinde descended in a smooth, elegant arc, landing among the violet-leafed trees with a gentle thud. The air shimmered with faint purple sparks warm, familiar, and quietly alive.

Kaelorn slid down from her back just as a familiar figure stepped from between the trunks.

Amara.

Her amethyst scales caught the light, gleaming in layered hues of lavender and starlight. Ong stood beside her, brushing stray leaves from her foreleg likely remnants of their recent battle over Goldmoor.

Amara gave a low, amused rumble.

"Welcome, Forestborne Warden."

Ong blinked.

"Forestborne Amara, that's Kaelorn. He is not a—"

"Ong," Amara said dryly, one luminous eye narrowing, "When will you learn not to argue with me?"

Ong opened his mouth. Closed it. Sighed the long-suffering resignation of a man eternally outmatched by an ancient dragon.

Kaelorn stepped forward, smiling.

"She is correct. I... was chosen by Aeliana. I am the Forestborne Warden now."

He scratched the back of his head sheepishly.

"Though I'm not yet certain I deserve it."

Amara snorted, half amused, half approving.

"She did. Because you care and not everyone does."

Ong nodded firmly.

"And if Aeliana trusts you, that's enough for all of us."

Kaelorn lifted his gaze to the glowing glade.

"So... this is Keisha's favorite forest. The one you two married in?"

Ong's expression softened, pride and affection weaving through memory.

"Yes. Right here in Purplefire. The trees glowed brighter that day even the fae wandered closer to watch."

Before Kaelorn could respond, a sudden rustling exploded behind the trees.

"Wait—what—?"

A blur of sleek black fur launched from the foliage.

"Pump—!"

The word cut off as Kaelorn was tackled clean off his feet.

Pumpkin the panther stood triumphantly on his chest, tail flicking, emerald eyes blazing with smug satisfaction. Kaelorn burst into laughter even as he tried — and failed to sit up beneath her very real weight.

Ong groaned.

"Pumpkin, you were supposed to stay with the scouts."

Pumpkin flicked her tail sharply against his legs in unapologetic defiance.

Amara rumbled with deep amusement.

"She approves of the new Warden. Consider that an exceedingly high honor."

Pumpkin purred thunderously, then finally stepped aside, allowing Kaelorn to sit up and brush leaves from his hair.

"I am... honored," he said breathlessly, grinning.

Then he rose, brushing off his clothes and his expression shifted, responsibility settling into place.

"I should continue my journey. Emberwoods is next."

Amara's amusement faded into quiet seriousness.

"Be cautious. The Topaz Dragon and the Mirage Dragon have both been seen there. Their presence strains the land."

She turned and released a resonant hum.

An adolescent amethyst dragon emerged from deeper within the woods, wings shimmering with violet light.

"Accompany them," Amara commanded. "Aid the emerald dragon if danger finds them."

The young amethyst bowed respectfully to Kaelorn.

Kaelorn inclined his head in sincere gratitude. "Thank you, Amara. I will not take that lightly."

Emberwoods — The Ember Pixies

Kaelorn turned back to Aeralinde, who pawed at the glowing ground with eager anticipation, wings twitching with contained energy.

"Emberwoods next, girl."

He mounted, settling into the saddle as the young amethyst and emerald dragons moved into formation around them. Aeralinde unfurled her shimmering wings, and with a single powerful beat, the Forestborne Warden and his guardians soared into the sky toward the fiery glades of Emberwoods.

Even Aeralinde's flight slowed as they neared their destination.

The closer they came, the thicker the air grew not with danger, but with warmth. Heat shimmered in gentle waves, and drifting embers floated through the sky like wandering fireflies.

The forest below glowed in molten gold and deep autumn flame. Leaves drifted from the branches like slow-burning motes of flame. Ancient runes pulsed faintly along the twisted trunks, marking land long claimed and respected by Copper Dragons.

Aeralinde circled once, scanning the forest below with alert precision.

Kaelorn stroked her neck.

"I know. We will be careful."

A sudden burst of laughter tiny, ringing, unmistakably mischievous rippled through the air.

Pixies.

Dozens of ember-pixies burst from the treetops, their wings blazing like copper sparks. The moment they spotted Aeralinde's radiant wings and Kaelorn's presence, they gasped in unison, scattering into excited spirals.

"Forestborne Warden!"

"He is here! Raelithar must know at once!"

They zipped away faster than Kaelorn could blink.

Moments later, the air trembled beneath the weight of massive wings.

Raelithar, the Copper Ancient, emerged from behind a ridge of flame-colored trees. His scales glowed like molten bronze, each plate etched with runes of age, memory... and fire. He landed with thunderous grace, scattering golden leaves in a drifting cascade.

Two younger copper dragons touched down beside him, bowing their heads toward Kaelorn and Aeralinde.

Raelithar's voice rolled deep and warm.

"Escort them to the heart of Emberwoods."

The younger dragons dipped their heads and guided Aeralinde downward through spiraling amber branches into the forest's glowing core.

There, Kaelorn saw it.

The Ember Maze.

A living labyrinth of copper-veined hedges glowing from within, its paths shifting subtly like a creature breathing. Legends whispered that only those with genuine intent or keen wit could navigate its ever-changing corridors.

Aeralinde landed beside it, snorting softly, as though assessing whether it planned to behave.

Kaelorn dismounted, eyes widening.

"I have heard rumors," he murmured. "But I never imagined it would feel like this."

A trio of pixies landed on his shoulders and tangled themselves in his hair, buzzing with irrepressible excitement.

"You want to go in?"

"You should go in! The maze likes you already!"

"We will guide you! We are the best maze-walkers in all Emberwoods!"

Raelithar lowered his head, amusement threading through his rumbling tone.

"If the Warden wishes to walk it, the maze will permit him. And the pixies are right he will be safe."

Two pixies crossed their arms in mock offense.

"Of course he will be safe! It is everyone else who should worry!"

Kaelorn laughed.

"Then... yes. I would be honored."

He approached the entrance. The copper-leafed archway shimmered, runes flaring brighter as if recognizing him. The air hummed alive, aware.

He stepped inside. For the briefest moment, Kaelorn felt the maze brush against his awareness — not as walls and paths, but as something living, curious, quietly testing the one who walked its heart.

Aeralinde moved to follow, but the maze rustled firmly, leaves shifting to block her path and gently nudge her back.

Raelithar huffed with laughter.

"Even the maze knows its rules. No winged creatures except pixies."

"We're special!" one pixie declared proudly.

Inside, Kaelorn followed winding paths filled with quiet wonder:

Hedges shifting behind him never threatening, only guiding.

Copper blossoms blooming at his passing like lanterns igniting.

Pools of molten-gold water reflecting visions of Emberwoods' past.

Fire sprites dancing along branches, trailing ribbons of living flame.

Hidden alcoves where ember-stags grazed peacefully, antlers glowing like burning branches.

The pixies darted ahead, chattering nonstop.

"Go left but not the first left the shiny left!"

"Do not step on that stone. It sneezes!"

"Ooh! This part smells like cinnamon!"

Kaelorn laughed softly, the weight of the world easing from his shoulders.

At the maze's center, they reached a small clearing.

A single ancient copper tree rose there massive, radiant, its bark glowing like heated metal. Its branches curved overhead like a protective crown.

Warmth pulsed through Kaelorn.

Recognition.

Acceptance.

Belonging.

One pixie whispered in reverence,

"The Heartfire sees you, Warden."

Kaelorn bowed his head.

When he turned back, the maze guided him gently outward paths opening smoothly, leading him home with quiet approval.

Aeralinde neighed in relief when he emerged, nudging him firmly with her muzzle.

"I'm fine," Kaelorn laughed.

Raelithar inclined his head.

"Emberwoods accepts you, Forestborne Warden. Remember that. And remember..."

His eyes gleamed knowingly.

"Not all who enter the maze are shown its heart."

Kaelorn swallowed.

"...Thank you."

But even as warmth lingered, Amara's warning echoed in his thoughts Topaz and Mirage near these borders.

Before he could remount, a pixie zipped forward, tugging gently at his sleeve.

"Wait! There is more to see!"

Raelithar bowed his great copper head.

"They speak true. Come, Warden. There is one place you must know before you leave."

They guided him along a winding path beneath molten-gold leaves. The two younger copper dragons stayed with Aeralinde while Kaelorn continued forward.

They stopped before a cave carved into the hillside, its entrance wide, its interior glowing faintly with warm amber light.

Kaelorn slowed.

He knew this place if only through whispered stories.

"This... is where Keisha and Ong once came seeking peace... and found suffering instead."

Raelithar's bronze scales dimmed with sorrow.

"Yes. Once, this cave was a place of torment. The Topaz Dragon and others twisted it into a prison of illusion, cruelty, and fear."

The pixies clustered near Kaelorn, wings dimming.

"We heard her screams..."

"We tried to reach her..."

"The illusions were too strong..."

Kaelorn felt his chest tighten as he stepped inside.

Where once there had been darkness...

Now there was healing.

Amber light filled the cavern.

Runes of restoration shimmered along the walls.

Soft moss grew where blood had once stained stone.

Tiny fire-flowers glowed in clusters, scattering sparks like fallen stars.

Raelithar spoke behind him, solemn and steady.

"We reclaimed this place. Emberwoods would not allow such darkness to linger."

Kaelorn rested his palm against the warm stone.

"You turned suffering... into sanctuary."

"The forest remembers," Raelithar replied,

"But it also heals."

After a moment, the Copper Ancient lowered his massive head, meeting Kaelorn's gaze.

"Tell me, Forestborne Warden..."

His voice lowered with quiet urgency.

"Can you help us drive the Topaz Dragon from our borders once more?"

Kaelorn straightened, resolve settling into his heart.

"I will. But first, I must report to Aeliana. Her guidance is vital. When she knows, Aeralinde and I will return."

The pixies erupted into cheers.

"We knew it!"

"The Warden will help!"

"We like him!"

Aeralinde stepped forward, wings shimmering in agreement.

Kaelorn rested a hand on her neck.

"Ready to fly again?"

She stamped once, feathers flashing emerald, gold, violet, and blue the forests calling her onward.

He smiled.

"Then let us go to Ardinia. We will return soon. I promise."

Raelithar bowed his great head.

"Go with Emberwood's blessing. And hurry back shadows stir near our borders."

Return to Ardinia — Aeliana's Acknowledgment

Kaelorn mounted Aeralinde as the emerald and amethyst dragons took up protective formation around them. Below, Emberwoods glowed warmly copper leaves burning like embers beneath twilight.

He cast one last look toward the restored cave a testament to resilience, healing, and hard-won courage.

"Soon," he whispered. "We'll help you soon."

Aeralinde surged upward in a sweep of radiant wings, carrying the Forestborne Warden toward Ardinia… and the next step of his destiny.

She flew with renewed vigor, wings shimmering brighter the closer they drew to the luminous realm. Kaelorn barely needed to guide her she moved with instinctive certainty, as though the forests themselves whispered directions through her veins.

When the first crystalline waters came into view, Kaelorn's breath caught.

Ardinia unfolded like a dream made real.

Sunlight refracted across ribbons of flowing water, each pool glowing with silver, sapphire, and pearlescent white. Trees rose like living sculptures, their leaves glowing with celestial radiance. Wisps of raw magic drifted through the air, trailing soft arcs of luminescence.

A herd of unicorns grazed along the water's edge, coats shimmering like moonlit snow, spiraled horns glowing with opalescent hues. They lifted their heads as Aeralinde passed, eyes serene and knowing.

Above, flocks of Pegasi glided through the sky, wings catching rainbows with every beat. They circled Aeralinde in greeting, dipping their heads respectfully toward Kaelorn.

He pressed his hand to his chest, overwhelmed.

"I... had no idea," he whispered. "Ardinia is more beautiful than I imagined."

Aeralinde descended through beams of crystalline light and touched down upon a field of soft silver grass.

Aeliana stood waiting.

Her presence radiated ancient serenity hair flowing like liquid silver-green light, delicate runes drifting along her arms like falling petals. Nymphs and fairies gathered around her, laughter chiming like bells in a spring breeze.

Kaelorn dismounted quickly and bowed deeply.

"Lady Aeliana."

Her smile was warm, knowing.

"You have visited the forests?"

"Yes," he replied. "Ivory Moonbeams. Purplefire. Emberwoods. All thrive... though Emberwoods will soon need aid."

"Good," she said with gentle approval.

"Then tell me, Kaelorn —" Her eyes sparkled with mischief. "Which forest was your favorite?"

Kaelorn flushed instantly.

"Oh—I—my Lady—I could never choose each forest is—there is no—um—favorites, truly—"

Behind Aeliana, the nymphs and fairies dissolved into laughter, wings fluttering wildly.

Kaelorn blinked, realization dawning. "...You were teasing me."

"Of course," Aeliana replied serenely. "A Warden must learn to endure many things including the humor of the fae."

Kaelorn sighed, embarrassed but smiling, as laughter rippled around them.

Aeliana motioned for him to walk beside her, and together they strolled through Ardinia's crystalline groves.

He spoke of:

- The Heartfire Tree in Emberwoods
- The quiet grace of the Ivory Moonbeams
- The vibrant spirit of Purplefire Woods
- And the looming threat of Topaz and Mirage

Aeliana listened with patient attentiveness, eyes thoughtful.

When he finished, she nodded.

"You have already begun to walk your purpose," she said softly. "Few wardens begin so quickly."

"And you have chosen your first task wisely. Emberwoods calls for your compassion... and your strength."

"I feel it," Kaelorn admitted.

"As though the forest itself is calling."

"It is," Aeliana replied. "Every grove, every root."

She touched his shoulder, her magic warm and grounding.

You are already becoming what the forests hoped you would be... long before you knew it."

They returned to where Aeralinde waited, her wings glowing with the colors of every realm she represented.

Then unexpectedly Aeliana embraced him.

Kaelorn stiffened in surprise, then gently returned the gesture.

Her voice was soft at his ear.

"Be careful, my Forestborne Warden. And do try to enjoy the pixies. They will test your patience... and brighten your spirit."

He laughed quietly.

"I'm beginning to understand that."

Aeralinde lowered herself so he could mount. Kaelorn swung into the saddle as Aeliana stepped back, raising her hand in blessing.

"Go with Ardinia's light."

Aeralinde lifted into the sky, the emerald and amethyst dragons following faithfully. Crystal waters shimmered beneath them as they turned toward the glowing horizon of Emberwoods once more.

Kaelorn exhaled, heart steady.

It is time," he murmured. "The forests are calling."

Aeralinde answered with a bright, determined cry ...they flew toward Emberwoods where the forest would soon be tested. As Emberwoods rose on the horizon once more, the warm glow of its copper leaves flickered strangely—embers drifting unevenly through the air, as though the forest itself sensed something approaching.

Chapter 22

Sparks Over Emberwoods

Emberwoods shimmered with warm copper light as Aeralinde descended through drifting ember-mist.

But Kaelorn felt the disturbance before he saw it a tremor running through root and leaf alike, like the forest itself whispering his name.

The air quivered. Branches shuddered. Sap pulsed faster through ancient trunks, as though Emberwoods had drawn a sharp, uneasy breath.

Something was wrong.

Aeralinde stiffened beneath him, wings angling defensively. The young emerald and amethyst dragons flying with them released low, warning growls, their instincts echoing his own.

Then Kaelorn saw the flashes jagged streaks of gold ripping across the sky.

Topaz dragons.

And Zarathos at their head.

They swept over the canopy in a storm of gleaming, razor-edged light. Below, Raelithar and his copper flight surged upward to meet them, wings blazing like molten bronze.

A copper dragon collided with a topaz attacker overhead, scattering showers of sparks through the trees. The sky roared with clashing magic, fire screaming against crystal-bright greed.

This was not a full invasion.

It was a calculated probe a Dominion tactic meant to test Emberwood's defenses, measure resistance, and map weakness.

"They are striking for the maze!" Kaelorn called. "Hold the inner paths!"

He barely had time to finish before Aeralinde landed.

Kaelorn leapt from her back as several topaz dragons shifted course and dove toward the Ember Maze.

Their breath weapons slammed into the luminous hedges. The maze vanished in a burst of golden fire only to re-form instantly, its copper veins blazing brighter, as though angered by the assault.

Another topaz dragon struck.

Another blast.

Another failure.

From above, Zarathos snarled, wings beating in open frustration.

"Clever tricks," he growled, voice like grinding crystal. "No construct holds forever. Break its pattern. Find the true path."

Raelithar barked a booming laugh as he grappled with a topaz lieutenant.

"You glittering fool!" he roared. "The Ember Maze is older than your pride, older than your greed. You cannot break what you do not understand!"

Pixies erupted into chiming laughter, their mirth cutting through the chaos—and driving the topaz dragons into sharper rage.

But then Zarathos' gaze snapped downward.

It landed on Kaelorn.

At first, the Topaz Ancient dismissed him a mortal, fragile, and insignificant. A creature beneath notice.

Then Kaelorn pressed his palms to the earth.

And the forest answered.

A surge of green-and-gold magic rippled outward from his fingertips, racing through root and branch in a luminous wave. The trees brightened in response. Copper leaves hardened into gleaming shields. Ancient fae resonance pulsed through the soil like a heartbeat awakening from slumber.

The Ember Maze's barrier flared brighter.

When a topaz dragon's blast struck it this time, it did not merely resist.

It rebounded fracturing the blast and hurling its force back in a violent surge.

The attacking dragon shrieked, spiraling wildly out of formation.

Zarathos froze midair.

His pupils narrowed.

"What..." he hissed, disbelief sharpening into suspicion.

"...What... is this construct?" he hissed. "...this is not illusion."

For a heartbeat, doubt flickered then the forest answered.

And doubt had no place to stand.

Kaelorn rose slowly, energy crackling around him not wild, not unstable but anchored. Rooted. Guided. Not his power alone... but the forest's will, moving through him.

Above, Aeralinde soared in a radiant arc, wings blazing with multicolored brilliance. Her presence did not grant him power it steadied it, aligned it, allowing the forest's strength to flow through him without breaking him.

Raelithar saw the realization strike Zarathos and grinned savagely.

"You face no wandering mortal, Topaz Ancient," he boomed.

"You stand against the Forestborne Warden of Vacari."

The topaz dragons screamed and renewed their assault, shifting tactics to overwhelm both the copper defenders and the forest's heart.

Copper dragons surged upward in response, colliding with their attackers in explosive bursts of fire and gemlight. Roars split the canopy. Sparks rained through ember-lit leaves.

Kaelorn thrust both arms skyward.

Roots tore from the earth in spiraling arcs. Copper sigils ignited midair. A living shield surged upward, intercepting another topaz blast.

It barely held.

Then the forest answered, surging upward and forcing the blast aside in a violent recoil.

The offending dragon slammed sideways, snarling in pain.

Zarathos beat his wings, sending a violent gust through the glade.

"You command the forest itself..." he growled, realization hardening into calculation.

"So, Aeliana has chosen her champion."

Kaelorn met his glare without flinching.

"I do not fight for titles," he said, voice steady and resolute. "I fight for the forest. I always will."

Zarathos' throat flared with gathering light fire ready, rage simmering but he hesitated.

The Ember Maze stood unbroken.

The copper dragons remained strong.

And this new Warden was far more dangerous than anticipated.

This skirmish was no longer worth the cost.

With a sharp snap of his wings, Zarathos signaled retreat.

The topaz dragons broke formation, circling him as they disengaged.

Before departing, Zarathos locked eyes with Kaelorn one last time.

"We will return," he promised coldly.

"And next time... we will come prepared for you."

Then he surged into the sky, golden fire trailing behind him as the topaz flight vanished into distant clouds.

The forest slowly exhaled.

And quiet returned to Emberwoods.

Ember-leaves drifted softly through the air the only lingering reminder of the chaos that had moments ago torn through the sky.

Raelithar landed heavily beside Kaelorn, steam curling from his nostrils as heat bled from his scales.

"Well done, Forestborne Warden," the Copper Ancient rumbled, pride warming his voice. "Few can force a Topaz Ancient to turn his back on a fight."

Kaelorn inhaled shakily, magic still humming through his veins like a fading storm.

"I only did what the forest allowed," he said quietly.

Raelithar let out a low, rumbling chuckle.

"Then the forest has chosen well indeed."

Pixies swarmed Kaelorn at once, tugging at his sleeves, darting around his shoulders, their wings chiming in breathless excitement.

"You scared him!"

"Did you see his face? All cracked and furious!"

"Do the big shield again!"

"Our Warden!"

Kaelorn laughed a breathless mix of relief, humility, and rising resolve.

This battle had not been a victory.

It had been a warning.

The Dominion was testing borders.

Probing defenses.

Searching for weakness.

And Kaelorn now understood something with chilling clarity:

He stood on a line that must not break.

Smoke drifted from the treetops where the last traces of topaz fire had guttered out. Copper dragons circled overhead, watchful now instead of fighting. Emberwoods exhaled slowly, tension loosening but not disappearing.

Kaelorn stepped beside Raelithar, brushing ash from his hands.

"The Topaz Ancient didn't withdraw because he was defeated," he said quietly. "He was measuring us. Just like Zylron. Just like Glaciera. Just like Mirage. They are not striking at random," Kaelorn said quietly. "They are testing us. Mapping us. Learning how we respond."

Raelithar rumbled deep in his chest.

"Aye. They mean to wear us down. Stretch us thin. Win through exhaustion rather than conquest," Raelithar rumbled. "Break the will... and the rest follows."

"And hope we lose heart," Kaelorn added, his gaze sweeping across the glowing copper canopy.

Raelithar flared his wings slightly, pride sharpening his tone.

"But Emberwoods will not fall. Not to Topaz. Not to Mirage. Not to any dragon who bends the knee to the Dominion."

Kaelorn nodded, determination settling into him like a steady flame.

"I'm staying here," Kaelorn said quietly. "This is where I'm needed." he said. "The forest answers me. If I can awaken Emberwoods the way Verdantia strengthened the Emerald Woods... the way Amara fortified Purplefire... then Emberwoods can defend itself. Not one forest alone but all of them... standing together."

Raelithar's bronze eyes glowed with approval.

"Emberwoods is old. Proud. Fierce. Stir its heart, and it will become a weapon the Dominion never expected."

Pixies whirled overhead, chiming eagerly.

"We'll help!"

"We know every root and every hidden flame!"

"We'll show him the Heartfire paths!"

Kaelorn smiled warmly at them.

"I was hoping you would."

Raelithar lowered his head, thoughtful.

"And perhaps others may lend their strength. Verdantia has awakened the emerald roots. Amara has reinforced Purplefire's defenses. Even Keisha... her bond with the forests runs deeper than most realize."

At the sound of her name, a faint ripple moved through the copper leaves above them, ember-light flickering as though the forest itself remembered.

Kaelorn's expression softened.

"Yes," he said quietly. "I may seek their guidance."

He lifted his gaze to the sky where the Topaz dragons had vanished a sky that would not remain peaceful for long.

"We'll be ready next time," he said firmly. "All of us. And Emberwoods most of all."

Raelithar spread his wings, casting a long copper shadow over the glowing forest floor.

"Then let us begin awakening it, Warden," he said, baring his teeth in a fierce grin.

"The Dominion believes we are weakening."

His eyes burned with molten resolve.

"They will learn otherwise."

And beneath drifting embers and whispering leaves, the Forestborne Warden, the Copper Ancient, and the flame-bright pixies began preparing Emberwoods for the battles yet to come not as a forest under siege...but as a forest awakening to war.

Chapter 23

Shadows at the Edge of the Sky

Lyra'el drifted in tranquil majesty above the Cerulean Expanse, its cloud-forged towers glowing with soft celestial light. The sky-city breathed serenity an illusion of peace suspended high above the struggles of the world below.

But peace, like cloudglass, was fragile.

At the outskirts of Lyra'el's drifting borders, darkness gathered.

Voraxia, Shadow Dragon of the Abyssal Dominion, glided silently through the high clouds, her wings slicing through vapor without sound. Beside her flew Vorathos, the Abyssal Dragon—her presence heavier, more oppressive, the sky itself seeming to recoil from her passage. Around them, their kin moved in slow, deliberate circles, dark shapes hovering just beyond the reach of Lyra'el's radiant wards.

They did not attack.

They waited.

Their purpose was unmistakable.

They wanted Radiantus.

They wanted Aurelius.

And this time, they intended to destroy what they could not corrupt.

Within the upper terraces of Lyra'el, Talhira felt it before she saw it.

A tremor rippled through the bond she shared with Radiantus subtle, precise, impossible to ignore. She stepped to the edge of a crystalline balcony, fingers tightening against the luminous stone as her gaze pierced the layered veil of clouds.

There.

Shadows where none should exist.

Her breath caught.

Without hesitation, Talhira turned and moved swiftly through the skyways, her steps ringing sharply against the glowing paths as she made for the inner sanctum.

Radiantus was already stirring when she arrived.

The great Platinum Dragon lifted his head, silver-white scales catching and refracting the surrounding light like living starlight. His eyes ancient, calm, and infinitely perceptive settled upon her.

"They are here," Talhira said, her voice low but steady.
"Voraxia... and another. Abyssal. Stronger than the rest."

Radiantus exhaled, a sound like wind moving across crystal towers.

"I felt them pressing against the outer currents," he said. "They do not come for skirmish or spectacle."

He rose smoothly, wings unfolding with measured power.

"Summon the Platinum kin. This is no mere provocation."

Talhira inclined her head. "At once."

She turned, signaling through Lyra'el's communication runes. Across the city, Platinum Dragons stirred, their riders responding with disciplined urgency. Armor was secured. Lances and spell-focuses were readied. Bonds flared with shared resolve.

High above them all, on a separate tier of sky, Aurelius waited.

The Celestial Dragon stood poised upon a halo of light, vast wings folded in quiet readiness. His kin gathered nearby—luminous beings of radiant essence and starlit scale. No rider stood beside him.

None was needed.

Aurelius watched the horizon where shadow pressed against brilliance, his expression unreadable.

This was not his first confrontation with the darkness.

Nor would it be his last.

Below, the Platinum flight assembled in formation, Radiantus at their head, Talhira mounting with practiced grace. Above them, the Celestial host aligned in silent unity, their light intensifying as one.

Lyra'el's bells chimed softly not in alarm, but in solemn acknowledgment.

All forces were gathering.

And beyond the cloud line, Voraxia smiled.

The hunt was about to begin.

The clouds above Lyra'el parted violently as Radiantus surged forward.

Platinum met abyss.

Vorathos answered with a roar that seemed to darken the sky itself, her presence dragging the light downward as though gravity bent toward her. The two Ancients collided in a thunderous shockwave radiance flaring against void-black force, sending tremors rippling through the surrounding cloudbanks.

Radiantus held firm, wings braced, light blazing from every scale.

"Have you learned nothing?" he thundered, his voice ringing like a bell forged from stars.

"The last time you tested us, you were cast back into the dark."

Vorathos hissed, abyssal energy curling around her talons.

"Each clash is a lesson, Platinum," she replied. "And the Dominion is a patient teacher."

Before Radiantus could answer, a familiar, chilling presence slid through the upper air.

Voraxia.

Her shadow spilled across the clouds like living ink as she glided into position, her eyes narrowing not at Radiantus, but beyond him.

Not at the Platinum Ancient.

At the one who needed no rider.

She felt it.

The light intensified.

She turned just as the heavens themselves seemed to open.

Aurelius had arrived.

The Celestial Dragon descended without sound, vast wings unfurling in a cascade of radiant brilliance. Around him gathered the Celestial kin beings of living light, their forms edged in starlight and quiet, inexorable power.

Voraxia's expression tightened.

Aurelius spoke, his voice calm, luminous, and utterly unafraid.

"Do not reach for your Black Sun, Voraxia. You learned before that shadow cannot eclipse what is eternal."

A flicker of irritation crossed Voraxia's face.

"Confidence suits you, Celestial," she replied coolly. "But even stars burn out."

Aurelius' wings shifted slightly, light pulsing brighter.

"Not before the darkness does."

The skies fell into a dangerous stillness.

Radiantus and Vorathos circled one another slowly, their movements deliberate and predatory. Below them, the Platinum riders held formation, Talhira 's grip tightening as she watched the two Ancients measure each other's intent.

Above, the Celestial host spread into a gleaming arc a living bulwark of light barring the advance of shadow.

No one struck.

Not yet.

This was not chaos.

This was calculation.

Voraxia's tail lashed once through the clouds.

Aurelius noticed.

Radiantus felt it ripple through the bonds of light.

Each dragon waited for weakness, for an opening, for the first misstep.

Lyra'el hovered beneath them all, silent and watchful.

And in the space between light and abyss, the coming battle drew nearer with every slow, circling breath.

The stillness shattered.

Vorathos lunged first, abyssal force coiling from her chest as she hurled herself at Radiantus. Platinum and void collided again, the impact cracking the cloudbank like splintered glass. Shockwaves rippled outward, tossing lesser dragons into tight corrective spirals.

Below, the Platinum riders surged forward as one.

Talhira raised her arm, Lightforged Shield flaring to life brilliant arcs of radiant geometry locking into place around her and the riders beside her. Abyssal fire slammed into the shields and skidded away in shrieking sparks, leaving the formation intact.

"Hold the line!" she called.

Platinum dragons wove through the sky, disciplined and precise, their riders striking in tandem lances of focused light and bursts of sanctified force meant not to kill, but to deny ground.

Voraxia darted through the chaos, shadows folding around her like wings within wings. She struck at a Platinum rider, tearing through the edge of a shield and sending the dragon reeling with a shriek.

Before the rider could fall light descended.

A Celestial dragon swept in, its presence washing the air in warmth and clarity. The wound sealed in a cascade of starlight. The rider gasped, steadied, and surged back into formation.

Another Platinum dragon took a glancing hit.

Then another Celestial was there.

Wings outstretched.

For a heartbeat, time itself seemed to reverse.

Again.

And again.

The Celestials moved with serene efficiency, healing each injury as it occurred, erasing momentum and denying the Dominion every inch of progress.

Voraxia snarled, her voice cutting through the air.

"They should be breaking."

Vorathos answered with a roar of pure frustration as Radiantus forced her back, platinum light blazing brighter with every healed ally returning to the fight.

Above them all, Aurelius glided through the upper arc of battle radiant and unassailable. His presence amplified the Celestial host. Each wave of healing strengthened the Platinum line. Each renewal sharpened their resolve.

Voraxia lunged toward him, shadow boiling.

Aurelius turned his head slightly.

Light flared.

The shadow recoiled as if burned.

"Enough," Aurelius said, his voice calm and inexorable.

"You cannot win a war of attrition against hope."

That was when Voraxia screamed.

Not in pain.

In fury.

She wheeled toward Vorathos, eyes blazing.

"Withdraw now!"

Vorathos resisted for a heartbeat longer then broke away as Radiantus advanced, platinum fire igniting the sky behind him.

The Dominion dragons retreated in snarling arcs, shadows unraveling as they fled beyond the outer currents of Lyra'el.

Silence returned in ragged breaths.

The Platinum riders regrouped, shields dimming but unbroken. Celestial dragons hovered among them, light still flowing as the last injuries faded.

Radiantus turned, surveying his allies with steady pride.

At the far edge of the clouds, Voraxia lingered her form half-swallowed by shadow, eyes burning with promises she could not yet keep.

This had not been their victory but neither had it been the Dominion's.

Lyra'el still shone untouched, defiant, and very much alive.

Before Voraxia could vanish entirely, Aurelius moved.

He did not pursue.

He did not threaten.

He spoke.

His voice carried across the sky clear, radiant, and impossible to ignore.

"You are running out of places to hide."

Voraxia paused.

The shadows around her stilled.

Aurelius continued, wings unfurled in quiet brilliance.

"We are close now. Closer than you realize.

We know your master served Vuarus in the Abyss.

We know they learned there... grew there... and waited."

A ripple of tension passed through the Dominion ranks.

Voraxia's jaw tightened.

"It is only a matter of time," Aurelius said evenly,

"Before the truth surfaces. And when it does, your master will no longer remain hidden behind servants and shadows."

For the first time, something flickered in Voraxia's eyes.

Not fear.

Unease.

She bared her fangs in a thin, dangerous smile.

"Bold words, Celestial," she said softly. "Be certain you are ready for what steps into the light."

The shadows closed around her like folding wings.

Voraxia vanished.

Vorathos and the remaining Dominion dragons followed, slipping into the upper darkness until the skies above Lyra'el were clear once more.

Silence returned broken only by the gentle hum of celestial currents.

Radiantus descended first, his platinum form glowing softly as he rejoined the Platinum flight. Talhira exhaled, lowering her Lightforged Shield at last.

The Celestial dragons regrouped in graceful arcs, their healing light fading as the last traces of injury vanished. Aurelius hovered above them all, radiant and still.

Lyra'el drifted on.

Unbroken.

Radiantus lifted his gaze to Aurelius.

"They are losing patience."

Aurelius inclined his head slightly.

"Because the veil is thinning."

Below them, the city's bells chimed not in warning, but in solemn acknowledgment.

They had held.

For now.

As the Platinum riders and Celestial host returned to their posts, one truth lingered heavier than any shadow:

The Dominion's master was no longer a distant threat waiting in the future.

They were close.

And with every clash, the final reckoning drew nearer.

Chapter 24

The Hidden Realm

Ixalia moved like a living mirage through the borderlands between the Emberwoods and the Emerald Woods, her vast wings barely stirring the air as she slipped between light and shadow. At times she was fully present, her dark opalescent scales catching embers of sunset at others she blurred, fractured, or vanished entirely, leaving only ripples where reality seemed to hesitate.

This place offended her senses.

The woods should have answered her.

Illusion always found something to cling to: fear, memory, desire. Yet here the land felt... veiled.

Not hidden.

Not warded.

Aware.

Ixalia's shifting opal eyes narrowed.

"E'vahona," she murmured, her voice folding upon itself like layered whispers. "You exist. I can feel you."

She circled lower, talons grazing the canopy without disturbing a single leaf. Light bent subtly around her passage; branches shimmered where her shadow passed, briefly revealing paths that were not there glades that dissolved the moment she focused upon them. The Mirage Dragon smiled, a slow and knowing curl of lip.

"So clever," she crooned. "To nest between fire and emerald. Between passion and permanence."

She exhaled, and the breath carried illusion with its phantom pathways unfurling through the forest, false clearings blooming and fading, echoes of laughter that never quite formed.

Ixalia waited for a response.

None came.

No resistance.

No answer.

No fear.

That, more than anything, unsettled her.

High above, where the emerald canopy thickened into ancient boughs older than memory, Verdantia watched in utter stillness.

The Emerald Dragon was immense, her form partially entwined with the living forest itself vines curling along her limbs, leaves growing across the ridges of her scales as though she were less a visitor and more a sovereign root given wings. Her eyes, deep and verdant, followed Ixalia's every movement without haste.

Beside her, perched upon a sun-warmed outcropping of stone streaked with copper veins, Raelithar lounged with exaggerated ease.

The Copper Dragon was restless energy barely contained by his wings, flexing once, twice, his tail tapping the stone in an irregular rhythm. His grin came easily sharp, mischievous and his eyes sparkled with barely restrained delight.

"Oh, she's getting annoyed," Raelithar whispered, his voice low despite the distance. "See how her illusions keep collapsing? It is like watching a bard forget the second verse."

Verdantia did not look at him.

"Restrain yourself," she said calmly. "This is not a game."

Raelithar snorted softly. "Everything is a game. Some simply carry higher stakes." He leaned forward slightly, lowering his voice further. "I could have her chasing her own shadow for days."

"I am aware," Verdantia replied. "Which is precisely why you will not."

Her gaze sharpened not with anger, but with quiet authority.

"This forest is not merely hiding E'vahona," she continued. "It is deciding."

Raelithar sighed dramatically, wings drooping a fraction. "You're no fun when you're right."

Still, he obeyed.

Below them, Ixalia paused midair, her form flickering as though reality itself could not decide where she belonged. Slowly she turned her head, eyes scanning the trees, the stone, the empty air.

For a breathless moment, it seemed she might sense them.

Verdantia's presence deepened, blending seamlessly with the forest's ancient awareness. Raelithar stilled completely.

The grin faded not into fear, but into calculation.

Ixalia frowned.

"No," she said softly. "Not here... but near."

She tilted her head, listening not with ears but with intent. The Mirage Dragon's wings folded slightly as she descended another measure, irritation creeping into her voice.

"You cannot hide forever," she warned the unseen realm. "The Dominion does not tire. And neither do I."

Above, Verdantia's eyes glowed faintly.

"She is probing," she murmured. "Testing the boundary."

Raelithar's tail twitched. "And failing."

"Not entirely," Verdantia corrected. "She has found where the forest allows her to look."

A distant wind stirred silver-cool, carrying with it a resonance both sharp and serene.

Verdantia lifted her head.

"They are coming."

Raelithar's grin returned, slower now tempered by anticipation rather than mischief.

"About time."

Far beyond sight, the Silver Dragons closed the distance Silvara and Talleoss, drawn not by summons alone, but by instincts older than dominion or war. Above the clouds, they moved with quiet certainty, unhurried and unstoppable.

Below, unaware of how completely the forest had turned against her, Ixalia spread her wings once more and pressed deeper into the liminal space between Emberwoods and Emerald.

The trap had not yet sprung.

But it was ready.

Ixalia's patience finally splintered.

The forest had ceased mocking her.

It now simply ignored her.

No illusions answered her call. No hidden paths unfolded beneath her will. Even the false glades she wove unraveled before they could take root, dissolving like breath against cold glass.

Her wings snapped open, scattering shards of refracted light as she surged upward, fury sharpening her focus into something dangerously precise.

"Enough," she hissed. "You dare bar me from what is owed?"

She could feel it already the distant, cold awareness of the Mysterious One turning toward her, not with fury, but with calculation.

And disappointment.

Within the Dominion, disappointment was far more lethal than rage.

Ixalia twisted in midair and froze.

The sky ahead of her shimmered.

Not with illusion.

With truth made visible.

Two vast forms descended from the higher currents, their scales reflecting the world as it was, not as it might be bent. Moonlight clung to them though the sun had not yet set, casting pale fire along elegant wings and crested spines.

Silver Dragons.

Ixalia's growl rippled downward through the canopy, bending leaves and shadow alike.

"So," she snarled, "Vacari bares its sentinels at last."

She rose to meet them, her form stabilizing into something unmistakably solid, illusion pulled tight and locked in place. Power coiled beneath her scales, waiting.

Dangerous.

Her shifting opal eyes fixed on the nearer of the two.

Taller. Broader.

Calm in a way that unsettled her far more than aggression ever could.

"What business have you here?" Ixalia demanded. "This place does not concern you."

The dragon she addressed did not bare his teeth.

Did not flare his wings.

Talleoss, Ancient Silver, simply looked at her.

And the weight of that gaze pressed down like winter settling into bone.

"I believe," he said evenly, his voice carrying quiet, inexorable authority, "That I am the one who should be asking that question."

Ixalia bristled.

"You mistake yourself, Silver," she snapped. "I tread where I will."

Talleoss tilted his head slightly, frost-light glinting along the ridges of his scales.

"You tread," he replied, "Where you do not belong."

A flicker of something sharp dangerous crossed Ixalia's expression. "Vacari does not own the skies."

"No," Talleoss agreed calmly. "But it knows its own."

Silvara drifted closer, her wings stirring currents that felt cleansing rather than cold. The air itself seemed to settle in her presence, distortion smoothing into clarity.

"You are not of this world," she said softly. "And your presence here is neither accidental... nor welcome."

Ixalia laughed, mirage-light fracturing along her jaws.

"You mistake caution for weakness," she said. "I seek only what was hidden from me."

"And that," Talleoss replied, "Is precisely the problem."

The tension snapped.

From the emerald canopy below came a sound utterly out of place in such a moment—

A chuckle.

"Well," Raelithar's voice rang out as he rose from concealment, copper scales catching the light like freshly stirred embers, "this brings back memories."

He surged upward to flank the Silvers, wings flaring with unapologetic confidence.

"Mirage Dragon," he continued, eyes gleaming with recognition rather than curiosity, "last time we crossed paths, you had me convinced the forest was turning itself inside out."

His grin widened. "I will give you this you are imaginative. Annoying. But imaginative."

Ixalia's gaze snapped to him, irritation sharpening as recognition surfaced.

"You," she spat. "You survived."

Raelithar bowed midair with exaggerated politeness. "Barely. And only because someone with better timing and far less patience showed up."

Before the exchange could deepen, the forest itself seemed to exhale.

Verdant light pulsed beneath the canopy as vines loosened and branches bowed. Verdantia rose with slow, inexorable grace, leaves clinging to her emerald scales as though reluctant to release their sovereign. Her presence carried the deep resonance of roots that remembered the world's shaping.

Her gaze settled on Ixalia steady, ancient, unyielding.

"I remember you," Verdantia said. "Your illusions sought to fracture us... and failed."

She sighed softly, the sound like wind through old growth. "You have not learned restraint since then."

Raelithar glanced sidelong at her, smirk intact. "To be fair, she did make things interesting."

Verdantia did not look away. "Interesting is not the same as wise."

Ixalia's wings spread wider, mirage-light rippling with restrained fury. Surrounded by four Ancients each distinct, each immovable she drew herself taller, pride refusing to bend.

"You will not bar me," she warned, her voice low and dangerous.

Talleoss' wings unfurled at last, silver light cutting cleanly through the air.

"We already have," he said.

The skies between Emberwoods and Emerald Woods grew heavy with intent. No fire loosed. No claws drawn.

But the balance had irrevocably shifted.

Ixalia had come hunting a hidden city.

Instead, she had found its guardians.

Her gaze slid once more to the Silver Dragons and for the briefest moment, her expression tightened.

Not with fear.

With memory.

She remembered the way her illusions had shattered like spun glass beneath Silvara's light. The humiliating clarity that had torn through her layered deceptions, leaving nowhere to hide and nothing left to twist.

Her lips curled.

"What a pity," Ixalia said coolly, her voice smoothing back into silk and shadow as her attention drifted toward Verdantia and Raelithar. "It would have been... amusing to play again. Your minds are so delightfully reactive."

Her opalescent eyes flicked back to Silvara.

"But you ruin the fun."

She rose higher, wings unfolding as illusion clung to her once more controlled now, deliberate, refined.

"Another time," she added lightly. "I am... needed elsewhere."

The pressure she carried loosened not retreat, but redirection. Dominion instinct recalibrating.

Before she could slip entirely into fractured light, Talleoss' voice cut cleanly through the space between them.

"You will never find E'vahona."

Ixalia paused mid-ascent.

"You may as well tell your master," he continued, silver gaze unwavering. "It is not hidden from you."

A beat.

"It is denied to you."

For a heartbeat, the Mirage Dragon hovered still.

Then she laughed softly.

"We shall see," she replied, already fading. "Denial has a way of... provoking curiosity."

And with that, she dissolved upward into refracted sky, her presence unraveling until even the forest could no longer feel her passing.

Silence reclaimed the space.

Verdantia exhaled slowly, her wings settling as she turned toward Talleoss.

"She will not abandon this," she said. "Frustration sharpens her. It always has."

Silvara inclined her head.

"We know."

Her gaze drifted toward the unseen heart of the forest, where E'vahona lay folded into secrecy and song.

"We will speak with the Eladrin and with Kadona. If Ixalia must be occupied, then let her chase something designed to hold her attention."

Raelithar's tail flicked thoughtfully, copper light glinting along its edge.

"A diversion," he mused. "Loud enough to feel like progress."

"And distant enough," Verdantia added, "to keep her from listening here."

Talleoss gave a single, solemn nod.

"Then it is decided."

One by one, they turned away.

Raelithar dipped first, vanishing back toward Emberwoods, already humming to himself half amusement, half calculation as though mischief and strategy were never far apart.

Verdantia descended next, her vast form melting seamlessly into the emerald canopy until forest and dragon were once more indistinguishable root, leaf, and sovereign united.

The Silvers lingered a moment longer, watching the skies Ixalia had abandoned.

Then Silvara and Talleoss turned as one, their wings catching the light as they departed toward council and consequence.

Between Emberwoods and Emerald Woods, the air stilled.

E'vahona remained unseen.

But the game had already begun to shift.

Chapter 25

Before the Next Strike

Flameford did not welcome failure.

Ixalia descended through the ashen skies, her form solidifying as the heat rose to meet her. Rivers of magma traced glowing scars through the land below, and the air tasted of sulfur and old violence. Illusion clung to her still, but it lay close now disciplined, restrained, a blade kept sheathed.

She entered the inner chamber without announcement.

The Mysterious One stood where they always did half-lit by fire, half-consumed by shadow their presence pressing against the cavern walls like an unspoken command. Power radiated from them not in spectacle, but in certainty.

Ixalia lowered her head.

"E'vahona remains beyond reach," she said, her voice steady despite the tension coiling beneath her scales. "It lies between the Emberwoods and the Emerald Woods, but it is... denied. The forest itself rejects illusion."

Silence followed.

Not the absence of sound, but the kind that waited.

Ixalia felt it then the displeasure. Sharp. Immediate. Not rage never rage but a cold recalibration, as though she herself were being weighed and measured anew.

"You failed," the Mysterious One said at last.

Ixalia did not argue.

"I was intercepted," she replied evenly. "The Silver Ancients have intervened. Verdantia and Raelithar stand watch as well."

That earned her a slow turn of the head.

"So," the Mysterious One murmured, "they guard it openly now."

Their fingers traced a sigil in the rising ash, symbols of command forming and dissolving in the heated air.

"This complication will not be addressed in isolation."

They turned sharply.

"Malrik."

From the shadows stepped the gaunt figure of their lieutenant, already bowing.

"Send the summons. All who are bound to the Dominion will gather at the Cavern of Ash."

Malrik hesitated only long enough to measure the weight behind the command.

"All of them?" he asked.

"All," the Mysterious One repeated. "This requires consensus... and obedience."

Their gaze returned to Ixalia. "You will wait."

Ixalia inclined her head once more, though her wings twitched faintly. "As you command."

The Cavern of Ash lay deeper within Flameford a vast hollow carved by ancient fire and conquest. Its ceiling vanished into darkness, while the ground below was layered with scorched stone, bones fused into the rock, and veins of ember that pulsed like a living heart.

Ixalia stood near its center, motionless, her illusions reduced to a faint heat shimmer along her scales.

The first arrivals came swiftly.

Shadows deepened along the cavern walls as Voraxia, Ancient Shadow Dragon, emerged soundlessly from the darkness, her form half-consumed by it. Beside her, the air seemed to tear as Vorathos, Abyssal Ancient, forced her way into the chamber, her presence heavy and corrosive, reality bending uneasily around them.

They took a position near Ixalia without a word.

Moments later, the stone itself groaned as Nocturna, the Obsidian Dragon, rose from below, her scales catching the firelight like fractured mirrors. She lingered just behind the Abyssal, silent and unreadable.

A blast of heat announced Zylron's arrival.

The Red Dragon landed with unmistakable force near the cavern's edge, molten light rippling across his scales as he folded his wings. His eyes swept the chamber once—assessing, already calculating.

Others followed, taking their places.

From the deeper tunnels slithered Xalzorath, the Black Dragon, acidic fumes curling around his form as he settled beside Zylron. The temperature dropped abruptly as Glaciera, the White Dragon, emerged in a plume of frost that hissed violently against the surrounding heat.

Last to arrive deliberate and unhurried was Zarathos, the Topaz Dragon.

His gem-like scales caught the firelight with unsettling brilliance as he settled near Zylron, his gaze sharp with pride and old resentment.

The formation was deliberate.

Ixalia, Voraxia, and Vorathos stood forward shadow and abyss unified, close to the heart of command.

The others remained farther back, clustered near Zylron: a line of restrained power, waiting not for unity but direction.

The cavern grew quiet again.

They had been summoned.

And none of them doubted why.

Zylron's molten gaze slid toward Ixalia, his expression sharpening with something close to satisfaction.

"Well?" the Red Dragon rumbled, his voice thick with heat and contempt. "Did you find it? This elusive jewel hidden between trees and song?"

Ixalia's head turned slowly.

She did not answer.

Her shifting opal eyes locked onto Zylron's, mirage-light flickering once dangerously restrained. The silence that followed was deliberate.

Pointed.

Zylron's lips curled.

"No answer?" he said softly. "How... predictable."

Before he could press further, the air in the cavern shifted.

Footsteps echoed measured, unhurried.

The dragons felt them before they saw them.

The Mysterious One entered the Cavern of Ash with Malrik at their side, ash and shadow folding away from their presence as though unwilling to touch them. The heat dimmed, the ember-veins along the floor pulsed more slowly, as if the cavern itself had learned caution.

Silence fell instantly.

Wings stilled. Tails ceased their restless movements. Even Zylron closed his jaws.

They stopped at the heart of the chamber and surveyed the gathered dragons not as equals or allies, but as instruments awaiting direction.

"E'vahona remains hidden from us," they said, their voice calm and precise. "Denied by design, not by chance."

A low scoff broke the quiet.

Zarathos shifted, gem-bright scales catching the firelight as pride surfaced unchecked.

"Of course it is," he said, disdain threading his tone. "You of all beings should have expected as much."

The cavern stirred subtle movements, exchanged glances, tension tightening.

Zarathos pressed on, emboldened by the stillness.

"An Eladrin stronghold woven into forest and ward?" His gaze flicked briefly toward the shadows. "Hidden by gods and Ancients alike?"

He huffed. "Did you truly believe it would yield to brute will?"

Zylron laughed, a harsh, crackling sound that echoed too loudly in the chamber.

"Even Phoenix failed to uncover it," he added. "Even Vuarus with all his sacrifices."

His molten gaze returned to the Mysterious One. "And yet you believed you would succeed where they did not."

The words hung in the air.

Dangerous.

Accusatory.

For a heartbeat, nothing happened.

Then the temperature dropped.

"Enough."

The command struck like a blade.

Ash lifted from the floor and froze midair. Shadows recoiled as if burned. The Mysterious One turned slowly toward Zylron and Zarathos, their authority hardening into something cold, absolute, and unyielding.

"I did not summon you here," they said evenly, "to indulge arrogance."

Their gaze sharpened.

"Nor to hear history recited by those who failed to learn from it."

Their attention swept the chamber measuring, weighing.

"You will be silent," they continued, "unless addressed."

The cavern obeyed.

Zylron lowered his head a fraction, molten fury compressed into restraint. Zarathos' brilliance dimmed, pride retreating beneath calculation. Even the abyssal presence near Ixalia stilled, sensing the shift.

The Mysterious One turned back toward the center of the chamber.

Control restored.

"E'vahona has not fallen," they said evenly. "Which means it must be pressured."

Their gaze settled on Ixalia not in rebuke, but in expectation.

"And that," they continued, "is why you are all here."

They turned toward the far edge of the formation.

"Glaciera."

The White Dragon lifted her head. Frost crept outward at the sound of her name, lacework ice threading across scorched stone as the cavern's heat recoiled.

"We will increase the pressure," the Mysterious One said calmly. "And we will do it in a way the realm cannot ignore."

A pause followed measured and deliberate. Long enough for every dragon present to feel the recalibration of intent.

"I require the Eladrin girl," they said, their voice precise, "Frozen and removed from Vacari's reach."

Glaciera's lips curved into a slow, satisfied smile.

She dipped her head in a shallow nod. "With pleasure."

Cold surged from her scales. The cavern hissed as frost overtook embers, fire and ice locked briefly in violent disagreement before the chill prevailed.

The Mysterious One continued without inflection.

"This is not the Abyss," they said, their eyes sweeping the gathered dragons. "We are not forcing the realm to choose between her life and its survival."

Mirage-light flickered faintly across Ixalia's expression interest sharpening.

"We are using her," the Mysterious One said, "As a beacon."

The cavern tightened. Attention drew inward like a breath held too long.

"When Keisha is taken," they continued, "they will come."

Names followed like falling stones.

"Kimras.

Amara.

Goldmoor.

The alliance."

Their gaze shifted first toward Ixalia, then back to Glaciera.

"They will tear open sky and forest to retrieve her."

Their voice lowered, certainty absolute.

"And when they move... E'vahona will be forced to react."

The implication settled heavily.

"A hidden realm can deny a hunter," the Mysterious One said softly. "But it cannot ignore the kind of disturbance a rescue creates."

They stepped forward once, ash whispering beneath their feet.

"Not when its people are bound to her."

Silence pressed in.

"We do not require E'vahona's surrender," they concluded.

Their voice dropped quiet, lethal. "We require it to expose itself."

The silence that followed was not uniform.

Ixalia inclined her head, mirage-light flickering with measured approval. Voraxia's shadow deepened receptive and unreadable. Vorathos radiated assent, abyssal energy pulsing like a slow, deliberate heartbeat.

Pressure.

Leverage.

Dominion logic refined.

A low chuckle cut through the silence.

Zylron laughed openly, fire rippling along his scales. "Still a foolish plan," he said bluntly.

The cavern stiffened.

Zylron stepped forward a fraction, molten eyes locked on the Mysterious One.

"You believe a rescue will expose E'vahona?" He snorted. "Phoenix tried to use her once. Vuarus tried. The alliance refused."

His lips pulled back in something grim. "They walked away."

Glaciera's smile faded. Frost crept softly along her jaw as she turned her head.

"What he says is true," she said coolly. "They have endured what should have broken them."

Her pale eyes narrowed. "And one such as you should have known that."

The air grew taut.

The Mysterious One did not flare.

Did not roar.

Did not defend.

They simply regarded them cold, patient, lethal.

"Endurance," they said quietly, "is not the same as stillness."

Their gaze settled first on Zylron.

"They walked away before because there was nothing they could reach. Nothing they could strike. Nothing they could save."

Then their eyes shifted to Glaciera calm as a blade drawn slowly.

"This time," they said, "They will have a location."

A subtle lift of the chin marked the shift.

"A trail.

A lair."

"And when hope believes it can act," the Mysterious One finished smoothly, "hope becomes predictable."

The cavern fell utterly still.

Zylron's molten fissures burned hotter, but he did not speak again.

Glaciera's frost shifted interest rather than obedience.

Malrik stepped forward then, careful and measured.

"What they say of the Abyss is true," he said quietly. "I was there when it collapsed."

He hesitated only a breath.

"If Kimras and Amara had not intervened, the sacrifice might have succeeded. But the alliance did not fracture."

A pause.

"And if we apply the same pressure again," Malrik finished, "we may only harden them further."

The words settled heavily.

The Mysterious One held the silence for a long moment.

Then they nodded once.

Not concession.

Calculation.

"Very well," they said at last.

Glaciera's attention sharpened instantly.

"You will not move," the Mysterious One continued, their voice even and absolute, "until I give the signal."

The message was clear.

This was not doubt.

This was timing.

A subtle shift rippled through the gathered dragons—some relieved, others quietly disappointed.

"Leave," the Mysterious One said. "Return to your lairs. Malrik will receive the final strategy when I am satisfied it cannot fail."

No objections followed.

One by one, the Dominion withdrew.

Voraxia dissolved into shadow without sound. Vorathos tore open a rift of darkness and vanished through it. Ixalia lingered only a heartbeat longer, mirage-light tightening around her form before illusion folded and she was gone.

Zylron departed among the last, wings stirring heat as he left without a word. Glaciera's frost receded reluctantly, her expression carefully unreadable. Xalzorath melted back into the tunnels, while Zarathos' gem-bright scales caught the firelight one final time before he disappeared into the depths of Flameford.

The Cavern of Ash emptied once more.

Only Malrik remained.

The ascent to the tower passed in silence.

Black stones loomed above Flameford, etched with sigils old enough to remember conquest, domination, and long things erased from record. The Mysterious One strode ahead, their pace controlled and measured until the doors sealed behind them.

Then the mask fractured.

Power exploded outward.

Ash and shadow whipped through the chamber, the air itself recoiling. Stones shattered beneath the force of their magic. Runes flared violently, dimmed, then flared again pulsing like a heart losing rhythm.

Malrik did not move.

He stood to the side, hands clasped behind his back, eyes lowered not in submission, but in practiced restraint. He had learned long ago that silence was not obedience.

It was survival.

The outburst burned itself out as suddenly as it had ignited.

Breath steadied.

Power receded.

The chamber stilled.

At last, the Mysterious One straightened.

"We will find another way," they said, their voice cold once more, fury buried but far from extinguished.

"Vacari will fracture. It always does."

They turned to Malrik.

"Go," they ordered. "Consider what remains that we have not yet exploited."

Malrik inclined his head.

"And bring you my ideas?"

"Yes," the Mysterious One replied.

"Every one of them."

Malrik bowed and turned away, already sifting through fault lines, old wounds, and fractures yet to be tested.

Alone again, the Mysterious One gazed out over Flameford, firelight reflecting in eyes that no longer bothered to hide their intent.

E'vahona remained hidden.

But the Dominion had only begun to adapt.

Chapter 26

A Necessary Deception

The veil parted without sound.

Silver light folded inward as Talleoss and Silvara stepped into E'vahona, the hidden realm welcoming them with a hush that felt less like greeting and more like recognition. The shimmer lingered only a heartbeat before the forest reclaimed itself, sealing the passage behind them as though nothing had ever disturbed it.

Here, magic did not pulse or flare.

It breathed.

Ancient trees arched overhead, their leaves catching light that had no visible source, their roots threading through soil saturated with power older than memory. The air carried awareness not watchful, not wary... but present.

The Sacred Grove lay ahead, untouched by time, a place where even thought seemed to slow.

Kadona would be there.

They did not hurry, but neither did they linger. The Grove revealed itself gradually, branches bowing aside as if acknowledging their right to pass. At its heart stood Kadona, her presence woven seamlessly into bark, light, and living earth.

She turned as they approached, her awareness already sharpened.

"You return sooner than expected," she said.

Silvara inclined her head. "Because the danger has grown."

Talleoss stepped forward, wings folding neatly against his sides. "Ixalia has begun searching for E'vahona."

The name rippled through the Grove like a stone across still water.

Kadona's expression darkened. Her gaze lifted toward the canopy, as though the Mirage Dragon's shadow might somehow reach even here.

"She should not have come so close," she said quietly.

"She was denied," Silvara replied. "But she is persistent. And frustration will only sharpen her."

Talleoss' voice remained calm, but warning edged every syllable.

"She has not abandoned the search. Nor will she."

For a long moment Kadona said nothing.

The forest felt it before she spoke.

Roots tightened beneath the Grove. Light dimmed a fraction not in fear, but in response. Her anger surfaced not as flame but as pressure controlled, deliberate, inevitable.

"If E'vahona is discovered," Kadona said at last, "The ancient magic bound here will no longer remain beyond reach. It will be taken. Twisted. Fed to the darkness."

Her gaze returned to the Silvers, resolve hardening into something absolute.

"That cannot be allowed."

She straightened, power gathering subtly around her like a rising tide restrained by will alone.

"This matter reaches beyond guardianship. The Eladrin Council must be informed."

With a single gesture, the Grove answered.

Light lifted. A low resonance spread outward through unseen pathways veins of magic older than roads or gates carrying her summons through E'vahona itself.

"I will call them here," Kadona said.

"What comes next must be decided together."

The forest stilled once more.

And far beyond its hidden borders, a Mirage Dragon continued to search.

The Sacred Grove filled slowly.

Light filtered through the living canopy as the Eladrin Council arrived one by one, their presence shifting the air with quiet authority and ancient grace. Roots parted for them. Blossoms unfurled in recognition. The hum of magic deepened as they formed a wide circle around Kadona.

Talleoss and Silvara remained just beyond the council ring, silver wings folded, watchful and still.

Kadona did not waste time.

She repeated what the Silver Dragons had brought to her: the Mirage Dragon's persistence, her growing frustration, her refusal to abandon the search. As the words settled into the Grove, unease rippled through the gathered Eladrin like wind moving through tall grass.

Lord Karrenen stepped forward, his expression grave.

"This is not like the others," he said. "Dark dragons have skirted our borders before. They have tested wards, sent creatures, whispered threats."

His gaze hardened.

"None of them have hunted E'vahona the way Ixalia has."

A murmur of agreement moved through the council.

"She is methodical," Karrenen continued. "Persistent. And far too curious."

His eyes flicked briefly toward the Silver Dragons before returning to Kadona.

"If she finds E'vahona, she finds more than a city. She finds ancient magic that must never fall into darkness."

Silence followed.

"We cannot allow that," one councilor said quietly.

"No," another agreed. "Never."

Heads nodded around the circle, yet uncertainty lingered.

Agreement was easy.

Solutions were not.

Kadona's expression remained calm, but something sharper gleamed in her eyes.

"Then we must change the game," she said.

Every gaze turned to her.

"We allow Ixalia to find E'vahona."

The reaction was immediate.

"No."

"That cannot be allowed."

"Absolutely not."

"Not E'vahona."

Even Talleoss shifted, silver eyes narrowing, and Silvara turned fully toward Kadona, surprise unmistakable.

Kadona lifted a hand, a trace of wry amusement threading her voice not mockery, but confidence born of foresight.

"Not the true E'vahona," she clarified. "An illusion."

The Grove stilled.

"One crafted carefully enough," Kadona continued, "to convince a Mirage Dragon that she has succeeded. One that reflects not what E'vahona is... but what Ixalia believes it to be."

Understanding began to take shape slow and cautious.

"A false city," Karrenen said, testing the idea.

"A decoy," Kadona replied. "A mirror."

Her smile was measured.

"If Ixalia is determined to find E'vahona, then let her find something worthy of her obsession. Something that draws her gaze away from what must remain untouched."

The Grove fell silent again.

But this time it was not fear that lingered.

It was calculation.

Karrenen's gaze sharpened.

"There is tremendous risk," he said carefully. "If Ixalia discovers the deception—"

"She will retaliate," Kadona finished for him. She inclined her head once. "Yes. The danger is real."

She moved slowly through the Grove as she spoke, her presence steadying the air.

"But consider the alternative. She will not stop searching. Every failure sharpens her focus. Every denial teaches her something."

Kadona turned back to them, her voice quiet but unyielding.

"We can guide her attention ...or we wait until she tears the veil apart herself."

No one spoke.

Then, one by one, the councilors nodded.

Reluctantly.

Grimly.

Talleoss broke the silence.

"If she is to be delayed," he said evenly, "this is the only path that buys us time."

Silvara added softly, "And time is what E'vahona needs."

Karrenen exhaled. "Then we proceed. With caution."

Kadona's expression softened not with relief, but with resolve.

"Then we prepare," she said. "And we do it together."

The Sacred Grove hummed faintly as plans began to take shape quietly, urgently, with full understanding that once set in motion, this deception would draw the Dominion's eye.

And that the calm surrounding E'vahona would not last.

"This must be done properly," Kadona continued. "The illusion must withstand scrutiny magic, instinct, intent."

"I will enlist Lysander," she said. "His mastery of depth and concealment will anchor what must feel ancient."

Talleoss stepped forward.

"We should also call upon Kaelorn. As Warden of the Forests, his power now runs deeper than before. He can bind growth, memory, and presence."

Karrenen nodded.

"And the illusion must be placed between the Emberwoods and the Emerald Woods. Anywhere else, and Ixalia will know."

Kadona smiled faintly.

"Pixies. Fairies. Nymphs. Let them shape what they believe E'vahona to be. Belief gives illusion weight... and permanence."

The plan settled not with enthusiasm, but with resolve.

"This will buy us time," Silvara said quietly.

"And time," Talleoss replied, "is what Vacari needs."

The council dispersed, each member turning toward their task as the Sacred Grove returned to its vigilant hush.

Above them all, E'vahona remained hidden.

But now deliberately so.

Chapter 27

The False Heart of the Forest

The place Kadona chose lay between truths.

Not within the Emberwoods, where flame-tinged leaves whispered of old battles and restless magic, nor within the Emerald Woods, where Verdantia's influence rooted reality too deeply to bend.

It rested instead along a narrow corridor of land where the two forests leaned toward one another, their canopies almost touching, their magics brushing but never fully merging.

Here, the air shimmered faintly, uncertainly.

"This will suffice," Kadona said softly.

She stood at the edge of a natural clearing, its soil pale and undisturbed, as though life itself had chosen not to linger too long. The light fractured strangely here, bending just enough to feel wrong a subtle imperfection that would draw a Mirage Dragon's curiosity rather than her suspicion.

Lysander emerged beside her, the scent of salt and storm preceding him.

Though far from sea or shore, he carried the quiet authority of tides.

His gaze swept the land, measuring not distance, but depth.

"It is far enough," he said, "yet near enough to echo what she has already sensed."

Kadona's expression remained taut.

"Ixalia will not abandon the search," she said. "She is too invested. If we deny her entirely, she will claw at the veil until something gives."

"And so," Lysander replied evenly, "we allow her to find something."

Kadona closed her eyes and pressed her palm to the earth.

Power stirred not violently, not forcibly but with careful precision. Ancient magic flowed through her, not summoned, but remembered, as though the land itself recognized her right to shape what lay upon it.

"This must feel real," she murmured. "Not merely seen... but believed."

Lysander stepped forward, lifting one hand as moisture gathered in the air despite the forest's dryness. The humidity thickened, carrying not the presence of water, but the memory of it—the pressure of unseen depths rather than surface reflection.

"I will anchor the illusion," he said. "Not with water, but with depth. Even a mirage must reflect something."

Together, they wove the deception.

The ground shifted not physically, but perceptually. Paths seemed to curve where none existed. Stone took on the suggestion of age. Light filtered downward in deliberate patterns, forming the illusion of ancient passageways long forgotten by time.

At the clearing's heart, Kadona traced a sigil older than written language.

A portal bloomed into existence.

It did not flare or roar.

It opened quietly so quietly it felt as though it had always been there.

Beyond it lay suggestion rather than certainty: arched silhouettes, pale structures half-veiled in mist, hints of a city shaped by reverence, restraint, and devotion.

A convincing echo of E'vahona.

Kadona studied it in silence, her expression unreadable.

"This will draw her," she said at last. "And when she steps through, she will believe she has won."

Lysander's gaze hardened slightly.

"And we will gain time."

Kadona nodded once.

"Time is all we are asking for."

The portal stabilized, humming softly hidden, patient, waiting.

And somewhere beyond the forests, a Mirage Dragon continued her search, unaware that the answer she sought was being carefully prepared to mislead her.

The illusion did not rise all at once.

It grew.

Under Kadona's guidance and Lysander's steady influence, the space between the Emberwoods and the Emerald Woods began to change not abruptly, but organically as though the land itself were remembering something it had never truly been.

The Eladrin Council moved with quiet precision.

Ancient magic flowed from their hands into the waiting earth, shaping walkways of pale stone that curved naturally between emerging clearings. The paths were etched with faint runes softened, weathered, deliberately uneven symbols that suggested age, purpose, and sacred intent rather than pristine design.

Bridges arched over shallow ravines where none had existed before, their spans elegant but imperfect, worn just enough to imply centuries of passage by uncounted feet.

Structures followed.

Not constructed but grown.

Halls and dwellings unfolded from root and stone alike, their forms blending seamlessly into bark and branch, mineral and soil. Walls leaned where they should. Stairways narrowed unexpectedly. Windows caught light at odd angles, as though designed by generations rather than a single hand.

They were not exact replicas of E'vahona, but they were close.

Close enough to feel convincing. Close enough to suggest a hidden Eladrin city shaped by time, reverence, and restraint the sort of place one would expect to exist precisely because it had never been meant to be found.

Kadona watched the weave intently, adjusting threads where necessary.

"It must feel lived in," she reminded them softly. "Not perfect. Never perfect."

At her signal, the nymphs stepped forward.

They sang to the soil, their voices coaxing life upward in waves of color and scent. Trees unfurled with deliberate asymmetry, their branches twisting as though shaped by ancient enchantments and forgotten storms. Leaves caught the light unevenly, suggesting spells layered upon spells, some fading, some renewed.

Flowers bloomed in abundance some luminous, some subtle spilling along pathways and clustering at the bases of dwellings as though they had always belonged there.

Animals answered the call.

Deer moved cautiously into the forming glades, ears flicking as though wary of memories they could not name. Birds settled into newly shaped branches, their songs threading through the air, stitching sound into the illusion. Even insects appeared beetles, moths, dragonflies—lending movement, rhythm, and breath to the space.

Life made the illusion believable.

Meanwhile, pixies worked where others could not or would not.

Invisible to most eyes, they darted through corridors and courtyards, weaving mischief into the city's foundation. Paths looped where they should not. Open doorways led into harmless but disorienting mazes. Light bent at corners subtly enough to unsettle instinct.

One pixie hovered near a newly shaped plaza, sealing the final thread of a secondary maze beneath the stone. She grinned to herself.

"She'll love this," she whispered.

Above it all, the fairies layered beauty like a final veil.

They intensified the bloom of flowers until the air shimmered with pollen and light. Petals drifted endlessly, catching on unseen currents. Soft glows lingered along walls and branches, giving the illusion a welcoming radiance the precise sort of gentle enchantment a Mirage Dragon would expect from a city steeped in ancient magic.

By the time they finished, the space no longer felt created.

It felt discovered.

Kadona closed her eyes briefly, sensing the weave settle, the illusion anchoring itself not in spellwork alone, but in belief.

"It will deceive her," she said at last. "At least for a time."

Far away still searching, still unsatisfied Ixalia's shifting opal gaze would soon fall upon exactly what she believed she had been hunting all along.

The forest stirred as Kaelorn arrived.

He did not descend from the sky nor step from any visible path. One moment the space between two ancient trees stood empty then it did not. The air bent inward, leaves whispering as though acknowledging an authority older than direction or distance.

The Forestborne Warden inclined his head once to Kadona.

"You will need this place to resist discovery," he said calmly. "Not hidden resistant."

Kadona's lips curved in quiet approval.

"Exactly."

Kaelorn lifted his hands, and the forest answered.

Paths folded subtly upon themselves. Clearings narrowed, then widened again depending on the angle from which they were viewed. Trails led forward only to circle back, while others vanished entirely unless approached with intent rather than sight.

This was not illusion alone.

It was misdirection layered with a living will.

"Let her search," Kaelorn continued. "Let her believe she is close. The nearer she thinks she is, the more certain she will become."

"And the harder it will be for her to accept doubt," Kadona replied.

He nodded once.

"That is the danger of certainty."

The forest settled into its new shape familiar enough to feel plausible, treacherous enough to delay even a Mirage Dragon. It did not resist her directly.

It simply refused to cooperate.

Above the false city, silver light began to gather.

Talleoss and Silvara circled once, their wings glinting as ancient magic threaded between them. Together they shaped a hidden entrance one not meant for the Dominion's eyes.

A veil of moonlight and frost settled into the air, forming a passage only those bound to silver truth could perceive.

"Our riders will need swift access," Silvara said quietly. "If Ixalia brings her mirage brood, subtlety will fail quickly."

Talleoss inclined his head.

"This is not meant to endure forever. Only long enough."

"Long enough," Silvara agreed, "to drive them away."

The entrance was sealed not closed, but waiting.

Below, the false E'vahona stood complete.

Its towers shimmered with believable age. Its walkways bore the marks of long use. Trees whispered with borrowed memory. Flowers bloomed with deliberate beauty.

And beneath glamour and grace, unseen traps waited.

It was not real.

But it was convincing.

Kadona surveyed the work in silence, then exhaled slowly.

"This will draw her," she said. "And when it does, the game changes."

The forest answered with a low, knowing murmur.

Somewhere between the Emberwoods and the Emerald Woods, a lie took root.

And the Dominion would come knocking.

Chapter 28

Before All Fires Fall

The temple beneath Flameford breathed with old heat and older malice.

Malrik moved through its depths alone, boots echoing softly against blackened stone as emberlight pulsed along the carved walls. The chamber he had chosen was lined with relics—fractured runes, scorched altars, remnants of strategies abandoned or broken.

This was where failures were entombed.

And where new ones were born.

He stopped before a stone table etched with sigils of binding and sacrifice, fingers resting lightly against its surface. The Dominion was pressing too hard. He could feel it in every failed maneuver, every repelled advance.

Force had failed.

Threats had failed.

Repetition had failed.

Which meant the solution could not be strength alone.

Slowly, carefully, an idea began to take shape.

Not immediate. Not clean.

But effective.

Malrik straightened, a thin smile touching his mouth as realization settled. He turned without hesitation, ascending from the temple's depths toward the tower above.

The doors parted at his approach, heat and shadow folding inward as he entered.

The Mysterious One stood near the far window, her silhouette cut sharply against Flameford's molten glow. She did not turn, though Malrik knew she had sensed him long before he spoke.

"I have an idea," he said carefully, stopping several paces away. "One that may help us deal with the noble dragons... and their riders."

Her attention sharpened.

"Particularly," he added, "Keisha."

At that, she turned.

Her gaze locked onto him cold, measuring, lethal.

"It had better be worth the interruption," she said softly.

She stepped closer, her voice lowering into something far more dangerous.

"Because if it is not, the creature you have been so diligently feeding will experience a change in its meal schedule."

The threat was not hurried.

It did not need to be.

Malrik did not flinch.

"I believe," he said evenly, "it will be worth your attention."

She studied him for a long moment, then gestured sharply.

"Speak."

Malrik inclined his head once.

"The difficulty is not the noble dragons themselves," he said, choosing each word with care. "It is that they never stand alone."

Her eyes darkened.

"You tell me nothing new," she snapped. "They protect one another. Their riders interfere. This is common knowledge."

Power tightened around the chamber like a closing fist.

"Perhaps," she said coldly, "the creature beneath the temple will have a different sort of meal after all."

Malrik felt the blood drain from his face.

For the briefest instant, his thoughts betrayed him slipping downward into the lightless depths beneath the stone. Into the place where something vast and patient waited. Something that had learned to expect specific offerings.

The memory of its hunger twisted his stomach.

He swallowed hard.

Then, forcing himself upright, Malrik raised his head.

"Listen to me," he said quickly. "Please."

She stopped.

Not out of mercy.

Out of curiosity.

Malrik seized the opening.

"They do not choose to help one another," he said. "They cannot help it. Their alliances are instinctive immediate. There is no hesitation. No calculation."

He drew a steady breath.

"That is the flaw."

Silence followed.

She did not interrupt.

She waited.

Malrik knew this was his only chance.

"If the problem is that the noble dragons and their riders always come to one another's aid," he continued carefully, "then the solution is simple."

Her expression did not change.

"We deny them the chance."

He let the words settle.

"We strike everywhere at once."

He stepped forward now, confidence threading into his voice.

"If coordinated attacks erupt across Vacari simultaneously, the noble dragons will be forced to remain where they are. They will have no choice but to defend their own lands."

Her fingers stilled against the arm of the chair.

"For example," Malrik continued, "if Goldmoor is attacked and Zylron and Glaciera strike together then Amara and Kimras, along with Ong and Keisha, will be locked into its defense."

He met her gaze.

"They will not be able to leave."

The silence deepened.

"And if those attacks are synchronized," he pressed on, "pressure applied in every major region, then no dragon will be able to reinforce another."

He gestured as though mapping the world between them.

"The Topaz and Mirage dragons will face Copper and Silver alone. Not Gold. Not Celestial. Not the full alliance."

A pause.

"Divide them," Malrik said quietly, "and their greatest strength becomes their greatest weakness."

The chamber fell utterly still.

The Mysterious One leaned back slowly, her expression unreadable as the implications unfolded.

For the first time since Malrik had entered the tower, she did not respond with anger.

She considered.

The silence stretched long enough for doubt to creep in.

Then she laughed.

Low at first. Controlled.

Then sharper. Satisfied.

"Perfect," she said.

She rose and turned toward him.

"Send the orders."

Malrik bowed deeply.

"Zylron and Glaciera will focus their assault on Goldmoor," she commanded. "And Glaciera is to do everything within her power to freeze the Eladrin."

Her smile thinned.

"Nocturna and Xalzorath will strike Crystal Vale."

She paced slowly.

"Voraxia and Vorathos will deal with Lyra'el."

Her gaze hardened.

"Zarathos will hit the Emberwoods."

She stopped.

"And Ixalia," she said quietly, "will find E'vahona and deal with the Silver Dragons."

Malrik nodded, committing every word to memory.

She turned away without dismissal or farewell.

High above Flameford, the Dominion's strategy shifted.

Not through brute force.

But through division.

Chapter 29

When the World Holds Its Breath

The Dominion Moves as One

The chamber of obsidian and ember lay in perpetual twilight, as though the world itself feared to intrude upon the audience taking place within. Black stone pillars coiled upward like the spines of slumbering beasts, their surfaces slick with shadow and old magic. Veins of molten crimson pulsed through the floor in slow, deliberate rhythm as if the mountain possessed a heart, and it beat in obedience to the will seated upon the throne.

Malrik knelt at the edge of the platform, one gauntleted fist pressed against scorched stone. The air tasted of sulfur and storm.

"It is done," he said.

The figure upon the throne did not move.

Light refused to settle upon them, bending instead around their silhouette as though even illumination dared not reveal what it served.

Only the faintest glimmer like dying starlight trapped in smoke outlined the suggestion of a crown that was no crown at all.

"All of them have been reached," Malrik continued. "Each dark ancient. Each warlord of shadow and flame. They have received their orders... and accepted the call."

A thin current of unseen power passed through the chamber, lifting ash from the floor and tugging at Malrik's cloak. The figure leaned forward only slightly but the pressure in the air sharpened instantly.

"And the timing?" the voice asked.

It did not echo.

It settled inside the mind, inside the bones.

Malrik's lips curved with something between reverence and hunger.

"They will strike as one."

He lifted his gaze, eyes burning now with conviction.

"No staggered assaults. No solitary campaigns. Each dragon will advance in concert, so the noble ones are drawn apart isolated within their own skies, their own territories, their own fires."

He exhaled slowly.

"By the time they understand what is happening..." His voice lowered, measured and satisfied. "...there will be no one left to answer their calls for aid."

Silence stretched.

Then the figure upon the throne inclined their head.

A single, deliberate nod.

The molten veins beneath the chamber flared brighter, responding to the decision as though the mountain itself acknowledged the turning of the age.

"Proceed," the figure said.

Malrik bowed lower, the weight of destiny settling across his shoulders like a mantle of war.

"As you will," he replied.

And in distant realms in caverns of frost and fire, in forests choked with rot, in peaks crowned by thunder the dark dragons stirred.

The sky was about to fracture.

The Emberwoods Targeted

The peaks of Etharyon thundered beneath a sky the color of old bruises, lightning winding through the clouds like living veins. Wind howled between jagged spires of crystal and blackened stone, carrying the scent of ozone and scorched earth.

High upon a fractured throne carved from crystal and slag, Zarathos unfurled his colossal form.

His scales burned with molten amber and fractured gold once a gem dragon of brilliance, now fallen into pride and fire, crowned in ruin. Heat bled from him in relentless waves, warping the air itself.

Around him gathered the Topaz brood.

Their wings folded like shattered suns. Their eyes gleamed with molten greed. Stone beneath their talons softened, scorched smooth by their presence alone.

Zarathos's voice cracked across the mountain.

"Emberwoods."

The word carried the promise of conquest.

"That forest is no mere stretch of land," he continued, talons carving molten channels through the rock. "It is a living defense. A labyrinth of ancient enchantments copper-born, fae-bound, woven into root and flame."

His wings flexed, scattering sparks.

"You will unmake it. Every vine. Every ward. Every whispering root. Reduce the maze to ash."

A low, eager rumble passed through the gathered dragons.

"And the Copper Ancients," Zarathos snarled, heat flaring brighter along his fractured scales. "Slay them. Hunt them until the sky itself runs molten."

His gaze hardened.

"Especially Raelithar."

The name fell like a blade.

"The riderless warden who hides among pixies and mockery. His death will be the signal proof that even forests kneel before the Dominion."

One of the younger Topaz dragons hissed, embers leaking from its jaws.

"The Warden remains."

Zarathos's eyes narrowed.

"Kaelorn," he said. "The Forestborne Warden."

He spat the name like a curse carved in sap and blood.

"Each forest bends to him differently. He speaks the old language of roots the hidden veins of soil and storm. If he interferes, the maze will regrow. The Copper will scatter. Our assault will fracture."

Zarathos leaned forward, vast and crushing, his presence bowing the storm itself.

"You will find him."

Silence pressed in.

"You will destroy him."

The mountain groaned beneath the weight of his will.

"Burn the forests around him if you must but he cannot be permitted to survive."

The brood bowed as one.

Heads lowered. Wings stilled.

Silence fell thick and expectant.

"Our forces are aligned," Zarathos said at last. "Routes mapped. Targets chosen. Flames prepared."

He lifted his gaze toward the storm-choked horizon.

"All that remains..."

Lightning split the heavens.

"...is the signal."

And Zarathos waited.

The Siege of Lyra'el

Far above the reach of mortal winds where clouds thinned into silver vapor and stars shimmered like watchful eyes the floating city of Lyra'el drifted in solemn defiance of gravity and time. Towers of pale crystal and living stone glowed with restrained celestial radiance, suspended upon ancient currents of magic that whispered of covenants long forgotten.

And beyond its light darkness gathered.

Voraxia emerged first.

The Shadow Dragon coiled through the firmament like a living eclipse, her vast form swallowing starlight as though it had never existed. Night clung to her scales not as absence, but as obedience. Her wings did not beat; they spread in silence, wide enough to veil constellations and still the heavens themselves.

Beside her descended Vorathos.

The Abyssal Dragon was immense and terrible, her form rippling with deep-sea darkness and ancient hunger. Where Voraxia embodied shadow, Vorathos carried depth the crushing weight of endless voids, drowned empires, and pressures meant to erase memory itself. The echo of things that should never have survived the abyss lingered around her like a curse.

They hovered upon unseen currents, gazing down upon Lyra'el.

"This time," Voraxia said, her voice threading directly into Vorathos's mind, smooth and merciless, "we do not fail."

Vorathos's eyes burned like suns smothered beneath black water.

"We will not be reinforced," she replied. "No hidden legions. No second chances."

Voraxia's gaze sharpened, fixed upon the distant shimmer of celestial wards.

"Aurelius is mine," she said. "The Celestial's light has lingered too long above this world."

Vorathos's claws flexed slowly.

"Then Radiantus falls to me," she answered. "Platinum healer. Guardian of the broken."

A low, abyssal resonance followed her words.

"I will drown his radiance in the deep."

Voraxia inclined her head acknowledgment without warmth.

"Do not underestimate their riders," she warned. "The Platinum bonds are... inconvenient. Their unity disrupts clean annihilation."

Vorathos's mouth curved into something between a smile and a snarl.

"Then we sever the bonds."

Below them, Lyra'el drifted serene and luminous its crystal terraces gleaming, its bells silent, its wards steady.

Unaware of the storm sharpening its claws in the dark.

The two Ancients turned their gaze toward the distant horizon, where fate gathered its breath.

"Await the signal," Voraxia said.

And they waited.

The Fall of Crystal Vale

Deep beneath a sky choked with ash and drifting cinders, where the earth fractured into towering crystal spires and emerald-veined cliffs, the horizon of Crystal Vale shimmered like a wound of living light.

It should have been beautiful.

Instead, it burned.

Beyond that radiance, two ancient horrors circled one another in the dark.

Nocturna hovered like a living shard of night, her obsidian form cutting through the air with unnerving stillness. Her scales drank in every trace of illumination, swallowing reflection and glow alike until even starlight seemed to die upon her hide. When her wings moved, they did so without sound—the quiet fall of unseen stars.

Cold, meticulous malice burned within her gaze.

Opposite her coiled Xalzorath.

The Black Dragon's immense form glistened with a corrosive sheen, fumes of poison and rot curling from his scales in slow, venomous spirals. Where Nocturna was restrained, Xalzorath had appetite. Old fury smoldered in his eyes, untempered and eager, as though every breath carried the promise of ruin.

Nocturna spoke first.

"Crystal Vale will break."

Her talons scraped faintly through the air as she angled her head toward the distant glow, her focus narrowing with surgical intent.

"Aurelia is mine," she continued. "The Crystal Dragon and her rider Prince Gailen, with that crystal bow. Their bond sustains the Vale's defenses. When they fall, the spires will fracture from within."

Behind her, obsidian-winged shapes shifted her brood, silent and poised, awaiting direction rather than encouragement.

"They will hunt the remaining crystal dragons," Nocturna said. "Strip the Vale of its guardians. I will carve out the heart."

Xalzorath's jaws parted in a slow, corrosive grin.

"Then Verdantia is mine."

The name dripped with venom.

"I still owe her," he growled. "And her rider Thalorian. That moon-elf who dared stain my sky with emerald fire."

His wings flexed, rot sizzling faintly where shadow met air.

"When I am finished, my black dragons will cleanse the rest of the emerald brood from the Vale."

Nocturna inclined her head once acknowledgment, not trust.

"Do not fail."

Xalzorath's wings spread wider, the air itself corroding beneath their span.

"I do not forget."

Silence followed.

Not the silence of uncertainty but of inevitability.

The planning was complete.

The targets chosen.

Hatred honed into weaponry.

Now there was only the waiting.

The Mirage Finds Its Prize

Far away, across realms and skies, the world held its breath.

Between the breathing magics of the Emerald Woods and the Emberwoods where reality thinned into shimmering distortion and the air hummed with unseen boundaries something ancient shifted.

The veil trembled.

Ixalia, the Mirage Dragon, hovered within that fracture of worlds, her immense form rippling like heat above desert glass. Her scales refracted light into a thousand false hues, each bending perception, each whispering suggestion into the fabric of the sky.

Where her wings passed, certainty unraveled.

Memory softened.

Truth hesitated.

She had felt it first.

A resonance beneath enchantment.

A pulse beneath patience.

A rhythm woven too deliberately to be coincidence.

And she had followed it.

"There," Ixalia murmured.

Before her, half-seen and half-imagined, the threshold revealed itself an unseen crossing masked by forest-born secrecy and ancient silvered wards. Not fully present. Not fully absent.

E'vahona.

The hidden realm of silver.

Her opalescent eyes flared with predatory triumph.

At once the mirage-call unfurled silent, instantaneous threaded through the illusion-bond of her brood. Across distant skies and fractured reflections of the world, Mirage Dragons answered, their awareness folding inward toward her signal.

It is found, Ixalia told them. *E'vahona lies open.*

Excited ripples of thought surged back, sharpened by anticipation and hunger.

Wait, she commanded. *Remain beyond the veil. When the signal comes, the silver will fall.*

She circled the threshold slowly, savoring the moment.

The way the air resisted her just enough to feel ancient.

The way the forest's magic recoiled subtle, restrained as though bracing for exposure rather than intrusion.

"How carefully they hid you," Ixalia murmured, admiration threading her voice like a blade wrapped in velvet. "And how futile."

Her wings angled, shadow and light folding inward.

"Do not underestimate the Silver Ancients," she warned, her voice sliding through the bond like silk drawn across glass. "Their minds are mirrors. They break what they cannot deceive."

A pause.

Then, with absolute confidence:

"Leave Talleoss and Silvara to me."

The forest sighed around her not wind, not movement, but something deeper. A sound of roots settling. Of memory choosing stillness. As though something older than illusion had felt the passing of a blade... and declined to react.

Now all fronts were set.

All claws poised.

All lies prepared.

And Ixalia like the others scattered across the tightening heavens waited for the signal, certain she had found the truth, unaware she stood at the threshold of a lie designed for her alone.

The Frozen Claim

Far to the north, where the world surrendered to frost and silence, the glaciers of Firornak groaned beneath a sky of pale steel. Ancient ice shifted and complained like a thing half awake, its slow movement echoing through valleys that had never known warmth—and never would again.

Within a cathedral of ice older than empires, Glaciera stirred.

Her white dragons answered her summons at once, vast wings carving slow, deliberate spirals through the frozen air. Snow lifted in shimmering sheets as they gathered, their forms pale and merciless against the storm, eyes bright with obedience and hunger.

"Go," Glaciera commanded, her voice cutting cleanly through the blizzard. "Find Zylron. Align our forces. I will follow."

They obeyed without hesitation, dissolving into the white fury beyond the peaks, leaving the glacier eerily still.

Glaciera remained.

She descended deeper into her lair, where the ice glowed with an inner moonlight and the walls sang softly with trapped winds. Here, frost did not merely exist—it listened. It remembered every scream ever stolen by the cold, every heartbeat stilled too soon.

With careful precision, she shaped it.

Spires rose at her will, flawless and merciless. A platform of crystal formed beneath her claws, ringed with frozen runes and layered wards that hummed with restraint, containment, dominion.

This was not a place of battle.

It was a place of claiming.

A throne.

"This will suffice," Glaciera whispered.

In her mind's eye, she saw it already Keisha encased in perfect, unmelting ice. Breath suspended. Firebound spirit preserved, not extinguished, not freed.

A living monument to inevitability.

A victory no rescue could undo.

"My prize," she murmured.

Satisfied, she turned and took to the sky.

Zylron's domain burned at the edge of the world, volcanoes vomiting smoke and molten rivers into churning clouds. When Glaciera arrived, frost and flame collided in a scream that split stone and sky alike, steam boiling upward in violent spirals.

Zylron's eyes narrowed as she descended.

"You are late."

Glaciera did not answer.

He snorted ash and embers, wings flexing.

"I will handle Kimras myself," he said. "You take Amara."

Glaciera inclined her head. "Agreed."

Then her gaze hardened, ice sharpening into command.

"But the elf is mine. Do not kill her."

Zylron's fire flared dangerously, molten fissures blazing brighter across his scales.

"She rides an Ancient Gold," he growled. "I will do what is required."

"You will dislodge her," Glaciera replied, voice precise and unyielding. "Nothing more."

For a long moment the volcano roared between them fire and ice locked in hostile stalemate, neither yielding, neither forgetting old grudges.

Zylron's jaw tightened.

At last, he gave a single, curt nod.

"Very well. But you keep Ong and Amara away from him. If they interfere, everything fractures."

Glaciera's wings spread, scattering frost across burning stone. "They will not."

The last of the agreements settled into place like locked blades.

Across realms across skies and forests and floating cities the dark dragons had chosen their targets. Lines were drawn. Paths set. Intent sharpened into inevitability.

The world trembled beneath the weight of what was about to begin.

And so they waited.

Every Ancient.

Every brood.

Every claw raised in the hush before ruin.

Waiting.

For the signal.

Chapter 30

Emberwoods remembers

The Emberwoods breathed uneasily.

Its ancient canopy whispered not with wind alone, but with memory old pain threading through bark and root, a scar the forest had never truly forgotten. Shafts of amber light pierced the towering leaves, illuminating drifting motes of pollen and the soft glow of pixie wings as the smallest guardians of the realm gathered within a copper-lit glade.

Their voices trembled like chimes caught in a storm.

“The forest remembers,” one pixie whispered, her wings flickering pale blue with worry.

“It still aches,” another said softly. “From when Vuarus and the Phoenix twisted it. From when it was forced to become something it was never meant to be.”

A hush followed.

They all remembered the corruption, the blackened roots, the screaming trees, the way the Emberwoods had writhed beneath a will not its own. Though the enchantment had been broken, though healing had come, the wound had never vanished entirely.

"Will it protect us?" a young pixie asked, voice small. "When the dark comes... will it answer?"

High above, copper wings folded.

Raelithar descended in a hush of wind and falling leaves, his massive form settling among the ancient trunks with reverent care. Copper dragons followed, their burnished scales catching the forest light like living flame.

Their presence brought comfort but not certainty.

Raelithar lowered his great head, eyes glowing with thoughtful concern.

"The forest is strong," he said. "But strength does not mean unscarred."

His gaze moved across the Emberwoods, reading its ancient language in every root and shadow.

"What was done here cut deeper than bark," he continued. "Corruption does not simply fade. It lingers. It changes how the forest answers when it is called."

The pixies exchanged uneasy glances.

"Then it might fail us?" one asked.

Raelithar did not lie.

"It might hesitate," he said quietly. "Not in weakness but in memory."

Silence settled again heavy and listening.

At last, Raelithar lifted his head.

"There is one who will know," he said. "One who hears forests the way others hear their own heartbeat."

The copper dragons inclined their heads as one.

"Kaelorn," Raelithar said.

The name carried weight prayer and warning intertwined.

"We go to him," he continued. "We bring this worry to the Forestborne Warden himself."

And so the decision was made.

Above them, unseen by any eye, the sky was already sharpening its claws.

They found Kaelorn where the Emberwood Maze began to breathe.

The living labyrinth coiled across the forest floor in slow, deliberate motion, its walls of ember-veined bark shifting like thoughtful giants, rearranging the forest's heartbeat. Kaelorn stood at its threshold, cloak threaded with leaves from a hundred realms, his staff rooted in the soil as though he himself were part of the land.

The pixies rushed him at once.

"The forest is frightened"

"It remembers the darkness"

"It may not protect us"

"Something feels wrong"

Kaelorn listened without interrupting, a gentle smile touching his lips.

Copper wind descended.

Raelithar landed in a quiet thunder of leaves and shifting roots, lowering his great head toward Kaelorn in greeting. He chuckled softly at the frantic storm of pixie voices.

"One at a time, little flames," he said kindly. "The Warden hears better when the forest is not shouting."

The pixies fell into embarrassed silence.

Raelithar's expression turned solemn.

"They fear the old wound," he told Kaelorn. "What the Emberwoods became during the corruption. They wonder if damage still lingers beneath the healing."

Kaelorn's smile faded into thought. He nodded.

"That is... very possible."

He lifted his staff, green-gold light whispering through the wood as he called softly,

"Aeralinde."

The air shimmered.

From between the shifting maze walls emerged Aeralinde, the Pegasus forest-spirit, her form woven of living light, leaves, and ancient breath.

Kaelorn knelt, pressing his palms to the soil.

Aeralinde bowed her luminous head, hooves sinking into the earth as the forest's magic stirred.

For a long while, nothing moved.

Then the forest exhaled.

Roots murmured. Leaves shivered. Memories opened like pages turned by unseen hands.

When Kaelorn finally lifted his head, his eyes carried the weight of centuries.

"The forest still hurts," he said gently. "But not with pain alone. It is... confused."

The pixies drifted closer.

"It remembers when it was only beauty," Kaelorn continued. "When it gave freely of shelter, color, and song. Then it was twisted into something cruel. Used to harm Keisha the one the forests chose."

The name rippled through the glade like falling rain.

"And though it was returned to itself," he said, tightening his grip on the soil, "the scars remain."

Raelithar's gaze stayed steady.

"Can we help it?" he asked.

Kaelorn smiled.

"Yes," he said. "But it will require all of you."

A pixie hovered forward.

"Should we call Keisha?"

Kaelorn shook his head.

"The forest remembers her. What it needs now is to remember itself."

The Emberwoods leaned closer, listening.

"Go," Kaelorn told the pixies.

They scattered like living sparks, weaving memory and light into every hollow, every wounded root, every place the forest still held its breath.

Raelithar lifted his head and released a low, resonant call.

The copper dragons answered.

One by one they lifted into the canopy, fanning out across the forest settling where the magic ran thin and the scars whispered loudest.

When the guardians encircled the Emberwoods, Kaelorn stepped forward alone.

He knelt.

Hands pressed into the soil like a healer against an old friend's heart.

Above him, Aeralinde rose beneath the canopy, her hooves glowing silver-green as she became the forest's beacon.

Kaelorn closed his eyes.

And he remembered.

The ritual did not roar.

It remembered.

And in remembering, it began to heal.

Hours passed.

Roots loosened.

Branches sighed.

Old magic surfaced slow and warm, like sunlight rediscovered.

Pixies poured their light into the soil. Copper dragons threaded courage through bark and stone. And Kaelorn spoke of Keisha of reverence, grief, and healing. Of love freely given, and fiercely defended.

The Emberwoods remembered her.

It remembered itself.

When Kaelorn rose at last, his smile was quiet and confident.

With a gesture he called the guardians back. Pixies and dragons gathered as Aeralinde descended, her presence shining like dawn through the leaves.

"The forest remembers," Kaelorn said.

"And when the darkness comes again... the Emberwoods will stand with you."

Above them, the canopy stirred not with fear, but with resolve.

And the forest prepared not merely to endure...but to fight.

Chapter 31

The Silver Accord

E'vahona lay wrapped in silver hush.

Mist curled between ancient trees and crystal-veined hills, drifting like breath from the sleeping heart of the realm. Above, the sky shimmered with soft luminescence, as though the stars themselves had stooped closer to listen.

Within the council grove, Lord Karrenen stood at the center of the gathered Eladrin and the silver-bonded riders. His gaze moved between the towering forms of Talleoss and Silvara steady, but grave.

"The mirage dragons will find E'vahona," he said quietly. "Ixalia already hunts its edges. When she does, she will bring the storm."

Talleoss inclined his great silver head.

"Then we meet her prepared."

"More than prepared," Karrenen replied. "We must let her believe we are not."

Silvara's eyes gleamed with understanding.

"There is an outer reach to E'vahona," Karrenen continued, gesturing toward the western rise. "The echo-realm. The forest there was shaped to mislead intruders. Let the silver train within it. Let them grow accustomed to shifting light, false horizons, and the way the land bends beneath expectation. When the mirage comes, the deception will not feel unfamiliar."

Talleoss' voice rolled like distant bells.

"A mirror for a mirror."

Karrenen nodded.

"And while they prepare, a handful of us will draw her gaze."

He turned to the Eladrin gathered at the grove's edge.

"We will approach the hidden threshold openly. We will linger. We will speak as though we do not know we are being watched. Then when we believe ourselves unseen we will pass through the true entrance."

A faint smile touched Silvara's lips.

"She will follow with her eyes."

"Let her," Talleoss rumbled. "Let her believe she has uncovered what was never meant to be seen."

The decision settled like falling snow.

The silver dragons and their riders moved first.

Wings unfurled as they entered the concealed passage leading toward the echo-reaches of E'vahona's outer veil. Their departure left only rippling light and quiet certainty behind.

Moments later, Lord Karrenen and a small group of Eladrin stepped into the open glade. Their movements were unhurried, their voices low, their caution carefully performed.

Beyond sight.

Beyond sound.

Within the shimmer of bent reality. Ixalia watched.

Her eyes glowed with mirrored starlight as she observed the Eladrin linger... hesitate... then vanish through the concealed threshold.

She did not move.

She did not signal.

Not yet.

The signal had not come.

Beyond the hidden passage, the Silver Ancients and their riders emerged into the echo-reaches of E'vahona, where certainty softened and the land itself seemed to dream.

Here, hills flowed like frozen mist. Distance bent and blurred, horizons shimmering as though the world could not quite remember its own shape.

Silver dragons spread their wings, luminous scales casting waves of moonfire through the haze. Their riders moved among them with effortless harmony—bonds forged over centuries requiring no command, no spoken word, only shared breath and instinct.

"This is not training," one Eladrin murmured softly. "It is remembrance of how truth feels when illusion begins to bend it."

They did not rehearse battle not truly.

Instead, they reacquainted themselves with the land. They traced paths that shifted beneath their feet, learning the angles of light, the way sound traveled strangely, the places where illusion might root itself if left unchallenged.

Spellweaver staffs were brought forth enchanted wood crowned with glowing runes. Designed by Kaelorn's hand as instruments of balance, they sang here in silver harmony. Wind, ward, and flame were woven into veils of protection, tested against the echo-realm's shifting breath.

The silver dragons answered with reflections of their own power, countering false skies with calm, anchored truth.

Talleoss glided low across the shifting fields, his rider keeping pace in flawless rhythm.

Silvara rose into the silver haze, her presence anchoring the drifting landscape with quiet authority.

"Remember this ground," Talleoss' voice echoed. "When the mirage comes, the land itself will attempt to deceive you."

"We will not be strangers to it," his rider replied.

Hours passed in measured silence and shimmering light.

By the time the silver host finally came to rest, the echo-realm no longer felt uncertain beneath their feet.

It felt like home.

When orientation was complete, Lord Karrenen stepped forward once more. Two Eladrin attendants followed, bearing relics wrapped in layers of living silk and starlight thread.

"E'vahona has kept its oldest covenant for you," Karrenen said, inclining his head to Lady Seraphina.

The wrappings were drawn back.

The air itself stilled as though the realm recognized what had been returned.

Argentis Aethern emerged in Seraphina's hands, moon-silverwood gleaming as though frost and starlight had learned to breathe together. Its runes whispered with ancient resonance, and the crystalline focus at its crown pulsed brighter as Talleoss lowered his vast head in reverence.

The staff answered him.

Across the glade, Karrenen turned to Lord Thaldir. "And for you."

Luminara Virell unfurled, its silversage heartwood glowing with pearl radiance. Delicate emerald currents drifted through its living grain, and the crystal blossom at its crown pulsed softly as Silvara's wings shimmered in reply.

No ceremony followed.

No speeches.

Only understanding.

Seraphina and Thaldir stepped back into the field. Silver dragons rose with them. Magic flowed.

Argentis Aethern lifted, argent resonance thickening the air as protective veils formed and reformed in perfect harmony with Talleoss' power.

Luminara Virell was planted, and a wave of luminous calm spread outward, steadying every heartbeat within its reach as Silvara's presence deepened the field.

Around them, the remaining Eladrin riders and Silver Ancients moved into formation, testing bonds, wards, and unity.

At the echo-realm's edges, Lord Karrenen and his mages selected anchor points places where ley-currents folded close to the surface. Crystals were placed. Sigils etched. Subtle enchantments woven, all designed to amplify the silver host when the mirage struck.

When the last shimmer of training light faded, the glade stood transformed.

Not into a battlefield but into a sanctuary of readiness.

Silver dragons stood poised. Eladrin riders held their staves with calm resolve. Wards hummed. The land itself listened.

And far beyond the veil of E'vahona the Mirage waited...certain she had already won.

Chapter 32

Shards of Light and Shadow

High above the crystalline spires of Crystal Vale, the sky darkened not with storm, but with intent.

Two shapes tore through the cloudline.

Nocturna, Obsidian Queen of Night.

Xalzorath, Black Dragon of rot and ruin.

Their descent did not merely disturb the air it forced it into obedience.

Around Nocturna, the sky fell silent, light devoured before it could touch her form.

Around Xalzorath, the wind rotted twisting into foul, corrosive currents that burned as they passed. The air shrieked and tore around their bodies, splitting into invisible blades that scythed across spires and skybridges alike. Crystal edges sang beneath the strain, their tones sharp and brittle as though the city itself recoiled from what approached.

Within the Vale, the alarms ignited.

Crystalline towers rang with shrill light as warning sigils flared across balconies, bridges, and elevated walkways. Bells of arcane resonance screamed through the streets sharp, piercing, unrelenting. The sound echoed from spire to spire, a chorus of crystal voices crying out in unison.

"Dark signatures in the upper western sky!"

"Obsidian and black confirmed!"

Panic rippled outward like a fracture through glass.

But panic did not hold.

Citizens scattered into sanctums and shielded corridors. Cloaks and robes streamed behind them as they hurried through luminous passageways. Dragon riders sprinted for launch platforms, armor half-fastened, weapons flaring to life as instinct overruled ceremony.

Prince Gailen burst onto the eastern platform, boots skidding across the smooth crystal surface. The air hummed around him, charged with the Vale's protective magic.

The Crystal Bow formed in his grasp as if summoned by his pulse alone. Living facets unfolded along its length, each surface catching and bending the light. Energy thundered within it, pulsing in perfect rhythm with his heartbeat already reaching for the presence above.

"Aurelia!" he called.

Above him, the sky answered.

Crystal wings unfurled, refracting sunlight into prismatic fire as Aurelia descended. She did not merely glide she cascaded from the heavens, each movement scattering rainbows across the towers below. Her presence rolled over the city like a living anthem of defiance a promise that the light of the Vale would not yield easily to shadow, no matter how deeply it pressed.

Across the city, Thalorian vaulted onto the ramparts as emerald light surged upward to meet him.

Verdantia rose from the garden terraces below, stone splitting as her immense form emerged. Leaf-laden branches burst apart in her wake as the Emerald Ancient climbed into the air.

Their eyes met rider and dragon, ancient bond flaring to life.

"We ride," Thalorian said, voice steady despite the thunder gathering overhead.

Verdantia's voice rolled across the sky like the breath of the world itself.

"Emerald brood to Crystal Vale. Now. The spires must not fall."

From the distant reaches of Vacari, emerald wings answered.

Streaks of living green tore through the sky ancient and swift. One by one, then in clusters until the heavens themselves seemed to turn green with their coming. Verdantia's brood converged upon their matriarch, guardians answering a call older than kingdoms, older even than the crystal foundations of the Vale.

On the northern parapet, the moon-elf mage Shael raised her staff.

Silver runes blazed to life along its length, casting cold brilliance across her resolute features.

"All mages defensive formation!" she commanded.

"Channel through the spires. Do not break the lattice if it fails, the Vale falls with it."

Magic surged.

The great crystalline towers of the Vale ignited in unison. Light threaded between them like woven stars, strands of power linking spire to spire. The energy climbed, locked, and expanded as the first layers of the defensive barrier rose a vast dome of living crystal and arcane force unfolding over the city like a second sky.

Just as the shadow of the Dominion fell across it.

Above it all, Nocturna's shadow slid across the sun.

Light dimmed.

The temperature fell.

Hope tightened refusing to yield.

And Crystal Vale braced for impact.

Aurelia surged skyward into a sky already bending against her.

Crystal wings scattered light like falling stars as she climbed, the air around her rippling with prismatic fire. Gailen remained steady upon her back while the Crystal Bow completed its living form in his hands facets locking into place, light tightening, purpose sharpening with every beat of his heart.

Each pulse echoed through Aurelia beneath him.

There was no hesitation.

They flew straight into the storm because there was nowhere else to stand.

From the southern reaches of the Vale, the wind split with emerald fire.

Verdantia arrived in a blaze of living green, the sky bending to the will of root and storm as her vast form tore through the air. The wind trembled in her wake as her brood surged in behind her emerald dragons streaking like blazing comets, ancient and relentless, their scales burning with the fury of guardians answering a call older than the Vale itself.

The sky seemed to widen around them, as though the heavens themselves made room for what was coming light and ruin alike.

Battle lines drew themselves in the air.

Gailen glanced across the churning currents and met Thalorian's gaze.

The emerald rider lifted one hand in a brief, unmistakable salute.

"Couldn't let you have all the fun," Thalorian called, his voice carrying cleanly through the roar of wind and wings.

Gailen allowed himself a tight smile.

"Try to keep up."

Together, crystal and emerald turned toward the encroaching darkness.

High above, Xalzorath's corroded wings beat against the clouds, rot and shadow trailing in his wake like a spreading infection that refused to die. His gaze locked onto Verdantia with venomous focus, ancient hatred coiling behind his eyes.

"Today," he snarled, the word dripping with centuries of hatred, "you will be destroyed."

Thalorian's laughter cut through the tension like drawn steel.

"Not if I have anything to say about it." He leaned forward slightly, eyes flashing. "And if memory serves, you didn't do a particularly respectable job last time either."

His grin sharpened.

"You had to slink back to Flameford."

Xalzorath's roar split the heavens raw, furious, corrosive. The sound seemed to rot the air itself, turning the wind sour and heavy.

Verdantia's voice rolled outward like living thunder, calm and unyielding.

"Your spite has not grown wiser, Black Dragon only louder."

The noble dragons did not slow.

Verdantia and Aurelia surged forward together emerald fire and crystal light converging as one. Their ancient wills aligned without word or signal as they closed the distance, wings beating in perfect, unspoken accord.

And the sky itself began to fracture beneath them.

Currents twisted. Light warped. The air rippled as reality strained beneath the weight of the coming clash.

High above the rising barrier of Crystal Vale, the dark host shifted formation.

The true battle was about to begin.

At a silent command from Nocturna, the obsidian host obeyed.

They swept toward the crystal-winged defenders, their bodies swallowing the light. Wherever they passed, the sky dimmed, their passage dragging night across the heavens like a wound sealing shut.

At the same instant, Xalzorath released a guttural snarl.

The black dragons tore from formation, veering hard toward Verdantia and her emerald brood. Their wings trailed streams of corrosive vapor that burned the clouds to tatters, leaving streaks of sickly darkness in their wake.

The sky divided.

Two wars unfolded across the same heavens.

At the center of it all, four Ancients Nocturna, Xalzorath, Aurelia, and Verdantia hovered in vast, coiled stillness. Ancient eyes locked across the widening gulf of air, each dragon a force capable of reshaping the battle with a single, irrevocable decision.

They did not rush.

They waited.

Below them, the barrier over Crystal Vale continued to rise, the city's spires blazing as magic surged through crystal and stone. Threads of light wove between the towers, strengthening the dome with relentless precision.

Above it, the heavens held their breath.

Then the first ranks collided.

The impact shattered the sky.

Obsidian met crystal in a screaming collision of brilliance against devouring darkness as the forward lines slammed together above the barrier. Crystal breath tore through the night like exploding starlight, while obsidian fire devoured the wind itself. Shockwaves rippled through the clouds, the force of the clash rattling the crystalline spires far below.

To the south, emerald flame and black rot crashed headlong into one another.

Verdantia's brood fought in disciplined arcs, their movements precise and ancient. Emerald fire carved luminous scars through the choking corruption pouring from the black dragons' jaws.

The heavens became a battlefield of falling stars.

Gailen loosed his first volley.

The Crystal Bow sang a sound like glass and thunder echoing through Aurelia's flight and the sky answered.

A storm of radiant shards tore into the advancing obsidian ranks, detonating across wings and scales in blinding bursts of silver-white brilliance. The explosions scattered the front line, fragments of fractured darkness tumbling through the air like broken pieces of night.

Above the chaos, Aurelia drove forward, her crystal wings blazing as she plunged toward the heart of the obsidian formation seeking its fracture point.

The true battle had begun.

Thalorian raised his staff.

Emerald sigils flared along Thalorian's staff as he wove living wind around Verdantia's brood. The currents curled like unseen rivers through the air—sharpening their turns, steadying their formations, driving their emerald fire hotter and truer.

The effect was immediate.

Non-ancient dragons clashed in violent spirals breaking, reforming, colliding again. Crystal wings flashed against the obsidian void while emerald flame carved luminous paths through blackened smoke. The air filled with streaks of light, fragments of darkness, and the thunder of beating wings.

Below them, Shael's barrier surged upward.

The growing dome of living crystal caught falling embers, fragments of shattered cloud, and stray blasts of corrupted fire. Slowly, the city vanished beneath its protective shell—sealed in living crystal and defiance.

The war for Crystal Vale had begun.

And the Ancients had not yet moved.

For a breathless moment they hovered four vast shapes suspended above the chaos, each one a storm waiting to break.

Then the standoff shattered.

Nocturna moved first.

Her vast obsidian form slid through the battlefield like living night given will. Where she passed, the light dimmed, swallowed by her presence. Shadows crawled across crystal wings, and the air itself thickened with cold, silent pressure.

She closed on Aurelia inevitable, unhurried.

"You remember the last time," Nocturna whispered, her voice sliding like a blade into Aurelia's mind.

"How easily light fractures."

Aurelia's wings flared.

Crystal brilliance surged outward, forcing back the creeping dark. Prismatic light spilled across the sky, scattering shadows like dust before a rising dawn.

"I remember," she said calmly. "And I remember that shadows only rule where light forgets itself."

Beside her, Gailen raised the Crystal Bow, its glow already answering Aurelia's rising power. The weapon resonated like a second heartbeat shared between them.

"The last time," he said, voice steady within the storm, "I was still learning what this bow could do."

The bow answered with a deep crystalline pulse alive, eager, almost proud.

"I am not the same anymore."

Light surged between rider and dragon.

The bond flared like a rising star breaking the horizon, crystal energy spiraling outward in expanding rings that rippled through the darkened sky.

Even the clouds recoiled.

The sky answered.

To the south, Xalzorath roared and lunged for Verdantia, his jaws spewing a torrent of hissing acid that devoured cloud and wind alike.

Thalorian was already moving no hesitation, no delay.

He drove the Arborblade into the rushing current of corruption.

Living green light erupted from the blade in a violent surge. The acid veered aside in a wide arc, scattering harmlessly across the open sky as emerald energy wrapped Verdantia in a shield of living forest root, leaf, and ancient will.

Xalzorath recoiled with a snarl.

Then the Ancients collided.

Crystal and obsidian exploded together in a blinding clash of power.

Emerald and black tore into one another in a storm of rot and green-fire.

Above Crystal Vale, the heavens broke open.

The battle fully ignited.

Nocturna vanished.

Not fled folded.

Her obsidian form fractured into a thousand overlapping shadows that slid between light and space. The sky fractured with her, blooming into false reflections of her body each one moving independently, each one lethal.

Aurelia's wings flared.

She did not chase the illusions.

She listened.

Crystal light rippled across her scales, refracting the battlefield into a vast lattice of mirrored brilliance and anchored truth. Where Nocturna's false forms crossed that prism, they began to destabilize their edges shivering, unraveling where reality refused to hold them.

"There," Gailen breathed.

The Crystal Bow answered.

He loosed.

The arrow did not fly.

It appeared forming in midair as a lance of living crystal and focused will that tore through Nocturna's true left wing in a detonation of prismatic fire.

Shadow screamed as the Obsidian Queen reeled, her web of illusions collapsing around her like shattered glass falling through night.

Nocturna shrieked, fury slicing through the pain.

"Little prince," she hissed into Gailen's mind, "you have grown bold."

She struck back, unleashing a consuming tide of night.

Shadowfire rolled toward Aurelia in a suffocating wave, swallowing light, sound, and breath until nothing remained but crushing pressure.

Aurelia dove straight through it.

Unyielding.

Her crystal scales burned white-hot, the darkness peeling away from her like smoke devoured by dawn.

"You rely too much on tricks," she said, voice ringing with calm certainty. "and too little on truth."

Above them, obsidian and crystal dragons clashed without cease.

The sky itself tore between shadow and brilliance.

Acid and rot poured from his jaws, a torrent of corruption that devoured the sky itself. Clouds collapsed into hissing poison rain, the air turning thick and sickly as the black dragon drove straight toward Verdantia.

She met the assault head-on.

Emerald fire surged from her chest a roaring tide of living flame that collided with the spreading rot. Green and black energy crashed together in a violent storm of light and corruption, the clash sending shockwaves rippling through the clouds.

Xalzorath burst through the turbulence.

His claws raked across Verdantia's flank, tearing deep into her scales with a grinding screech of stone and bone. She roared not in fear, but in fury and drove into him, emerald wings beating with immense ancient power as she forced him backward through the choking air.

Thalorian lifted the Arborblade.

The forest answered.

Roots of living energy erupted from the blade in a violent surge, spiraling outward like awakened vines. They lashed through the sky and coiled around Xalzorath's wing mid-flight. The living strands tightened, piercing between corrupted scales and anchoring deep as green fire spread through tainted flesh.

The black dragon shrieked and thrashed, rot spraying from his jaws as he fought against the tightening grip.

Verdantia seized the opening.

She slammed into him.

Their bodies collided with the force of colliding mountains, the impact sending a shockwave rolling across the southern sky. Scales cracked. Clouds tore apart. The air thundered with the sound of ancient power unleashed.

The emerald brood closed in.

They did not strike wildly.

They moved in disciplined arcs, each dragon taking position as if following an unspoken pattern older than memory itself. One by one then in coordinated bursts they unleashed emerald flame into the black dragons' ranks.

The corruption faltered.

Formation shattered.

Black dragons reeled under the assault, driven into disarray as emerald fire carved luminous wounds through the choking darkness.

The southern front tilted toward life.

To the north, Nocturna surged again.

Her damaged wing trailed ribbons of shadow as she tried to fold herself from sight once more, her form blurring as illusion gathered around her like a cloak of living night.

Aurelia anticipated it.

Crystal light detonated outward from her body in a vast radiant flare. The sky filled with a lattice of perfect refraction countless shards of prismatic brilliance locking the battlefield into merciless clarity.

Light bent and multiplied.

Every shadow fractured.

There was nowhere left to hide.

Gailen drew again.

The Crystal Bow pulsed like a living heart in his hands, its facets blazing with contained power.

This time it did not sing.

It thundered.

The arrow formed between his fingers a storm-shard of living light and focused will, dense and blazing, as though a fragment of the sun itself had been carved into crystal.

He loosed.

The projectile screamed across the sky, trailing a comet-tail of prismatic fire, and struck Nocturna square in the chest.

Shadow shattered violently.

The impact detonated in a blinding explosion of crystal light, ripping through the darkness wrapped around her body. The force of the strike drove the Obsidian Queen backward, her wings convulsing as the illusion-laced shadows collapsed around her.

With a roar that shook the heavens, Nocturna was hurled from the sky.

She spiraled downward through the clouds a falling storm of fractured shadow and fading illusion as the northern front flooded with returning light.

Above Crystal Vale, the balance of the battle shifted.

To the south, Xalzorath bleeding green fire lunged for Verdantia's throat.

Corruption streamed from his jaws, his eyes blazing with desperate fury. He hurled himself forward in a final reckless strike, determined to drag her down with him in ruin.

Thalorian stepped forward.

"Not today."

He drove the Arborblade into the space between them.

The blade answered like the living heart of the forest.

Roots of radiant green energy erupted outward, coiling and expanding as the forest's wrath detonated into a shockwave of emerald light that slammed into Xalzorath's chest.

The impact hurled the black dragon backward.

His massive form skidded through shattered clouds, rot and acid scattering behind him as he fought to regain control of his wings.

The remaining black dragons faltered at the sight formation breaking as fear rippled through their ranks.

One by one then in clusters they turned and fled, scrambling after their wounded master in panicked retreat.

Silence rushed in after them, as though the sky itself exhaled.

Moments later, the obsidian dragons followed.

With their queen cast from the heavens, they dissolved into the torn clouds, retreating into distant shadow.

Above Crystal Vale, only crystal and emerald remained.

Aurelia hovered, her wings burning with silver-white fire, light cascading from her scales in soft, fading streams. Verdantia steadied herself beside her, wings lowering slightly, emerald breath steaming in the thinning air. The glow of life still pulsed beneath the wound along her flank.

Gailen slowly lowered the Crystal Bow, its facets dimming as the tension drained from the sky.

Thalorian exhaled, his shoulders easing as the Arborblade's glow softened.

Below them, the barrier over Crystal Vale shimmered cracked, scorched, and webbed with faint fractures of light.

But it still stood.

The city was wounded.

But it lived.

The battle for Crystal Vale was over.

The sky no longer roared.

It breathed.

High above the wounded clouds, Aurelia and Verdantia lingered in the thinning light. Their vast forms were outlined by drifting embers and fractured reflections of crystal, the air around them still trembling from the violence that had just passed.

Far on the horizon, the retreating shapes of Nocturna and Xalzorath diminished dark specks against the fading glow.

Driven back.

Not destroyed.

Not finished.

Gailen watched them go, the Crystal Bow dimming gradually in his hands. Its living facets softened from blazing brilliance to a quiet glow, as though the weapon itself understood the battle was only paused.

Thalorian's gaze followed the same distant shadows.

"This was only a probe," he said quietly. "They were testing our strength."

"No," Aurelia replied, her voice calm but certain. "They were testing our separation."

Verdantia tilted her great head, emerald eyes narrowing in thought.

"They fought as one front," she said. "Shadow and rot, moving with purpose. Not chaos. Not rivalry."

Aurelia inclined her head.

"They are learning," she said. "And someone is teaching them how to divide us."

The quiet that followed was fragile the kind that came only after violence. The air still trembled as currents of magic settled reluctantly back into place, as though the sky itself needed time to remember its natural shape.

Then Aurelia turned toward the city below.

"We must tend the wounded."

Verdantia cast one last look toward the retreating darkness before folding her wings.

Together, crystal and emerald descended toward Crystal Vale toward shattered spires, trembling streets, and the waiting hearts of their people.

The first front of the war had ended.

And Vacari scarred, shaken, but unbroken still stood.

Chapter 33

The Price of Crystal

The sky over Crystal Vale was quiet again.

Not whole but quiet, for now.

The clouds still bore the scars of battle, torn into ragged ribbons that drifted slowly across the horizon like the remnants of a broken storm. Faint motes of crystal light and shadowfire embers glimmered as they fell, dissolving before they could reach the city below.

High above the wounded sky, Verdantia turned to her brood. Her great emerald wings steamed faintly, wisps of green-lit vapor curling from the shallow wounds along her flank.

"Return to the Emerald Forests," she commanded. "Watch the roots... and the skies. If the dark dragons move again, you will know before the wind does."

The emerald dragons answered with low, resolute calls deep, harmonious notes that rolled through the thinning clouds.

One by one, they broke formation, their glowing forms streaking southward like falling stars of green fire.

Verdantia watched them go, her ancient gaze lingering until the last flicker of emerald light vanished beyond the horizon. Only then did she turn to Aurelia.

"We will go with you. This is not yet finished."

Aurelia inclined her crystalline head, light gliding across the facets of her scales.

"Crystal Vale will need both of us."

Together, crystal and emerald turned back toward the city.

Below them, the shimmering barrier still arched across the skyline, flickering under the strain of lingering magic. Its surface was no longer flawless. Fractures of light spiderwebbed across the dome, and each pulse of energy sent faint, unstable ripples through the air.

As the people of Crystal Vale caught sight of their returning guardians, the city stirred.

Voices rose uncertain at first, then growing.

Bells rang not in alarm, but in fragile relief.

On the northern parapet, Shael lifted her staff, silver runes dimmed but still glowing.

"Lower the barrier," she called. "They are home."

Light unraveled.

The great dome of crystal magic folded inward, dissolving into threads of fading brilliance. The sky above the city opened once more as Aurelia and Verdantia descended side by side, their riders steady upon their backs.

They landed in the heart of the city.

Crystal towers glimmered around them many cracked, some blackened by shadowfire. Entire balconies had sheared away, their fragments scattered across the streets below. Skybridges hung at uneven angles, some split clean through, others warped by heat and corruption.

The streets bore the scars of falling embers and shattered sky.

But the people were alive.

And they were running toward the square.

Gailen dismounted first, his boots striking crystal stone with a sharp, echoing note. The Crystal Bow dissolved in his hands, its light folding inward until only a faint glow lingered along his fingertips.

Thalorian followed, one hand resting against Verdantia's glowing scales. He felt the steady pulse of life beneath his palm slower now, but unbroken.

They had won this front of the war.

But the war itself had only just begun.

Now they would see what it had cost.

Aurelia turned slowly, her crystal gaze sweeping the city.

Near the eastern spires, several crystal dragons rested upon fractured terraces, their wings folded tight. Some bore long cracks across their scales, while others smoldered with the faint residue of shadowfire. Mages and medics moved among them, hands glowing with healing light as they worked to seal wounds and purge lingering corruption.

Nearby, two wounded emerald dragons lay upon the marble bridge, their massive bodies stretched across the span. Healers knelt beside them, weaving strands of restorative magic through torn scales and scorched flesh.

The air hummed with the scent of living energy and faint acrid rot life and corruption still at war.

Verdantia moved at once.

She crossed the square in long, careful strides, her immense form moving with surprising gentleness. She lowered her great head beside her injured kin, emerald light spilling softly across their bodies.

The effect was immediate.

The wounded dragons' breathing steadied. The tension in their limbs eased. Even the healers seemed to draw strength from her presence, their magic steadying beneath hers.

Aurelia watched the scene in silence before her attention shifted as King Manard approached.

His robes were dusted with crystal ash, and a thin line of blood marked his temple, yet his posture remained straight.

"How stands your city?" Aurelia asked.

"There is damage," Manard replied, his gaze lifting to the scarred skyline. "But not as much as there might have been. Your stand saved us from ruin."

He looked around the square at the wounded dragons, the exhausted mages, the citizens helping one another to their feet.

"We still have a home because of you."

Aurelia inclined her head, the gesture both regal and solemn.

Then she turned to the assembled crystal dragons.

"Clear the city," she commanded. "Lift the broken stone and shattered spires. Carry the debris beyond the outer ridges. Destroy what cannot be mended and return. Crystal Vale must be made whole again."

The crystal dragons answered with low, resolute calls.

One by one they rose into the air. Some carried fractured towers in their talons, others entire sections of broken spire. Others lifted shattered crystal slabs in careful, balanced grips.

They moved with deliberate precision, carrying the debris beyond the city's borders before returning to begin the long work of repair.

Above them, the sun broke through the thinning clouds.

Its light spilled across the damaged spires, turning the fractures into rivers of gold and brilliance.

Crystal Vale still stood.

And now, it would heal.

Thalorian and Gailen moved at once, joining the lines of mages and builders already restoring the shattered avenues and fractured spires. Spellweaver light and raw determination blended as the people of Crystal Vale worked side by side.

Gailen knelt beside a fallen crystal column, placing his hands against its fractured surface. Light flickered from his palms, spreading like veins of living crystal as the break slowly sealed.

Across the square, Thalorian raised the Arborblade once more. Gentle emerald energy flowed from the blade, coaxing warped crystal back into shape and strengthening weakened structures.

All around them, the city began to breathe again.

Aurelia crossed the square toward Verdantia, the two ancients standing side by side as they watched the slow rebirth of the Vale. The air shimmered between crystal and emerald light as they shared a silent understanding.

"This was no reckless assault," Verdantia said at last. "They came with purpose. With coordination and intent."

Aurelia's gaze darkened with quiet resolve.

"Yes. Someone is teaching them to fight as one and to divide us."

The thought settled heavily between them.

For the first time in many ages, the war felt different.

But Aurelia lifted her head, crystal light hardening along her scales.

"Then we prepare," she said, her voice steady as crystal. "We strengthen this city. And when the next storm comes... it will not find us unready."

Verdantia nodded once, slow and certain.

Below them, Crystal Vale shimmered once more wounded, scarred, but unbroken.

And in its heart, hope still burned, unyielding.

Chapter 34

When the Forest Fights

While the skies of Crystal Vale burned with crystal fire and shadow, the war did not wait for victory or defeat.

Far from the shattered spires, deep within the heart of the Emberwoods, another front ignited.

The Emberwoods whispered with restless breath.

Light filtered through towering boughs and ember-veined leaves, the glow pulsing faintly like a slow heartbeat beneath the bark. Paths curved where they had not curved before. Roots shifted just beneath the soil, tightening like muscles preparing for a strike.

At the edge of the living maze, Kaelorn stood among a swirling cloud of pixies male and female alike each blazing with stubborn color and flickering light. Their wings hummed with restless energy, scattering sparks of gold, crimson, and violet through the air.

“It may be wiser,” Kaelorn said gently, “for you to return to Ardinia. You would be safe there.”

Beside him, Raelithar inclined his great copper head. Emberlight glinted between the plates of his scales, his presence warm and steady amid the uneasy forest.

"No one wishes to see you harmed," the Ancient rumbled. "Least of all by a Topaz warflight in a temper."

A hush fell across the glade.

Then one of the male pixies shot forward, his wings flaring bright gold.

"I'm not leaving."

The others surged in agreement, their voices rising like a storm of chiming bells.

"We are not leaving."

"This is our forest."

"We grew up in these roots!"

A female pixie darted upward and hovered before Kaelorn, her glow steady and fierce.

"They will need us," she said. "Every time the Topaz dragons try to burn the maze away, we will be the ones who make it grow again."

Kaelorn's gaze softened.

Raelithar released a low, approving rumble that vibrated through the roots beneath them.

"Spoken like true children of flame and leaf," he said. "Stubborn to the last spark."

Kaelorn inclined his head slightly.

"Very well," he said at last. "But you will remain hidden even while you hold the maze together. The forest needs your magic more than it needs your heroics."

The male pixie's eyes gleamed.

"I have an idea."

He swept upward into the leaves, vanishing briefly among the ember-lit canopy.

"The males will take the heights," he called. "We'll harry their wings blind their turns, pull their fire where it does the least harm."

A ripple of mischievous excitement spread through the upper branches, sparks of light darting between leaves.

The female pixies exchanged sharp, knowing smiles.

"And we will hide among the flowers and roots," one said, her voice lilting and dangerous, "and twist their senses until they no longer know which way is sky... or ground. Let them burn illusions until they tire themselves out."

Kaelorn allowed himself a faint smile, though his eyes drifted toward the deeper shadows between the trees.

Raelithar turned to his waiting brood, copper scales catching the forest's shifting glow.

"Be ready," he commanded. "A nymph has warned us the Topaz dragons are coming."

"We do not meet them in the open sky," Raelithar continued, voice low and certain. "We meet them where the forest chooses to fight."

At those words, the Emberwoods seemed to lean closer.

Roots tightened beneath the soil. Leaves trembled. Paths quietly rearranged themselves, curling into new turns and hidden loops.

Somewhere deeper in the forest, a distant branch cracked.

The air grew warmer.

Not with flame but with pressure.

Heat that pressed rather than burned.

Heat that promised something vast was already moving toward them.

The forest was ready.

And it would choose how the battle was fought.

The sky over the Emberwoods darkened as Zarathos arrived.

Topaz wings blotted out the sun, molten-gold scales reflecting harsh, electric light as the fallen gem dragon descended at the head of his brood.

Heat and static rolled through the canopy in suffocating waves, the air crackling with tension.

Leaves shivered.

Roots tightened beneath the soil.

The forest answered with a low, uneasy sigh.

With a single silent command from Zarathos, the Topaz formation split apart like a blade dividing flesh.

Several of the Topaz dragons veered toward the living maze. Their jaws opened in unison, and forked bolts of searing lightning crashed into the shifting walls. The strikes split trunks, blasted corridors through tangled roots, and left smoking scars across the maze.

Thunder rolled through the forest.

Trees shattered.

Vines snapped.

The earth trembled beneath the assault.

For a moment, it seemed the forest would break.

And then the maze answered.

Roots surged upward from the soil like rising serpents. Bark reknit itself, glowing faintly with ember-veined light. Blackened trunks straightened, their charred surfaces flaking away as new growth pushed through.

Within heartbeats, the corridors stood whole again.

Paths twisted.

Branches shifted.

The forest closed its wounds as if the lightning had never touched it.

One of the Topaz dragons snarled in disbelief, sparks crackling between his fangs.

“Impossible. We reduced it to splinters.”

Another lashed his tail through the lingering smoke.

“It should be nothing but charred roots!”

The forest answered.

Voices drifted through the leaves soft, laughing, ancient.

"You strike what you do not understand..."

"You burn what does not fear you..."

"This forest does not belong to you..."

The words came from everywhere and nowhere at once, woven into the wind, the rustle of leaves, and the faint crackle of cooling bark.

A Topaz dragon wheeled sharply, jaws snapping at empty air.

"Show yourselves!"

The ground seized him.

Not slowly instantly.

Roots erupted from the soil, coiling around his legs and wings in a violent surge. They tightened like living chains, dragging him down with a thunderous crash that shook the clearing.

The forest closed in.

Branches bent low. Vines wrapped around his limbs. The earth itself swallowed his movements as he roared in fury, lightning crackling uselessly against the living wood.

The Emberwoods were not prey.

They were fighting back.

On the far side of the burning glades, Zarathos moved alone.

He did not waste his strength on the maze.

He watched it.

He stalked between the trees, molten claws sinking into the scorched earth. Each step left faintly glowing impressions in the soil, heat lingering in his wake. His eyes tracked the shifting paths, irritation simmering beneath the surface.

"Kaelorn..." he growled, his voice low and cutting.

"You hide behind roots and tricks."

A step forward.

Slow.

Deliberate.

"Come face fire."

The forest did not answer.

It only shifted.

Paths curved where they had not curved before. Branches bent, closing sightlines. The air carried the faint scent of living sap and emberlit bark.

Zarathos took another step.

The earth shook.

Not from him.

Copper wings unfurled before him.

Raelithar descended between Zarathos and the forest path, his vast form slamming into the clearing with the weight of an avalanche.

For a single breath, the two Ancients regarded one another recognition passing not as greeting, but as challenge.

Copper scales gleamed like living fire, reflecting the glow of the smoldering glade, while roots instinctively curled around Raelithar's talons as though greeting an old ally.

"Have you no sense at all?" Raelithar thundered. "You will not lay a claw upon the Forest Warden. This forest has already suffered once beneath your kind."

His voice deepened, resonant with ancient fury.

"It will not be broken again."

Behind him, unseen, but keenly felt the Emberwoods gathered its strength.

Leaves stilled.

Roots drew tight.

Even the air seemed to hold its breath.

Magic coiled through bark and stone alike, as though the forest itself listened for the outcome of the confrontation.

The true battle for the forest was about to begin.

Zarathos's eyes narrowed, molten light flickering between his fangs.

"Then I will break you first."

He lowered his body, lightning gathering along his scales in crackling threads of gold-white energy.

Before he could strike the forest stirred.

Light rippled through the trees like dawn spreading across a valley. The air grew warmer, brighter, filled with a quiet, ancient harmony.

Aeralinde rose from the heart of the Emberwoods.

Her great wings unfolded in a cascade of radiant color greens, golds, and earthen hues flowing together like a living tapestry. Each feather shimmered with the tones of deep forests, sunlit glades, and hidden groves. As she stepped forward, the ground beneath her hooves glowed faintly, roots stirring in gentle reverence.

Kaelorn stood upon her back, staff blazing with ancient runes.

The ground itself answered to his presence. Roots shifted. Leaves lifted. The forest leaned toward him like an old friend.

Zarathos turned, eyes blazing.

He surged forward, molten power coiling in his jaws, gathering into a spear of crackling gold.

The world answered with light.

A brilliant shield formed around Kaelorn and Aeralinde a living barrier woven from forest-song and elder magic. It shimmered like layered leaves caught in sunlight, every strand humming with ancient protection.

Zarathos's lightning crashed against it.

The impact exploded across the surface in a blinding flare of gold and green. Thunder rolled through the glade. Bark split. Leaves tore free in a storm of color.

But the shield held.

His dark sorcery followed threads of corrupted energy lashing against the barrier.

Neither left a mark.

Zarathos reeled back, disbelief twisting instantly into fury.

" What trick is this?" he bellowed. "He is the Forest Warden and she a mere pegasus! How is this holding?"

Raelithar's laughter rolled across the glades like thunder.

"Only a Pegasus?" the Copper Ancient echoed. "Look closer, Topaz. Each feather carries the colors of every forest of Ardinia itself."

His eyes hardened, his voice turning sharp as hammered bronze.

"Kaelorn is the Forest Warden. The roots of every forest in Vacari know his name."

Behind Zarathos, the remaining Topaz dragons descended in a storm of crackling gold, lightning dancing across their scales as they swept through the smoke and broken canopy.

The real battle for the Emberwoods had begun.

Zarathos whirled on them, fury sharpening his command.

"Burn it all. Leave nothing standing!"

The words tore through the glades like a thunderclap.

And the Emberwoods answered.

The forest roared not with sound alone, but with will. Something ancient shifted beneath the soil, vast and waking. The ground trembled. Leaves shivered in sudden waves. Deep beneath the surface, ancient roots stirred as though something enormous had awakened.

At Zarathos's command, the Topaz dragons surged forward.

Lightning gathered in their jaws crackling in molten-gold arcs.

Then they unleashed it.

Forked strikes tore through the canopy.

Trees split with thunderous cracks. Branches exploded into splinters. The air filled with smoke and the sharp scent of scorched bark.

But the copper dragons met them head-on.

Burnished wings cleaved the smoke as they slammed into the advancing Topaz brood. Acid breath streaked through the air in molten lines, hissing as it struck lightning-scarred scales.

Slowing gas followed deliberate, controlled spreading in drifting clouds that dulled wingbeats and turned precise Topaz dives into clumsy, faltering charges.

Above them, Raelithar tore into the heart of the Topaz formation.

His roar shook the roots of the world as he seized one attacker by the shoulder and drove him down into the earth with bone-crushing force. The impact split the ground open, roots tearing free as the forest reacted to the blow.

And the Emberwoods joined the war.

At Kaelorn's command, the ground itself rose.

Roots erupted from the soil, coiling around Topaz wings and limbs. Vines lashed through the air, snapping like whips. Trees bent and struck, their massive trunks sweeping dragons from the sky.

Lightning flashed in desperate retaliation.

Bolts tore through branches, blasting holes in the canopy but the damage began to heal even as it formed. New growth surged through scorched wood. Roots reknit themselves.

The forest refused to remain wounded.

High in the canopy, the male pixies unleashed their mischief.

They vanished and reappeared in flashes of light, darting between branches as they hurled illusions and stinging sparks of magic. Distances twisted. Shapes blurred. Depth and direction warped.

"Too slow, gold-crest!"

"Try the other sky!"

"No, not that tree!"

A Topaz dragon lunged at a copper shape only to collide with a trunk that had not been there a moment before.

Below, the female pixies wove their magic through petals, roots, and ember-veined flowers. Clouds of shimmering dust drifted through the air, glowing softly as they settled over the battlefield.

Gravity bent.

Reflexes dulled.

Perception slipped just enough to betray instinct.

"Down is up now..." one whispered sweetly.

"And up is wherever we say it is," another chimed.

Lightning struck empty air.

Claws closed on shadows.

Topaz dragons crashed into trees that were not where they thought they were.

Zarathos roared in fury, tearing through the chaos. Entire sections of the maze vaporized beneath his strikes cleared in an instant before the forest could reclaim them.

But even Zarathos could not move through it unchallenged.

The Emberwoods closed around him branches rising, roots surging, the land itself rebelling against his presence. Every step he took met resistance. The ground shifted beneath his claws. Vines snapped at his wings. The air thickened with the scent of living sap and smoldering bark.

Kaelorn stood radiant atop Aeralinde, his staff blazing with green-gold fire.

Roots stirred in answer to his voice. Leaves lifted toward him. Even the wounded trees leaned as though listening.

He spoke the ancient language of growth and storm.

"This forest will not fall."

And the land itself answered.

Copper and Topaz clashed in the burning sky while the woods below writhed with movement, light, and wrath.

For the first time since the ancient corruption, the Emberwoods were not merely surviving the darkness.

They were fighting back.

A scream tore through the canopy.

One of the Topaz dragons broke through the chaos, lightning trailing from his jaws as he dove toward a towering ember-tree. A lone pixie clung to one of its upper branches, wings flashing in frantic bursts of light—too exposed, too visible.

The Topaz's jaws opened.

Before he could strike a copper dragon slammed into him.

The impact cracked through the glade like a falling mountain. The air itself seemed to buckle as bark exploded outward. Leaves ignited in the sudden rush of heat and motion as the two dragons tumbled through the canopy, tearing branches free in their wake.

The pixie was hurled loose, spinning through smoke and drifting sparks as the copper dragon drove the attacker away from the tree.

But the victory came at a terrible cost.

Too slow.

Too close.

The Topaz's claws tore deep across the copper's chest and wing, raking through scale and into flesh. Lightning flared between his fangs as he kicked free, leaving long smoking gashes across copper scales.

The copper dragon lost control.

He crashed through the canopy, snapping branches like brittle bones. Each impact tore away more leaves and splintered wood until he struck the forest floor with thunderous force, shaking the surrounding roots.

Dust rose.

Leaves drifted down like slow-falling embers.

The copper dragon lay too still amid shattered roots and scorched earth.

A hush rippled through the battle.

Pixies fell silent.

Copper wings faltered.

Even the forest seemed to pause, as though something within it recoiled its branches trembling with the shock.

Raelithar saw him fall.

For a heartbeat, the world narrowed sound dimming, motion blurring until there was only that single, motionless form on the forest floor.

Something old and terrible ignited in the Copper Ancient's chest.

A memory of Caleum.

Of fire and open sky.

Of laughter carried on the wind.

Of the day Zylron had torn his friend from the world.

Grief did not fade.

It hardened.

Became fury.

Raelithar's roar split the heavens.

And he turned on Zarathos.

The two ancients surged toward one another, copper and topaz colliding with the force of worlds meeting in violence. Their impact cracked through the burning glade, a shockwave ripping outward as wings, claws, and lightning clashed in a storm of ancient power.

The forest buckled beneath their fury not breaking, but straining beneath the weight of it.

Roots tore free from the soil. Ember-veined trunks bent and groaned. Leaves spiraled into the air as the ground trembled beneath their clash.

The battle for the Emberwoods entered its final most savage phase.

At the heart of the burning glade, the ancients fought in a storm of fury.

Zarathos struck first.

Lightning exploded from his jaws in blinding arcs, gold-white bolts tearing through the smoke as they crashed toward Raelithar. The air split with thunder, branches shattering under the force of the strikes.

Raelithar answered in the same breath deliberate, measured.

A cloud of shimmering slowing gas poured from his jaws, spreading like a living haze. The air thickened around Zarathos, dragging at his wings, dulling the precision of his movements, turning deadly speed into heavy, sluggish motion.

Around them, the copper dragons shifted tactics.

Illusion unfurled.

Phantoms of copper and flame bloomed across the battlefield false forms weaving between the real ones, mirages so complete that even the air seemed to ripple with their presence. Some charged. Some dove. Some roared with convincing fury.

The Topaz dragons struck at them.

Claws passed through light.

Lightning tore through shadows.

And in those brief, fatal moments of confusion, true copper talons struck from unexpected angles, ripping into exposed flanks and driving the Topaz formation into growing disarray.

Distance bent.

Direction collapsed.

Panic crept into molten eyes.

Zarathos roared in fury and hurled a storm of lightning into the forest, splintering trees and blasting holes through the canopy.

But Raelithar was no longer where he had been.

The Copper Ancient's **Aura of Deception** rolled outward like a silent tide.

The air thickened with uncertainty. Shapes blurred at the edges. Even the ground seemed to shift beneath claw and talon. Sounds echoed from the wrong directions. Shadows moved when they should have stood still.

Reality bent.

For the first time, doubt crept into Zarathos's mind unwelcome, unfamiliar.

Was that the true Raelithar or another illusion?

Was the ground beneath him real or a trick of the forest?

The hesitation lasted only a heartbeat.

But it was enough.

Snarling, Zarathos surged forward anyway, refusing the doubt. He struck through the haze and raked Raelithar's wings with his claws.

Scales tore.

Blood flashed like molten copper, bright and searing against the firelight.

Raelithar staggered, his wings faltering for a single dangerous moment, but he did not fall.

Above them, Kaelorn saw the strike.

His staff flared.

The pixies answered.

The forest moved.

Roots burst from the ground in a violent surge. Branches coiled like grasping arms. Entire trees bent inward, their trunks groaning as the Emberwoods themselves closed around Zarathos.

The earth rose to meet him.

Roots wrapped around his legs and wings, dragging him toward the soil. Vines lashed across his chest. Branches struck at his sides like battering rams.

Zarathos roared and tore free in a storm of fury. Lightning exploded from his jaws, blasting bark, stone, and roots into splinters.

The forest recoiled but only for a moment.

Then it surged again.

New roots erupted.

Fresh branches closed the gaps.

When Zarathos finally wrenched himself free and rose into the air, hovering amid smoke and drifting embers, he saw the truth clearly.

The Topaz dragons were losing.

Some were entangled in roots. Others wheeled blindly through illusions. Several limped through the air, copper acid smoking along their scales.

They were confused.

Injured.

Hemmed in by copper flame, living forest, and relentless misdirection.

Zarathos's wings beat slowly as the realization settled over him.

This was no simple burn-and-break assault.

He lifted his head and gave the signal.

Retreat.

The Topaz brood broke away at once, fleeing into the scarred sky. Lightning flashed in scattered arcs as they climbed, the forest's canopy glowing faintly beneath them.

Behind them, the Emberwoods roared not in triumph, but in defiance.

Leaves trembled.

Branches lifted.

Roots tightened in the soil as if daring the invaders to return.

Zarathos lingered a heartbeat longer.

He locked eyes with Raelithar.

"This is not finished," he snarled. "Next time, I burn this forest to its roots and you with it."

Raelithar met his gaze wounded, bloodied, but unbroken. Copper blood still gleamed across his wing, dripping slowly onto the roots below.

"Then come," he rumbled, low and steady. "And bring more than pride. You will need it."

For a moment, the two ancients hovered in silent challenge, the wounded forest breathing beneath them.

Then, with a final thunder of wings, Zarathos turned and vanished into the burning clouds.

Silence followed.

Not empty silence but the slow, living quiet of a forest that had endured.

Below, the Emberwoods still stood.

Scarred.

Smoking.

But alive.

The Emberwoods had survived.

And this time they had fought back.

Chapter 35

Ash and Greenfire

The sky over the Emberwoods no longer burned.

Smoke drifted in long, tired ribbons above the shattered canopy. Where lightning had split the trees, faint embers still glowed along blackened bark. The scent of scorched wood lingered in the air, mingling with the slow, stubborn perfume of living sap.

High above the wounded forest, Raelithar hovered for a moment longer, watching Zarathos and the retreating Topaz dragons vanish beyond the distant ridgelines. Their molten forms shrank as they fled toward the mountains of Etharyon, lightning flickering faintly around them like dying stars.

He turned to one of his own.

"Follow," Raelithar said. "Not close. Just far enough to know where they go."

The Copper dragon dipped his wings and vanished into the scarred clouds.

Below, the Emberwoods breathed.

Not easily. Not fully.

But it breathed.

Ash drifted through glowing leaves. Embers hissed softly against living bark. Where trees had been split apart, new shoots already pushed through the cracks. Roots shifted beneath the soil, knitting the wounded ground together.

The forest had survived.

But it had not escaped unscathed.

When the scout returned, the smoke had thinned enough for the damage to be seen clearly. Entire groves were blackened. Some ancient trees leaned at dangerous angles. Patches of the maze still flickered with unstable magic where lightning had torn through illusion and growth alike.

"They crossed into Etharyon," the Copper reported. "But they were not alone for long. Mercury dragons intercepted their path silent and swift. They signaled they would shadow the Topaz brood and ordered me back to report."

Relief flickered across his features.

Then his gaze shifted and the relief vanished.

He saw Raelithar.

The Copper Ancient lay upon the forest floor, vast wings spread wide, scorched and torn. Copper blood darkened the roots beneath him, steaming faintly where it touched the soil, as though the forest itself felt the wound.

Kaelorn knelt beside him, staff glowing softly as streams of green-gold light flowed across shattered scales and torn membrane.

Pixies hovered in trembling constellations around the ancient dragon, their lights dimmed to anxious embers. Some whispered soft, wordless songs. Others simply drifted close, unwilling to leave.

The younger Copper rushed forward.

"Will he be all right?" he asked, his voice breaking.

Kaelorn lifted his gaze from the wounded wing.

"He will live," the Forest Warden said. "But he will need rest. The forest itself must finish what my magic begins."

Raelithar's breathing was slow but steady. The roots beneath him had already begun to coil gently around his body, drawing strength from the ancient dragon and feeding it back into his wounds.

Before anyone could speak again, a pixie burst through the drifting ash. Her wings were dulled with soot, her glow flickering unevenly.

"The Copper who saved us," she cried. "He is badly hurt very badly. We should have seen it sooner... we should not have been so careless."

Her voice broke.

Raelithar's great head lifted at once.

"Kaelorn," he rumbled, "go. I can wait."

The Forest Warden did not argue.

He rose immediately, the pixies parting to guide him. Raelithar struggled to his feet, pain rippling visibly through his wings as torn membrane pulled against healing scales.

"Do not move," Kaelorn said sharply.

Raelithar ignored him.

"I must," the Copper Ancient replied. "He is my own."

Together they followed the pixie through broken branches and scorched roots. The forest parted for them, its paths opening in quiet sympathy.

They reached a small clearing where the young Copper dragon lay crumpled against the earth.

His breathing was shallow. One wing hung nearly torn through at the joint, the membrane shredded and useless. Deep claw marks scored his chest, copper scales peeled back to reveal dark, smoking wounds.

Blood stained the leaves beneath him.

Several pixies hovered close to his side, their lights dimmed to soft embers. They whispered to him in gentle, trembling voices, too afraid to leave him alone.

Kaelorn knelt and pressed his staff into the soil.

"Pixies," he said gently, "gather the healing herbs. All of them. From every hollow and root the forest still holds."

Some scattered in flashes of light.

Others remained, hovering near the wounded dragon, their glow steady and warm against his scales.

The Emberwoods wounded but willing opened its hidden places. Small flowers bloomed where there had only been ash. Roots pushed aside stones to reveal hidden caches of herbs and glowing moss.

Healing answered the call not swiftly, not easily but with quiet, determined resolve.

Raelithar lowered his great head beside the fallen dragon.

For a moment, he said nothing.

He simply breathed, his warm copper-scented breath stirring the pixies' lights.

"You fought well," he murmured. "Better than I had any right to ask of you."

The young dragon's eye fluttered weakly open.

"I... did not want them to reach the tree," he whispered.

Raelithar's voice softened.

"And they did not."

Kaelorn's magic flowed in a steady current, knitting torn flesh and sealing the worst of the bleeding. The forest's roots curled closer, their energy seeping into the dragon's body.

Around them, the other Copper dragons began to return, landing quietly among the wounded groves. Some carried injured kin. Others bore fallen branches or fragments of lightning-split stone, already beginning the work of clearing and healing.

Kaelorn rose slowly and turned to them.

"Search the forest," he instructed. "Find every wound this battle left behind. Bring me the truth of what was lost nothing hidden, nothing softened."

They lifted into the thinning smoke and vanished between the scarred trees.

Raelithar remained beside the fallen dragon, his gaze never leaving the trembling form.

Ash drifted down around them like gray snow.

The forest would heal.

The Emberwoods always did.

But Raelithar knew that some wounds those carved into memory and heart were not mended by magic alone.

And those were the ones that endured.

He would carry this one for a long time to come.

Chapter 36

Where Stars Bleed

While the forests of Emberwoods still smoldered with ash and greenfire, the war spread beyond root and stone, rising into the heavens above Lyra'el.

The sky tore open not with storm, but with something far worse.

From the void beyond the clouds came Voraxia, the Shadow Dragon, and Vorathos, the Abyssal Dragon colossal forms barreling out of the darkness like living cataclysms. Shadow and void trailed in their wake Voraxia's darkness devouring light, Vorathos's abyss swallowing even the space between it.

The heavens dimmed around them.

Clouds twisted into spirals of black and violet. The wind faltered, then surged again in jagged, unnatural gusts. Even the light of the upper sky seemed to recoil, as if the firmament itself recognized the intruders.

Lyra'el shuddered, its floating foundations trembling against the unseen force pressing down upon it.

On the western spire, Talhira saw them first.

Her breath caught then shattered into motion.

"Signal the city!" she cried.

The warning bells rang.

Pure. Piercing. Relentless.

Their tones cut through the high air, echoing between crystal towers and skybridges as citizens and guardians alike turned their eyes upward.

Talhira sprinted across the skybridge, boots striking crystal glass. She did not slow at the edge.

She leapt.

Radiantus, the great Platinum Dragon, swept beneath her in a flawless arc, lowering his wing mid-turn with perfect precision. She landed upon his back as his scales ignited with silvery-white fire, the glow spreading across his vast form like rising dawn.

Across the platforms, the other Platinum riders mounted in perfect rhythm. Harnesses snapped into place. Commands rang out. Dragons lifted as one, thunderous wingbeats shaking the air as disciplined formations formed around their leader.

Above them all, Aurelius rose.

The Celestial Dragon unfurled in radiant gold-white brilliance, his immense wings scattering starlight like falling embers. One by one, the Celestial dragons ascended with him a living constellation rising into the heavens, order against the unraveling dark.

Below, the city moved with practiced urgency.

Mages raced across the terraces, staffs blazing. Arcane barriers flared into being, curving between towers in shimmering domes of light. Healing sanctums awakened across the upper platforms, their wards humming in preparation for the wounded yet to come.

The air filled with layered magic sharp, luminous, and humming with restrained urgency.

Lyra'el braced itself.

Above its towers, platinum and celestial wings gathered in luminous formation, facing the approaching darkness.

The sky was about to fall.

Voraxia surged forward, shadow rolling from her wings like living night. Darkness poured behind her in long, tattered ribbons, devouring the pale light of the upper sky. Her gaze locked upon Aurelius with murderous intent.

"This ends," she hissed, her voice sliding through the air like a blade through silk.

"Here. Now."

Aurelius did not retreat.

His radiant form blazed brighter with every beat of his wings. Gold-white light spilled from his scales, pushing back the creeping darkness as he closed the distance. The air around him shimmered with quiet celestial power.

"You have fallen before. You will fall again."

His voice was calm as dawn over still waters.

Below them, the platinum formations faltered for a heartbeat, every rider and dragon feeling the gathering pressure in the sky. Light and shadow drew toward one another like opposing tides.

The clouds between them twisted, caught between radiance and void.

Voraxia's jaws opened, darkness coiling within her throat like a starless abyss.

Aurelius answered with a surge of pure celestial light, his wings flaring wide as though he carried the sun itself upon his back.

They collided.

Shadow met radiance in a blinding detonation that tore through the heavens. Light exploded outward in every direction, clouds vaporizing as the air screamed beneath the strain of their impact.

For a moment, the sky turned white.

At that same instant, Radiantus drove straight toward Vorathos, intercepting the abyss before it could reach the city, platinum scales burning with celestial fire. His vast wings cut through the darkened sky, each beat leaving trails of silvery brilliance in the air behind him.

Talhira rose in her saddle, voice ringing across the formation.

"This is no ordinary battle," she called. "Lightforged now!"

The Platinum riders raised their weapons in perfect unison.

Blades, staves, and lances ignited with radiant power as one, their light flowing outward and upward, weaving together into a vast living lattice.

The Lightforged Shield formed.

Bands of brilliant energy arced between the Platinum dragons, linking scale to scale, rider to rider, until the entire formation was wrapped in a dome of living radiance.

It shimmered like a second sun in the sky pure, unwavering, and unyielding.

Below them, the towers of Lyra'el gleamed in its reflection.

Then the Abyssal host descended.

They plunged from the void like a storm of living nightmares jagged wings, hollow eyes, and claws outstretched in hunger and mindless fury. Their shrieks tore through the air as they dove straight for the Platinum formation.

They struck the shield.

Light thundered across the heavens, the sound rolling outward like a breaking world.

Talons scraped against impossible brilliance. Abyssal claws screeched across the radiant lattice, sending showers of starfire cascading into the clouds below.

The impact rippled through the formation, but the riders held fast. Their weapons blazed brighter. Their dragons tightened their formation.

The shield did not break.

But it trembled.

Radiantus threw back his head and roared, the sound echoing across the sky like a divine proclamation carried across creation itself.

The battle for Lyra'el had begun.

And the heavens erupted.

Shadow and abyss crashed into light and starlight as the sky above Lyra'el became a storm of wings, radiance, and shattered constellations.

Dragons wheeled and collided across the heavens. Platinum scales flashed like falling stars. Celestial wings carved radiant arcs through the smoke-streaked sky.

Against them surged the darkness shadow dragons slipping between the lines like living wounds in the air, while Abyssal dragons hurled themselves forward in savage, relentless waves breaking, reforming, and breaking again.

They struck with hunger and fury, uncaring of wounds or loss.

Some broke through.

A Platinum dragon reeled as an Abyssal claw tore deep across his flank, silver blood scattering like dying sparks in the wind. His formation wavered, the Lightforged lattice flickering where his strength faltered.

Nearby, a Celestial dragon was struck by a blast of shadowfire. Darkness clung to his radiant scales, smothering his glow as he spiraled downward, light flickering like a fading star.

Below, the towers of Lyra'el loomed closer.

Before either could fall far, the Celestial dragons surged forward keepers of the sky's last mercy.

Great wings of gold-white light swept through the smoke-filled air as they intercepted the wounded. Their voices rose in resonant harmony deep, ancient tones that rolled across the battlefield like sacred hymns.

Golden radiance poured from their wings and throats, living light wrapping around the fallen where they drifted.

The wounded dragons were caught in those glowing currents, cradled by celestial power.

Torn flesh reknit.

Broken scales reformed, gleaming whole once more.

Shadowfire hissed and dissolved beneath the touch of radiant breath.

The falling dragons slowed... then rose again, lifted by celestial light, returning to the burning sky to rejoin the fight.

Lyra'el refused to let its guardians fall.

Across the battlefield, Voraxia saw it.

Her fury ignited sharp, focused, immediate.

The healing light, the rising formations, the unbroken resolve of the skyborne defenders—it enraged her more than any blade.

With a snarl, she abandoned the chaos of the wider war and fixed her gaze solely upon Aurelius.

Shadow coiled tighter around her form. Darkness thickened along her wings, pooling like liquid night. The space between them dimmed as her power swelled with lethal intent.

The sky itself seemed to falter.

Light thinned.

The air grew cold.

And the heavens darkened around them.

The war narrowed... to two.

Around them, dragons still clashed, light and shadow tearing across the sky but at the center of the storm, the world seemed to draw inward.

Voraxia's gaze never left Aurelius.

Darkness gathered at her claws as she drew upon the void itself. The air warped around her, space bending inward like cloth pulled too tight. Starlight dimmed. Even the glow of the Celestial dragons faltered at the edges.

Light bent toward her talons, stretched thin as though caught in a closing fist.

Between her claws, a seed of nothingness began to form.

A black sun was born.

It devoured the stars around it as it swelled. Gravity screamed as space collapsed toward annihilation. Clouds spiraled toward it. The air howled as the heavens themselves seemed to slide toward the growing void.

Even the dragons nearby felt its pull.

Formations wavered. Wings strained against the invisible current. Riders shouted to hold formation as dragons fought the drag of the gathering abyss.

Aurelius felt it.

He did not retreat.

Before the void could fully form, he answered.

The Aura of Righteousness surged from his form a wave of living radiance spreading outward in silent, unstoppable brilliance.

It was not merely light.

It was presence.

Truth.

The unyielding weight of celestial purpose itself.

The radiance struck the forming void.

Light met darkness not as force, but as certainty. Not as power, but as truth.

The brilliance pierced the heart of the black sun, unraveling the spell at its core.

The void faltered.

Cracks of brilliance spread through the dark sphere.

Then the black sun collapsed violently inward.

It vanished with a thunderous crack that split the clouds and sent shockwaves rippling across the heavens. The air roared outward, scattering shadow and light alike.

Voraxia screamed a sound of rage and ruin and hurled herself at him.

Her claws tore across Aurelius's side, shadow and void ripping into celestial light. Radiance spilled from the wound like molten dawnlight, scattering through the air in fading sparks.

Aurelius staggered.

His wings faltered for a single, dangerous moment.

The sky itself seemed to tremble at the faltering of its brightest light.

Radiantus saw.

With a roar that shook Lyra'el itself, the Platinum Dragon surged upward to answer.

Radiantus climbed through the smoke-streaked heavens and placed himself between Voraxia and Vorathos, his vast form blazing with unbound celestial fire. His platinum scales shone like a newborn star, radiance spilling from him in waves that pushed back the creeping darkness.

For a moment, the shadow recoiled.

At once, the remaining Celestial dragons closed ranks around Aurelius. Their luminous wings formed a living shield of gold-white light as they encircled him in the sky.

Healing radiance poured into his wounded side, sealing torn light and reforming fractured scales.

Celestial voices rose in steady harmony, their ancient tones weaving together as light flowed across the torn flesh. Shadow burned away beneath their touch. Celestial scales reformed.

The glow of Aurelius's form steadied, though he remained within their protective ring, not yet returned to full strength.

Above and below, the war spiraled on shadow, abyss, platinum, and starlight locked in violent orbit.

Dragons wheeled in blazing arcs. Lightning and shadowfire tore through the clouds. Trails of radiance streaked the heavens like falling stars.

The fate of the sky itself hung in the balance.

"Raise the shields," Talhira commanded.

"Higher tighten them around Aurelius."

The Platinum riders answered as one.

Their weapons blazed, Lightforged Shields expanding outward. Bands of radiant energy arced between them, interlocking into a vast lattice that wrapped Aurelius in a fortress of living brilliance.

Within its glow, the Celestial dragons worked without pause their voices steady, their light unbroken as wounds knit closed beneath their touch.

Then the Platinum host surged forward.

Radiant wings tore through the sky as the Platinum dragons drove straight into the Shadow and Abyssal ranks.

Their charge fell like a star of silver fire through the dark formation.

The impact scattered them like ash before a storm.

Shadow dragons were hurled aside, spiraling into the clouds. Abyssal forms tumbled from the heavens, their hollow screams fading as they fell toward the distant earth below, swallowed by cloud and distance.

Vorathos saw them fall and something ancient snapped.

Her fury ignited.

She turned on Radiantus with a scream of abyssal wrath, her massive form plunging in a killing dive.

Vorathos fell from the upper sky like a comet of devouring darkness, wings folded tight as the void coiled around her body. The air howled in her wake. Shadows trailed behind her like torn banners as she drove straight for the Platinum Dragon.

Radiantus did not retreat.

He watched her descent, his silver-white fire burning brighter with every heartbeat. The light around him intensified, his scales blazing like molten starlight.

At the last instant, he moved.

He rolled aside in a sweeping arc, the abyssal dive tearing past him close enough to rattle his wings.

As Vorathos passed, Radiantus struck.

His talons flashed.

They raked across her wings with the force of falling stars unleashed. Abyssal flesh tore open, dark ichor spraying into the burning sky, hissing where it touched the light in long twisting streams.

Vorathos howled, the sound echoing across the heavens like a wounded storm.

The impact rippled outward. Nearby dragons staggered in the air. Clouds shattered beneath the shockwave of their clash.

Above and below, both armies felt it.

The war for the heavens of Lyra'el had reached its breaking point.

For a moment, the sky began to quiet not in peace, but in tension held too long. Light and shadow drifted apart, as though the heavens themselves waited to see which force would claim them.

The battle hung on a single fragile breath.

Voraxia saw Vorathos falter.

Abyssal blood stained the clouds, drifting in dark ribbons through the smoke-streaked sky. Below them, the dark silhouettes of their younger dragons were already falling away some wounded, some in full retreat, their formations breaking under the relentless pressure of platinum and starlight.

The tide had turned.

Voraxia's gaze hardened.

She turned back to Aurelius, shadow coiling tightly around her form, darkness gathering like a storm about to break.

"You may live," she said coldly. "For now. But you are wounded perhaps enough to keep you from the wars yet to come."

Her eyes flicked once toward the blazing shields of the Platinum host. The Lightforged lattice burned bright and unbroken, the Celestial dragons still working within its radiant heart.

Calculation replaced fury cold and immediate.

She turned to Vorathos.

"Withdraw," Voraxia commanded. "We have done what was required. They will not aid the others."

Vorathos snarled, rage churning in her abyssal eyes. Dark ichor still dripped from her wounded wings, hissing where it touched the light.

But she did not argue.

"As you will," she growled. "This sky is not worth dying for today."

Shadow folded around them.

Abyss answered.

Darkness gathered like closing wings of a world without light, swallowing their forms as void and shadow wrapped tight around their bodies. In a single heartbeat, Voraxia and Vorathos vanished taking the deepest shadows of the sky with them as they fled.

The dark host followed, dissolving into streaks of retreating night.

Silence crept back into the heavens slow and uncertain.

The sky above Lyra'el finally exhaled.

Starlight seeped back into the heavens as the last echoes of battle faded.

Clouds thinned and drifted apart in slow, weary currents, as though the sky itself had released a long-held breath. Trails of silver fire and shadow slowly dissolved, leaving only the quiet shimmer of distant stars.

Radiantus turned at once and flew to Aurelius's side.

"Solae vethra, kaelith," he murmured, the words flowing like quiet starlight. "Easy, old friend... the light has not finished with you yet."

The Celestial dragons parted to let him through. Their wings lowered in silent respect as the Platinum Dragon drew close, his radiance softening to a gentle glow.

Aurelius's light flickered but it did not fade.

Radiantus eased himself alongside him, shielding the wounded Celestial with his vast gleaming wings.

Together, they began their slow descent toward the floating city below wounded, but unbroken.

Around them, the surviving Platinum and Celestial dragons formed a silent escort.

No commands were needed.

No words were spoken.

The sky itself seemed to bow as they passed.

Above them, the constellations returned one by one reclaiming the heavens from shadow.

Dawnlight crept across the clouds, pale and fragile at first, but growing stronger with every breath.

Below them, Lyra'el hovered scarred, shaken, but intact.

Cracked spires still glowed with warding light. Platforms bore the marks of falling fire.

But the city lived.

The war for the heavens was over.

And Lyra'el scarred, shaken, but unbroken still stood.

Chapter 37

The Sky Still Stands

The barrier around Lyra'el lowered slowly, its radiant lattice dissolving into drifting threads of light. The last fragments of the Lightforged shields faded into the sky like embers carried on the wind.

Along the outer platforms and skybridges, there was damaged scorched stone, fractured spires, shattered balustrades. Crystal inlays had been blasted loose. Sections of railing lay twisted and blackened. Shallow craters marked where shadowfire had struck.

Wounds the city had never known before nor believed it could.

The people moved through the wreckage in quiet lines, clearing broken crystal and gathering fallen fragments of the sky. Their faces were drawn, their voices hushed. Even the children, usually quick to speak or laugh, worked in solemn silence, as though the sky itself had taught them stillness.

Nothing had ever pierced the shield before today.

And now they knew it could.

That truth weighed heavily.

And yet they stayed.

They worked.

They refused to flee.

Lyra'el would not abandon its guardians.

A murmur rippled across the terraces.

Tools stilled. Voices quieted. Eyes lifted.

High above, the Platinum and Celestial dragons were returning.

They came in slow formation not in the fierce order of war, but in the careful rhythm of protectors escorting one of their own. Starlight clung to their wings as they descended, dimmed but unbroken.

At the center of the formation, Radiantus flew close beside Aurelius, one great platinum wing braced beneath the wounded Celestial's side, guiding him carefully toward the landing platforms.

The sight spread through the terraces like a pulse of emotion.

When Aurelius touched down unsteady but upright the people of Lyra'el dropped their tools and began to run.

Toward the light.

Toward their wounded guardian.

Toward hope that still lived.

Some fell to their knees as he passed. Others reached out, as though the warmth of his presence alone might steady their hearts.

As the dragons settled across the platforms, the Platinum riders immediately moved among them, checking wings, scales, and joints, calling out injuries and summoning healers.

But Talhira was already running.

She leapt from Radiantus's back and sprinted across the terrace toward the healing sanctum, her breath sharp with urgency, her steps never slowing.

Inside, she nearly collided with Thump, the little fox racing in frantic circles, his tail thumping anxiously against the stone.

"Where is he?" Talhira murmured.

Thump darted down the corridor.

She followed.

She found Valeon surrounded by drying herbs and open satchels, the scent of crushed leaves and oils thick in the air.

"Valeon," she said, gripping his arm, "you are needed. Bring your healing herbs. Aurelius has been injured."

Valeon's face drained of color.

For a moment he simply stared at her unable to process the words, as though they did not belong to this world.

Then urgency took hold.

He seized his satchel and followed her at once, neither of them noticing as Thump slipped after them, silent and intent.

They reached the landing platform where Aurelius lay supported by the Celestial dragons, his wound still dark against his radiant scales.

The air around him shimmered faintly, as though the sky itself were reluctant to let his light dim.

Valeon knelt beside him, his hands trembling only for a moment before steadiness returned. He opened his satchel, selecting leaves and crushed blossoms with careful precision, already working to cleanse the torn flesh.

"I... I hope I can do this," Valeon whispered.

Aurelius turned his luminous gaze toward him.

"I have faith in you," the Celestial Dragon said gently.

And the healing began.

Valeon worked carefully, crushing the gathered herbs together and pressing the glowing mixture into Aurelius's wound. The air filled with a warm, living fragrance as the torn flesh began to seal, light slowly threading back through the Celestial's scales fragile, but returning.

Around them, the Celestial dragons stood in silent vigil, their wings partially spread, forming a quiet ring of radiance.

"You must rest," Valeon said softly.

Aurelius gave a quiet laugh.

"That is what I tell all who are wounded."

Valeon smiled then frowned.

"Thump... no."

The little fox had climbed boldly onto Aurelius's chest, curling near the wounded place as if standing guard over the light itself.

Aurelius shifted just enough to make room for him.

"Thump is welcome," he said.

Several of the nearby Celestial dragons gave soft, amused rumbles, their tension easing just slightly.

Valeon shook his head in quiet disbelief before rising to see what else he could tend.

Nearby, Radiantus watched him go.

"Well done," the Platinum Dragon said to Talhira. "You were right to bring him."

Talhira nodded. "I've seen his progress."

Aurelius's eyes glowed with agreement.

Talhira turned and moved back toward the city, joining the others in clearing the damage along the terraces. All across Lyra'el, people and dragons worked side by side lifting stones, repairing wards, and tending the wounded.

Radiantus lowered his great head toward Aurelius.

"You pushed yourself too far, old friend."

Aurelius smiled faintly.

"Perhaps," he said. "But the light still stands."

Radiantus exhaled, a soft plume of silver warmth drifting into the thinning air.

Above them, the sky of Lyra'el shimmered once more scarred, but unbroken its returning starlight settling gently across the wounded terraces.

The city endured.

And the light though tested had not fallen.

Chapter 38

Heart of the Storm

While the heavens above Lyra'el still bled starlight and shadow, war thundered across the golden city of Goldmoor.

Their thunder rolled across fields and towers alike, and every eye turned skyward.

From the burning horizon came Zylron and his Red dragons, fire rippling along their wings like living banners of destruction. Heat shimmered beneath them, the air itself warping as they advanced.

Beside them flew Glaciera and her White dragons, their pale forms cutting through the sky like shards of winter. Frost spread in their wake. Clouds froze and cracked apart as bitter cold poured outward, devouring the warmth of the late afternoon sun.

Heat and cold advanced together fire and frost, ruin in twin forms.

The city moved as one.

Mages and medics surged to their stations. Dragon riders ran across the towers and launch platforms, armor catching the light as they took their places. Orders snapped through the streets, sharp and steady, as practiced resolve overtook the first stirrings of fear.

Keisha was already moving.

She reached Kimras just as the great golden dragon unfurled to his full ancient height. His scales burned with molten light, and when he spread his wings, lightning crawled along their edges like living veins of stormfire.

Keisha vaulted onto his back in a single fluid motion, already part of the storm.

Kimras roared deep, thunderous, unyielding and surged skyward. The ground trembled beneath the force of his ascent as golden fire trailed behind him like a rising sun.

One by one, the noble dragons followed, wings beating in powerful rhythm as they climbed to meet the coming storm.

The instant the last cleared the city's edge, the mages sealed Goldmoor's barrier. A dome of living magic rose from the towers, threads of radiant energy weaving together until the city vanished beneath a shimmering shield of light.

On the western tower, Queen Jeanne stood beside Casper, her hands resting against the cougar's thick fur as King Alex joined the other riders above.

"Please," she whispered, her fingers tightening in the animal's fur. "Be careful... and come back to me."

Above them, the armies of the sky closed.

Then streaks of amethyst tore across the heavens.

Kimras cast a sidelong glance toward Amara as the distance between the opposing forces narrowed, his voice carrying with calm, ancient assurance.

"Storm-sister," he said, "you once claimed these dark dragons plagued you like a winter migraine. Yet here you fly to greet them."

Amara's laughter rang like crystal struck by lightning, storm-light flashing in her eyes.

"They do trouble my thoughts," she replied, her voice smooth and amused.

"But the quickest cure for a headache is to remove the cause."

Ahead of them, the sky darkened with the approaching shapes of red and white wings.

The heavens churned with fire and frost as the distance closed. Heat shimmered from Zylron's formation. Glaciera's cold rolled outward in pale, cracking waves. The air between the two hosts twisted, caught between burning wind and killing chill.

Then the sky cracked open.

The battle for Goldmoor had begun.

Ong tightened his grip on his dragonlance as the wind howled around Amara's wings. A low, thrumming pressure pulsed through the air felt more than heard as her psionic field spread outward like an invisible tide, brushing against the minds of friend and foe alike: unsettling, probing, impossible to ignore.

He cast a glance toward Kimras and Keisha, then back to Glaciera, his brow tightening.

Keisha saw it.

She smiled, her eyes bright despite the gathering storm.

"Don't worry," she called across the wind. "She will have to pass through all of us before she ever reaches me. And Glaciera is no match for Kimras."

She tilted her head slightly, teasing warmth threading her voice.

"Besides, she didn't care much for your dragonlance the last time you met."

Ong let out a quiet laugh, the tension in his shoulders easing just a fraction even as fire and frost closed in around them.

Amara angled toward the White Dragon, her crystalline wings cutting through the churning air. Around her, the sky bent as waves of psionic force rippled outward, distorting sound and space alike. The wind twisted around her form, drawn into silent, invisible currents that hummed with pressure.

"You again, Glaciera?" she called, her tone bright with mocking ease. "I see the last beating didn't leave a lasting impression."

For a heartbeat, the sky held still.

Then frost exploded outward.

Glaciera answered with a scream of glacial fury, her pale wings snapping wide as a storm of ice and killing cold surged from her body. The temperature plummeted in an instant. Clouds crystallized and shattered. Needles of frost spiraled through the air as she lunged forward, jaws glowing with freezing power.

At the heart of the storm, Kimras dove toward the jagged rock spires below.

"Zylron favors his claws," he rumbled to Keisha, his voice steady despite the roaring sky.

"I will draw him high. Your magic will serve us better from the ground and I would have you beyond his reach."

Keisha nodded once.

"I trust you."

Kimras swept low over the stone outcropping, golden wings stirring dust and sparks as he leveled his flight.

Keisha leapt from his back.

She landed upon the outcropping with impossible grace, already gathering power. Raising her hands, she let ancient Eladrin magic surge through her veins. Protective wards blossomed outward sigils of living light locking into place, anchoring themselves against fire and frost alike.

Overhead, Kimras met Zylron's talons head-on.

The sky shattered.

"Do not kill the elf," Glaciera snarled toward Zylron as they closed on the battlefield, frost streaming from her jaws.

"She is mine. A trophy."

Zylron's molten gaze flicked toward Keisha far below, his lip curling as heat shimmered along his fangs like molten breath.

But Kimras heard her.

The Golden Ancient wheeled in the burning sky, his vast wings scattering firelight as he rose between them and the spires below. His roar tore across the storm, shaking frost from the clouds and rattling the towers of Goldmoor beneath them.

"Lay a claw upon her," he thundered, his voice rich with ancient authority,

"and you will answer to me, ice-witch. I have buried tyrants older than your frost ever dreamed of becoming."

The air trembled with the weight of his promise.

He surged upward into the clouds, vanishing into the thunderhead as Amara, her psionic brood, and the Gold dragons held their line beneath him. The air around them tightened pressure building, minds sharpening, space warping subtly as Amara's psionic field spread like an unseen tide.

The formation held.

Then the sky changed.

From within the clouds, Kimras unleashed his power.

The thunderhead thickened, turning heavy and unnatural. Light dimmed behind rolling masses of storm-dark cloud.

The air slowed.

A shimmering **Cloudkill** poured outward, spreading like golden mist through the Red and White ranks. It rolled between their wings and jaws, thick as molten fog burning lungs, dulling senses, turning breath itself into a weapon against its wielder.

Fire faltered.

Frost cracked and sputtered.

The dark dragons faltered.

Their wings labored against the choking air. Their movements dulled as if the storm itself resisted them. Fire and frost both lost their edge, turning uneven and unreliable as breath grew thick and uncooperative.

Zylron's fury ignited.

From within the storm above, Kimras's voice rolled outward deep, resonant, and edged with terrible amusement.

"You forgot, did you not?"

"Even mountains kneel when the golden storm remembers its strength."

The golden haze deepened, swallowing the enemy ranks in choking brilliance.

Even Glaciera screamed as the magic seized her. Her pale wings shuddered as the poisoned air clawed at her breath, each motion growing heavier. Frost sputtered along her scales, cracking apart as the choking haze dulled her strength.

"What sorcery is this?!" she snarled, thrashing against the thickening air.

Amara answered her.

The air screamed.

A banshee-like psychic shriek tore from Amara's jaws silent to the ear, yet devastating to the mind an impact felt rather than heard. The invisible force rippled outward in a widening wave, crashing into the dark formations.

Minds recoiled.

Balance shattered.

Several White dragons veered wildly, their wings stuttering as terror and disorientation slammed into them at once, breaking instinct and formation alike. Their carefully aligned ranks unraveled into jagged spirals of confusion.

"It's called strategy," Amara said lightly, her voice echoing through the warped air like a mocking chime.

"You should try it sometime. It works wonders for persistent headaches."

The tide of battle turned.

High above the barrier of Goldmoor, chaos thundered through the clouds golden mist, splintering frost, and rippling psionic force colliding in a violent storm.

Then one White dragon broke formation.

Its icy gaze locked onto King Alex as he rode into the storm, separated for a single, dangerous moment.

The beast screamed and dove straight for him.

On the western tower, Queen Jeanne gripped the stone parapet, her breath caught as the world narrowed to that single falling shadow.

Then fire split the sky.

A Gold dragon surged in from the flank, its rider driving it forward with fierce precision. The golden form cut across the White dragon's path just as it descended upon King Alex.

Golden flame erupted from its jaws.

The blast tore through the ice dragon's chest in a blinding arc of fire. Frost and flame exploded together in a violent burst of steam and shattered crystal.

The White dragon screamed once sharp and brief before its wings faltered. Its body twisted, spiraling helplessly into the clouds below.

On the western tower, Queen Jeanne exhaled, her knees weakening as the tension finally broke. Casper pressed against her side, steady and warm, anchoring her to the stone.

Above them, the battle raged on.

Gold and Amethyst dragons struck in coordinated waves, their movements precise and deliberate, each strike reinforcing the next. Golden fire swept across the dark ranks while the Amethyst dragons reshaped the battlefield itself.

From their formation came concussive bursts of psionic force visible only in their impact. Shockwaves rippled through the clouds, hurling Red and White dragons off course. Space buckled. Formations collapsed.

Then came the crystal barrage.

Amethyst dragons spat jagged shards that detonated midair, scattering bursts of psychic force through the slowed enemy ranks. The explosions rippled through the golden haze, amplifying the disorientation.

Red dragons reeled beneath waves of golden fire.

White dragons scattered as their freezing breath shattered against Eladrin wards and invisible psionic barriers, their attacks slipping wide or rebounding without control.

Above it all, Kimras's Cloudkill continued to poison the sky.

The storm no longer obeyed the dark.

The storm belonged to the nobles.

And the dark dragons were bleeding.

Through the choking gold haze, Glaciera caught sight of the rocky outcropping below.

Of Keisha.

Her fury twisted cold, focused, and terrible.

"We may be losing this battle," Glaciera shrieked, "but I will still claim what is mine. The elf will leave this sky encased in ice!"

She plunged.

Her pale form knifed downward through the storm, frost streaming behind her like a falling comet. The golden haze tore around her wings as she forced through it, ice forming in jagged sheets across her scales.

The rocky outcropping rushed closer.

But Amara and Ong were already moving.

They cut across Glaciera's path in a surge of warped air and flashing steel. Space folded around them as Amara's psionic field compressed, bending distance and momentum in their favor.

"Not while I'm breathing, Glaciera!" Ong roared. "You want her, you go through me first!"

He drove the dragonlance forward.

The blade struck true.

It sliced through Glaciera's wing in a violent spray of frost and pale blood, the impact jolting her entire body off course. Ice shattered. White scales split. Her descent broke into a wild, spiraling tumble.

Glaciera screamed, fury and pain mingling in a single, piercing cry as she veered away from the rock, spinning back into the storm.

Above them, Zylron surged toward Kimras, talons extended, molten rage blazing in his eyes.

The Red tyrant cut through the golden haze like a falling inferno, heat rippling along his wings as he drove straight for the ancient.

Kimras twisted aside at the last instant.

Zylron's claws raked along the Golden Ancient's flank, carving a burning line across radiant scales. Sparks and molten light scattered through the storm but the wound was shallow, the strike glancing rather than fatal.

Kimras answered with thunder.

The sky shook as the two ancients tore past one another, wings beating in explosive bursts of heat and stormfire. Clouds shredded in their wake as gold and crimson flames streaked across the heavens.

The heart of the storm was breaking.

Kimras surged forward, talons closing as he reached for Zylron—but Zylron remembered.

He pulled back at the last instant, twisting away before Kimras could seize him. The memory of their previous battle flashed in his eyes, and for a heartbeat fear flickered beneath his fury.

Kimras's laughter rolled through the storm.

"Ah... at last, a lesson remembered," he rumbled. "Even a tyrant may learn, given enough defeats."

Then he unleashed hell.

A torrent of golden flame erupted from Kimras's jaws a roaring river of living fire that tore across the sky and crashed into Zylron. The Red dragon answered in kind, his own inferno surging forward.

Gold and crimson collided.

The heavens ignited where their powers met, fire blossoming outward in blinding waves as the sky itself seemed to burn.

And then Zylron saw the truth behind him.

Glaciera was wounded, her pale wings trailing frost-stained blood.

Red and White dragons were falling faster than Gold and Amethyst. Dark forms spiraled from the clouds while golden fire and psionic shockwaves continued to tear through their ranks.

The storm no longer favored the dark.

The tide had turned.

Zylron's rage twisted into cold, calculating fury. He drew in a breath that burned like a furnace and roared the signal.

"Retreat!"

Glaciera shrieked in fury, her wounded wing trembling as she hovered in the thinning storm.

"I will not leave without the elf!"

"Another day!" Zylron bellowed. "You are injured and I will not lose you for a trophy. Fall back!"

Glaciera screamed her defiance, frost exploding from her jaws but she obeyed, wrenching herself free as the dark host began to withdraw.

"This is not over!" she cried, her voice echoing across the clearing sky. "I will have that elf!"

The storm thinned.

Golden haze drifted apart. The clouds parted. Fire and frost faded into distant streaks along the horizon as the dark dragons retreated.

The sky cleared.

Kimras descended to the rocky outcropping where Keisha stood waiting. The great golden dragon landed with heavy, controlled grace, wings folding slowly as the last sparks of battle faded from the air.

Keisha ran to him at once, her hands already searching his wounded flank.

"You're hurt."

"I have endured worse," Kimras rumbled, a low thread of draconic warmth beneath his words.

"But your concern honors me, little flame... vethira shal'en."

She rested her forehead briefly against his scales before climbing onto his back once more.

Amara and Ong descended nearby, landing beside them on the clearing stone. Together they turned toward the horizon, watching the dark dragons retreat into the burning distance.

No one spoke.

They all knew the truth.

They would be back.

And Goldmoor would be ready.

Chapter 39

What the Fire Leaves Behind

The sky over Goldmoor was clearing.

Smoke and frost drifted apart in slow, weary currents, revealing patches of blue between thinning clouds. The golden haze of Kimras's storm faded into the distance, leaving only the quiet echoes of battle behind.

When Queen Jeanne saw the returning silhouettes of the dragons, she lifted her hand at once.

"Lower the barrier."

The shimmering dome of magic unraveled, folding back into the towers in threads of fading light as the noble dragons descended.

She watched the sky with her breath held.

King Alex was among them.

The moment his boots touched stone, she ran.

She reached him and wrapped her arms around him, holding him as though the storm had nearly stolen him away. He held her just as tightly, one hand resting against her back, the other brushing dust from her hair.

For a moment, the war did not exist.

Casper pressed close, nuzzling Alex's side with a soft rumble of relief. Jeanne laughed quietly through her breath, and the three of them stood together in the quiet that follows battle.

Around them, the people of Goldmoor began to emerge from doorways, towers, and sanctums. Some wept openly. Others simply stood and stared at the sky, as though still expecting another wave of fire or frost to descend.

But the dark dragons were gone.

Nearby, Amara turned to her brood.

"Return to Purplefire," she commanded. "Guard the forest. I will follow shortly."

The Amethyst dragons answered at once, veering toward the distant horizon in streaks of violet light. As they departed, the subtle pressure of their psionic presence slowly faded from the air, leaving the sky strangely quiet.

Amara drifted down beside Kimras, and together they descended into the glen beyond the city's edge.

Queen Jeanne released Alex's hand only long enough to look at him, her eyes searching his face as if to be certain he was truly there. Then she took his hand again as they walked toward the two ancients the heart of the battle now resting before them.

Goldmoor still stood.

And so did its people.

King Alex paused at the edge of the square and looked out across the city.

The barrier had spared much of it but not all. Scorched stone, broken towers, and shattered streets marked the storm's path. Roofs had collapsed. Balconies hung crooked. The smell of burned timber and frozen mortar lingered in the air.

He raised his voice.

"Divide into crews. Clear the debris. Begin rebuilding the damaged quarters at once."

The people of Goldmoor obeyed without hesitation. Workers and mages alike began moving through the streets, forming lines, lifting rubble, and weaving spells to stabilize cracked stone.

Above them, Kimras turned to his own.

"Gold dragons, lend your strength to the city," he commanded. "Remove the heaviest wreckage. Carry it beyond the walls and see it undone."

Golden wings lifted. One by one, the great dragons took to the air again not for war, but for labor hauling massive fragments of stone and shattered earth away from the city.

Below, Keisha was already at Kimras's side.

She found the wound at once.

"You are hurt," she said, concern sharpening her voice.

"It is nothing of consequence," Kimras replied.

Amara turned on him, psionic light flickering faintly along her scales.

"I will decide that," she said dryly.

She lifted one talon and inspected the torn gold scales. Kimras muttered something under his breath.

Ong only laughed as he stepped closer and pulled Keisha gently into his arms.

Then a streak of black shot across the square.

It slammed into Ong's legs and sent him sprawling.

Keisha burst into laughter.

"Pumpkin!"

The great black panther skidded to a halt and immediately began purring, entirely unapologetic, her tail swishing with satisfaction.

Amara gave Keisha a slight nod.

Keisha stepped forward and placed her hands along Kimras's wounded side. Eladrin magic rose to meet Amara's psionic current, the two currents weaving together in a slow, luminous flow.

The wound sealed.

The heat faded.

Kimras grumbled, "Two against one. Hardly a fair arrangement."

But he lowered himself into the grass and allowed the healing to finish, his great wings settling around him like folding banners.

Amara shook her head, then turned her gaze to Keisha.

"Are you well?" she asked softly. "After Glaciera's... enthusiasm?"

Keisha's expression softened but did not waver.

"She still troubles my thoughts," she admitted. "But I know all of you will stand between her and me. And I will not let her threats keep me from defending Goldmoor."

Nearby, Ong climbed back to his feet and looked down at Pumpkin, who was already purring loudly. He smiled, scratched the great panther behind the ears, then pulled Keisha close again.

"They'll be back," he said quietly.

Kimras's eyes burned gold.

"Yes. And they will continue to come until we find the one who commands them—and end her dominion over the dark."

Keisha nodded.

"They're learning to fight together."

Amara lifted her gaze to the darkening sky.

"That is... inconvenient," she said softly. "But it will not save them. Vacari is not so easily claimed."

Above them, Goldmoor rebuilt.

Around them, the world endured.

And the war was far from over.

Chapter 40

The War of Silver and Lies

While thunder and flame still scarred the skies above Goldmoor, illusion crept along the hidden paths of E'vahona.

Silence ruled the false realm.

Within the folded layers of deception, Lord Karrenen and his mages waited unseen, unmoving their wards threaded through stone, wind, and light. Rings of subtle Eladrin runes shimmered across the ground, hidden among roots and moss, anchoring the true shape of the land beneath the illusion.

The enchantments around them did not exist to hide truth, but to mislead those who believed they already understood it lies crafted carefully enough that the mind completed the deception for itself.

Paths bent where none should.

Hills appeared where there were none.

Reflections drifted across the air like memories of places that had never existed.

And beneath it all, the Eladrin held the real world in place.

High above, against the ghost-lit sky, Talleoss and Silvara hovered with their silver kin, wings barely stirring the air. Their scales caught the faint, shifting light of the mirage, reflecting it back in cool, steady glimmers.

Beside them, Lady Seraphina and Lord Thaldir sat poised in their saddles, the glow of their Eladrin Spellweaver Staves casting quiet halos around their forms.

Seraphina's hand rested upon Argentis Aethern, its runes breathing with sovereign light measured and patient, like a crown waiting to be raised.

Thaldir's grip tightened around Luminara Virell, verdant sigils flowing like living script along the staff's length, ready... but restrained, like roots coiled beneath still earth.

No one spoke.

Below, the Eladrin mages stood in silent circles, their spells woven deep into the soil, keeping the illusion from unraveling or turning against them.

They all waited.

For Ixalia.

Thc illusion rippled.

From the false horizon of E'vahona emerged Ixalia and her Mirage dragons, their forms wavering between color and shadow as they slipped through the hidden entrance. Reality bent around them. Reflections stuttered. Mirage-light refracted against mirage-light until even the sky seemed uncertain of its shape.

Ixalia's laughter drifted softly through the fabricated heavens.

"So," she purred, her voice rich with delighted arrogance,
"even the Eladrin cannot hide their precious sanctuary from one who sees what others refuse to."

She circled through the illusion, wings casting fractured reflections across phantom spires and silvered valleys. Each sweep of her gaze fed her pride. The false city gleamed beneath her just convincing enough to satisfy her hunger for conquest.

The Silver dragons did not move.

High above the false realm, Talleoss and Silvara hovered in perfect stillness, their wings barely stirring the air. They watched her roam. They let her savor the lie. They let her believe she had outmaneuvered not only the Eladrin, but the ancient Silvers themselves.

Below, Lord Karrenen smiled faintly.

He lifted one hand.

The mages stiffened breath held, power poised. Runes along the ground brightened, their glow spreading in quiet, living lines beneath roots, stone, and moss.

The trap was set.

Talleoss inclined his great silver head.

Across the false sky, Silvara answered with a slow, deliberate tilt of her wings a signal not spoken, but remembered from battles older than kingdoms.

The silence sharpened.

No longer waiting.

Now coiled to strike.

Silvara moved first.

She swept forward, her radiant form cutting cleanly through the shimmering air. Where she passed, the illusion steadied silver light asserting truth where mirage flickered and warped.

Her presence alone demanded attention.

Ixalia turned.

She smirked, her wings fluttering with prismatic distortion.

"It seems we have found E'vahona at last," she said.

"Now we take it for the mysterious one..."

Her gaze hardened, ambition sharpening her tone. "...and Vacari will kneel."

Silvara did not answer.

She and Thaldir began to circle slowly, deliberately. Luminara Virell glowed in Thaldir's hands as he wove its power, verdant sigils spiraling outward in layered, interlocking patterns.

The magic did not surge.

It settled.

It sank into the air like roots seeking soil, anchoring the space around them—binding it so nothing within could easily slip away.

Then the sky shifted.

Talleoss descended.

With him came Seraphina, laughter bright and fearless as she raised the Argentis Aethern, its runes flaring with sovereign clarity. Silver-white light rippled from the staff steady, unwavering.

"Oh, Ixalia," Seraphina said lightly, her voice touched with musical amusement. "An ancient dragon of illusion..."

She inclined her head, almost kindly. "...and yet you walk so willingly into another's design."

She lifted her staff and nodded toward the ground.

The world shattered.

The false realm dissolved in cascading light. Phantom towers fractured. Silvered valleys peeled away like mist burned off by the sun. Reflections splintered into drifting shards of brilliance.

Illusion collapsed inward layer by layer until nothing remained but raw sky, warded stone, and waiting power.

Ixalia recoiled.

Her eyes widened as the true shape of the illusion-field revealed itself around her: rings of Eladrin runes blazing across the ground, Silver dragons poised above, their formation already closing.

The trap had never opened.

It had only been waiting.

Shock flared then ignited into fury.

"How dare you turn illusion against me!" Ixalia roared. "You will answer for this insult!"

The sky answered instead.

From the veiled clouds above, the Silver dragons descended in gleaming waves measured and deliberate, each movement guided by unerring clarity. Their riders came with them, moonlight and starlight blazing along their wings as they closed ranks around the battlefield.

Their approach was silent at first.

Then the air trembled.

They did not hesitate.

The moment truth took hold, they struck.

Silver flame and focused spellcraft tore through mirage and shadow. False images collapsed like brittle glass, unable to endure the weight of anchored reality. Illusion-doubles flickered, stuttered, and vanished as the Silver dragons carved clean paths through the distorted sky.

Mirage dragons faltered.

Their tricks failed them where reality held fast. Wings struck empty air. Phantom allies dissolved. Distances snapped violently back into their true shape.

At the heart of it all, Silvara and Talleoss drove straight toward Ixalia, their riders steady, intent, and unwavering.

Talleoss's voice rolled across the field, deep and absolute.

"You were warned. You are not welcome here. You do not belong in Vacari or in truth itself."

His wings flared, silver light cutting cleanly through the last of the distortion.

"Now you will pay the price for forgetting where illusion ends."

The heavens tore open.

The decisive battle erupted.

Around Ixalia, the air fractured.

Reality bent.

And truth began to slip.

Her scales shimmered then shattered outward.

A dozen identical forms burst across the battlefield as Shattered Reflection bloomed into existence. Each Ixalia moved independently. Each could strike. Each was impossible to trust.

The false dragons laughed in overlapping voices, the sound folding into a haunting chorus Echoing Lament until even the wind seemed to scream in voices that did not belong to it.

At the same time, a fog of illusion poured from her wings.

Thick.

Luminous.

Swallowing.

The battlefield vanished beneath swirling color and drifting mirage as Reality Warp twisted gravity and distance. The ground stretched and tilted beneath the Silver dragons. The sky pressed too close. The earth seemed to fall endlessly away.

Up and down lost meaning.

Several Mirage dragons exhaled their Illusory Breath, vivid dream-images erupting through the fog.

Phantom armies surged from nowhere.

Collapsing skies cracked overhead.

False wounds bloomed across silver scales pain that felt real, lingered real... and then vanished without cause.

Others scattered **Hallucinogenic Spores**, glittering motes drifting like starlight beautiful, invasive, and impossible to track once breathed.

For a heartbeat, the world became a nightmare.

For longer than a heartbeat, it held.

A Silver dragon snapped at a shadow wearing Ixalia's face teeth closing on nothing but glittering air. Another Silver plunged downward, certain the ground lay below, only to lurch mid-flight as the world tilted, the horizon sliding beneath him like a rug pulled by unseen hands.

Riders shouted warnings that contradicted one another.

"Left flank no, that's not—! Hold the line—she's behind us—she's everywhere—!"

Even sound betrayed them.

Direction became a lie.

The Echoing Lament twisted voices into false directions so commands seemed to come from the wrong side of the sky. For a moment, discipline frayed not from fear, but from the mind's instinct to make sense of what refused to be understood.

Below, Karrenen's mages felt the illusion bite deeper.

The earth stretched beneath their feet, stone turning to water in the corner of the eye, roots becoming serpents, paths rearranging themselves with living malice. One mage staggered, reaching for ground that seemed to fall away beneath her feet.

Karrenen seized her wrist and pulled her back into the circle.

"Anchor," he snapped. "Not sight—truth."

The Eladrin staves flared.

Wards tightened.

Runes awakened beneath moss and stone, threading through the hidden paths like veins of light. A low hum rose from the ground steady, insistent as reality answered their call.

Above them, Seraphina's gaze sharpened.

"She's trying to make us react," she said, her voice calm through the chaos. "To chase the wrong thing until we tear ourselves apart."

Thaldir lifted the Luminara Virell, the staff's verdant sigils spiraling outward like living script.

"Then we stop chasing," he said. "We make her come to us."

Talleoss drew in a slow breath.

Silver light gathered along his throat.

Then the Silvers answered.

But not all at once.

For a moment, even the ancient silvers faltered within the warped sky. Talleoss lunged for a Mirage dragon that dissolved into drifting color. Another Silver struck what appeared to be Ixalia herself only for the form to burst into glittering fragments that sliced harmlessly through empty air.

Below, the Eladrin mages felt it too the strain creeping into even the anchored world.

The ground beneath them stretched and tilted. Paths twisted. Distances warped into impossible angles that refused to hold still. One mage staggered as the earth seemed to drop away beneath her feet only for another to seize her arm and anchor her back to reality.

"Hold the wards!" Karrenen commanded. "Do not chase the illusion let it break against the truth!"

Staves flared. Sigils tightened. Threads of stabilizing magic anchored the battlefield, pinning fragments of reality in place like stakes driven into a raging storm.

Above, Talleoss drew a deep breath.

Then he roared and the sky itself seemed to freeze.

A sweeping cone of cold tore through the illusions, crystallizing mirage-light into brittle prisms. Half of Ixalia's false forms shattered into gleaming shards, their laughter breaking with them as they dissolved into nothing on the wind.

But the nightmare did not end.

Several Mirage dragons dove from impossible angles some falling upward, others striking sideways through warped gravity. One struck a Silver's flank with a claw that seemed to come from nowhere. Another exhaled a wave of hallucinogenic breath, and for an instant a Silver rider cried out as phantom flames crawled across his armor heatless, yet agonizingly real.

Silvara moved.

A breath of paralyzing gas rolled outward silent, absolute silver mist flooding the Mirage ranks. Wings locked. Jaws stiffened. Movements died mid-flight as terror seized them.

Above them, the Silver brood vanished into conjured clouds as Control Weather reshaped the sky. Stormbanks thickened. Winds shifted. Visibility dropped. Illusion-fog tangled with stormcloud until even the heavens struggled to decide what was real.

Then, from within the storm, they fell.

Silver shapes dropped like falling stars, bursting from the clouds to strike with claws, tails, and crushing force ancient aerial precision guiding every blow. Mirage dragons reeled as the disciplined assault carved through their fractured formations.

Ixalia felt the shift.

For the first time, the illusion-field resisted her.

She tried to flee.

Space folded around her as she triggered Dimensional Rift, slipping from one point in the sky to another in a blink distance collapsing to nothing beneath her will. One moment she was surrounded by silver wings —and the next she appeared behind Thaldir, claws outstretched.

Her magic snapped closed.

Mind Maze wrapped around him like chains of thought, illusion tightening with cruel, suffocating precision. The sky twisted. Distance warped. Phantom forms closed in on him from every direction.

But Luminara Virell blazed in his hands.

The staff flared with living green light, its sigils surging outward like roots tearing through stone. The illusion shattered where the staff's power touched it, severing the maze at its core before it could close completely.

Seraphina surged beside him.

Argentis Aethern released a pulse of sovereign light that spread across the air like a rising dawn.

The remaining fragments of illusion collapsed under its glow, dissolving into drifting motes.

Ixalia screamed.

She vanished again space folding around her in a flash of distortion.

Then she reappeared directly in front of Talleoss.

"You cannot strike what you cannot truly find."

Talleoss did not hesitate.

His Frightful Presence rolled across the sky a wave of ancient Silver terror that burned into the Mirage host. The air itself grew heavy with memory and judgment.

Several Mirage dragons faltered. Wings trembled. Illusions flickered as courage fractured and minds unraveled.

Silvara rose behind Ixalia.

Without a word, she unleashed Reverse Gravity.

The sky inverted beneath them.

Mirage dragons were hurled upward, their bodies spinning helplessly as the air itself betrayed them. They shot toward the clouds like leaves caught in a violent updraft only to meet waiting Silver claws.

The Silvers struck.

And this time nothing in the sky moved to deceive them.

They seized the disoriented dragons and dragged them screaming back into the heart of the battle, silver talons closing with unyielding precision.

Below them, the illusion-field trembled.

Cracks of silver light spread through the remaining distortions. False horizons flickered. Phantom terrain dissolved into open sky.

The illusion-field finally began to break apart.

Ixalia felt the fractures spread.

Not merely in her spell—but in the control she wielded.

She struck out with fury, dragging the remnants of Reality Warp into a final, desperate twist. The sky lurched. Gravity shuddered. For an instant even the silver storm wavered clouds folding in impossible directions, winds snapping sideways as though the world had forgotten which way it should turn.

A Mirage dragon lunged for Seraphina through the distortion claws aimed not at her armor, but at the staff in her hands.

Argentis Aethern flared.

Sovereign light burst outward in a blinding pulse, and the Mirage dragon slammed into an unseen boundary and recoiled violently.

Silvara moved like moonlight made a blade.

Her wing cut cleanly through the last heavy fold of mirage, and the battlefield steadied hardening into something the mind could finally grasp.

Karrenen lifted both hands.

"Now," he commanded.

The ground wards answered with a single, unified surge.

The hidden paths of E'vahona are locked.

Not sealed denied.

Ixalia's eyes widened as her Dimensional Rift sputtered, space resisting her in a way it had not moments before refusing to yield.

Talleoss rose before her, his silver presence absolute.

"Enough."

The word itself carried the weight of law.

For the first time, Ixalia did not smirk.

She bared her teeth, pride cracking into raw hatred. Then she snapped her head toward what remained of her host.

For the first time in centuries, Ixalia knew fear.

The shattered illusions stilled at last.

Fragments of false sky and broken mirage-light drifted away like dying stars as Ixalia hovered in the torn heavens, her many reflections collapsing back into a single, wounded form the illusion of perfection finally broken. Her breath came in furious bursts, shadow and light twisting unevenly along her scales. The magic that once cloaked her in flawless deception now flickered like a cracked mirror.

"I will return," she hissed. "And next time, your truths will not save you."

Talleoss rose before her vast, immovable, unyielding. Silver light gathered along the edges of his wings, not in threat, but in certainty.

"And we will be waiting."

Beside him, Silvara's wings gleamed with restrained silver fire, her presence calm and absolute like moonlight no shadow could swallow.

"Forget E'vahona," Silvara said. "It lies beyond your reach. You will never find it. Not again."

Ixalia's eyes burned, rage and wounded pride battling beneath the fractured sheen of her scales. For a heartbeat it seemed she might strike again—might throw herself at the Silver ancients in one last desperate assault.

But the battlefield had already spoken.

Around her, the Mirage dragons faltered, their illusions unraveling into drifting strands of colorless light. False wings flickered. Phantom doubles collapsed into nothing. The power that once made them untouchable now bled away into the open sky.

Ixalia snarled a sound like broken stars grinding together. "Withdraw." The command snapped through the air.

The Mirage dragons scattered at once, discipline dissolving into fractured retreat. One by one the last remnants of false sky collapsed, the layered illusions peeling away like mist burned off by a rising dawn.

Truth returned.

Above them, the real heavens stretched wide and clear.

Below, the hidden paths of E'vahona lay untouched, their wards still humming with quiet, ancient strength.

The Silver dragons hovered in silence, watching the last flickers of mirage-light vanish beyond the horizon.

No cheers rose.

No victory cries.

Only calm, steady vigilance.

Silence returned to the hidden realm.

The war of this age had not ended.

But E'vahona still stood unbroken, and unseen.

Chapter 41

The Shattered Veil

The hidden paths of E'vahona opened once more.

Through them came Lord Karrenen, the Silver host, and their riders Talleoss, Silvara, Seraphina, Thaldir, and the others returning from the broken illusion-field where the war of silver and lies had raged.

The air within the hidden realm felt different now.

Not wounded.

But watchful.

Silver dragons descended among the ancient groves, their wings stirring drifting petals and soft motes of light. Riders dismounted quietly. No one celebrated. Even victory carried weight when it came wrapped in deception and shadowed by how near loss had come.

Along the forest floor, Eladrin healers moved to meet them. Gentle magic rose from their hands as they checked scales, wings, and armor, sealing shallow wounds and easing the strain of battle. Their magic settled like falling leaves against worn scales.

A few Silver dragons rested near the roots of ancient trees, their sides rising and falling slowly as the tension of the illusion-war finally left their bodies.

Talleoss folded his wings and lowered his great head, letting the calm of E'vahona settle over him like cool rain.

"We held the line," he murmured. "But the darkness presses closer now than before."

Silvara stood beside him, her silver scales catching the soft glow of the hidden realm.

"And it will press again," she said. "This was only one front of a greater design."

Together they moved into the heart of E'vahona, where Kadona awaited beneath the towering boughs of the central grove, her presence steady as the roots beneath them.

She listened in silence as the account was given, her eyes reflecting both the victory and the cost carried home with it. When the final words faded, she allowed herself a small, measured smile.

"Let us hope," she said, "that Ixalia has learned something from this."

Silvara inclined her head, calm but unyielding.

"She may not attempt to find E'vahona again. But I do not believe she is finished with us."

Kadona's expression sobered.

"Then we must be ready."

Beyond the glimmering boughs of the hidden realm, the echoes of war still lingered in the wind.

The Silver dragons and their riders had scarcely finished landing when a ripple of unease passed through the glades.

A nymph burst from the hidden paths, breaking the stillness like a snapped thread, her Pegasus skidding to a halt behind her. She was breathless and shaken, her words tumbling over one another until only a single truth could be understood.

"Battles... battles..."

Kadona moved to her at once.

"Peace," she said gently. "All will be well. Breathe and then tell us what has happened."

The nymph obeyed. She steadied herself, guided her Pegasus aside, and stepped into the clearing. Silence fell as every eye turned toward her.

"The realms were attacked," she said. "Crystal Vale. Emberwoods. Lyra'el. Goldmoor. All of them."

A murmur rippled through the assembly.

Lord Karrenen stepped forward, his voice low and grave. "Why were we not called to their aid?"

The nymph lowered her gaze. "Because the assaults were carried out... simultaneously. All fronts—at once."

The truth settled over E'vahona like a gathering storm.

Talleoss lowered his great silver head, sorrow dimming the light in his eyes.

"So," he said quietly, "the darkness grows more cunning. It strikes not with fury alone, but with design—dividing us, that we may not stand as one nor come to one another's aid."

Silvara turned back to the nymph.

"What of the wounded?" she asked, her tone steady and precise.

The nymph swallowed. The names came like falling stones.

"Raelithar was injured. Aurelius as well. And Kimras... he too was hurt."

She hesitated.

Lord Karrenen stepped closer, his expression softening.

"Take your time," he said gently. "There is no shame in sorrow. Speak what must be spoken."

Her voice dropped to a hush.

"It has been discovered that Glaciera was targeting Keisha seeking to freeze her and take her as a prize."

The clearing went utterly still.

Even the leaves seemed to pause in their gentle motion.

Karrenen lowered his head for a long moment before lifting his gaze again.

"Did she succeed?" he asked quietly.

"No," the nymph said quickly. "She nearly reached her, but Amara and Ong blocked her path. Glaciera's wing was injured."

A collective breath escaped the assembly quiet, but heavy with what might have been.

Talleoss straightened, resolve hardening like silvered steel.

"Then the bonds between them remain strong," he said. "And that strength has spared us a greater sorrow."

His gaze swept the clearing over dragons, riders, mages, and spirits alike.

"Send word at once. Let every noble dragon and every rider be summoned to the Hidden Isles. No realm stands alone any longer."

His voice deepened, ancient authority ringing through the grove.

"It is a single shadow and it must be faced together."

The nymph bowed and departed, her Pegasus lifting into the shimmering paths beyond E'vahona.

When the clearing fell silent again, no one spoke.

They did not need to.

The war was no longer distant.

It had come to every realm of Vacari.

And when it ended...

it would end with all of them standing together.

Chapter 42

The Return to Flameford

Deep within Flameford where molten stone wept and the air shimmered with heat the mysterious one waited with Malrik in the Cavern of Ash.

The chamber breathed fire. Slow. Relentless. Alive.

Ash drifted like black snow from the ceiling. Rivers of magma crawled between jagged spires of obsidian, casting the cavern in a slow, pulsing glow. Smoke and scorched metal clung to every breath, thick enough to taste.

The first to arrive were Nocturna and Xalzorath.

The Obsidian Queen and the Black Dragon swept into the cavern and landed with the sound of cracking stone. Without a word, they moved to the far end of the chamber, wings folding like closing blades taking position, not waiting.

The mysterious one's voice cut through the heat.

"Is Aurelia dead?" she asked.

A pause.

"Or Verdantia?"

Nocturna's eyes slid toward her cold, unreadable, as if the question itself were beneath answer.

Xalzorath's growl rolled against the cavern walls, low and corrosive.

"If you truly possessed the power you boast of," he said, "you would not need to ask at all."

The air tightened, heat rippling outward in a sudden surge.

The mysterious one's gaze hardened, but they did not rise to the bait.

They waited.

The cavern shuddered as Zarathos arrived not in greeting, but in warning.

The Topaz Dragon crashed down in a spray of molten stone and stalked forward to join Nocturna and Xalzorath, his scales scorched, his eyes burning with unspent fury.

The mysterious one turned to him.

"Was Raelithar destroyed?"

Zarathos's lip curled, contempt flashing across his molten features.

"He was broken," he said. "But not ended."

The words were deliberate. Final. A refusal to grant her the victory they wanted.

The mysterious one opened their mouth to speak.

Zarathos turned his head away, dismissing them before they could speak.

The magma flared. Heat rolled through the cavern like a rising storm as their fury pressed outward, silent but suffocating.

Before they could answer, the air twisted.

Shadow folded inward as Voraxia and Vorathos emerged from the dark. They landed near the center of the cavern, and the mysterious one's gaze locked instantly onto Vorathos's wounded wing.

"Again?" they said, their voice edged with frozen steel.

Voraxia's eyes gleamed with quiet satisfaction.

"Yes," she replied. "Radiantus struck her down."

She let the words linger just long enough to sharpen the wound.

"But take comfort," Voraxia continued. "Aurelius was wounded as well."

For the first time, the cavern fell truly silent.

Even the magma seemed to still.

Malrik stood beside the mysterious one, feeling the heat of their fury coil tighter like an inferno denied release.

He did not speak.

He had learned not to.

He waited.

The cavern shook once more as Zylron and Glaciera arrived not as guests, but as a storm already in motion.

Glaciera's wing hung torn, frost-streaked blood dripping onto the obsidian floor, hissing where it touched the heat. The mysterious one took one look at the wound and drew breath to speak.

Zylron cut them off.

"Quiet," he snarled low, commanding. "All you ever do is complain."

The word complain echoed too loudly in the chamber, ringing against stone and fire alike.

"You know Kimras is powerful," Zylron continued, molten fury sharpening his tone. "And Amara is the most dangerous of the gem brood. Yet you stand there as though defeat were beneath you."

He jerked his head toward Glaciera's injured wing, a silent accusation.

"Kimras was wounded. And she earned that scar chasing the elf."

The cavern went cold.

The magma dimmed as though even the fire held its breath.

The air tightened.

The mysterious one's restraint finally gave way, heat surging outward in a silent, suffocating wave.

Nocturna turned her head toward Zylron and laughed, the sound thin and cutting as shattered glass.

"Brave," she said softly. "Or foolish. I have not decided which."

Zylron's eyes burned brighter, embers flaring beneath his scales.

"I spoke the truth," he replied. "If it burns, he said, "then perhaps it was meant to."

Without another word, he turned away. Glaciera followed, her movements stiff with pain and simmering fury as they moved toward the rear of the chamber.

They took their place beside Nocturna, Xalzorath, and Zarathos carefully skirting the space claimed by Voraxia and Vorathos.

Malrik watched it all.

The way the dragons grouped.

The distance they kept.

The unspoken lines forming in ash and shadow.

The balance of power was shifting and no one had yet claimed it.

The dark host was changing.

The cavern's shadows twisted listening.

And Ixalia arrived last.

The Mirage Queen swept into the cavern last, her form shimmering with fractured light as though reality itself refused to settle around her, as she landed beside Voraxia, her gaze already cold, already calculating.

The mysterious one turned toward her.

"Well?" they demanded impatience cutting through the heat. "Did you at least find E'vahona?"

Ixalia's lips curled in faint disdain.

"No," she said. "What I found was an illusion meticulously prepared by the Silvers, the Eladrin... and likely Kadona herself."

She glanced briefly at Voraxia, then returned her gaze to the mysterious one.

"They are not fools," she said flatly. They knew you desired E'vahona. You misjudged how they would protect it." Her voice sharpened, edged with pride and irritation. "For one who claims such power, you should have understood the strength of Talleoss and Silvara... and their riders."

A ripple passed through the chamber.

Ixalia did not stop.

"One thing you did correctly," she continued almost reluctantly, "was ordering us to strike simultaneously. That tactic carried weight. But perhaps you should reconsider attempting to take E'vahona at all."

The cavern trembled.

The mysterious one screamed and the cavern answered.

Lava burst from the stone in blazing arcs, molten fire ripping across the floor in searing waves. Heat roared. Shadows leapt. The air itself howled with her fury.

The dragons did not move.

They only watched.

And waited.

Malrik stepped quietly to their side and lowered his voice.

"You must reclaim your dominion over them," he said quietly. "Rage without purpose only weakens your command."

The mysterious one drew in a slow, deliberate breath.

Silence fell.

Then she turned her gaze upon Xalzorath.

Power surged.

The cavern darkened as an invisible force slammed down upon the Black Dragon absolute, suffocating. Xalzorath froze mid-motion unable to move, unable to breathe his limbs locking beneath the crushing weight.

Zylron's head snapped toward her, molten eyes blazing.

The pressure vanished instantly.

Xalzorath collapsed to one knee, dragging in a ragged breath.

The mysterious one straightened, their fury now sharpened into something colder, more dangerous.

"Enough," they said.

The word struck like a blade.

"You have failed me again. I grow weary of this. You were meant to destroy these dragons."

Zylron's chest rumbled with a low growl but he did not speak.

Nocturna.

Voraxia.

Ixalia.

Zarathos.

Glaciera.

Vorathos.

All stood in silence, their attention fixed on the one who commanded them.

The balance of power trembled in the heat.

The mysterious one surveyed the assembled dragons, their gaze cold and unyielding.

"You will return to your lairs," their voice cold with finality. "Regather your strength. And you will wait."

A pause.

"For two more dark dragons to join this war."

A ripple of interest moved through the chamber subtle but unmistakable.

Nocturna tilted her head, silver streaked with violet eyes narrowing with predatory curiosity.

"And who are these new guests?" she asked, her tone smooth as midnight glass edged with quiet hunger.

"Nyxathor," the mysterious one replied. "The Onyx Dragon."

Nocturna's smirk spread slowly.

"A gem dragon," she murmured almost amused.. "And one born of Vacari's own mountains. How... appropriate."

From the shadows, Glaciera's voice drifted forward thin with frost and malice.

"Yes. The Onyx make their home in Firornak. In the far mountains. Cold places breed useful monsters."

Zylron's molten gaze narrowed.

"And the other?" he demanded.

"Voraxus," the mysterious one said. "A Dreadfang."

Voraxia's wings twitched.

"From the Void," they said softly, something darker stirring beneath the words.

Zarathos growled low.

"Another outsider," he muttered, displeasure rumbling beneath his breath.

The mysterious one raised their hand.

"Go."

One by one, the dark dragons turned away vanishing into smoke, shadow, frost, and flame each returning to the element that defined them,

When the cavern was empty, the mysterious one turned to Malrik.

"Make sure the creature is ready," they said softly. "Our next target is the merfolk."

A pause.

"Vacari will feel this one from the depths."

Their gaze sharpened, something colder settling behind her eyes.

"And most of all... Lysander."

The Cavern of Ash fell silent.

Even the magma seemed to slow, its glow dimming as though the fire itself listened.

And the war deepened.

Chapter 43

Council of the Hidden Isles

The winds of Vacari carried the call.

Across forest and flame, sky and sea, the nymphs carried their messages to the noble dragons and their riders, to the guardians of the realms, to all who still stood in the light. Each carried the same summons.

All were called to the Hidden Isles.

One nymph flew far beyond the western ranges, crossing into Etharyon, where the mountains gleamed with strange metallic light. There she found Argentus, the Ancient Mercury Dragon, newly returned to Vacari after long years beyond its borders.

His silver form coiled along the peaks, liquid and luminous, as his brood gathered around him. Their bodies shifted and flowed like living metal, reflecting the fractured light of Etharyon's peaks.

The nymph delivered the message.

Argentus inclined his great head in acknowledgment. The living-metal sheen of his scales rippled as he turned to his dragons, the movement sending waves of mirrored light cascading across the mountainside.

"Let the people of Etharyon know we have returned," he commanded. "Establish our protection between Silvaraen and Aerindral. Keep watch for the Black and Topaz broods. They will test those borders."

The mercury dragons bowed their heads, their forms rippling in silent unity.

Then, with a thunder of living metal, Argentus lifted into the sky his body flowing upward like a rising blade of liquid silver and set his course for the Hidden Isles.

The gathering had begun.

The first to arrive were Kimras and Amara, with Keisha and Ong riding upon the wind.

They descended upon the grandest of the Hidden Isles—Drakonhart—where ancient stone arches rose in sweeping curves and floating crystal terraces circled a vast sky-lake, its mirrored surface reflecting the endless blue above like a second horizon suspended in air.

Kimras landed first, golden wings folding with measured power. Amara followed in a ripple of psionic distortion, the air bending subtly around her as she touched down.

Keisha and Ong dismounted, their boots meeting ancient stone worn smooth by ages of gathering.

Soon after, Aurelia and Verdantia arrived with Gailen and Thalorian.

Crystal and emerald light swept across the terraces as they descended, their presence adding a quiet brilliance to the growing assembly. As Verdantia's wings settled, Thalorian's gaze lifted and stilled.

Far across the sky, a form of shifting silver moved like living metal beneath the sun.

"Argentus..."

The name left him in a breath.

Without hesitation, Thalorian stepped away, crossing the terrace with purpose as he approached the Ancient Mercury Dragon, offering a warrior's respect forged not in ceremony but in memory.

Argentus inclined his great head in return, recognition passing between them without the need for words.

Nearby, Ong and Gailen exchanged a glance before turning toward Keisha, curiosity bright in their expressions.

Keisha followed their gaze and smiled softly.

"That is Argentus the Ancient Mercury Dragon," she said. "Before many of the dragons ever left Vacari, he and his kind watched over Etharyon. They were its silent sentinels."

Both men nodded, awe settling over them as they watched the metallic giant glide with effortless fluidity toward the isle, his form catching the light like flowing silver.

The air shifted again.

Silvara and Talleoss descended from above, their silver wings cutting clean arcs through the sky. They landed with quiet authority, their presence steadying the gathering like the calm before a storm fully understood.

The skies shifted once more.

From the southern winds came Dirona, the noble Bronze Dragon, her scales gleaming like sunlit dawn. Close behind her soared Aurix, the ancient Brass Dragon, his laughter already threading faintly through the air before his talons ever touched stone.

They descended near Argentus, and at once both dragons moved to greet him.

"Welcome home," Dirona said, warmth steady and sincere.

Aurix inclined his head, a familiar grin touching his voice.

"If trouble stirs in Etharyon," he said, "send word. My Brass will fly from Afor to stand beside yours. Old alliances should never gather dust."

Argentus's liquid-silver eyes softened, his form rippling faintly as though stirred by memory itself.

"My thanks, old friend. Your words carry the weight of years, and I remember every one of them."

For a moment, the past stood beside the present.

Then, together, they turned their gaze back to the open sky.

The council waited.

For the rest to arrive.

The next presence came on wings of deep blue fire.

Azurina, the Ancient Sapphire Dragon, descended from the skies of Ardinia, her form wreathed in cool, radiant flame. Her arrival did not shake the air like thunder but steadied it, like a calm that refused to break.

At her side flew Kaelorn.

She guided him forward before the council, her great wings folding with quiet authority as she regarded the gathered assembly.

"This is Kaelorn," Azurina announced, her voice clear and resonant. "The new Forest Warden. The forests of Vacari speak through him now."

A subtle shift passed through the gathering.

Dragons inclined their heads. Riders followed. Not in ceremony but in recognition.

Kaelorn did not bow deeply. He simply stood, grounded and still, as though the roots of every forest stretched unseen beneath his feet.

A hush fell.

Many among them had already heard the whispers carried on wind and wing of battles across the realms... of wounds taken... of sacrifices made.

Of Raelithar.

Of Aurelius.

Concern moved through the assembly like a quiet tide, unspoken—but deeply felt.

Then the air shimmered again.

From the eastern horizon came Radiantus, bearing Talhira.

Beside him flew Aurelius.

His wings were held tight with pain, his once-unbroken radiance dimmed at the edges but not extinguished. He was supported in flight by Valeon riding close and by the small, steadfast presence of Thump, who refused to be left behind.

Radiantus did not conceal his displeasure.

"I told him to remain in Lyra'el," he said, his voice low, edged with restrained frustration. "But he would not listen."

Aurelius's reply was calm unshaken.

"A council of the ancients is not something I would miss," he said gently. "Wounds or no wounds, I am still of this world... and I will stand with it."

They landed.

Valeon moved immediately, hands already at work, checking the wounded Celestial's side with practiced care. The soft glow of healing herbs began to stir once more as he worked.

Around them, the council fell into reverent silence.

Not out of fear.

But respect.

Before that silence could settle fully another shadow crossed the sky.

Raelithar arrived.

The Copper Ancient descended with measured strength, each movement controlled despite the fresh wounds marking his scales. His wings bore the cost of battle, and yet he did not falter.

Around him fluttered a constellation of pixies, their dimmed lights flickering with stubborn devotion as they refused to leave his side.

He was not alone.

Several among the gathered stepped forward at once dragons and riders alike voices low with concern as they moved to examine his injuries.

No command was needed.

No rank required.

Only understanding.

The cost of the war now stood before them visible, undeniable, carried in flesh and scale.

And still they came.

And still they stood.

When at last all had taken their places upon the high terraces of Drakonhart, a deep quiet settled over the gathering.

Not empty silence—

but the kind that forms when every voice knows what is at stake.

Many eyes turned to Kimras, expecting him to begin.

But the Golden Ancient did not rise to speak.

Instead, he inclined his great head.

"Radiantus," Kimras said, his voice carrying both authority and quiet respect, "you have returned to us. The council is yours to open."

Radiantus inclined his great head once and stepped forward, his platinum form catching the mirrored light of the sky-lake.

"The first truth we must face," he said, "is that these attacks were not chaos. They were planned carefully, deliberately."

His gaze moved across the gathered assembly, lingering on each dragon, each rider.

"Every strike occurred at the same time, severing our ability to come to one another's aid."

Murmurs rippled through the terraces.

Then silence.

For every gaze turned to Aurelius...and to Raelithar.

Their wounds needed no explanation. The cost of that strategy was written plainly in celestial light dimmed at the edges... and in copper scales marked by fire and claw.

Radiantus's voice softened, though it did not waver.

"This is the price of that design."

The words settled heavily.

The war was no longer distant.

It stood among them.

They spoke then of the Silver response of illusion met with illusion, of deception unraveled by deeper truth.

Silvara allowed herself a faint, humorless laugh.

"Ixalia was... displeased," she said. "To be fooled by those she believed beneath her."

A quiet voice offered, "Perhaps it will deter her from seeking E'vahona again."

Talleoss answered at once, his tone steady as winter stone.

"It will not deter her from striking us. Pride wounded is often more dangerous than pride satisfied."

The council fell still once more understanding settling where hope might have lingered.

Then Raelithar lowered his great copper head.

"There is... other news," he said.

The words carried weight before they were even spoken.

He told them of the young Copper of the moment of choice... of the shield raised not for glory, but for others... of the cost that followed.

No embellishment.

No grandeur.

Only truth.

When the final words came, they were simple.

"He did not survive."

The council bowed their heads as one.

No command was given.

None was needed.

A moment of reverence passed measured only by breath... and the slow, steady rhythm of wings at rest.

When Raelithar lifted his gaze again, something in him had changed.

Grief remained.

But it had hardened into resolve.

Then Aurelius spoke.

"There is... some good news."

Every eye turned toward him.

Radiantus inclined his head slightly, granting the floor.

Aurelius's light flickered but held.

"We requested the council of Lyra'el to investigate the origins of Vuarus," he said. "In doing so, they uncovered something... troubling."

A pause.

"The one we call the mysterious person is connected to him. Deeply."

Stillness spread across the terraces.

"Vuarus trained her in the Abyss," Aurelius continued. "And she is the daughter of one of the Dark Sorceresses of that realm."

A low tension rippled through the gathering quiet, but unmistakable.

Kimras's eyes gleamed with ancient fire.

"So," he said, voice calm but resolute, "her secret begins to unravel. Do we know her father?"

"Not yet," Aurelius replied. "Nor her true name. But we will."

His gaze lifted steady, unwavering.

"No shadow remains unchallenged forever."

Argentus spoke then, his voice like molten metal given thought.

"Even in absence, the Mercury keep their watch," he said. "The nymphs of Vacari still whisper to us. These truths reached Etharyon long before I returned."

Understanding passed between the ancients.

The threads were connecting.

The enemy was no longer faceless.

The council began to shift wings stirring, riders preparing when the wind changed.

From the eastern sky came Aeliana, Guardian of Ardinia, her presence bright as first dawn.

"Forgive my intrusion," she said, bowing her head slightly, "but I bring news. I have sent my fairies and nymphs to seek the Sky Nymphs to draw them from hiding, so they may aid us in the battles to come."

Radiantus inclined his head.

"May their answer come swiftly. The heavens will be stronger for their return."

The gathering dissolved.

Not in disorder but in purpose.

Dragons and riders took to the skies once more, returning to their realms scarred… strengthened… and no longer divided.

Above Drakonhart, the sky remained clear.

But beneath that calm, something had changed.

The war had revealed its shape.

And Vacari united at last would endure.

Epilogue

When the World Begins Again

The war had not ended.

But everything about it had changed.

Across the realms of Vacari, the noble dragons, their companions, and the guardians of every land came to the same understanding:

The enemy no longer struck in isolation.

The dark dragons were learning.

Learning to organize.

Learning to think as one.

Learning how to fracture the world by striking everywhere at once.

That could never be allowed to happen again.

No longer would Goldmoor stand with only gold.

No longer would the Emberwoods be guarded by copper alone.

No longer would the skies of Lyra'el belong solely to platinum and light.

The age of the solitary watch was ending.

In its place, something greater began to rise Mixed wings. Shared vigilance.

Alliances no longer bound by territory, but by purpose.

A defense not divided by realm but united by will.

And with that change came another.

The noble dragons set aside the word *rider.*

It was a name born of distance of command and hierarchy... of an age when survival demanded masters and servants.

That age had passed.

Those who flew beside the noble dragons were no longer riders.

They were bound kin.

Family forged not by blood alone, but by trust... by choice... by shared fate.

Not masters.
Not servants.

But hearts bound to wings.

There would be those who did not yet understand.

Mortals who still spoke the old word.

They would be given time.

For learning like trust could not be forced.

It had to be chosen.

But when the dark dragons spoke the word *rider*—

They were answered.

With fury.
With defiance.

With roars that shook the heavens and left no doubt.

Domination would never be mistaken for kinship.

If darkness was learning unity then the light would answer with something stronger still.

Not alliance.
Not command.
Not necessity.

Family.

And when the storm returned as it surely would Vacari would not stand divided.

It would rise as one.

Teaser

Tides of Darkness

Far beneath the surface of Vacari's seas, where sunlight fades and ancient currents whisper through forgotten ruins, the deep waters stirred.

For ages the oceans had belonged to Lysander.

But the Dominion had begun to look beneath the waves.

In the silent trenches where even the bravest swimmers dared not descend, a new presence gathered in the dark watching the war above with patient, calculating intent.

And deeper still... something moved.

Not born of the sea.

Not shaped by nature.

A creature wrought by the Dominion's will.

Its first breath rippled through the abyss like a wound in the water.

Far above, the tides rolled gently against Vacari's shores.

But the deep had begun to change.

And soon even Lysander would feel the rising pull of darkness.

Battlecraft of Vacari

Enchantment of E'vahona Edition

Battlecraft of Vacari

A record of the legendary weapons, gear, and craftsmanship that shaped the Dragon Wars and the rise of the alliance.

Characters of Vacari

Key Figures

- **Caryth Shadowmere (Umbral Elf)** — A figure of quiet menace within the Umbral ranks, moving through shadow and influence with deliberate precision.
- **Gailen (Human)** — Prince of Crystal Vale, bonded to Aurelia, the Crystal Dragon, and wielder of the sacred Crystalbow.

- **Kaelorn (Luminara)** — Forestborne Warden of the Emerald Woods, appointed by Aeliana to preserve the balance between realm, root, and dragonkind. A leader devoted to harmony, he walks the living paths as both guardian and guide.

- **Keisha (Eladrin)** — Courageous and resolute, gifted in elemental magic and masterful archery, bonded to Kimras, the Gold Dragon.

- **King Alex (Human)** — Noble ruler of Goldmoor, steadfast in duty and unwavering in his loyalty to the alliances that safeguard his realm.

- **King Manard (Human)** — King of Crystal Vale, a stabilizing force whose reign preserves the legacy and strength of his people.

- **Lady Seraphina (Eladrin)** — A powerful sorceress trained by Lord Karrenen, wielder of Argentis Aethern and a leading voice within the Silver Accord.

- **Lord Karrenen (Eladrin)** — A master of arcane craft, whose command of magic has shaped many of Vacari's most enduring enchantments.

- **Lord Thaldir (Eladrin)** — A revered elder and keeper of ancient lore, guiding the Silver Dragon Concord with wisdom and foresight.

- **Lyra Dreadcrusher (Druchii)** — A cunning sorceress once allied with Phoenix and Vuarus, her ambitions forged through power, survival, and control.

- **Maldrak** — Exiled ruler of Shadowhaven, now bound to the will of the Dominion, his fate entwined with forces far darker than before.

- **Malrik** — Once the Chief Priest of Vuarus, now in service to a mysterious power, his path marked by corruption and veiled intent.

- **Ong Swifthammer (Human)** — A loyal warrior of unyielding resolve, husband to Keisha and rider of Amara, the Amethyst Dragon.

- **Qellaun Dreadcrusher (Druchii)** — A ruthless warrior once in service to Phoenix and Vuarus, driven by strength and an unrelenting will to dominate.

- **Queen Jeanne (Human)** — Queen of Goldmoor, a dignified and steady presence beside King Alex, her strength revealed in both quiet endurance and rising courage.

- **Rhys (Umbral Elf)** — A shadow mage of the Umbral Order, his true motives concealed beneath layers of secrecy and shifting allegiance.

- **Thalorian (Moon Elf)** — A skilled warrior and guardian of the natural world, bonded to Verdantia, the Emerald Dragon.

- **Talhira (Human)** — Chosen rider of Radiantus, the Platinum Dragon, bearing the weight of celestial purpose and unwavering light.

- **Valeon (Human)** — A healer of Lyra'el, his path shaped by restoration and quiet purpose as he learns to mend both body and spirit within a realm touched by celestial light.

Noble Dragons

- **Amara (Amethyst Dragon)** — A being of spiritual depth and psionic power, her presence bridges arcane energy and emotion, guiding those bound to her with quiet, unwavering strength.
- **Aurelia (Crystal Dragon)** — Ethereal and radiant, bearer of ancient knowledge, her wisdom refracts across time like light through crystal.
- **Aurelius (Celestial Dragon)** — An ancient embodiment of mercy and light, a quiet guardian whose presence restores balance wherever it falters.
- **Kimras (Gold Dragon)** — A regal force of wisdom and benevolence, his authority tempered by compassion, guiding others with both strength and grace.
- **Radiantus (Platinum Dragon)** — Brilliant and unyielding, an embodiment of divine purpose whose radiant power stands firm against even the deepest darkness.
- **Raelithar (Copper Dragon)** — Cunning and unbound, a solitary ancient whose wit and unpredictability veil a deeper, ever-watchful purpose.
- **Talleoss (Silver Dragon)** — Eldest of the Silver Ancients, composed and resolute, his presence inspires unity and commands respect in times of uncertainty.
- **Silvara (Silver Dragon)** — Gentle yet enduring, a keeper of restoration whose strength is found in healing, memory, and

quiet resilience.

- **Verdantia (Emerald Dragon)** — Guardian of the living realms, deeply entwined with nature's vitality, her power moving through root, leaf, and breath alike.

Dark Dragons

- **Glaciera (White Dragon)** — Ruthless and relentless, the embodiment of winter's cruelty, where even breath stills and freezes in her wake.

- **Ixalia (Mirage Dragon)** — Mistress of illusion and distortion, she fractures reality itself, turning certainty into deception.

- **Nocturna (Obsidian Dragon)** — Cold and unyielding, her obsidian form reflects nothing, as though even light refuses to linger upon her.

- **Vorathos (Abyssal Dragon)** — Born of the abyss, a terror that does not merely destroy, but consumes—leaving only silence in its wake.

- **Voraxia (Shadow Dragon)** — Shadowed Empress of darkness, her dominion spreads not through force alone, but through fear that takes root and festers.

- **Xalzorath (Black Dragon)** — Cunning and merciless, a patient predator whose cruelty is measured, deliberate, and absolute.

- **Zarathos (Topaz Dragon)** — Fallen and bound by pride, his brilliance twisted into dominance, where power exists not to protect, but to rule.

- **Zylron (Red Dragon)** — Treacherous and volatile, a living inferno whose fury leaves ruin in every beat of his wings.

Divine and Significant Beings

- **Aeliana** — Guardian of Ardinia, bound to the living essence of the forests, her will shaping and preserving the balance of her realm.
- **Kadona** — Goddess of Light and protector of the Eladrin, a radiant force of guidance and unwavering hope against encroaching darkness.
- **Lysander** — God of the Sea, sovereign of the vast and restless tides, his power governing both tranquil depths and rising fury.
- **The Mysterious One** — An enigmatic force within the dark divine realm, felt through shadow and subtle influence, their design unfolding without ever revealing its true form.

Companions

- **Aeralinde (Pegasus)** — A rare and sacred Pegasus whose wings mirror the living forests of Vacari and Ardinia, their colors shifting like leaves in wind and light. Gifted to Kaelorn, she serves as both companion and guide to the Forestborne Warden, her nature attuned to the harmony and motion of the natural world.

- **Casper (Cougar)** — Protector of Queen Jeanne, steadfast and watchful, a silent guardian against threats that linger unseen.

- **Pumpkin (Panther)** — Fiercely loyal to Keisha, mischievous in spirit yet formidable when it matters most, moving with quiet grace through shadow and battle alike.

- **Thump (Fox)** — Valeon's clever and ever-curious companion, gifted by Lord Karrenen, known for his persistent tail-thumping and sharp, observant nature.

Bonded Flight Doctrine — Use of Saddles and Harnesses

Eladrin-crafted saddles and harnesses are masterworks of enchantment, designed to secure and support riders through the rigors of early training and extended travel. Yet they are not the foundation of true dragonflight.

As the bond between rider and dragon deepens, reliance on such gear often diminishes.

In battle and moments of urgency, most bonded pairs abandon saddles and harnesses entirely, favoring unrestrained movement and complete synchronization. The bond itself provides the awareness, balance, and unity required to endure evasive maneuvers and the chaos of aerial combat.

Saddles are therefore most commonly retained for:

Early-stage training

Riders not yet fully attuned to their dragons

Long-distance or endurance-based flights

Among the most experienced pairs, to fly without such support is not recklessness—it is a mark of trust, mastery, and unity.

The Celestial Calendar of Vacari

Archived within the Battlecraft of Vacari: Chronicles of Creation, Flame, and Balance

"Time is no master in Vacari. It is a tide—ebbing, surging, and reshaping with the breath of dragons and the whisper of gods."

— Archivist Thalenor of the Shimmering Keep

The Cycles of Creation

Vacari's reckoning of time is not divided by months or mortal invention, but by the celestial dance of its twin moons, Lunara and Veyr, and the pulse of its elemental ley lines. The world turns through Four Great Cycles, each reflecting the elemental dominion that reigns for its span.

The Emberturn — Cycle of Flame and Awakening

When fire returns to the land, the Copper and Gold Ancients stir from slumber. The Emberwoods ignite with radiant blossoms, and forges across the realms burn brighter. It is a time of renewal, courage, and the forging of oaths.

The Veil of Silver — Cycle of Reflection and Moonlight

Beneath twin moons and shimmering frost, illusion veils the world. The Silver Ancients preside over this tranquil season, when truth hides behind beauty and the Eladrin practice their rites of remembrance beneath argent skies.

The Frostweave — Cycle of Stillness and Endurance

Winter's dominion. The White and Silver Ancients draw cold clarity through air and stone. It is a season of introspection and survival—when mortals honor endurance and the silence between heartbeats.

The Verdant Tide — Cycle of Renewal and Balance

Life surges anew beneath the guardianship of the Green and Aquanor Ancients. Rivers thaw, forests awaken, and magic hums through the roots of the world. It is both ending and beginning—where balance renews itself.

The Eladrin Reckoning

The Eladrin do not measure time by sun or moon, but through Phases of Bloom—each reflecting the rise and fall of their innate magic:

Moonbloom — growth and enlightenment

Twilightfall — introspection and art

Waning Veil — fading power, wisdom gained

Evershine — rebirth, when ancient magic renews

Their calendars are living works of art—petals etched with silver runes that shift in hue with the moonlight, no two ever the same.

The Sylvan and Aquanor Reckoning

The Sylvan Elves follow the Breath of Seasons, guided by the forest's own pulse. Their year begins when the Great Oak of Thal'Sien blossoms and ends with the fall of its final leaf. Their seasons are named for what the forest gives: **Seedwake, Leafsong, Harvestshade, and Slumberfall.**

The Aquanor, kin of sea and storm, follow the tides of Lunara and Veyr. Each lunar phase shapes currents, migration, and prophecy. Their reckoning divides time into Four Depths—**the Rising, the Crest, the Falling, and the Still**—each bound to their reverence for the Tidefather and the Whispering Goddess.

The Human Reckoning

Mortal kingdoms, ever pragmatic, mark their history through wars and harvests. They follow the Solar Reckoning—a calendar of twelve Houses, each named for a virtue or ancient hero.

Though less poetic, this system governs trade, diplomacy, and record-keeping across the continents. Yet even they yield to greater celestial rhythms, for armies march and crops bloom according to the dragons' cycles—not human decree.

The Druchii and Umbral Reckoning

The darker kin—the Druchii and Umbral Elves—measure not the passage of time, but its decay. Their calendars are carved into obsidian, each mark a memory of conquest or loss.

The Druchii follow Cycles of Shadow, believing each ends only when a dominion falls and another rises.

The Umbral mark time through Echoes, holding that history repeats until vengeance is fulfilled.

To them, time is a weapon—sharpened by patience, wielded through hatred.

The Dragons' Reckoning

To dragons, time is not a straight path but a spiral of elemental recurrence. Their lore speaks of Eras of Flame, Frost, and Balance—each ruled by different dragon flights.

When a new Era dawns, the world itself shifts: mountains rise or fall, seas reshape their shores, and even mortal magic is rewritten.

The Nobles track these changes through the constellations—the Draconic Crown, the Coiled Flame, and the Weeping Star. Each alignment signals the rise or fall of ancient power.

Only the Celestial and Platinum Ancients are said to know the true count of the world's ages.

The Divine Reckoning

Above all mortal and draconic measures lies the Divine Cycle—the rhythm by which gods shape destiny.

It is said there have been only three true Ages in Vacari:

The Age of Flame — Creation, when gods and dragons walked as one

The Age of Frost — Division, when mortals turned from divine light

The Age of Shadow — The present, when balance trembles and the Dominion stirs

To the divine, time is not measured in days, but in deeds—for its weight lies not in duration, but in consequence.

"The world's heart does not beat to seconds or suns. It beats to dragons, to gods, and to the will of those who remember."

— From the Battlecraft Archives, Volume VII: *The Celestial Reckonings of Vacari*

Dragon Rider Academies

Following the first alliance victories, dragon rider training evolved from individual mentorship into formal academies established across Vacari. These institutions teach the core disciplines required of all riders—flight coordination, aerial recovery, mounted combat, and bond strengthening—while also providing specialized instruction in advanced techniques and unique weaponry.

Certain methods, such as Standing Combat, are reserved for riders whose equipment or fighting style demands greater balance and precision. As the alliance continues to adapt, new weapons and tactics—such as Lightforged Shields—are steadily integrated into academy training programs.

Eladrin Physiology & Traits

Eladrin Ocular Luminescence:

Eladrin eyes reflect the strength and balance of their life-essence. In times of illness, poisoning, magical disruption, or grave injury, the natural brilliance of their color fades—often paling to a washed or diminished hue.

As vitality is restored, the true color returns, growing more vivid in moments of heightened emotion or awakened power.

Eyes of Vacari: Unique Colors & Meanings

A record of the distinctive eye colors among the people and dragons of Vacari, each revealing heritage, magic, or deeper truths.

Thalorian — *Jade-Fire eyes*; a rare emerald brilliance threaded with inner flame, revealing his fierce bond to nature and the living energy of the forest.

Kaelorn — *Glade-Fire eyes*; a vibrant green kindled with golden sparks, carrying the vitality and quiet radiance of Vacari's sacred glades.

Nocturna (Dragon) — *Silver eyes streaked with violet*; an uncommon fusion of wisdom and shadow, suggesting ancient power held in tension with something far more volatile beneath.

Radiantus (Dragon) — *Diamond-Silver eyes*; a radiant gleam like cut crystal catching the sun, signifying purity, healing light, and the unwavering clarity of celestial purpose.

Aurelius (Celestial Dragon) — *Luminous White eyes*; a calm, enduring radiance, aglow with timeless wisdom and celestial harmony.

Voraxia (Shadow Dragon) — *Silver-White eyes*; a spectral gleam that cuts through darkness, hinting at veiled power and the cold dominion of shadow.

Vorathos (Abyssal Dragon) — *Abyssal-Blue eyes*; a depthless glow, vast as the void, carrying the weight of ancient hunger and endless consumption.

Ixalia (Mirage Dragon) — *Opalescent shifting eyes*; ever-changing hues that ripple like fractured light, concealing truth beneath illusion and bending perception with every glance.

Forged Gear & Equipment

A chronicle of exceptional craftsmanship, forged to endure the trials of war and the bond between rider and dragon.

Bonded Dragon Rider Armor

Crafted of reinforced, enchanted leather and interwoven with stardust enchantments by the fair folk of Vacari, this armor is not merely protection—it is an extension of the bond itself.

Form-fitting and seamlessly adaptive, it moves with the rider in fluid precision, allowing full aerial agility without restriction. The armor responds to the presence of its bonded dragon, its hues shifting to mirror the dragon's essence—golden flame, emerald shimmer, or crystalline light—marking the unity between sky and soul.

Each piece bears ancient engravings that recount the legacy of past dragon riders, their stories preserved in quiet reverence within the weave. Matching gauntlets are finely enchanted to enhance grip, spellcasting precision, and control during high-speed maneuvers.

Primary Functions:

Bond Resonance — Strengthens the connection between rider and dragon, enhancing instinctive coordination in flight and combat.

Impact Dispersion — Absorbs and redistributes force from aerial collisions, falls, and glancing strikes.

Arcane Conduction — Allows controlled magical flow through the armor without disrupting spellcasting or dragon-linked abilities.

Despite its elegance, this armor is forged for war. It is neither ceremonial nor ornamental—it is built to endure the violence of the skies.

Eladrin Dragon Saddles

Masterworks of Eladrin craftsmanship, these saddles are formed from supple, enchanted materials and inscribed with stabilizing runes that bind rider and dragon in seamless harmony.

Created within the sacred enclaves of E'vahona, each saddle is tailored not only to the dragon's form, but to the nature of the bond it supports. The enchantments woven into their structure do not replace trust—they reinforce it, acting as a safeguard when the skies turn hostile.

Primary Functions:

Aerial Anchoring — Secures the rider during evasive maneuvers, dives, and violent shifts without restricting movement.

Endurance Support — Reduces physical strain during extended flights, preserving combat readiness over great distances.

Bond Alignment — Enhances synchronization between rider and dragon, particularly during coordinated attacks or rapid directional changes.

As the bond deepens, reliance on saddles often fades. Many experienced pairs forgo them entirely in battle, trusting wholly in one another. Yet for training, long-distance travel, and large-scale formations, these saddles remain essential to Eladrin warcraft.

Eladrin Spellweaver Staves (Silver Dragon Legions)

Crafted within the sanctified groves of E'vahona and the Emberwoods, the Spellweaver Staff stands as a cornerstone of modern Eladrin warfare. Unlike singular relics reserved for champions or bloodlines, these staves are issued as standard armaments for Eladrin warriors bonded to Silver Dragons—ensuring each rider enters battle with both shield and storm at their command.

Each staff is formed from living enchanted wood, harvested only from trees that willingly yield their branches during sacred moon rites. The shaft is carved with ancient Eladrin runes that glow in response to the wielder's magic, shifting between argent, sapphire, and ember-gold depending on the nature of the spell.

Primary Functions:

Elemental Amplification — Enhances the strength, reach, and precision of offensive spellcasting.

Ward Generation — Conjures layered protective barriers capable of deflecting physical strikes, elemental assaults, and hostile magic.

Arcane Conduit — Allows complex spells to be shaped, stabilized, and released with heightened efficiency.

Corruption Stabilization — Anchors unstable magic, countering illusion and dark influence before it can spread.

When paired with a Silver Dragon, the staff's runes harmonize with the dragon's innate purity, creating a unified magical field between rider and mount. This allows coordinated warding of both aerial and ground forces, making Eladrin–Silver formations among the most resilient units ever fielded in Vacari.

Though uniform in purpose, no two Spellweaver Staves are identical. Each develops subtle variations as it bonds with its wielder—a reflection of the Eladrin belief that even in standardized craft, the soul of the warrior shapes the weapon.

Lightforged Shields (Platinum Riders)

Concealed for centuries within the celestial reaches of Lyra'el, these radiant shields were revealed only when the balance of Vacari stood on the brink of collapse.

Forged from celestial alloys infused with living starlight, each shield responds not to strength alone, but to the purity of the wielder's intent.

When awakened, it projects a luminous barrier that extends beyond the rider, enveloping both dragon and sky in protective radiance.

Primary Functions:

Radiant Barrier Projection — Generates a protective field capable of shielding both rider and dragon from concentrated assaults.

Dark Magic Reflection — Weakens and redirects corrupted energies, diminishing their impact and destabilizing their source.

Unity Amplification — Strengthens nearby allies, reinforcing formation integrity when multiple shields are wielded together.

Though each shield adapts subtly to its bearer, all share a singular purpose—to stand unbroken when all other defenses fall, and to hold the line when darkness presses hardest against the light.

Herbal Origins Index

This document lists the primary regions across the realms and bordering worlds where notable herbs can be found.

Afor (Veiled Desert Realm within Vacari)

Afor lies beyond the Emberwoods, concealed beneath shifting sands and sealed pathways. Its scorching winds and forgotten trails conceal potent, volatile herbs—used by survivors, smugglers, and shadow-walkers alike.

Scorchroot Bulb — A pungent, fire-veined root used in tonics to sustain stamina and guard against dehydration.

Dustpetal Bloom — Pale golden blossoms that ease fever and cleanse minor toxins when steeped into tea.

Cindermoss — A heat-tolerant moss that grows beneath stone in volcanic sand, commonly used in burn salves and heat-warding charms.

Ashthorn Needle — A wiry, spine-like growth that induces swelling and painful numbness if ingested raw; often harvested and used in poison-tipped darts.

Serpentblight Resin — A thick, adhesive sap drawn from desert thorns. In small doses, it induces severe cramps and hallucinations; favored by assassins and smugglers for its debilitating effects.

Cerulean Expanse

A water-drenched region of tide kingdoms and oceanic mystery, where herbs thrive in salt spray, moonlit shores, and abyssal depths.

Mistral Coralbud — A soft blue-pink bloom that forms along drifting reef roots. When dried and steeped, it soothes internal swelling and treats lung ailments caused by water inhalation.

Tidefern Silk — A silver-green aquatic frond used in dream elixirs and scrying rituals. When smoked or brewed beneath a full moon, it enhances divination, though it often leaves the user disoriented on land.

Abyssfruit Pearl — A translucent, sea-plum fruit formed within deep pressure trenches. Extremely rare. Consuming its flesh strengthens magical wards, but excess use induces temporary deafness and pressure-born hallucinations.

Brineleaf Cluster — Thick, oil-rich leaves with a bitter edge. Commonly applied in poultices for sea-creature venom and wounds from jagged coral. Its scent carries a sharp blend of kelp and iron.

Sirenshade Algae — A bluish-black growth that clings to wreckage and submerged stone. Brewed into tea, it suppresses the voice and weakens magical projection—favored by underwater assassins and silence-casters.

Glimmerkelp — A softly luminous strand of seaweed. Dormant in daylight, it awakens beneath starlight or moonlight, where it radiates a calming energy. When brewed, it reduces magical burnout and tempers emotional surges.

Emberwoods

A region of smoldering growth and living flame, where heat, ash, and renewal intertwine. The flora of Emberwoods carries both destructive force and vital resilience.

Coalshade Vine — A smoky-black creeper that releases choking fumes when burned; inhalation causes dizziness and disorientation.

Feverthorn — A bramble infused with searing sap. Even brief contact ignites the skin, leaving a lingering burn and persistent irritation.

Embermint Leaf — A fiery red herb used in warming tonics, known to stimulate blood flow and ward against deep chill.

Smokeflare Bud — When steeped, its vapor soothes the lungs and restores breath after smoke inhalation or ash exposure.

Pyrewine Berry — A rare, ember-hued fruit used in enchanted elixirs. When properly distilled, it can heighten magical potency or sharpen emotional clarity—depending on the wielder's intent.

Emerald Woods

A realm of living harmony and quiet vitality, where growth, balance, and restoration shape every root and branch. Its flora nurtures both body and magic, though not without hidden risk.

Lifesap Bloom — A vibrant green flower that thrives near healing springs. Its nectar is prized in regeneration elixirs and calming balms.

Verdant Lace — A soft-fronded herb known for its stabilizing influence on magic. Often brewed by Moon Elves to steady volatile spells.

Thorncurl Spindle — A spiral-shaped plant adorned with fine crimson thorns. Contact with bare skin triggers intense itching and disorienting confusion.

Greenmire Pollen — A fine, drifting pollen carried on the wind. In concentrated amounts, it induces sleepiness and a dreamlike state of disassociation.

Everdew Pearlcap — A pale, rounded mushroom flecked with glimmering spots. Revered as sacred, it is used in vision quests and rituals of divine communion.

Etharyon (Mystic Forest Realm within Vacari)

Veiled in mist and bound by ancient magic, Etharyon rests near the southern coast. Here, time and memory bend within enchanted groves, and the flora reflects that lingering stillness.

Starleaf Bloom — A radiant blue flower that sharpens mental clarity, often used in spells requiring heightened focus.

Aethergrass — A shimmering reed that grows near leyline pools; when steeped, it amplifies light-based magic.

Silvertuft Vine — A soft, pale vine used in healing salves, known to close shallow wounds with unusual speed.

Moonlace Root — When crushed and brewed into tea, it calms anxiety and stabilizes volatile magic.

Thornless Celain — A gentle culinary herb with restorative properties, commonly used in broths to aid recovery.

Duskleaf Fern — Often mistaken for Moonlace Root; induces magical dulling and a trance-like sleep when consumed.

Frostpetal Bind — A delicate white flower found near enchanted springs. Improper preparation leads to emotional detachment and memory fog.

Fel Thalor

A land of ruin and lingering corruption, where ancient magic festers beneath broken stone. Its flora thrives in decay, feeding on shadow, memory, and the remnants of forgotten power.

Blackthorn Coil — A parasitic vine lined with needle-like leaves. When brewed, it induces paranoia, a racing heartbeat, and vivid hallucinations.

Gravemoss — A pale lichen found clinging to ancient ruins. When ingested, it dulls the senses and disrupts dream-based magic.

Ashlure Root — When ground into powder and inhaled, it implants false memories and severe confusion; often used in manipulation rituals.

Bleeding Shroud Fungus — Releases a dense red mist when crushed. Prolonged exposure leads to violent coughing and destabilization of magical control.

Dusksage — A rare silvery herb that, when carefully distilled, soothes nightmares and serves as a component in protective charms.

Verdant Hollowcap — A soft green mushroom that calms the mind and is often used in truth-serum blends when paired with Moonlace Root.

Friornak (Frostbound Northern Realm of Vacari)

Hidden within Vacari's upper reaches, Friornak endures beneath eternal snow and icebound caverns. Its flora embodies preservation, numbness, and the quiet resilience required to survive the cold.

Frostveil Bloom — A delicate blue flower that grows beneath ice-crusted stone. When steeped, it calms the mind and numbs pain, often used in winter survival brews and deep meditative rites.

Shiverthorn — A jagged white herb lined with needle-like leaves. Contact with bare skin induces numbness and creeping stiffness; at times used in frost-forging rituals or as a tool of punishment.

Icelace Moss — A thin, silver moss that drapes from frostbitten trees. When burned as incense, it slows the heart and mimics death, making it valuable in escape rites and burial traditions.

Wintersap Root — A thick, pale root that retains internal warmth. When chewed, it sustains stamina and slows the onset of hypothermia.

Snowgloom Cap — A dome-shaped fungus found deep within ice caverns. Its spores dull emotion and memory, often brewed into draughts of forgetfulness.

Ivory Moonbeams

A realm of silvered light and quiet enchantment, where moonlit canopies blur the boundary between waking and dream. Its flora bends perception, memory, and magic in subtle, often unpredictable ways.

Dreamwillow Bark — Ground into powder and steeped into tea, it enhances meditation and dreamwalking rituals; favored by Sylvan seers.

Mistfern Veil — A rare trailing fern that, when burned beneath moonlight, amplifies healing and is often used in purification rites.

Duskgloom Thorn — A barbed plant that releases a disorienting vapor, inducing vertigo and nausea; especially dangerous in enclosed spaces.

Twilight Creep — A low-growing vine with delicate blooms. Contact or ingestion slows movement and delays reaction time, leaving the body heavy and unresponsive.

Whispersting Pod — Releases a fine numbing pollen. In high concentrations, it disrupts memory and suppresses internal magical flow.

Lyra'el (Celestial Realm)

• *A skybound realm of celestial grace and refined living, where floating gardens and luminous terraces cultivate both delicate sustenance and subtle, often dangerous flora. Here, even beauty may conceal quiet harm.*

Veinroot Briar — A dark, basil-like plant that, in small doses, induces joint stiffness and tremors; particularly dangerous for mages and warriors reliant on precision.

Glassvine Thorn — Bearing translucent petals, this plant slows blood flow and blurs vision, creating a subtle yet disorienting effect.

Whispermoss — Found near still pools and quiet terraces, it dulls focus and disrupts short-term memory, making sustained concentration difficult.

Moonblister Pod — When crushed into broths, it gradually induces fatigue and physical weakness over time.

Hollowshade Bloom — A fragrant flower that weakens magical auras and disrupts spellcasting without causing direct harm.

Culinary and Subtle Restoratives

Thistledawn Petal — A delicate addition to teas, offering floral sweetness while gently easing minor inflammation.

Glowmint — Cool and refreshing, often infused into wine or cider to sharpen flavor and soothe the senses.

Ironfern Root — Earthy and grounding, used in pastes or broths to enrich thin meals with depth and body.

Sunberry Leaf — Sharp and tangy, used sparingly to balance rich meats and heavy oils.

Purple Fire Woods

A volatile region where flame burns with unnatural hue, and the land itself pulses with searing energy. Its flora thrives in extreme heat, offering both resilience and peril to those who dare harvest it.

Blazeblossom — A vibrant crimson flower that blooms in intense heat. Used in energizing tonics and brews that grant resistance to fire.

Flaregrass — Thin, golden blades that shimmer with retained warmth. Commonly used in forging rites and in salves designed to preserve body heat.

Cinderpetal Balm — A soft orange bloom that yields a soothing oil, prized for treating burns and reducing inflammation.

Ignistalk Mold — A fungus that grows along smoldering roots. Its spores, when inhaled, trigger violent coughing and temporary blurring of vision.

Singeweed — A small, ash-colored herb that scorches the throat when consumed, causing dryness and disorientation even in minimal doses.

Sacred Grove (E'vahona)

A hidden sanctuary of ancient balance, where living magic flows in quiet harmony with the will of the Eladrin. Its flora carries both restoration and consequence, shaped by forces older than memory.

Lunaria Bloom — A shimmering petal used in moonlit rites and calming draughts, known to enhance clarity and restore emotional balance.

Heartroot Vine — Brewed into restorative teas, it strengthens the heart and grounds the spirit; often used by the Eladrin in rites of healing and renewal.

Silverdew Moss — Found upon ancient stone, this soft moss is used in salves to mend magical burns and soothe overstressed arcane channels.

Wyrdfern — A rare, sacred fern that heightens sensitivity to divine presence and compels truth-speaking in those attuned to its influence.

Gloamshade Berry — Small, dark berries with a deceptively sweet taste. In excess, they slow the heart and dull magical awareness.

Twilight Fangleaf — A delicate lilac leaf that induces vivid hallucinations and disorienting confusion when smoked or brewed.

Shadowhaven — Alchemy, Smuggling, and the Unregulated Trade

"Not all herbs are grown. Some are... acquired."

Black Market Blends of Shadowhaven (Codex Add-on)

In Shadowhaven, nothing grows—yet everything can be bought, brewed, or stolen. The substances traded here are absent from formal archives, spoken of only in hushed tones, bartered in iron flasks, and tested on the unwary.

Siren's Poison — A deep blue extract distilled from stolen Coraluna kelp and smokeleaf. It induces vivid hallucinations and a fleeting infatuation with the nearest voice; favored by pirates for interrogation... or seduction.

Wakevine Spoor — A powdered stimulant mixed with ground bone ash and Duskleaf. It drives the body without rest for up to three days, before collapsing into violent nightmares and nerve tremors.

Tideburn Draught — A volatile tonic brewed from fermented sea-bramble and stormroot shavings. It numbs pain and ignites a berserker fury; outlawed across most ports.

Moonblind Ink — A diluted alchemical blend used in tattoos and binding contracts. It glows beneath moonlight, but gradually erodes memory and fosters deep paranoia. Its origin remains unknown—possibly tainted by Etharyon's influence.

Gutterroot Balm — A greasy salve scraped from alley-grown molds and scorched herbs. It seals wounds quickly, but leaves lasting discoloration—and in some cases, a heightened sensitivity to shadow magic.

Twilight Grove

A realm suspended between light and shadow, where dusk lingers and the veil between calm and danger thins. Its flora embodies both quiet restoration and subtle peril, shifting with the balance of the grove.

Nightcoil Stem — A slick, dark vine that seeps paralytic oil when split. Even brief exposure can numb the limbs for hours.

Emberblight Spore — A faintly glowing orange fungus. Inhalation scorches the lungs and triggers fevered hallucinations.

Shivershade Root — A chilled, fibrous root that, when improperly brewed, induces uncontrollable tremors.

Moonveil Nectar — Drawn from a soft-scented bloom, this nectar soothes emotional distress and restores mental clarity.

Gleamsprig — A pale herb touched by twilight, known to heighten magical sensitivity and sharpen vision in darkness.

City-Based Exceptions

While many regions are represented within the Herbal Origins Index, certain cities—such as Crystal Vale and Goldmoor—are not listed as primary sources. Though firmly within the world of Vacari, their herbal practices draw from nearby regions, most notably the Emerald Woods and Purple Fire Woods.

Within these cities, herbalists focus not on harvesting, but on refinement, enchantment, and ritual preparation—transforming gathered materials into elixirs, salves, and arcane compounds of higher function.

Fel Thalor Exception

Though part of Vacari, Fel Thalor exists apart in nature and influence. Its volcanic terrain and abyssal corruption distinguish it from other fire-aligned regions, such as the Emberwoods.

The flora found within Fel Thalor is shaped by ruin, instability, and lingering dark magic. For this reason, it is classified independently within the Herbal Origins Index, despite its proximity to the gateway leading toward Afor.

Legendary Weapons

Argentis Aethern — The Sovereign Spellweaver of Lady Seraphina

Legendary Eladrin Relic

Forged within the sanctum-groves of E'vahona during the first Silver Convergence of the modern age, Argentis Aethern was created not merely as a weapon, but as a living covenant between Lady Seraphina and Talleoss, eldest of the Silver Ancients.

Its form is shaped from moon-silverwood—a rare, living timber that grows only where ancient dragon magic saturates the roots of the world. Frosted light glimmers through its grain, as though starlight were woven into its core. Runes of elder Eladrin script trace its length, their language known now only to the most learned.

At its crown rests the **Heart of Talleoss**—a crystalline focus formed from the dragon's own breath during a celestial forging rite. Within it coils a perpetual storm of argent light, pulsing in time with an ancient heartbeat.

Powers & Attributes

Sovereign Arcane Conduit — Amplifies Seraphina's spellcasting beyond mortal thresholds, allowing simultaneous weaving of multiple schools without destabilization.

Dragon-Bound Resonance — When Seraphina and Talleoss act as one, wards strengthen, illusions fracture, and corruption recoils as if burned by living moonfire.

Dominion of the Argent Aegis — Manifests a vast protective dome, shielding allies, dragon, and terrain while weakening dark magic and unraveling illusion.

Voice of the Ancient — In moments of dire need, the will of Talleoss may speak through Seraphina, a force that shakes the fabric of reality itself.

Legacy

Argentis Aethern is not merely wielded—it is shared. A living testament to the Silver Accord, it embodies the unity of Eladrin wisdom and dragon eternity.

Crystalbow — Relic of Crystal Vale (Gailen)

Forged within the radiant sanctums of Crystal Vale, the Crystalbow is a sacred inheritance bound to royal lineage and awakened only through the bond with a true Crystal Dragon.

Its form appears carved from living crystal, yet moves with fluid grace, pulsing in rhythm with Gailen's heartbeat. It requires no quiver—each arrow is formed through intent, shaped by will, emotion, and the presence of Aurelia.

Powers & Attributes

Manifested Crystal Arrows — Arrows form from pure arcane crystal, shifting into explosive bursts, piercing lances, or radiant dispersals.

Dragon Resonance — In Aurelia's presence, the bow fully awakens, its power stabilizing and intensifying.

Harmonic Convergence — Channels ambient strength from allied dragons, infusing arrows with their elemental signatures.

Magic Disruption — Fractures unstable or corrupted magic, particularly effective against illusion and Dominion influence.

Legacy

The Crystalbow is a symbol of unity, purpose, and rightful inheritance—a bridge between legacy and becoming.

Arborblade — Living Relic of the Emerald Accord (Thalorian)

Forged by the Moon Elves in communion with the ancient forests, the Arborblade is not shaped—it is grown.

Its form shifts between blade and spear, composed of condensed emerald light threaded with living essence. It pulses with the rhythm of the land itself.

Powers & Attributes

Living Edge — Adapts between slashing and piercing forms in response to the wielder's intent.

Verdant Resonance — Draws strength from living terrain, growing more powerful in forests and natural environments.

Guardian's Reversal — Deflects incoming force and redirects it outward as controlled bursts of energy.

Balance of Life and War — Strikes with precision—capable of restraint or finality as balance demands.

Legacy

A covenant between the Moon Elves and the living world—power guided by preservation, not domination.

Dragonlance — Relic of Unity and Ascension (Ong)

Crafted by Lord Karrenen and blessed by Kadona, the Dragonlance was forged for one who stands between worlds.

Its shaft bears intertwined runes of Goldmoor and E'vahona. At its core glows amethyst light, resonating with Amara.

Powers & Attributes

Amethyst Conduit — Channels Amara's energy through the lance, amplifying each strike.

Aerial Momentum Strike — Builds kinetic and magical force during flight, releasing it in devastating impact.

Bond Synchronization — Strengthens Ong's connection to Amara, compensating for his non-traditional lineage.

Symbol of Unity — Embodies alliance between once-divided peoples.

Legacy

The Dragonlance represents choice over birthright—unity forged, not inherited.

Eladrin Longbow of Serena — Legacy Relic of the Eladrin Archers (Keisha)

Forged by Lord Karrenen and gifted to Serena, this bow was crafted for unmatched precision. In Keisha's hands, it awakens beyond its original design.

Powers & Attributes

Elemental Infusion — Arrows carry wind, flame, or natural force shaped through Keisha's magic.

Living Alignment — The bow responds instinctively to intent, adjusting trajectory and tension.

Silent Precision — Enables seamless, fluid motion between shots.

Awakened Potential — Continues to evolve beyond its original limits.

Legacy

A legacy transformed—what was inherited has become something entirely new.

Luminara Virell — The Verdant Chronicle of Thaldir

Legendary Eladrin Relic

Forged beneath moonlit boughs, Luminara Virell is not a weapon of conquest, but of restoration and memory.

Its form is grown from silversage heartwood, its runes living and ever-changing. At its crown blooms the **Tear of Silvara**, a crystalline embodiment of restorative breath.

Powers & Attributes

Wellspring of the Everbound — Continuously restores wounds and stabilizes magic.

Chronicle of Ages — Holds ancient knowledge, revealed as living visions.

Sanctuary of Silver Grace — Creates a protective domain where pain fades and corruption weakens.

Breath of the Gentle Star — Calms, heals, and dissolves destructive magic without violence.

Legacy

Where Argentis Aethern commands, Luminara Virell restores—together forming the dual pillars of the Silver Covenant.

Radiantus's Shield — Celestial Bond Relic (Talhira)

Forged at Radiantus's command, this Lightforged shield is a living extension of celestial will.

Powers & Attributes

Celestial Synchrony — Amplifies Radiantus's light through Talhira.

Radiant Aegis — Generates a barrier of immense defensive power.

Unbreakable Bond Field — Strengthens both rider and dragon simultaneously.

Light of Judgment — Weakens and unravels corrupted magic.

Legacy

Not a shield—but a vow made manifest.

Locations of Vacari

A categorized index of the known cities, realms, and wild domains of Vacari and its neighboring lands. Some lie open beneath the sun, others remain veiled by enchantment or shadow, and all carry legacies that shape the balance of the world. Expanded histories and travelogues are available on the author's website.

Cities & Realms

Crystal Vale — The radiant jewel of Vacari, renowned for its crystalline towers and the legacy of unity forged through the bond of Gailen and Aurelia.

Etharyon — Realm of the Moon Elves and dwarves, where forested valleys rise into mountain strongholds along the Shimmering Beach. Though always part of Vacari, it was once cut off after the assault upon its king—its roads broken, its people left to endure in isolation. In those years, it came to be spoken of as distant. Now its halls stand open once more, gleaming with moonlit stone and the quiet glow of hidden forges.

Fel Thalor — A Druchii stronghold steeped in blood rites and abyssal corruption, its foundations scarred by ancient ruin and dark dominion.

Flameford (Old Flameford) — Once the seat of Phoenix Shadowwalker, now a city of fractured ruins and lingering shadow, where dragon lairs rise among the remnants of its fallen power.

Goldmoor — The shining capital of Vacari, where elven elegance and human craftsmanship are woven into a unified and enduring realm.

Shadowhaven — Maldrak's refuge of exile, a lawless city of pirates and outcasts, veiled in twilight and governed by shadowed ambition.

Forest Realms

Emberwoods — A smoldering forest bordering volcanic lands, where heat and illusion intertwine and dragon-pixie magic veils the paths near Fel Thalor.

Emerald Woods — A lush and living passage leading to Crystal Vale, known for its deep-rooted magic and the place where Ong and Keisha's bond was sealed.

Ivory Moonbeams — The mystical domain of the Sylvan Elves, where silver light filters endlessly through moonlit canopies.

Purple Fire Woods — An enchanted forest of violet flame and radiant growth, remembered as the sacred site of Ong and Keisha's wedding.

Twilight Glade — A liminal woodland resting between Ivory Moonbeams and Shadowhaven, where light and shadow exist in fragile balance.

Hidden Sub-Realm inside Vacari

E'vahona — The hidden jewel of the Eladrin, veiled from the wider world and preserved beyond mortal sight. Bestowed as a sacred gift by Kadona, Goddess of Light, it endures as a sanctuary of balance, ancient magic, and unwavering harmony.

The Sacred Grove — At the heart of E'vahona lies a living sanctuary where divine light gathers. Here, a breathtaking garden flourishes beneath Kadona's gentle influence—its roots steeped in restoration, its air alive with quiet radiance, and its presence felt as both refuge and reverence.

Waters & Coastal Realms

Abyssal Sovereign — A vast and awe-inspiring underwater dominion, watched over by Lysander, God of the Sea. Its depths are both sanctuary and mystery, where divine will shapes the tides and ancient forces stir beneath the surface.

Cerulean Expanse — The great ocean bordering Vacari, its endless waters home to hidden kingdoms, ancient currents, and secrets long lost to the depths.

Coraluna — A majestic merfolk kingdom of living coral and flowing architecture, ruled by King Oceanous, where oceanic grace and sovereign strength are held in balance.

Luminaqua — The radiant city of the Aquanar Elves, illuminated by bioluminescent coral and woven currents, a place where magic and water exist in seamless harmony.

Shimmering Coast — A sunlit shoreline where land and sea converge, serving as a meeting place between landfolk and the merfolk of the deep.

Sub-Realm inside Vacari

The Hidden Isles — Concealed behind a shifting mystical barrier, these isles remain unseen by most of the world. They serve as a sanctuary of breathtaking beauty and quiet gathering, where ancient forces and noble dragons may dwell beyond the reach of conflict.

Ardinia — A secluded realm of enchantment, shielded by powerful magic and shaped by the will of Aeliana. Here, nature reigns in its purest form—untouched, vibrant, and deeply attuned to the living balance of Vacari.

Regions & Wilds

Vast landscapes beyond crown or council, where the land itself is as perilous as the creatures that claim it.

Firornak — The Frozen Wastes, a realm of endless ice and jagged peaks where blizzards erase all trace of passage. Beneath its frozen surface lie cavern networks that echo with the presence of Glaciera, Sanguis, and Nyxathor—their dominion carved into frost and shadow. Few who cross its expanse return, for the cold itself is as unforgiving as the dragons who rule it.

Fel Thalor Wastes — A scorched and volatile expanse shaped by relentless eruptions and rivers of molten stone. These lands serve as the domain of Zylron, where fire and fury reign unchecked, and the ground itself trembles beneath his presence.

Specialized Aerial Techniques

Standing Combat Techniques

A rare but vital discipline among Vacari's dragonriders, standing combat allows a rider to fight upright upon their dragon's back while in flight. This technique is essential for weapons requiring full reach and leverage, such as the Dragonlance and the Arborblade.

Training begins with balance drills at a controlled hover, gradually advancing into maneuver adaptation, weapon integration, and combat responsiveness under shifting aerial conditions.

Not all riders employ this method. Certain styles—such as Keisha's magic and longbow—are best executed from a seated stance, where stability enhances precision and control. In these cases, training instead emphasizes accuracy, magical focus, and aerial recovery readiness.

Due to its inherent risks—including loss of harness security, extreme balance demands, and physical strain—standing combat is reserved for highly experienced riders and employed only when the demands of battle require it.

Aerial Recovery

All Vacari dragonriders are trained in emergency aerial recovery, regardless of combat specialization. This discipline prepares riders to survive an unplanned fall—whether caused by enemy assault, sudden turbulence, or failed maneuvering.

Instruction includes controlled freefall positioning, spin reduction, protection of vital areas, and precise timing for magical or dragon-assisted interception. Riders are taught to maintain composure in open sky, as panic often proves more dangerous than the fall itself.

Keisha's controlled descent during her fall from Kimras stands as a foundational example within rider academies—transforming a potentially fatal moment into a recoverable one. In such instances, trust between dragon and rider becomes paramount, with the dragon adjusting position and speed to ensure a successful recovery.

Dragons of Vacari Series

Part I — The Age of Unbound Darkness

The dawn of conflict and the first fall of shadow.

(Books I–III)

Before the Dominion rose again, chaos reigned without purpose. The first dragons and their companions emerged in fractured alliances, facing ancient betrayals and awakening powers.

This was the era when the light first learned to fight back—
but unity came at a terrible cost.

Book 1 — Rise of the Ancients

Ancient powers awaken, and the first fault lines of darkness fracture the skies.

Book 2 — Shadows of Betrayal

Old loyalties crack as the Dominion's influence slips deeper into the world.

Book 3 — Celestial Convergence

The forces of light rally to withstand the Dominion's rise...
The first great arc reaches its turning point.

Part II — The Abyssal Dominion

Darkness learns purpose, and the war of minds begins.

(Books IV–VI)

Darkness has learned discipline.

No longer wild, the shadows move with intent, spreading deception through the realms.

Dragons and their bound kin must confront illusion, corruption, and the weight of their own divided hearts as the Dominion tightens its hold.

Book 4 — Enchantment of E'vahona

Illusion and shadow invade the hidden realms, and the war for Vacari spreads across every sky and forest.

Book 5 — Tides of Darkness

Beneath the waves of Vacari, ancient powers stir as the Dominion carries the war into the deep.

Book 6 — Whispers of Doom

In the deserts of Afor, the Dominion's schemes tighten as their fury turns increasingly toward Keisha.

Part III — The Age of Unity

Light stops defending and begins to lead.

(Books VII–IX)

Hope stirs once more—fragile, defiant, unstoppable.

From the ruins of war, old enemies begin to recognize the truth: only together can Vacari survive what is coming.

The final convergence approaches, when light and shadow will decide whether harmony or ruin shapes the world's destiny.

Book 7 — Echoes of Despair

In Ardinia and the forests of Ivory Moonbeams, nymphs and Sylvan Elves rise as hope struggles against gathering darkness.

Book 8 — Shattered Realms

The skies themselves fracture as the Sky Nymphs return and the war spreads across every realm of Vacari.

Book 9 — Final Dawn of Renewal

In the last stand between light and shadow, the fate of Vacari—and the hope of every realm—will be decided.

The saga continues in the volumes yet to come.

Acknowledgements

Jean McEvoy

To my wonderful mother—your red pen and unwavering belief in me will never be forgotten. Thank you for always standing by me.

Caroline Otto

To my best friend from high school, Caroline—thank you for taking the time to read the rough drafts and for always being there for me. Your friendship has meant more than words can say. You have always been like a sister to me.

Steven Thomas

To my dear friend Steven—thank you for taking the time to read early drafts of the chapters. Your friendship and thoughtful feedback mean the world to me.

Special Acknowledgements to the Fur Babies (whose names are used in the book

Special Acknowledgements to the Fur Babies

(whose names appear in the story)

Pumpkin

I rescued my little black panther over five years ago, and her playful spirit became the inspiration for Pumpkin in this book.

Casper

Casper, my best friend's beloved kitty, inspired the loyal companion who appears in this story. His quiet presence and gentle spirit earned him a place in the world of Vacari.

About the author

T.A. McEvoy grew up in heels and high fantasy, despite being told girls weren't supposed to love dragons, elves, or galaxies far, far away. She never saw a reason to stop.

Though she avoids camping (unless it involves a bed, a shower, and zero bugs), she's drawn to darker tales with quiet strength, broken heroes, and healing that matters as much as vengeance.

In her world of Vacari, forests mourn, dragons remember, and love comes in many forms, none of them asking you to change to be worthy.

She writes for readers who never quite fit in, who carry their softness like armor, and who crave fantasy with heart and teeth.

Her dragons love deeply, but it's not always romantic love. Because love takes many forms.

They are guardians.

And sometimes, they are the only ones who truly understand.

Every tale she writes takes place somewhere in Vacari—a living world of dragons and elves whose stories intertwine across time. Some are sweeping sagas, others quiet legends—but all are part of the same heartbeat.

"Thank you for reading Enchantment of E'vahona. If you enjoyed the book, we would be immensely grateful if you could take a moment to leave a review at the location where you purchased the book. Your feedback is invaluable to us and helps other readers discover our work. Thank you for your support!"

Also, by T.A. McEvoy

The Elves of Vacari Series:

The Wicked Published 11-01-2023

Shadows Unveiled- Published 12-05-2023.

Vacari's Resurgence: Healing Bonds 04-12-2024

Dragons of Vacari Series:

Rise of the Ancients 12-02-2024

Shadows of Betrayal 04-21-2025

Celestial Convergence 09-25-2025

Enchantment of E'vahona 04-01-2025

Tides of Darkness (Coming Soon)

The print editions of my books are produced through Lulu, whose print quality is second to none. For the best experience — and to explore more about each book and series — please visit:

https://www.tamcevoy.com

www.ingramcontent.com/pod-product-compliance
Lightning Source LLC
LaVergne TN
LVHW041052080826
845145LV00007B/1548

* 9 7 8 1 9 6 4 2 5 0 2 3 6 *